The Master of Jalna

Mazo de la Roche was born in Toronto and spent her childhood on her father's fruit farm in Ontario. Educated at Toronto University, she disliked city life and lived in the country. Her first novel, *Explorers of the Dawn* (1922), attracted little notice, but she achieved fame with *Jalna* (1927), which won the *Atlantic Monthly*'s ten thousand dollar prize, and was followed by a whole series of sequels forming a family chronicle which have recently been made into a highly successful television series under the title *The Whiteoaks of Jalna*.

She also wrote a comedy, *Low Life* (1925), several other plays, and a *History of the Port of Quebec* (1944). In 1930 she moved to England and in 1938 she was awarded the Lorne Pierce Medal of the Royal Society of Canada. She died in 1961.

The 'Whiteoaks' novels in
chronological order

Mazo de la Roche

The Master of Jalna

Pan Books in association with Macmillan London

to Hugh Walpole ·

First published 1933 by Macmillan and Co Ltd
This edition published 1954 by Pan Books Ltd,
Cavaye Place, London sw10 9pg
9th printing 1978
in association with Macmillan London
all rights reserved
ISBN 0 330 20262 6
Made and printed in Great Britain by
Cox & Wyman Ltd, London, Reading and Fakenham

CONTENTS

THE WHITEOAK FAMILY

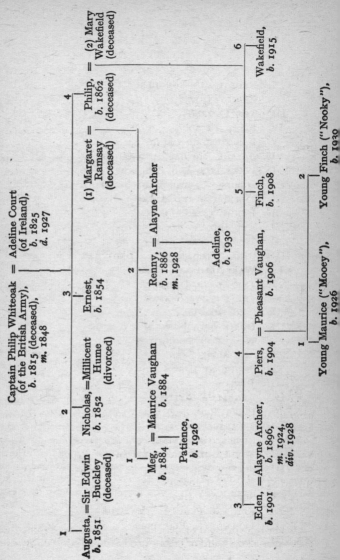

Captain Philip Whiteoak (of the British Army), *b.* 1815 (deceased), *m.* 1848 = Adeline Court (of Ireland), *b.* 1825, *d.* 1927

1. Augusta, = Sir Edwin Buckley (deceased), *b.* 1851
2. Nicholas, = Millicent Hume (divorced), *b.* 1852
3. Ernest, *b.* 1854
4. Philip, = (1) Margaret Ramsay (deceased), = (2) Mary Wakefield (deceased), *b.* 1862 (deceased)

1. Meg, = Maurice Vaughan, *b.* 1884, *b.* 1884
   Patience, *b.* 1926
2. Renny, = Alayne Archer, *b.* 1886, *m.* 1928
   Adeline, *b.* 1930
3. Eden, = Alayne Archer, *b.* 1901, *b.* 1896, *m.* 1924, *div.* 1928
4. Piers, = Pheasant Vaughan, *b.* 1904, *b.* 1906
   1. Young Maurice ("Mooey"), *b.* 1926
   2. Young Finch ("Nooky"), *b.* 1930
5. Finch, *b.* 1908
6. Wakefield, *b.* 1915

ELDEST AND YOUNGEST

RENNY WHITEOAK stood with his brows drawn together but a smile softening his lips while a wire-haired terrier belonging to his brother Piers strove with controlled energy to dig her way into the burrow of some small animal. The digging was not easy because a root of silver birch-tree made a barrier across the entrance. The terrier's white coat was covered with earth, and Renny was remembering how Piers had spent an hour that day in washing from her the stains of some foul encounter. He had titivated her as though for a show. And already she had come to this!

Still it was clean dirt, good honest earth that, when it dried, would fall from the stiff white coat. The terrier lay on her side now, throwing the brown soil against her pink belly. She tore at the root with her teeth. She tore so hard that the splinters she spat out were blood-stained. Renny remembered that it was spring, that there was probably a terrified little mother with young down there. He picked up the terrier by the scruff and, tucking her under his arm, strolled away. The little dog knew that it was useless to struggle. She turned up a beseeching muzzle, caked with earth, and seeing a face that promised no relenting, wagged her tail and panted toward the next excitement.

Renny walked on through the still radiance of the June day. Earth and sky were of an ineffable brightness, and the smooth path beneath his feet was his own. He thought of this as he followed its turnings through the birch wood. There was something odd and personal about the possession of a path. It was unlike the fields that surrendered themselves to cultivation or the woods that held themselves apart. The path gave itself—stretched itself supine for you to walk on—but it did not surrender. It led you where it willed, and, if you would not follow it, if you turned aside among the bushes or the tree-trunks, it ran on without you in the appointed way marked by the footprints of your fathers.

He liked the thought of that. It heartened him to think that this path—that all the paths of Jalna—had been made by his own people

7

or those who worked for them. It had been nothing more than a forest when his grandfather, Captain Philip Whiteoak, had come here from England. Uncle Nicholas, Uncle Ernest had run over these as little boys. He, himself . . . well, if these paths could speak, they could tell a lot about him . . . forty-five he was now.

The smile that had been lurking about his mouth became a grin. He tossed the terrier on to the path in front of him, and it sped like an arrow after something that moved among the bracken. A little devil, Biddy. You couldn't keep her down. Her joyous acceptance of life made him happier. That was the way to take it. If you couldn't have what you wanted, go at top speed after something else.

What had been worrying him? Oh yes, that account from Piers for the winter's feed. He let the farm-lands to Piers. Then he bought the fodder off him. Piers was always ready with the rent, but of late he often had to ask Piers for time. It was humiliating because Piers was younger than he and had a way of staring at one as though he were holding himself in, keeping back some unpleasant truths which he would have taken pleasure in uttering. Well . . . if anyone could make anything out of horse-breeding with conditions as they had been for two years . . . getting worse and worse . . . he'd like to see how it was done. The smile faded on his lips and the frown groping across his forehead settled between the reddish brows.

The terrier reappeared on the path leaping about the legs of a slender youth of seventeen who came toward his eldest brother with an air at once petulant and ingratiating.

"Oh, there you are, Renny! I've been all over the place after you. Are you on your way to the fox-farm?"

"Well, I might drop in there."

"I'll come with you, if you don't mind."

"All right."

Renny shot an inquisitive look at him. Wakefield seemed to be always ready to go to the fox-farm. Was it possible that he was a bit gone on Pauline Lebraux? It was ridiculous to think of his being gone on anyone. He was little more than a kid. Yet—looking at him as an outsider you'd say—"Here's a tall fellow, handsome as the devil. The girls will be after him." But an outsider wouldn't know what a kid he was, how dependent and nervy, though he had almost outgrown his delicacy.

They had come to an open grassy space where the white-boled silver birches cast their lacy shadows. Renny suddenly grasped Wakefield's arm and stopped.

"Do you remember?" he asked.

8

Wakefield looked blank. "Remember what?"

"The day you read me a poem you'd written. It was on this very spot. It must be almost two years ago."

Wakefield was gratified. "You remember? Well, I had completely forgotten it. I've even forgotten the poem."

"Thank God for that! I was afraid you were going to turn out like Eden. You showed all the symptoms."

"It was only a phase. I have quite outgrown it."

Approval shone out of the elder's eyes. Wakefield saw it and thought the moment propitious.

"The school is giving a dinner to Professor Ralston," he said, "and a presentation. I have to subscribe to both. And I think I should have a dress-suit. I am one of the tallest fellows in the school, and I shall feel very awkward in ordinary things. I felt awkward at the last dance, and I expect that I looked as I felt."

It was impossible to think of his looking or feeling awkward, seeing him standing there in the sunshine, as straight and slender as one of the young birches. Renny said:

"There is a suit of Eden's in the attic cupboard. A dinner-jacket. I guess that it would fit you. You are just about the size he was then."

Wakefield looked horrified. "That old suit! I should look like the devil in it. Why, even Finch refused to wear that."

"Finch couldn't wear it. He is too long in the arm. But I believe it would fit you. It could be altered if necessary."

Wakefield turned away. "Very well, Renny"—he spoke with sad dignity—"I'll give up going. I don't mind so very much, but I do mind making myself into a figure of fun."

Renny followed him along the path grinning in appreciation of his methods of getting what he wanted, at the old-fashioned turn of speech which he cultivated. How different he was from what the others had been at his age! In a similar position Finch would have backed down at once, agreed to wear anything rather than be insistent. A good boy but rather spiritless. Piers would have sulked. Eden argued excitedly. . . . Well, it was a great thing that Wake had grown up to want a dress-suit. It had often seemed doubtful if he would. He was an extravagant youngster too. Money spilt through his fingers like water. It was a pity he had come along when it was so scarce. He was formed for easy living and extravagance. Renny said, in a grudging tone:

"I suppose I can do it. But money is terribly tight. Well—I shouldn't say tight—I simply haven't got it."

9

Wakefield threw over his shoulder:

"Let Piers wait."

"He is waiting."

"Let him keep on waiting. He really should not charge you anything for the feed."

"What would he live on?"

"You—like everyone else does!"

Renny broke into loud laughter, then suddenly sobered.

"Look here, Wake," he said rather sternly, "you're growing up too fast."

"Just the same," persisted the boy, "I don't like to see Piers so high and mighty about managing his farm profitably when he and his wife and two kids get their living at Jalna for absolutely nothing."

"You don't understand," returned his elder, rather stiffly. "Piers helps me in a lot of ways." How could Wakefield understand his clannish desire to have his family under the same roof with him, his pride in keeping the old house full!

"Well, I'm glad to hear that." Wakefield's tone was grandfatherly. "And thanks very much for the evening things. You can always get credit at Fowler's, can't you?"

Fowler's! The most expensive tailoring place in town. This lad hated himself!

"I suppose it's possible."

"And you'll remember about my subscription to the dinner and present?"

"Hm-hm."

They had crossed a field, passed through a gate, and emerged into the public road. It was deserted, and not far off they could see the white picket-fence that enclosed the fox-farm.

Clara Lebraux had had a hard fight to keep it afloat in the two and a half years since her husband's death. But somehow—and with help from Renny Whiteoak that both kept secret—she had escaped failure. She had done well with the poultry that got her up so early every morning.

She and her daughter Pauline were standing together at a window in the kitchen as the brothers appeared at the gate. Pauline said hurriedly:

"Oh, don't let us be caught in the kitchen! They'll think we live in it. Last time Renny came we were washing dishes."

Clara Lebraux laughed curtly. "It's a late hour for me to begin prinking for him. He has seen me looking my worst for over three years now." There was a curious note of satisfaction in her voice as she said this. She added—"And married men aren't supposed to look at anyone but their wives."

"I wonder why they don't ring the bell."

"They've gone round to look at the foxes."

"Mummie, shall I run upstairs and change my dress? This is so abominably short."

"Yes, do . . . I like you to look nice."

Pauline hesitated at the door. "It's hard to think of him as married, isn't it? We see so little of her."

"Oh, he's very much married!" Clara Lebraux spoke abruptly. She went quickly to the oven, drew out a pan of scones she was baking, looked at them suspiciously and thrust them back, banging the oven door.

Pauline disappeared up the stairs as the bell sounded. Clara wiped her hands on a scorched oven-cloth and went to the door. She glanced in the mirror in the hall in passing, saw that her hair that had been tow-coloured and was now turning dark in streaks, was dishevelled, and that there was flour on her cheek, but she marched straight to the door and opened it.

She and Renny greeted each other familiarly, but Wakefield stood somewhat aloof. He was conscious of his new height and his imminent manhood.

"Where is Pauline?" asked Renny, when they were in the living-room that had an air of comfort in spite of its extreme shabbiness.

"Upstairs. She'll be down directly."

"How is the injured fox?"

"Quite recovered. But we had a time with him. The others had torn a foot almost off. They are devils when they're roused. But Pauline never loses patience with them. I do. Sometimes I'd like to turn all the foxes in together. Then throw the poultry to them. Have a general massacre."

Wakefield's eyes brightened. "If ever that climax arrives, please let me know. I'd love to see it."

She asked with sudden gravity—"Have you —but, of course, you have—heard of the proposed massacre of the trees?"

Renny, turning his head sharply toward her, demanded—"Whose trees?"

"Everyone's. The road is to be widened. The curve just beyond Jalna straightened out. I thought, of course, you'd have heard, as your property is the most affected."

He stared at her, stupefied. He could not take it in. Wakefield looked uncomfortable. He had heard something of this before.

Piers also. But they had kept it to themselves. Renny would make a row and the old people would be upset.

She repeated—"They're widening the road, you see. Those huge old oaks are in the way. They want to make it a better road for motorists. The curve is supposed to be dangerous. It's the Government, so I suppose we must put up with it. Pauline is mourning over our nice cedar hedge. We shall lose that."

He understood now.

"How long have you known this?" he asked.

"Just since yesterday."

He turned to Wakefield:

"And you?"

The boy answered in a muffled voice:

"For two days."

"And Piers knew of it?"

Wakefield nodded.

Renny gave a bitter laugh. "By God, I like this! It's splendid! The road is going to be widened—the front of my property disfigured—and everyone knows of it but me!"

Wakefield said—"We knew you'd find out soon enough."

"Well, I have. . . . I won't allow it. There has been no meeting of the ratepayers."

"Yes. There was. When you were in Montreal."

Renny grinned savagely. "Oh, they waited till I was out of the way—the curs! Well—it can't be done! I won't allow it. Why, those trees have stood there——" He stopped, swallowed, and got to his feet as he saw Pauline coming down the stairs.

Her eyes were fixed on his as she came into the room.

He said—"They've just told me about the trees, Pauline."

"Oh, I knew you'd be sorry! Can't you please do something about it?"

"Do something! Well, I should like to see them touch my trees!"

Wakefield spoke, in a high judicial tone:

"After all, we must always consider the good of the many. There is no doubt that the road is narrow for motors."

"Let them keep off it, then."

"And the curve is dangerous. Perhaps you've forgotten, Renny, how you knocked over Noah Binns just there with your own car."

"He wasn't hurt."

"He might have been killed."

"So much the better."

"Oh, well, there's no convincing you."

"Look here," interrupted Renny savagely, "do you want the trees cut down?"

"No—but if the majority of taxpayers do, we're helpless, aren't we?"

Clara Lebraux added—"I suppose what has really happened is that the Minister of Highways, or some such person, has been influenced by someone with a pull."

Renny broke in—"He'll have me to reckon with. Why, those trees were old when Gran first came here. She and Grandfather always protected them. There are few enough beauty spots left in this country. No stranger ever comes to Jalna without admiring those trees."

"I know," agreed Wakefield, "but we have hundreds like them—almost as fine."

"Yes! You'd better put in that 'almost.' We've nothing else to equal them."

"They're paying compensation."

"As though I'd accept their filthy money!"

Clara Lebraux and Wakefield exchanged a look.

Pauline went to Renny and touched his sleeve with her hand. "I knew you'd feel as I do about it," she said.

He pressed her hand against his arm. "We'll throw their compensation in their teeth," he said. His face cleared as he looked down into her eyes. He could never quite make out their colour, but he knew they were deep and beautiful and that the lids had a foreign look.

She wanted to be near him. But yet she could not bear the nearness. It was as though she, being cold, could not bear the heat of the fire. She had loved her father with all the force of her sensitive child nature. Her father had loved Renny Whiteoak. She told herself that her feeling for Renny was a sacred heritage from her father. She moved away and went to Wakefield's side.

The fire of his presence was a softly burning fire. She could comfort her spirit there. Yet there was something in him too that frightened her. There was something watchful about him. He watched but he did not let himself be seen. . . .

As the brothers returned along the path they had come, Renny talked of the trees, of the beauty of the road as it stood, of the outrage of suggesting that the boundary of Jalna should be moved back from the road so much as a foot. He talked of the winding roads of old England. He would not enter the house without first going to the edge of the meadow beyond the lawn to see that the ancient

13

oaks were still intact.   He took off his hat as though to salute them.
He stood beneath the summer spread of their green leaves, the serene
strength of their branches, with head thrown back, his fiery brown
eyes penetrating their sunlit heights with an expression of passionate
protectiveness.

II

FAMILY TREE

The first real heat of summer had come that day, and it was delicious.
The new leaves, bright and smooth as though waxed, sunned themselves in it.   Each spear of grass stood up, full of life, as though de-
claring—"I am the lawn."   The flower blossoms that hitherto had
opened with discretion, now cast caution aside and threw wide their
petals like welcoming arms.   The earth that till now had only been
warmed on its surface, absorbed the fire of the sun deeper and deeper
into its fibre.   Jock, the bob-tailed sheep dog, left the porch where he
had been sunning himself, and stretched his shaggy body in the shade
of a balsam.

But it was the old house itself that most greedily drank in the heat.
Its walls, which had cracked in frost, shivered in bitter winds, now
turned a mellow rosy red in the bright radiance.   Pigeons strutted
and slid up and down its warmed roof.   Its windows—those windows through which old Adeline, for seventy-five years the centre of
its activities, had so often stared—beamed tranquilly.   A blue smoke-
wreath from the kitchen chimney settled above it like a rakish halo.

Ernest Whiteoak sat in an armchair with cushions piled behind him,
on the gravelled sweep in front of the house, where his long, thin
body received the full force of the sun.   He had been seriously ill
of influenza two months before and he still clung to the pleasant ways
of convalescence.

It was so nice to stand in the doorway, watch Wragge, the Cockney
manservant, who had been Renny's batman in the War, carry out the
weighty chair, one of the women-folk follow with the cushions, his
brother Nicholas seek out the most sheltered spot, then himself follow, leaning on the ebony stick that had been his mother's.

He had been sitting there an hour and twenty minutes.   In another
twenty minutes it would be one o'clock—time for dinner.   His
appetite was good, his digestion better than for some time.   He
looked forward to the hot meal and the long nap afterward on his

own soft bed.   He was already drowsy because of the heat, and the sun gleaming on the bright hair of Renny's wife sitting close beside him actually made him wink.   She was trimming his nails for him, an office she had undertaken when his hands had been shaky after the fever.   He was quite able to do it himself now, but one day when Nicholas had suggested it he had become very peevish and exclaimed —"I suppose you don't mind if I cut off the ends of my fingers !"

Alayne was thorough in all she did.   Each nail was trimmed to correspond with the curve at its base.   They were well-shaped nails. She had brought out her own polisher and was now rubbing them briskly.   Ernest's eyes were on his fingers in bland concentrated interest.   He was barely conscious of the brightness of Alayne's hair in the sun and the pretty curve of her wrist.

Nicholas slouching in a deep wicker chair watched the two of them, a mocking light in his eyes beneath the heavily marked brows. Spoiled old boy Ernest was.   And this illness had made his comfort all too precious to him.   If mamma were living she would take the kink out of him.   In fancy Nicholas could hear her say—"Don't act like a ninny, boy !"   She would still call him boy, though he would be seventy-eight this summer.   Well . . . it was splendid to see him about again, after the scare he'd given them, with his cough and his fever and all his aches and pains.   He looked good for a score or more of years yet.

Alayne, he thought, looked considerably older since her baby was born.   She was something more than a charming girl now.   She was a woman of experience, the character of her face making one wonder what lay behind.   Well, she loved Renny, that was evident, and it must be no joke for a woman of Alayne's sort—for there would be always something strait-laced about her—to love a man like Renny.   She had had a deal of tough experience since she had first come to Jalna as Eden's wife.

"There," said Alayne, returning Ernest his hand, "you're all fixed up for another few days."

"Next time he'll be able to do it for himself," observed Nicholas.

"I am mending slowly," Ernest returned mildly.

"You're getting a look of positive brute strength," said his brother.

"Did you have your egg-nog?" asked Alayne.

"Yes, thank you."

Nicholas scoffed—"And now going in to devour a hot dinner !"

Alayne gave him a look of affectionate reproval.   "He must be built up," she said, "and nourishing food is better than medicine."

A contralto voice asked from the porch:

15

"Is Renny hereabout? Someone wants to speak to him over the telephone."

All three looked around. They saw Lady Buckley, sister of Nicholas and Ernest, tall and distinguished-looking, still holding herself upright, though she had passed her eighty-first birthday, her Queen Alexandra fringe still of a strange magenta black. In spite of the warmth of the day she wore a dress of woollen material, a very dark brown with wide velvet hem, a shade not at all kind to her speckled sallow skin. She still held her head high, her chin drawn in, the full eyes wide open with an air of startled offence, but her cheeks had grown hollow, thus giving greater prominence to the mouth with its curve of tolerance. She had had an anxious time over her brother Ernest and it had told on her. She had come from England to be with him in March, enduring a stormy voyage and an exhausting journey by rail. She felt happy at sight of the little group in the sun, with Ernest, flushed a delicate pink, as its centre.

"I have not seen him since breakfast," answered Alayne. "I'll go to the telephone, Aunt Augusta." She went swiftly into the house and Lady Buckley joined her brothers.

"Whatever," she demanded of them in her deep voice, "should we do without Alayne? I quite *lean* on her."

"And so do I," said Ernest. "She is so sensible and so thoughtful for one's comfort!"

Nicholas said—"I suppose Renny is at the fox-farm." He gave a humorous glance at his brother.

"I suppose so. That friendship persists, though Alayne shows so plainly that she dislikes Mrs. Lebraux."

"I dislike her too," declared Augusta. "I disliked her from the first moment I saw her. She struck me as unfeminine."

"Perhaps that is what attracts Renny," said Nicholas.

"Never! An excessively masculine man like Renny cares only for the truly feminine in woman. Look at Alayne. She is all feminine."

"I spoke of attraction, not love," returned Nicholas testily.

"He is very fond of the child—Pauline—" put in Ernest, "and she has clung to him since her father's death."

"Well," growled his brother, "here comes Redhead himself. Let us ask him what is in his heart."

Renny, followed by Wakefield and the terrier, was striding along the drive, his every movement vibrant with temper. As soon as he was within speaking distance he said loudly:

"I suppose you have all heard of it!"

The three old people looked at him startled, and, even in his anger, he noticed the family resemblance among them, a resemblance deeper than and beyond feature and colouring. They answered simultaneously:

"Heard of what?"

"Why, the trees! The fool Council, or Public Works or something, is out to butcher them! I thought everyone but me knew about it."

Augusta looked warningly at him. This excitement was not good for Ernest. He gave no heed to the look but went on, in his rather metallic voice:

"They're widening the road and they propose to take a few feet off Jalna—you know what that would mean—the oaks—and they're straightening the *dangerous curve*—my God, I'd put a curve on their sterns if I had them here!"

Alayne emerged from the house just as he shouted these words. A shadow darkened her eyes, her lips tightened. He was in a mood she hated, one of noisy rage. That had been bad enough in his grandmother, an old woman of violent temper, but in a man, and that man her husband . . . For the hundredth time since their marriage she compared him unfavourably with her father. She realised that it was stupid of her to compare them, for one had been a gentle New England professor and the other was a horse-breeder—a country gentleman—but still a breeder of horses, a companion of grooms and horsy, rough-talking men. She had loved and revered her father, who would have referred to Renny's remark as "indelicate." She loved Renny with all the passion that was in her but she moved toward him with disapproval hardening her face. He saw it and his eyes, which had eagerly sought hers, turned quickly away. He callously repeated what he would like to do to the Council.

"But they dare not touch *our* trees," said Augusta, on a deep note.

"Why—why—" stammered Ernest, "it would be too horrible. Why—they must be mad!"

"It would be the last straw," muttered Nicholas heavily. "I shall interview the Minister myself."

"We'll all go," said Renny. "You, too, Auntie! You ought to have a say in it. We'll all go." He looked proudly at his elders, confident of the weight of their personalities. He was suddenly cheerful and gave a laugh. He ran his fingers through the hair on the top of his head, making it rise in a crest.

"I pity them if they interfere with us," he said confidently.

His uncles and aunt began a vigorous discussion of the case. They recalled former instances, some of them sixty years ago, when attempts had been made to impose the will of the community on the Whiteoaks, always without success. Yet no family in the neighbourhood, probably not one in the Province, was held in such affectionate regard.

This discussion inflamed their pride so that they appeared younger. Nicholas heaved himself out of his chair and strode up and down before the house, now and again casting inquiring looks at it, as though seeking its commendation. He flung out his gouty leg with scarcely an effort.

Ernest stretched himself in his chair, displaying his full length. He folded his arms and stared truculently up at the others, with nostrils dilated. "Thank heaven," he said, "that I am sufficiently recovered to go with you. We'll give these coarse-grained vandals something to think about."

More than ever Augusta looked affronted. She drew in her chin, on which a few grey hairs curled, her eyes brightening with emotion. "Mamma and Papa," she said, "walked under those trees, a stately young couple, when I was a babe in arms. It was on that very curve that their carriage collided with old Mr. Pink's and he had a thighbone fractured."

"I should think," said Alayne, who had come down the steps, "that that proves the curve to be dangerous."

"Not at all," returned Augusta. "Mr. Pink was a man of the poorest judgment. He could not dance a quadrille without collisions."

"As an infant," said Wakefield sententiously, "I was wheeled in my baby carriage around that curve, under those oaks. My first feeble speculations were concerned with their girth. My earliest——"

A look from Renny cut him short.

"Even Wakefield," remarked Augusta, "is deeply affected."

"Yes," agreed Ernest, "and no wonder, for the day he was born and his mother lay dying, a gale tore one of the finest up by the roots and laid it across the road."

"Well," said Renny, "we'll not worry any more about the trees. We will go to headquarters and put a stop to it."

The dinner-gong sounded from within. Wakefield hastened to help Ernest to rise. Nicholas took his sister by the arm and Renny and Alayne followed last. She took a pinch of his sleeve in her fingers and delayed him in the hall. She looked up into his face half provocatively, half accusingly.

"You have not kissed me today."

"I have not seen you."

"Whose fault is that?"

"Not mine. I knew that the kid had disturbed you last night, so I kept away this morning. Right after breakfast I had business at the stables."

"That was something new, wasn't it?"

He was quick to notice the sarcasm in her voice and to take offence where his horses were concerned. He answered hotly:

"I should like to know where we should be if it weren't for the horses!"

"In pocket, I sometimes think," she answered.

"Oh, well, I can't expect any sympathy from you." He jerked himself away and moved toward the door of the dining-room. From there came the appetising smell of chicken pot-pie, and the animated mingling of voices.

She caught his arm and held it. "Renny! You're unjust, and you know it. I do sympathise in everything you do. But I think it hard that I should have to ask for kisses."

He turned to her and gave her a kiss that had no more tenderness in it than a bite. She pushed him toward the dining-room with a little laugh. "Please go and have your dinner. Don't think about me." Her cheeks were flushed angrily.

He drew out her chair, pushed it under her with more force than politeness, then took his place at the head of the table. Wragge regarded them out of his shrewd grey face with pessimistic understanding. Alayne resented his watchful attitude, resented still more his leaning over Renny and whispering something in a tone of commiseration. She caught the words "grand old trees" and "knew as 'ow upset you'd be, sir."

Renny was serving the stewed chicken and dumplings with speed and discrimination. Breast and a wing for each of the women, breast alone for Ernest, breast and the little oyster-shaped pieces from the back for Wakefield, the upper part of a leg to Nicholas, who preferred dark meat, a drumstick to his small nephew, Maurice, and what was left to Piers and himself, well flanked by dumplings. Every eye was on him. If he had faltered in his serving of the dinner, his hard-won prestige would have suffered, the solidarity of table tradition been shattered.

On one side of the table Augusta sat between her two brothers. On the other Piers, his wife, Pheasant, and Wakefield. Between Piers and Renny, six-years-old Maurice industriously scooped up his gravy with a spoon.

Piers gave Renny curious side glances out of his full blue eyes. He wondered where his feelings of outrage for the trees would carry him; how far he would go if his efforts to bring the authorities to his way of thinking were futile. He himself was sorry about the trees, about the picturesque curve in the road, but—one must move with the times, and the times moved with motor-cars. He asked casually:

"What shall you do if—well, if they won't listen to reason?"

Renny thrust a piece of hot dumpling into his mouth and stared at Piers. Alayne took the opportunity to speak. She said in a tone of restrained calm, which was obviously intended to be an example to her husband:

"What could he do, Piers, but submit as any gentleman must?"

Piers grunted, without taking his eyes from Renny's face.

Wragge gave a sneering grin which he hid behind his sallow fingers and a cough.

Renny bolted the dumpling.

"Do"—he repeated—"do—why, I will take my gun down to the road and put a shot into the first man who lays an axe to one of my trees!"

Such an abrupt silence—made more intense by the suspension of even mastication—followed this outburst, that little Maurice laid down his spoon and looked from face to face, astonished.

Then Nicholas broke into subterranean laughter, followed by a high-pitched giggle from Pheasant. Ernest turned deep pink.

"That's the way to talk," he said.

"Yes," agreed Piers, "if he wants to get into trouble."

"Trouble nothing," retorted Nicholas. "We'll show them from the start that we'll not be browbeaten. My God, when I think of our trees . . ."

Augusta added:

"And the road that was once absolutely ours. . . ."

"And it," said Ernest, "disfigured by bungalows."

"And now the kink taken out of it," put in Wakefield.

Augusta drew a deep sigh. "Things are changing both here and in England." She looked about the table as she said this as though expecting astonishment at her announcement.

"And for the worse, too," came from young Pheasant.

"They can change as fast as they like," said Renny, "if they'll just let me alone."

Rags spoke in a sentimental tone from the doorway.

"Ah, I expect I'd see great chynges in old London if I was to go back naow!"

Lady Buckley looked through him. Alayne looked down her nose. But Renny ejaculated warmly:

"I'll bet you would, Rags! We must go over some time before long." He had finished his chicken and now set his plate, swimming with gravy and scraps, on the floor in front of Piers' terrier.

Piers, who had not seen her since her bath, when she had left his hands white as the snow, gazed down at her with a scowl.

"Where has she been?" he demanded.

"Taking a walk with me."

"You might have kept her out of burrows. I'm taking her into town this afternoon to show her to a man who is interested in her next litter." He bent down to take the plate from her. "She's not allowed to eat table scraps."

Renny, who always gave his dogs titbits from his plate, also bent and caught Piers' wrist and held it. "Let her alone," he said. "She looks half starved."

"That's what I say!" cried Pheasant. "She never has enough to eat."

"What do you know about it?" growled Piers, still trying to remove the plate while Renny still held his wrist.

"I know what it is to have young," she declared.

There was a laugh at Piers' expense. He sat up, red-faced. The tablecloth had been pulled askew between the brothers, and Mooey's mug of milk was overturned. The terrier, who had been fearful of losing her dinner, had in great haste licked the plate clean and now turned her attention to the milk that dribbled like manna from above.

"Look what you've done, you young idiot!" said Piers to his son.

"You did it yourself," returned Renny, straightening the cloth. Alayne looked apologetically at Augusta, who suddenly exclaimed: "Enough! Enough! You are making the child unruly."

"What I want to know," interrupted Ernest, "is how soon we can go to the office of this official. I must conserve my energy."

"Directly the meal is over," said Renny, attacking the black currant roly-poly that Wragge had placed in front of him.

Ernest eyed it longingly.

"Uncle Ernie?"

"Perhaps I had better not."

"Do you good."

"A small helping then."

Circular pieces of the suet pudding oozing purplish black jam hastened after each other down the board.

"Mooey, you tripe, we've come to you! Much or little?"

"Much!" shouted Mooey, joggling in his chair.

"Strange how unruly he grows," said Augusta.

Piers put his hand on the child's head and pressed it down. He said: "It would be better to find out if the Minister is in town before you go. You should make an appointment."

Nicholas answered—"No, no. He might try to get out of seeing us. We'll risk not finding him at home. Better strike while the iron is hot."

Piers shrugged. "You'll find it a stifling drive at this hour."

"We shall take the new car," said Renny.

It was still called the new car though it had been bought three years before. Piers gave an astonished look at Renny, who had always refused to use it.

"Why, look here," he said, "I'm taking it myself this afternoon. I'm sorry"—but after all, it was his car.

"You may take the old one," said his senior pleasantly.

"Certainly," agreed Nicholas. "We must not go in looking shabby. It is just possible that the man may not have heard of us. We must appear as people of substance."

"Not heard of us!" exclaimed his sister.

"Well"—Nicholas' voice was sombre—"you never know who these fellows are."

Ernest interjected—"Yes, we must appear as people of substance. I shall wear my silk hat, I think."

"For God's sake . . ." mumbled Piers.

The telephone rang loudly in the sitting-room. It had been installed at the time of Ernest's illness. Its most frequent use since had been for conversations between Renny and his horsy friends. He sprang up now to go to it, leaving his pudding. One of his Clumber spaniels came sedately from under his chair and laid its muzzle on the seat as though to guard it for him.

He left the door open behind him and all that he said was audible in the dining-room.

"Hello! Yes—it's Whiteoak speaking. . . . Certainly I wanted to see the mare. You were to let me know. . . . I got no message. . . . No—not a word. . . . And Collins bought her? It's a damned shame! . . . Why didn't you call again? . . . My wife! She gave me no message . . . yes, I suppose—thinking about a new dress . . . yes, women all alike . . . yes, I'll give her your reproaches . . . yes, I'll tell her you said she was a naughty girl—ha! ha! Oh no, she'd not be annoyed. . . ."

He came back to the table grinning, but the grin faded when he saw his wife's expression.

"No wonder," exclaimed Pheasant, "that Alayne looks mortified. Playful messages from that old Crowdy! I wonder at his cheek."

Renny gave a deprecating glance at Alayne from under the thick black lashes that lent his looks an added charm for women. "Crowdy is a decent head and Alayne has no reason for feeling hurt," he said. "It is I who ought to be feeling hurt at not getting his message. It was very important that I should see that mare."

Alayne made no answer. She was in a mood of helpless childlike anger against him. Hot tears were behind her eyes and a cold smile on her lips. But why was she angry? She scarcely knew. Perhaps it was just because she loved him so fiercely, and fierce love was against her nature and hurt her. Perhaps it was partly because all he did was so important to her that she saw his faults under her magnifying absorption in him. It was possible that she had a perverse pleasure in being hurt by him. But her unhappiness of the moment was real. She excused herself from the table, after a stiff apology for her forgetfulness, and went upstairs to relieve the nursemaid who was looking after her child.

As she entered the shabby attic room which they had turned into a day nursery she noticed how hot it was up there under the sloping roof, and the thought crossed her mind, as it had often before, that if the family were not so large she might have arranged a beautiful modern nursery next her own room. She despised Alma Patch, the young girl who came in by the day to help with the children. She disliked her ill-kept hair and nails, her wet underlip, her timid whispering voice, and she allowed her to have as little to do with her child as possible. It was nervous, highly strung. She had its crib in her bedroom and devoted the greater part of the day to its care.

Pheasant's younger son, named Finch, but called Nooky, was still sitting in his high chair emptying the last drops from his mug of milk. He was two years old, a delicate, shy child, with sleek fair hair and hazel eyes. He was very fond of Alayne, and she often wished that her own child would show so much affection for her.

That child came toward her now with the triumphant walk she had just acquired, her dense, dark-red hair on end, her small being overflowing with vitality. She was not a pretty child, for she had too large a nose for her infant face, and the expression of her mouth showed little of the appealing softness of eighteen months. She looked at Alayne out of Renny's eyes, and in some strange way that intense gaze was a barrier between them. For in the babe it was feminine and antagonistic.

She lifted up the child and kissed it. It grasped her neck fiercely,

23

pressed its knees spasmodically against her stomach and rubbed its satin cheek against hers.

"Gently, Baby," she begged. "You *must* not be so rough!"

"Me, too! Me, too!" cried the little boy.

She bent over and kissed the top of the silky head. Before she could prevent it the baby had grasped a handful of his hair and pulled it vigorously. He broke into loud wails, his mug was knocked to the floor and broken.

Alayne set down the baby, forcing back a desire to shake her, and exclaimed:

"Adeline, you *must* be more gentle! See how you have hurt dear little Nooky!"

Alma Patch, picking up bits of broken china, said:

"She's after him all the time, ma'am. She takes his own playthings off him and, if he don't give them up quick enough to please her, she pulls his hair. It's really awful to see her sometimes."

Little Adeline was angry at being put down. With head and heels on the floor, she arched her plump diaphragm and rent the air with her shrieks. Alayne picked her up and carried her swiftly down the stairs and into her own bedroom. Again she sat her down, regarding her with an expression more suspicious than maternal. Would she hurl herself on the floor again? And, if she did, would it be better to go out of the room and leave her to her rage, or stay and try to control her?

Adeline did not throw herself down, however. She stood, with chest expanded, screaming, and hitting savagely at her mother when she laid a restraining hand on her. Alayne was almost frightened at the anger which her own child had the power of rousing in her. She abhorred the cruel desire to hurt which she felt battling within her. Yet to see her child suffer would have been terrible to her.

Adeline held her breath for a more sustained effort and in the interval Alayne heard Nooky still wailing above. Children—how she once had idealised them!

She heard Renny's step in the passage. Adeline heard it too, and the scream she had been preparing issued from her scarlet lips in a gurgle of laughter. She ran to the door and rattled the knob. Alayne, fearful that the opening door might strike her, swept her up and was rewarded by kicks and writhings.

They faced Renny as he came in, mother and daughter, with no trait, mental or physical, in common, antagonistic, yet loving each other and him.

He took the child from Alayne's arms, tossed her up and kissed her.

There had been no tears in her eyes. Now they shone like stars. Her exertions had flooded the cream of her cheeks with a delicious pink. Renny regarded her with pride.

"Wouldn't Gran have gloried in her?" he demanded.

Alayne nodded. She was too disturbed by the fracas for speech.

"She's a wonder," he continued, "a wonder, and a peach of peaches. I wish Gran could see her! She'd appreciate her. She's in a class by herself—the prize filly—aren't you, my pet?"

The object of his ecstasies well knew that she was being praised. She preened herself, drew in the corners of her mouth, and looked at him out of the sides of her dark eyes.

Then he drew her close and, planting his mouth on hers, devoured her with kisses. . . . Alayne stood looking at them, remembering how she had wished for a child, had felt that, with her child in his arms, the bond between him and Wakefield, which seemed to her neurotic, would be naturally loosened. This had not been the case. Renny's heart had only expanded to make room for the new love. And his demonstrations of love for the small Adeline were too extravagant, too reminiscent of his grandmother, to please her. How could she properly train her child with Renny's laughter, Renny's scowl, or his boisterous praise, always intervening at the wrong time? Even now Adeline showed plainly that her mother's opinion was of little value to her as compared with her father's.

She laid herself out to please him, changing her expression from that of a small fury to one befitting a seraph, at his approach. She would show off her tricks before him like an actress. She delighted in pulling the ears and tails of the dogs but, at the sound of his step, she would stroke and blandish them. All the family (except Wakefield, who was jealous of her) spoiled her. "How she favours dear Mamma!" "She is a perfect Court!" "Do not cross her! Her high spirit should not be broken!" Or "She's the spit of dear old Gran." These were the exclamations Alayne was constantly hearing. She was beginning to despair of ever training her as she should be trained.

"She has been behaving very badly," she said. "Pulling Nooky's hair for nothing at all."

He kissed her again. "She loves the feel of hair in her hands. She doesn't realise that it hurts. Pull your Daddy's then! He has a tough scalp."

The baby filled her hands with his strong red hair and pulled until she drew herself upright in his arms.

Suddenly he set her on her feet. "I must be off," he said.

After a moment of astonishment she broke into screams and beat her little hands in anger on the door he had shut behind him.

III

THE FELLING

The interview between the elder Whiteoaks, Renny, and the Minister of Highways had been partially successful. The road in front of Jalna was to be widened entirely on the opposite side. The trees that shielded the old house from the gaze of the public were to be spared. But the beauty of the road would soon be a thing of the past, living only in the memory of those who, like the Whiteoaks, had grown up beside it.

The noble oaks, serene in their strength, proud, sound as saplings, had completed the green galaxy of their summer foliage before the first blow from the axe bruised their bark. They formed an arch above the white road, stretching out their leaves like hands, to touch those opposite. The strong sun threw the mantle of their shadows on the worn paths beneath. Squirrels, chipmunks, blackbirds, and orioles flashed in and out of their sheltering boughs. Bright drops of resin oozed from them in their exuberance.

The day on which the first one was felled was a day of mourning at Jalna. The uncles were sunk in melancholy, but Augusta, leaning on Pheasant's arm, walked down the road as far as the bend to look at their unbroken ranks for the last time. It was a lovely day and the path was smooth with pine needles. Pheasant's short brown hair blew in the breeze. She pressed Augusta's arm against her side in a comforting way, as they passed under the trees. They might have been entering a chamber of death.

"To think," Augusta exclaimed, "that there are people so insensate as to cut these down!"

"It is a blessing," said Pheasant, "that Gran did not live to see this."

"She would never have allowed it!" declared Augusta. "And I will do these people the credit of thinking that they would never have suggested it in her lifetime. They look on my brothers as younger and less firmly attached to tradition."

"Yes, of course. We're none of us nearly so old as Gran."

Augusta looked down into the small oval face with its pencilled brows.

"You are very young," she said. "I hope that you are happy with Piers."

"Oh yes! And with dear little Mooey and Nooky. I really think I am a happier woman than Alayne. We've both been through a good deal."

"You have," agreed Augusta deeply. "It was so different with me in my married life, which was complete bliss."

"Married life like that must be wonderful." Pheasant remembered the photographs of Uncle Edwin, looking out of pale eyes between thin whiskers.

"Wonderful. . . . He has been in his grave for many years."

"Shall we turn back, Auntie? It will be quite a long walk for you."

Walking back they forgot the trees in their own thoughts. Scenes from Augusta's childhood and girlhood came back to her with remarkable clearness, and Augusta's question as to her happiness turned Pheasant's thoughts back to her affair with Piers' brother Eden. That had almost wrecked her life with Piers. Seven years ago . . . she had been only eighteen then . . . and it was more than four years since Eden had gone off with Minny Ware! He had not been home since. His name was not mentioned—in front of her, at any rate—but she knew that Renny heard from him occasionally, for she had seen letters addressed in his hand. She wondered if Alayne often thought of her married life with him, and if he had become shadowy, like a figure in a dream, to Alayne, as he had to her. She could not clearly recall his features, but his smile—that veiled, half-sad smile—and the touch of his hands—the memory of them was branded on her soul. . . . She shivered as she walked under the trees. Never, never did she want to see him again! She would be glad if she could hear that he had died in foreign parts. The hands of her spirit stretched out toward Piers and her children. She quickened her steps to return to them. Oh, perhaps it had been well that this nest which she and Piers had built had been almost broken, for she would ever fly back to it with the greater ardour. . . .

As the trees were felled and lay with shattered limbs across the path, Renny, of all the family, could not bear to be long away from the scene of destruction. He would tear by the workmen in his dilapidated old car at a rate so furious that they would have to leap aside to save their lives. Sometimes he would stop the car beside them and point out to them how they were ruining the beauty of the road. They were Italians and, even if they did not understand half of what he said, they understood his gestures and his love of the beautiful

27

trees. He managed to waste a good deal of their time for them, so that their foreman hated the sight of him.

As the devastation progressed he took to visiting the scene on horseback so that he might draw closer to the men and thread his way among the fallen trees. It was a spirited beast he was exercising, and more than once a panic was caused by its rearing and plunging when a tree fell. He knew that the foreman hated him, so he kept as near to him as possible, shouting occasionally:

"Good for you! Keep them at it! You'll soon have the place looking like hell!"

The farmer from whom Clara Lebraux rented her fox-farm had had been one of the petitioners for widening the road. When Renny met him he called to him:

"You may thank God that I have good control of myself!"

But when the old trees were laid flat and the road stretched bare and hideous, he suddenly ceased to worry about it. Such things would happen, and he was thankful that the authorities had been persuaded to spare his own oaks. He drove his car past the gang of workmen without looking to right or left.

He found his gate shut and got out of the car to open it. As he turned, the comforting feel of it under his hand, he looked, with a sense of bewilderment, along the disfigured road. After this he would take the back road whenever it was possible. He was an alien on this.

He saw a man walking slowly along the path who seemed strangely familiar. Surely it was someone he knew very well. He must have passed him without noticing him. He narrowed his eyes, trying to make out the features. His heart gave a quick throb of mingled pleasure and pain as he recognised Eden. Pleasure at seeing him again after nearly five years, pain at his changed looks. He had always been slender, but now he was terribly thin. His cheeks were hollow and there was a feverish light in his eyes. He hurried forward at the sight of Renny waiting by the gate.

"I recognised you in the old bus!" he exclaimed, "but you went by so fast I couldn't make you see me." He added petulantly, as they shook hands—"I should have liked a lift. That's a beastly walk from the station."

Renny wrung his hand. "Too bad I didn't see you! But surely the walk from the station . . ." He left the sentence unfinished, looking anxiously into his brother's face. He asked:

"You've been ill, haven't you?"

Eden gave the shadow of a shrug. "Well, not exactly down on

28

my back, but rather rocky. I may as well tell you that I haven't a cent—or a job. If I had one, I'm not well enough to hold it." An abrupt, harsh cough escaped him, and he added quickly:

"I wasn't coming in. I was going over to Meggie's to see if she'd have me for a bit."

For a moment Renny did not speak. He drew back a pace from Eden and stood looking at his slender form against the background of the desolated road. Behind him the fallen trees, the young green foliage, bruised and broken. He had a horrible sense of foreboding. He said, with an effort:

"Of course, Meggie will be glad to have you. And Maurice, too. I'll drive you over now. Have you any baggage?"

"It's at the station. I thought I'd walk. I'd forgotten how far it is. God, what a mess they're making of the road! It used to be pretty at this time of year."

"Yes. But they're letting our trees alone, I'm glad to say. Get into the car and I'll have you at the Vaughans' in time for dinner."

Eden sank on to the warm seat with a sigh of exhaustion. Renny started the engine and the old car, with a preliminary lurch or two, bumped up the road toward Vaughanlands.

"What have you been doing with yourself?" asked Renny. "I haven't heard anything of you for over a year. Young Finch wrote then that he'd met you in Paris."

"Yes. . . . I've been there, and in London."

"What about that girl—Minny Ware?"

Eden laughed easily. "Oh, she and I parted—quite amiably. Boredom on my side. A rich Jew on hers. He was fond of music and he fell in love with her voice."

"Hm. . . . Well, I'm glad you separated."

"Perhaps. But I shouldn't be in this state if Minny were with me. She always took good care of me—saw that I went to bed in decent time—fed me well—when she could manage it. I haven't had what I should to eat lately." He spoke lightly, but the sight of his thin knees, the thin hand lying on the knee, pierced Renny. He muttered:

"Why didn't you come home before?"

"I had a job on a newspaper in Paris—for a while. Then I lost that, and—Minny. Then I went over to London. I did some writing, but it was hard to sell things. I had pretty uncomfortable lodgings and I caught a chill; oh, I don't know—everything went wrong, and how could I come home without the money for my passage?"

"You know I would have sent it."

"Good old fellow! How are things with you?"

"I'm just hanging on. Times are rotten. Nobody wants to buy horses."

"And Alayne?"

Eden succeeded in making his tone casual but Renny reddened. "She's all right. She's got a child, you know."

"Yes, I heard. Good for Alayne. The image of you, Finch says."

"More like Gran. . . . When did you see Finch?"

"Just before I sailed. He dug up the money for my passage. He has just come to the last of Gran's legacy—but he'll get on. He's attracting attention in London. I heard him play in his recital there. I was proud of him. He'd been frightfully nervous before it but he didn't show a trace when he played. There were two musical critics behind me. They said such nice things about him that I couldn't restrain myself. I turned round at the end and told them that I was his brother. He composes too. Has an idea for an opera in his head. Queer stuff. But, I believe, good. As I have said before, Finch is the flower of our flock."

Renny looked gratified, but sceptical. He said:

"Wake's coming on. You'll be surprised when you see him. He's as tall as you are. Has almost no trouble with his heart now. He's just got his first dinner-jacket."

"Does he write any poetry now?"

"Not a line!" Renny's voice had a jubilant ring.

Eden gave a short bitter laugh. "He'll be popular with his family, then."

"Oh, poetry is all right. But I don't think too much of it is good for a young fellow. . . . Have you been writing any lately?"

"Not a line!" He imitated Renny's tone, but this was lost on his elder, who inquired:

"How is Finch? Has he put any flesh on?"

"He's looking tired out. He spoke of coming home for a rest."

"We'll be glad to see him."

The car had turned in at the Vaughans' gate and now drew up before the door. It was wide open, and at this moment their sister appeared inside, carrying an armful of pink peonies.

She was like a peony herself, full-bosomed, fragrant, exhaling feminine sweetness. She smiled as she saw Renny, looked startled when she became aware of Eden's presence, ran rather heavily down the steps and threw an arm about his neck. They kissed repeatedly.

"Oh, my dear boy, how ill you look! But I'm so glad to see you! It seems such ages! Why didn't you tell me he was coming, Renny?"

"Because I didn't know myself." He added, with a sardonic smile that brought out a resemblance to Nicholas: "He has a way, you know, of going and coming without letting his family know."

Eden, feeling a boy again in Meg's presence, looked sulky.

She said, with a plump arm still around him:

"Never mind! We'll go straight in and I'll have places laid for you. You're just in time for dinner."

She led them into a comfortable sitting-room, bright with flowered chintz. A canary sang noisily; a cat purred in the most comfortable chair; a raucous female voice declaimed culinary recipes from the radio. Renny flicked a finger sharply against the wires of the cage, pushed the cat from her nest, and turned off the radio. His sister watched him tolerantly. She said:

"I wasn't listening-in. But the noise encourages birdie. And it intimidates the cat. It's so useful in that way."

Six years-old Patience came running in. She had her mother's smile and her father's grey eyes. She clambered to Renny's knee, hugging him closely. He kissed her demonstratively, and asked:

"Do you know who that is?"

She stared dubiously at Eden, who did not like children.

"That's Uncle Eden," said Renny.

"Aren't you going to give me a kiss?" asked Eden.

She went to him gravely and they kissed without enthusiasm. Then she flew back to Renny's knee.

Meg said—"I must go and see about the dinner. Oh, it is so nice to have you!"

When she had gone Eden asked:

"Does she eat a decent meal now or does she still live on snacks?"

"She's the same old Meggie. Little trays—scones and honey—bread and jam—pots of tea. They set a rotten table."

"We do not!" exclaimed Patience.

"Don't be cheeky! And don't tell your mother I said that or I'll skin you alive."

She looked momentarily subdued, and Eden remarked:

"I hope they won't starve me."

"Meggie will delight in feeding you up. She was wonderful with young Finch that time he was ill."

Eden said maliciously—"Oh yes, the time he tried to drown himself."

Renny scowled and looked at the child.

She said defensively—"I'm not going to tell."

He hugged her to him and burst out laughing.

31

Maurice Vaughan came into the room. He had heard from his wife of Eden's arrival. With the greying of his hair, his complexion had become clearer. He had put on flesh. He and Meggie were a solid pair.

After shaking hands with Eden he gave Renny an only half-concealed look of foreboding.

Eden said—"You're looking well, Maurice. You fellows are so beastly healthy. It's rather hard lines that I should have inherited my mother's weakness."

"You'd be all right," said Renny, "if you'd take care of yourself."

"It's the proper thing for poets to be consumptive, isn't it?" observed Maurice.

Meg returned to the room, beamed at her brothers and daughter and frowned slightly at her husband.

"Dinner will be ready in a few minutes," she said, and seated herself on the arm of Eden's chair and stroked his hair. "The same beautiful hair, Eden. Do you notice how grey Maurice has grown?"

"Yes. I suppose you've had something to do with that, Meggie?"

She answered with conviction—"He never got a grey hair on my account."

"He certainly looks well fed."

Patience wriggled on her uncle's knee. "Daddy," she said plaintively, "I don't want to be skinned alive!"

"Be a good girl then," said Daddy.

"The remarks she makes!" exclaimed Meg. "Sometimes I'm almost afraid for her, she's so deep."

"Don't take any notice of what she says," said Renny, "that's the best way."

"But fancy her having ideas like that in her little head!"

Eden turned to Maurice. "They've been making a shambles of the road, haven't they?"

"I only wish," returned Maurice in a low tone, "that the road had been widened in this direction. I'd have been glad of the compensation for my land and trees."

But Renny overheard him and broke in, heatedly:

"I'm ashamed to hear you say such a thing! Better starve than do that!"

Maurice gave his rather hang-dog laugh. "Well, it looks as though we'd starve in any case. My dividends have dropped almost to zero."

"It's a mercy," cried Meg, "that Finch holds the mortgage on our place or we might be turned out."

"He is coming home," said Eden. "Perhaps that is his object."

"Never! Finch would never turn his only sister out of her home!"

She had no sense of humour. The three men looked at her kindly. Maurice said:

"Finch is a good fellow. I can't say that I quite understand him. But—as Meggie says—he's kind-hearted." He sat in silence a moment, tapping his teeth with his nails, obviously trying to say something that he hated to say.

At last he got it out. "Meg and I have been thinking that it would be a good idea if we'd subdivide some of our property into building lots. Put up some bungalows. People are anxious to get out of the city. I think there must be lots of people who would be glad to sell their houses and move into nice little bungalows where taxes are low and they could have a bit of garden." All the while he spoke he fingered the leather bandage he wore on the wrist that had been shattered in the War.

Renny set Patience on her feet.

He glared at his brother-in-law, his eyes showing white around the iris. "You're not in earnest!"

"Absolutely. Why not?"

"You know very well why not. You're not quite a fool."

Maurice's face reddened. "It's all very well for you to talk. But what are you going to do about it? We've got to live."

"If you're hard up I'll lend you money."

"Where will you get it? I don't want to be inquisitive but—well, I thought you were pretty hard up yourself."

"I am. But I'll not stand seeing the old properties cut up."

"This won't affect Jalna."

"Don't talk rot! Of course it will affect Jalna. What sort of people are coming into those bungalows?"

"I'd see that the right sort came."

"Don't deceive yourself! You'll plant a shack town at our door." He got up and strode about the room.

"That can't be helped," said Meg fiercely. "We must have money. We can't get on any longer without it. I economise in every way possible. I set a very very plain table. . . ."

"Oh, no, no, no!" interrupted Patience, and burst into tears.

Meg gathered her child to her breast. "Whatever is wrong, my darling?"

"I don't want to be skinned alive."

Meg faced her brothers in her maternal splendour.

"You see. The child is unnerved. She knows that something is hanging over us—like the sword of Damocles."

Eden gave an hysterical laugh.

"You may laugh," said Renny, "but this is a serious matter. I could not have believed that Maurice would suggest such a thing. And for you to back him up in it, Meggie! Why, it is horrible. Gran would turn over in her grave."

"You talk," said Maurice, "as though I were subdividing Jalna."

"You are our nearest neighbour. Your people and my people have always kept up the old traditions."

"What good does it do us to hang on to land that brings in nothing? My God, man, we've got to move with the times!"

"You can't make me believe that the times are moving forward. They're just rotting."

"That may be true, but—I must have money."

"I wonder," said Meg, "if Finch could help us."

Eden answered—"No chance of that! He's sucked dry."

Meg shook her head sorrowfully. "I think it is terrible the way Finch has gone through Gran's money. I could not have believed he would be so extravagant."

"So generous, you mean," retorted Eden. "He has given most of it away."

Meg ignored this. "If only the money hàd been left to me—her only granddaughter—it would never have been frittered away."

Renny interrupted—"That has nothing to do with what we are discussing."

"It has everything to do with it! If Gran had left me her money it would not be necessary for us to sell our land."

Maurice added—"And we must think of the youngster's future. If I had some rents coming in, things wouldn't be so bad."

Renny said—"Meg talks of selling, and you of renting. Which is it?"

"Well—our plans are indefinite."

There was something aloof in Maurice's voice—something of a cold withdrawal into himself that made Renny turn away. He picked up his hat, which he had thrown on a couch, and went toward the door.

"Why, you're not going!" exclaimed Meg.

"You must stay for dinner," added Maurice, half-heartedly. He shrank from the thought of a meal dominated by Renny's arrogant opposition to his project.

"I must go. I've a man coming out to see a horse at two o'clock."

The same formula was always the ready excuse on his lips. And as he uttered it he moved, with something of the restiveness of a nervous horse, away from the others. He gave Meg a look in passing and she followed him to the porch.

"Eden is in a pretty bad way," he said in a low tone. "He needs a rest and lots of good food. I had to bring him here to you—well, I couldn't have taken him to Jalna, you know."

She clasped his arm in her hands. "I will nurse him back to health. No matter what happens he shall lack nothing. Thank goodness, we have quantities of Jersey milk."

"Good. I'll send some stout and sherry. And I can give you some money next week. You'll need it."

"No, no. You must not. Tell me—where is Minny?"

"They've separated. I think that's a good thing. He's very thin, isn't he?"

"Yes, the poor boy! But don't worry! I'll look after him. Don't let us worry about anything!"

He smiled rather grimly but kissed her with affection, and, after half a dozen attempts, induced his car to start homewards.

IV

FINCH RETURNS

Two months later Finch Whiteoak came out of the house after having eaten his breakfast in company with Wakefield on the first morning after his return from abroad. He slowly crossed the lawn, his head thrown back, his eyes closed, drinking in the familiar scent of the air with closed eyes, so that it might permeate his entire being, in the fiery darkness beneath his lids. "I am here," he thought, "home again, where the very air has a smell all its own. A dry, sweet stinging smell that tickles my nostrils. Every foot of this lawn has been stepped on a thousand times by every one of us. No matter where I've been or what I've seen, this place has gone with me. I could not uproot myself from it if I tried. I've seen places so much more beautiful, so much more spectacular that this is tame compared with them, and yet it is so dramatic to me that the rustle of the trees makes me shiver with excitement, the neighing of that stallion in the stable is like a peal of bells to me, the sight of Rags' shiny coat with the fringed cuff makes me want to cry. I'll bet anything that I can walk straight across the lawn with my eyes shut and pick a golden-brown zinnia from the middle of the border." He walked on without wavering, made a scallop to avoid the great balsam-tree, and stopped just at the edge of the grass. He bent and stretched out his hand and closed it on a crisp flower-head. His fingers slid down the stalk. He broke it off and opened his eyes. He held a golden-brown zinnia with a crimson heart.

He was laughing when he heard steps on the grass behind him. He turned and saw Wakefield.

"What are you doing?" Wake asked.

"Passing a test. I came down the lawn with my eyes shut and picked a golden-brown zinnia."

"Brilliant youth," returned Wake, sitting down on the grass. "Here's your reward!" He held up a harvest apple, smooth as yellow silk, with one green leaf still clinging to its stem.

Finch took it and dropped to the grass beside his young brother. He sniffed the spicy sweetness of the apple, bit into its white flesh and said:

"Lord, I had forgotten what an apple could be!"

Wakefield looked at the hand and wrist that held the fruit. "You're very thin," he observed. "Thinner than I remember you. And Eden came back in an even worse condition. It's strange. I always envy you fellows who go abroad, and yet you come home—after all your adventures and your triumphs—looking half-starved."

"It is queer," agreed Finch. "But I have worked frightfully hard and it's natural to me to be thin. It's not natural to Eden. I feel worried about him."

"Oh, you mustn't worry now. He has picked up wonderfully. I had a talk with him yesterday and he was looking awfully handsome, with a most beautiful colour—as fit as can be. He was wondering if those rich friends of yours, the Leighs, could help him get a job."

"Have you seen anything of them lately?" asked Finch, trying to make his tone sound casual.

"No. They've been somewhere down the St. Lawrence all the summer, but before that we saw them occasionally."

"What did you make of Sarah, Wake?" He was curious to know how that strange girl, whom he had loved and hated, would affect this sensitive, rather supercilious young brother

"Young Mrs. Leigh? Well, Meg says she's as deep as the sea, and I'm inclined to agree with her. I'm sure of one thing, and that is that her in-laws hate her."

"What makes you sure of that?"

"She told Pheasant so. And Pheasant told me. I never guess at things. And she as much as told Pheasant that you and she had had an affair." Wake peered sideways at him.

Finch's heart had begun to tap sharply against his side. He said, plucking a handful of grass and slowly scattering it:

"That amounted to nothing. We rather liked each other, but she and Leigh fell in love at first sight. I don't suppose you have heard how they get on?"

"No—but Pheasant told me that, in her opinion, they're an ill-assorted pair. However, as far as I can make out, most married couples are. Except, of course, Aunt Augusta and Uncle Edwin. There was a marriage of souls!"

He looked so earnest as he said this that it was hard to know whether or not he were laughing in his sleeve. What a self-possessed, conceited young devil he was! The old admiration for him, the old desire to treat him roughly, came over Finch. But he finished his apple in outward acquiescence and tossed the core into the border. Then he asked irrelevantly:

"Do you often see Pauline Lebraux?"

"Almost every day since the holidays began. You'll be surprised at the way she's improved. I used not to think much of her looks, but she's grown almost beautiful. Beauty just comes on her like a flash. She may be standing near you looking rather round-shouldered and sallow, and she turns and smiles at you—or perhaps she doesn't even smile—and suddenly she's beautiful and you feel like shouting to her—'Don't move—don't change—stay like that always!' It's a most extraordinary thing."

Finch, watching his animated face, felt a sudden glow. Wake was growing up. They could be friends. He had never had a real friend among his brothers—a friend in the sense of close companionship.

"Tell me more about Pauline," he said.

"Well, for one thing, I took her to a dance not long ago. I knew she could dance. I knew that Renny had danced with her a good deal to the gramophone at the fox-farm. But I had no idea she was so wonderful. She simply floats. You feel that you could go on for ever."

"I'd like to see her."

"We'll go over this afternoon!"

"I can't. I'll have to go to the Vaughans."

"We'll go there first."

"All right. . . . I say, what's this I hear about Maurice subdividing some of his land?"

"My God! Don't ask me! I'm fed to the teeth with that. I've heard about nothing else all the holidays. Deputations of every shape and form have waited on him from Jalna. Then, for a week, the whole thing is hashed over and a new deputation is formed. According to the oldsters, Gran must be ceaselessly turning over in her grave. And Renny is almost as unreasonable as they are. Only one fact remains—Maurice and Meggie have got to have money or apply to the Consolidated Charities for help."

"I wish you wouldn't be so glib," said Finch. "You make everything sound awful."

"Do I? That's interesting."

"You're a callous little brute."

"Better callous than callow."

"Lord, when I think what I was at your age!"

"Yes," agreed Wakefield pityingly. "I remember. And Piers was always ragging you. And Renny was rather hard on you. But he's proud of you now. We all are. You're going to be famous, aren't you? I wonder if I shall. Perhaps I'll be a famous criminal. I believe I have a flair for crime."

"I shouldn't wonder." Then he added seriously—"What do you think you'll be, Wake?"

"I don't know. Renny wants me to be a clergyman. Thinks it would be a nice easy life for me and keep me near Jalna. But the truth is that I'd rather be a flier than anything, but I know he'd never let me go in for that."

Wakefield had lowered his voice, for he saw Renny coming toward them across the sun-warmed grass.

"I am going over to the fox-farm," he said. "Would you two like to come?" He looked down at them kindly, asking them if they would like to go with him as though he proposed a treat to two children.

Wakefield got to his feet at once. "Just the thing! I've been telling Finch that I must take him to see Pauline. He'll immediately fall in love with her, won't he, Renny?"

Finch still lolled on the grass. "I don't think I'll go," he said, twirling the zinnia in his fingers.

Wakefield looked down at him mockingly. "Very well, let's leave him," he said, and then sang, in a silky tenor:

"If he's content with a vegetable love which would certainly not
    suit *me*,
  Why, what a most particularly pure young man this pure young
    man must be!"

Renny gave his short jeering laugh that always had the power to make Finch flush with annoyance at himself, and began to walk away. Wake followed him, and Finch, after a short hesitation, rose and joined them.

"It was just," he explained, "that I suppose they have forgotten me. I hate butting in."

"Don't you worry," said Wakefield. "They haven't forgotten you. Renny and I never let anyone forget you. We're always bragging about you. When you were rich we bragged about your riches, and, now that they've gone, we brag about your fame, don't we, Renny?"

Finch could gladly have throttled him. He was scarcely home, he thought bitterly, before he was being ragged. And he had no power of retaliation.

Renny laughed again and then turned abruptly to Finch. "How much have you got left?" he asked.

The question came as a shock to Finch. His money and what he should do with it had so long been a sore point, Renny had so arrogantly refused to discuss it with him, that this sudden demand to know what remained of it startled and confused him. One reason that it confused him was because he had purposely given Eden the impression that there was almost nothing left of the one hundred thousand dollars Gran had bequeathed to him. He had felt contemptible in deceiving Eden who was ill and penniless, but he had done it instinctively to protect his own art. If he were to have a career he must have something to live on in the meantime. But if Eden knew he had money . . . well, he never could refuse Eden. Now, here was young Wake listening, ready to carry the news to him—yet he could not lie to Renny. And, after all, what was fifteen thousand dollars? Almost nothing! No one knew better than himself how quickly it would melt.

He stammered—"Oh, I think—I'm not perfectly sure—but I guess—about fifteen thousand."

"Hmph! Well, you've parted with it fast enough. Just what I expected."

"I have enough to see me through."

"You're lucky. I wish I had."

Finch burst out—"Renny, if I can do anything . . ."

Wakefield looked encouragingly at Renny, but he muttered:

"No, no. I don't want any of your money!"

"It must be good fun," said Wakefield, "to have spent all that and still have so much left."

"Oh, I don't know," said Finch.

Renny interrupted—"On our way to Mrs. Lebraux's I must show you what our dear Maurice has been doing. You've heard that he's planning a shack town along the ravine?"

"Yes. . . . Look here, Renny, I don't believe I want to see. It's so beastly depressing."

Renny gave his objection no more heed than if he had been a small boy, but led the way through the wicket gate in the hedge, along the winding path across a paddock, then down into the ravine where the stream hid itself among the watercress and honeysuckle. They stopped for a moment on the rustic bridge, for no Whiteoak could pass over it without this tribute. A group of cat-tails grew beside the stream, and one of them had already unloosed its velvet pile and the bright particles glistened on the air. A sumach tree of the deepest red sheltered the gay plumage of an oriole while he sang of late summer joys and eyed the purple elderberries spread out beneath him. The stream, talking secretly, showed itself for a space before sliding under the bridge, and into the sunlit pool thus formed Finch dropped his zinnia. A moment it stood upright, spreading out its leaves as though in a vase, then reclined gently and gave itself to the soothing movement of the stream.

Renny held out his cigarette-case to his juniors.

"It seems only yesterday," he said, "since I carried Wake down here in my arms to see the water and you ran alongside."

"I remember," said Wakefield, lighting his cigarette. "And Finch would sail paper boats, and you'd hold me over the railing head downward and the pool would look like a deep well."

Finch did not speak. The remembrance of his childhood filled his heart. He saw it complete, tangible. He felt that he could hold it in his hand, drop it down into the stream as he had dropped the zinnia.

The smoke from their cigarettes lay on the air in bluish-grey planes. Renny looked at his brothers with an amused, reminiscent expression, seeing them as he had seen them then.

At last, with one accord, they moved from the bridge and climbed the steep on the far side of the ravine. They passed through a wood of young oaks and Renny observed:

"This is where Piers and Pheasant used to meet on the sly."

They came to open fields which showed here and there the stakes of the surveyors.

"Good Lord!" exclaimed Finch. "Is this where Maurice is planting his bungalows? Why, it's right beside us!"

40

"We shall need to put up a barbed-wire fence," said Wakefield.

Renny grunted derisively. "No fence will keep the sight and sounds of them out. No—it's the thin end of the wedge. If we let this happen, God knows where it will end." He turned, with the ingratiating smile so like his grandmother's, to Finch.

"Here's your chance to become a landowner, youngster. You could buy the land off Maurice and save the situation."

"How much does he want for it?" asked Finch heavily.

"Ten thousand dollars, or even less, would buy it. But of course you can't be expected to do that. We'll just have to grin and bear it, I suppose." He looked bitterly over the fields and then turned away as though he could not bear the sight of them.

They walked over the rough ground to the road in the direction of the fox-farm.

"I wonder if they'll mind our coming in the morning," asked Finch, as they turned in at the gate. "They're not expecting us, are they?"

"We'll go round and have a look at the foxes," returned Renny. "That will give them time to tidy up, if they want to. Mrs. Lebraux is not at all fussy."

"Neither is Pauline," said Wakefield. "I've never known such an unaffected girl. She's just as natural and beautiful as one of her own foxes."

Renny gave a sly look across him at Finch.

Finch thought—"So—the kid is falling in love with Pauline."

Somehow the thought of that did not please him. Wake was too young for real love, and the idea of Pauline as the object of his first amorous flutter was irritating.

There was a scurry among the foxes as they approached. Tawny streaks slid into kennels or burrows. All except a dog fox who sat on top of one of the kennels looking contemptuously about him. He had the expression of a fox that has been hunted a score of times and has learned to sneer at his pursuers, but he had spent all his life behind wire-netting, had his food without danger, his courtships without rivals, and had never heard the cry of a hound. He had been a sickly cub nursed to health by Pauline. He was her pet and would let her handle him with no more objection than the lifting of his lip. Now he knew that she was in her seat in the apple-tree from where she could become acquainted with the habits of the different foxes unobserved.

She watched the three brothers approaching with a feeling of nervous excitement. If she could, she would have fled to the house, unseen by them. She drew back among the foliage of the apple-tree and listened, hoping, with a kind of mischievous fear, to hear what they might say.

They stood looking at the dog fox. She could see them distinctly, hear Renny whistling between his teeth. She was conscious of his peculiar inaccessibility. Although she had not seen Finch for nearly two years, it was Renny at whom she gazed with yearning surprise, as though she recognised in him an antagonist whom she loved and feared.

Finch said—"They've made some improvements here. It looks better cared for than when I saw it last." Something new in his voice held her. It was deeper. It had lost the hollow sweetness of youth. It was a man's voice, easy, careless, pleasant to hear. There was a new look in his face too, as though he had learned to wear a mask.

Wakefield answered eagerly—"Mrs. Lebraux is splendid. She works like a man. And as for Pauline—she's a marvel with the young foxes—she's as tender with them as though they were babies—*and* she's beautiful too. You'll agree with me in that, Finch."

Pauline's cheeks blazed. She was terrified lest they should go on talking about her. She could not bear to hear more, but that Wakefield had called her beautiful filled her with a wild, voluptuous joy. She stared down at him through the leaves, joyous and terrified.

Renny's voice cut in. "I should never call her beautiful. She's got that startled look, like a foal, that is rather nice to see in a young girl, but beautiful, why—I wish you boys could have seen a girl named Vera Lacey I was gone on when I was your age. *There* was a beauty, if you like."

Oh, how cruel he was to deny that she was beautiful when Wakefield had so positively said that she was!

Wakefield was asking—"Is that the one you have eleven photographs of, Renny?"

"Yes. She was always being photographed."

"Ah, then I have you," said Wake. "You admit that she was a beauty. Pauline is beautiful. There is a great difference."

Renny threw Finch a delighted look, as though to say—"See how this young one is coming on!"

Finch looked glum.

Pauline peered down at the three, scarcely able to breathe for the pounding of her heart. What if she were discovered? She would never be able to face them again. She saw the faces of the two younger, each feature clear in the morning light. But Renny's face she could not see clearly. She saw it distorted as though through tears

Clara Lebraux appeared from the stable, carrying on her back a sack filled with straw. She wore a man's overalls, and her cotton shirt, open at the neck, showed her rounded throat and chest as brown as mahogany. Her hair was the colour of a straw that was caught in its short denseness. Her round eyes regarded her visitors with an expression of confident friendliness.

She threw down the sack and shook hands—an agreeable smell of clean straw and warm clean flesh coming from her person.

"What have you there?" asked Renny.

"Litter for the cubs."

She looked appraisingly at Finch. "You've improved," she observed in her brusque way. "I hear you're becoming famous."

He blushed. "Heavens, no!"

"Well, you've given recitals in London."

"I've a long road ahead before I become famous."

"Are you giving any here?"

"I hope to."

Renny said—"He is going to rest and play about for a while first. I've brought him over to see Pauline."

"I thought she was out here," answered Mrs. Lebraux. She glanced up toward Pauline's accustomed seat, glimpsed her warning face and turned hastily away. "We'll go indoors and find her," she said, moving in the direction of the house.

Finch, too, had seen Pauline and followed the others, amused and curious.

They went into the shabby dining-room, and Mrs. Lebraux produced a bottle of Scotch and a syphon of soda. Both boys refused a drink, but Renny mixed one for himself and another slightly weaker for Clara Lebraux. With hers in her hand she went to the foot of the stairs and called—"Pauline!"

A voice answered from above and in a moment the young girl appeared, tall, pale, her skirt much too short for fashion, revealing her thin straight legs. She had the look, as Renny had said, of a startled foal, and Finch's first thought was one of disappointment that she had not developed more. Then he saw her beautifully shaped eyes, her smile of a proud child, and thought—"She's not what Wake said, but she's fascinating."

Her eyes searched his face, for she was afraid that he had seen her. But he successfully hid his knowledge and gave her a gently re-

43

assuring look. He held her long cool hand in his a little longer than was formal.

Renny said—"I've been showing Finch the sight of Vaughan's subdivision."

"I hope he was properly horrified. We think it a great shame," said Clara Lebraux.

"He was so horrified that he is inclined to buy the land from Vaughan and become a bulwark of Jalna."

"He's the moneyed one of our family, you know," put in Wakefield.

"What a splendid idea," said Clara Lebraux.

Finch laughed uncomfortably. "My brothers are joking."

"Of course we are," agreed Renny heartily, and turned to talk in an undertone to Pauline.

Clara said to Finch—"Renny is more deeply disturbed by this talk of subdividing and building bungalows than he shows."

Finch nodded sympathetically, but could not agree as to Renny's reticence.

"I'm afraid nothing can be done," he said, a note of firmness, of self-defence, in his voice.

"No. Nothing can be done. First it was the trees. And now this. It's hard luck for him."

"I think all the family feel it," said Finch.

"Of course." But her glance in Renny's direction said—"He is the only one who matters to me."

"I'm sorry for the Vaughans too," she added. "They feel that they must do it, and yet they feel guilty."

Wakefield had gone to a gramophone that stood in the small bay-window and was looking over some records. Finch had a sudden vivid recollection of him as a small boy investigating the contents of the cabinet of Indian curios while his elders were too busy with their talk to notice him.

Wakefield said—"Let's have a dance. I've brought Finch over especially to see what a lovely dancer Pauline is."

"At eleven o'clock in the morning!" exclaimed Clara Lebraux. "You forget that Pauline and I are farm hands!"

"I am paintng," returned the boy, "to dance with you in your present costume. Do let us be merry, as my grandmother used to say, for in fifty years or so we die."

Pauline looked eagerly from one to the other. "Whom shall I dance with?" she asked. "Mummy needn't pretend that we don't dance at this hour, for we do. She and I do tangos at any odd moment."

"Listen to that!" exclaimed Renny. "She'll show you up for the laggard you are, Clara!"

"Shall we shoot the dining-table into the parlour?" asked Wakefield. "Or shall we dance round it and into the hall?"

"Shoot it out," returned Clara Lebraux briefly.

The table was pushed through the archway into the parlour. Wakefield put on a record and gave it a little push. Outside a fox was barking, but the sound was quickly drowned by the arrogant passion of a syncopated one-step.

"Let joy be unrefined!" cried Wakefield, and danced toward Clara Lebraux with inviting arms.

They were an amusing sight dancing together, he in his well-fitting grey flannels, she in her baggy overalls and ruffled tow hair. Finch watched, smiling and rather shy. He did not want to dance this dance with Pauline, and he was relieved when Renny laughingly put his arm about her and swept her into it.

The two couples danced up and down the room. Finch watched them with a smile that had both indulgence and deprecation in it, as though he were watching children whom he longed to join, yet fearing that he could not sufficiently let himself go. His mind vibrated between the hope that he might remain an onlooker and the desire to hold Pauline in his arms. What was the expression in her eyes as she looked up into Renny's face? Utter trust—pleading—or a moth-like fascination? Her movements were extraordinarily supple and showed unexpected strength. And Renny danced as well as he rode. . . .

The record was finished. Only a protesting buzz came from the gramophone. Wake dashed to it, wound it up, turned the record over, and bowed in front of Pauline. What a vain youngster he was! Always dashing about, posturing, even though it was scarcely noon and he danced to a tinny gramophone. Finch hoped he would not have to dance with Mrs. Lebraux in that overall. He should feel idiotic. He turned to the window embarrassed and showed a pretended interest in a controversy going on among small birds in an apple-tree.

This was a languid, sensuously stressed waltz. The beat of it swept through his nerves with passionate melancholy. When he looked back into the room the partners had changed. Wakefield and Pauline floated together in a happy embrace. Mrs. Lebraux and Renny, with impassive faces, turned and turned again, their heads encircled by the wreath of smoke from a cigarette she had lighted.

45

When the waltz was over Renny looked at his wrist-watch and exclaimed that they must be off as he had something to attend to before dinner.

V

FAREWELL TO LEIGH

A fortnight later Finch picked up a paper and read an account of the drowning of his friend Arthur Leigh at a resort on the St. Lawrence. He and his wife had been caught in a squall while sailing and their boat had been swamped. They had clung to the overturned boat, but Leigh had soon become exhausted and let go. Several hours had passed before Mrs. Leigh had been rescued, but she was, although suffering from shock and exposure, progressing favourably.

After the first painful start Finch read and re-read the account with a numbed feeling. He said nothing of it to anyone, but went to his room, trying to realise what had happened, trying to believe that he would never see Arthur again, trying to put out of his mind the thought of Sarah.

One thing filled him with an aching surprise, and that was his lack of any poignant grief. Arthur . . . his dearest friend . . . his first passionately loved comrade . . . and he could think without any agony of his tragic death and wonder—with a quiver of the nerves —what it would mean to him !

Sarah. . . . How her coming had changed his feeling toward his friend ! He had never really forgiven Arthur for taking her from him, even though he had done it unknowingly. He recalled how Arthur had poured out to him the ecstasy and fear of his love. He remembered too how the ecstasy seemed always to be shadowed by the fear, how Arthur had seemed to dread being alone with Sarah. What had they made of their married life ? he wondered. He had ceased even to write to them, allowing a coolness unacknowledged to grow up between him and them.

He sat down and buried his face in his hands, in order that he might recall their two faces the more clearly. Arthur's, smooth, bright with the brightness of an untroubled boyhood. Had he ever in his life been crossed, gibed at ? Not unless Sarah . . . But could she, could any woman with a heart, bear to hurt Arthur ? Had Sarah a heart ? She had passion but that was different. . . . He saw her white, still face, her small withdrawn mouth, secret between the arched nose and prominent chin. He saw her small cold-looking

46

ears, the rigid plaits of her black hair. . . . Arthur's face retreated from him, submerged, lost in the waters of the St. Lawrence; only Sarah's was left in its tormenting sweetness. . . .

At last he could bear thinking of her no longer. He got up and went quickly down the stairs to Augusta's bedroom. He tapped on the door and her deep voice said—"Come in." She was sitting by the window sewing a button on a large white nightdress. She took off her spectacles and looked at him encouragingly, for in her opinion Finch needed encouragement.

"Auntie," he said jerkily, "I've had bad news."

She drew in her chin and her eyes widened.

"Yes? What is it, my dear?"

"It's about Arthur Leigh. You liked him, didn't you, Auntie?'

"Very much. . . . Is he dead, Finch?"

"Yes. He was drowned yesterday." He repeated what had happened.

Augusta's sallow skin had turned pale. She reiterated:

"This is very sad! Dear me—the poor boy's mother!"

Finch asked—"What about Sarah, Auntie? Don't you pity her?"

"Sarah will bear up," said Augusta cryptically.

Nicholas came in, following a loud knock. He carried the newspaper in his hand.

"I see that you know," he said. "I was just coming to find you. It is a great pity, isn't it?"

"It's awful for Sarah, isn't it, Uncle Nick?"

"Yes, yes, of course. But it is the poor lad himself I am thinking of. That girl always struck me as a heartless hussy."

Finch was strangely glad to hear these words on his uncle's lips. . . . "A heartless hussy," he repeated to himself.

Some days after he sought out Eden, who had known Arthur and Sarah during their short courtship. Eden was looking splendid, he thought. It was difficult to think of him as having been ill a few months before. Meggie had done wonders for him. He had quite taken possession of the Vaughans' sitting-room and they thought twice before entering it. He sat now, with writing things about him, and a worried expression on his handsome face.

"It's very disappointing," he said, "that Leigh should go off like this just when I counted on him to help me to some sort of job."

Finch was not shocked at Eden's callousness. Indeed he was not at all sure that it was callousness. Eden simply bowed his head to the arbitrary workings of fate. He was not given to self-pity, except in the form of occasional petulant remarks.

47

"It is too bad," agreed Finch. "What did you think of doing?"

"Anything! I can't sponge indefinitely on Meg and Maurice with the wolf at their door. I had thought that Leigh, with his connections, might get me appointed as lecturer in English somewhere or other. Or even in an office or bank. I've tried all the newspapers but the editors don't want anything. I showed one of them some articles on Paris and London but he wasn't interested in Paris or London. I suppose I'll end in running an elevator."

"I should think that any of those indoor jobs would be bad for you. You should have outdoor work."

Eden drew a woman's face of the classic type on the blotter in front of him and said irrelevantly:

"I suppose Sarah will be left awfully well off?"

"She'll be rich. Leigh's mother and sister are well provided for. I expect he would leave everything to Sarah."

A mischievous smile lit up Eden's face.

"Now is your opportunity. That girl was crazy about you. She cared nothing about Leigh. Meg tells me that they were unhappy together. You're a fool if you don't——"

"Shut up!" exclaimed Finch. "If you have no sense of decency, I have. You talk like this, and they probably haven't found Arthur's body yet!" His voice broke. "Don't you care in the least that he is dead?"

A bleakness came over Eden's face, giving it a closed-in look. He ran his hand quickly over his hair and picked up a freshly sharpened pencil. He said:

"I wish you wouldn't come bothering me, just when I've something worth while in my head."

Finch sprang up offended. "Sorry. . . . I'm going now. I want to find Meg." He reddened with anger.

Meg was all sympathy, crying over young Leigh as she ate toasted currant bun from a tray in her own room.

"That's just the way," she said. "The young and beautiful are taken. As for me, I've never really got over Gran's death. Sometimes I see her in my dreams, clearer than life. And the strange thing is, Finch darling, that she always says to me—'Margaret'—and she never called me that—'Margaret, I intended that you should have my ruby ring.' Isn't it uncanny?"

"Very uncanny, Meg."

"And isn't it impressive?"

"Awfully."

"Why do you suppose she calls me Margaret in the dream?"

48

"Well, they go by contraries, don't they?"

"Yes, but there is nothing contrary about her way of telling me that she intended me to have the ruby ring. . . . Just think—all that I—her only granddaughter—got from her beautiful belongings was her huge gold watch, which I couldn't possibly carry, and her old Indian shawl that her parrot used to make a nest in. Even little Patience thought it very strange when I told her. She said—'Mummie, those were funny things for great-grannie to give you.'"

"Why, look here, Meggie," said Finch suddenly, "I'd like to have Gran's watch and shawl, if you don't mind parting with them."

The Vaughans were considerably behind with the payments of the interest on the mortgage which Finch held on their house. Meg looked flurried. "Do you mean——" she stammered, "do you want—I know we're behind with the interest——"

"No, no, I was not thinking of the interest. I was just thinking I'd buy those things off you—if you don't mind." He gave his deprecating, rather troubled smile.

Meg laid her hand on his arm. "I'm sure you'd love to have the watch and the shawl, dear. As you got all her money it would be nice for you to have some of her personal belongings too."

Finch winced, and mumbled—"Oh, I don't know—I only thought—well, I always liked her watch and the colours in the shawl. . . ."

"Of course! And so do I! They're perfectly lovely, and if I had got the ring too—I'd have adored them. But you must confess that it's rather hard for me—her only granddaughter—to see other women wearing her jewellery. I don't mind Aunt Augusta, because she is Gran's only daughter, and I can endure Alayne, because she is Renny's wife, and all he got was her painted bedstead, but to see Pheasant—an illegitimate girl and the wife of a younger brother —sporting that gorgeous ruby, stirs me to my deepest depths!"

"Yes, it is hard," agreed Finch heavily. "Look here, Meggie, I don't believe you had better part with those things. After all, it would hardly be right, when Gran left them to you."

"But I want you to have them!" cried Meg dramatically. "The moment one of my brothers expresses a wish for anything, my one desire is to get it for him if it is within my power."

"Yes, but Meggie . . ."

"Not a word! You shall have the watch and the shawl—even though they are all I have."

A tightness came in Finch's throat at the realisation of Meg's

49

selflessness. She saw that he was deeply touched, and the ready tears filled her own eyes.

"Well," he said, "since you insist. But, of course, I must pay you a decent price for them."

A pucker dented Meg's smooth forehead. "Oh, I wish I were in a position to give them to you absolutely! It is so cruel to have always to think of money."

"I know. I know."

"But—since I must! Let me see—a watch like Gran's could never be worth less than two hundred dollars, and—do you know, they say those old Indian shawls are a fabulous price. Queen Victoria used always to give them for wedding presents."

"Did she really?" Finch looked rather alarmed.

"And I suppose Gran would scarcely have left it to me—her only granddaughter—if it had not been worth a good deal. . . . But I'd never dream of asking you more than a pittance for it. Give me— say, four hundred—no, a bare three hundred and fifty for the two and I'll be perfectly satisfied. . . . Except for wishing that I could afford to give them to you!"

Finch, by this time, almost felt that she was giving them to him. How kind Meg was! Indeed, she was perfect. . . .

"I'll write you a cheque for them this minute!" he exclaimed, and took out his book of blank cheques and his fountain-pen that had been a present from Aunt Augusta.

"Oh, any time will do for that!" But she allowed him to go on with the writing of it, and her eyes followed the movements of his pen as though it were the wand of a magician.

It was a relief to Finch to do something that took his mind—even for a moment—from the thought of Arthur, and from the sorrowful thought that the loss of Arthur came as no deep grief.

He left Vaughanlands with the shawl in a parcel and the watch in his pocket. As he crossed the fields he felt an extraordinary happiness in possessing them. Gran had brought the shawl with her from India eighty years ago. How many times its soft, richly coloured fabric had lain about her strong graceful shoulders, had covered her breast when it was full and firm. What intimacies of her passionate heart it had shielded! And the watch. . . . He took it from his pocket and it lay on his palm, shining in the hot sunlight. On it was en- graved—"Adeline, from her Philip, 1862." Finch remembered having been told that it was a present to celebrate the birth of his father. And his father and his grandparents were dust, and the watch was as quick as ever. . . . How the sight of it brought back Gran!

He could see her peering into the golden face, winking fast as she deciphered the time, her ornate cap rather askew, a look of lively anticipation lightening her strong features. "Dinner-time! Ha, that's good! I like my dinner. Exercise or no—I like my hot dinner." And she would thrust her head forward to catch the first sound of the gong.

As he walked homeward he had the feeling that virtue entered into him from the possession of her belongings, resilience against the blows of life. Zest for life and fortitude seemed to emanate from these things so long associated with her.

These feelings did not prevent his shrinking painfully from the thought of Arthur's funeral. Yet it happened that he was not able to go to it. He got a chill and was in bed when the day came. It was a week before he was about again. Now he found himself dreading the inevitable meeting with Sarah. While he lay in bed he had successfully put the thought of her out of his mind during the day, though at night her troubling presence had darkened his dreams. He had thought deliberately of Pauline Lebraux, her face, the sensitive reflector of her emotions, against the background of her tumbled dark hair, her supple body eager as a bird's for movement. When Wakefield had come in to see him he had, as he thought, subtly brought the talk around to the fox-farm, but, though Wakefield talked eagerly enough on the subject of the foxes, he drew back, lightly but warily, from more than a passing reference to Pauline. "He's too quick for me," thought Finch. "He knows what I'm after almost before I know myself."

After that the thought of Pauline was always accompanied by the thought of Wakefield. The two thoughts zigzagged about each other like amorous butterflies. It was impossible for him to draw the face of the young girl out of the darkness beneath his eyelids without drawing with it the face of the still younger boy. It was peering over her shoulder. It was half-hidden under her chin. Its eyes were her eyes, and its mouth her mouth. It made Finch angry, for the boy was too young for love, and he had hoped they would be happy companions together. And was this all he was to get out of Wake's growing up? A rival! The idea made him laugh. The idea hurt him and frightened him. Yet he did not love Pauline. But he wanted no one else to love her. He wanted her to remain for a little while as she was.

The second day he was downstairs he found the drawing-room empty, and he sat down before the piano, not intending to play, but only to feel its nearness, to let his mind rest on the mysterious harmonies hid within it. He drooped above it, his angular body expressing submission and receptiveness. His hands lay on the keyboard like the hands of a lover on the breast of his beloved.

He did not hear the door open but he was conscious that someone had come into the room. He turned his face, its expression preoccupied and grudging, toward the intruder. It was Sarah Leigh, dressed in mourning, her deep-set eyes shining like jewels in her white face.

"Sarah!" He got up and went quickly toward her. She seemed to recede from him as she always receded from him in dreams, as he approached. He hesitated, drew back, and she advanced, as she always advanced in dreams. He found himself looking into her eyes, holding her hand, while her voice was uttering words he could not form into sense. They came to him brokenly, like the lispings of a young child. He saw then that there were tears on her cheeks.

He led her to a sofa, and still held her hand as they were seated. Her black garments made her remote, but he felt the strange flame burning in her that once before had seared the wings of his spirit.

"Do you feel able to talk?" he asked hesitatingly.

"Not of that."

"No, we must not talk of that."

But of what else could they talk while Arthur's drowned figure loomed between them?

"You talk, Finch. Tell me of yourself."

"There's not much to tell, Sarah. Just a lot of hard work."

"But talk of it. Tell me of your life. It is three years since we met."

He began to talk, telling her of his study in London and Germany. Repeating it to her it became romantic, a desirable life. He told her of his recitals and his compositions, not looking at her but holding her small, firm hand in his. She sat motionless, as though cut out of ebony, except for the nervous tapping of her narrow black suède shoe.

"You have done so much," she said, "and I have done so little."

"You have travelled. You've been—married." He had not intended to say that, but he could not help himself. She did not wince but her fingers closed on his.

"Yes—I've travelled. Yes—I've been married." She spoke as though she reiterated—"How little I've done."

"It is three years since we have met," he said. "Am I changed, do you think?"

She turned and looked into his face. He saw then the blue circles about her eyes and the weariness on her lips.

"Yes, you have changed. But you still have your beautiful expression. I'm glad of that. It comforts me."

He dropped her hand and, in confusion, clasped and unclasped his fingers between his knees. For something to say, he said:

"I had no idea you were coming here today."

"Alayne expects me. She asked me when she came to see me. She thought the change would do me good."

At that moment Alayne came into the room. She was followed by Renny. The sight of Sarah's black clothes and her pallor startled him, filled him with unease. To cover it he began to talk loudly, as soon as the first subdued greetings were over. The smell of carbolic soap did not quite conceal the smell of horse and leather that emanated from him. He was saying:

"What do you suppose was keeping us? Well, I'll tell you! We were quarrelling over our youngster. It's a never-failing bone of contention. It's the very spit of my grandmother—what a pity that you never saw dear old Gran—and Alayne is trying with all the mettle in her to turn it into a proper young person. But it's putting up a good fight. I admire its spunk, I can tell you!"

VI

FATHER, MOTHER, AND CHILD

IT was true that the small Adeline was a bone of contention between Alayne and Renny. Again and again Alayne determined that this should not be so, yet, in her own mind, she felt herself powerless to prevent it. The child was almost two, strong on her legs, intelligent, sly, already seeming to know and relish the fact that she was an unsolvable problem to her mother. Already she would look shrewdly from one face to another, when her parents exchanged a sharp word. If Renny reprimanded her or gave her a slap, as he sometimes did, she would fly into a tantrum, stiffen herself, pull his hair or bite him. This violence of hers charmed him. He would hug her to him, covering her distorted face with kisses, and, when the storm subsided, dandle her as though she were a model of infant propriety.

Sometimes Alayne was in despair over her arrogance and lack of consideration for the other children. Nooky was hopelessly afraid of her. He dropped whatever he had when he saw her blazing brown eyes fixed on it. Even six-years-old Mooey thought twice before he crossed her. And Piers encouraged her in her predatory habits, as did Renny.

She had odd ways with her too. She liked the dark, and, being a poor sleeper, would lie awake talking and laughing to herself. At first when Alayne rose from her own bed and went to her, she would become quiet and, being turned over and tucked in, would settle down and fall asleep. But, as months went on, she took more and more pleasure apparently in the perversion of night into day. She would sleep for five or six hours, then wake refreshed just as Alayne was settling into unconsciousness.

A sudden chuckle would startle the darkness. This would be followed by a loud laugh. Nothing Alayne could do would stop the wild laughing. Sometimes she would roar like a bear, moo like a cow, or chatter unintelligibly. Unless Alayne took her up and carried her about the room, or took her into her own bed, she would not be quiet. Now the nights were growing cool and it was a hardship to be up. Neither could one rest with a kicking little body beside one. Alayne grew wan and irritable from loss of sleep.

Adeline disturbed Nicholas and Ernest too, but Renny, once he was asleep, was almost impervious to noise. Yet he did sometimes hear her and advised Alayne to slap her or dash cold water on her.

One night he came into the room and found mother and daughter facing each other, the one pale and almost in tears, the other flushed and wearing an unchildlike grin. It was almost three o'clock.

"What's this?" he asked.

Alayne answered tragically—"She has been awake for two solid hours, laughing and talking. I am positively unnerved. I don't know what to do with her." She looked at the child, almost hating her; at the man, almost hating him for having given the child to her.

Renny, lithe and striped in his pyjamas, advanced toward Adeline.

"Why were you laughing?" he asked.

She only stared at him, sitting upright in her cot, her dark red hair massed above her forehead.

"Why do you laugh?" he repeated sternly.

"I must," she answered, in her baby accents.

"Why?"

"I must."

He sat down on Alayne's bed and took the child on his knee.

"What do you see?"

She smiled and pointed in front of her.

"Do you see funny things?"

She nodded and put half her hand into her mouth.

"Look here," he said to Alayne, "this won't do! You're tired out. Now I've got an idea. . . . The old-fashioned way was to give kids a good hiding when they persisted in anything they were told not to do. But now it's different. You're supposed to study them. Find out what they need and give it to them."

"Yes." Alayne looked at the two of them, feeling hypnotised.

"Now I think," he went on, dandling the child, "that Adeline has a laughing complex. Just because you are always so serious with her, d'you see?"

"Yes." Alayne leaned against the dressing-table, tired through and through.

"What she needs is someone to laugh with her."

"She has the other children to laugh with her all day. Why should she want to laugh at night?"

"At night she wakes and she is lonely and she thinks life is strange and—well, you know, Gran was a sardonic old bird, and Adeline takes after her."

"It seems hard that Pheasant's children should both be so gentle and mine——"

"Now, look here, you get right into bed and forget everything. I'll take the kid."

"Where?"

"To my room. I'm going to laugh with her."

"Renny—it's too ridiculous."

"No. It's modern psychology."

"Will you bring her back?"

"Yes, as soon as she is asleep. I'll tuck her in and never wake you."

With the child on his arm he led Alayne to her bed and drew the eiderdown over her. She caught his hand and kissed it, half sobbing.

"I'm a perfect baby myself. I don't know what's come over me."

"Sweet girl." He patted her cheek.

She lay, still as an animal in its burrow, listening as he crossed the passage, opened and shut the door of his room. His presence had comforted her, but the touch of his hand had set her pulses throbbing, filled her with a terrible unease. She drew deep breaths, drinking in the stormy sweetness of the night. . . . Oh, why had he left her? Why did the passionate tears flow at the thought of him? Once they had lain in this house, separated by the walls of her marriage with Eden, suffering their anguish of desire. . . . Now, they belonged, each to each—and still they were separated, still her spirit called to him and beat against its walls.

She had heard the child give a crow of delight at being carried into his room. Then there was silence, and she hoped it had quietened, perhaps fallen asleep. But before long her strained ears caught the sound of its laughter. Then came an answering muffled roar from Renny. . . . She dragged the bedclothes over her head. But curiosity, a sudden amusement, overcame her. She threw them back and listened.

Adeline's laughter grew louder and so did her father's. She screamed in fantastic mirth and his muffled roars became shouts.

"As though anyone could sleep in such a maddening noise! They'll have the whole house up!"

She lay listening. After a little a heavenly silence fell and she hoped the child had succumbed. But no—the laughter broke out again, shout upon shout. They took turns in a wild duet. Alayne heard other voices in the passage, opening and shutting of doors. "Oh, those poor old people! Uncle Ernest will get his death! And Aunt Augusta, at her age!"

Renny should be ashamed. From loving him her heart swung to hate. Dishevelled, she scrambled out of bed, pulled on her dressing-gown and slippers, and hurried to his room. She found the whole family crowded into it: Augusta, with her hair in curlers and a bottle of smelling-salts in her hand; Nicholas looking like an old lion with his crest of iron-grey hair; Ernest, sleek-headed, and in a handsome robe; Piers and Pheasant like two figures from a stage bedroom scene; Finch looking about sixteen, with his hysterical boy's grin; and Wakefield, sitting up in bed, with the bored expression of an elderly man.

Alayne took them all in, in one furious glance. Her glance also took in Renny, seated in the one chair, his daughter on his knee, while, for the moment, they desisted from their unbecoming mirth.

Nicholas turned to Alayne. "What do you think of this new psychology?" he asked.

Ernest put in—"I don't like it. It's too noisy. I'll lie awake for hours after this."

"Well," said Piers, "I'm for the rod. If one of mine carried on that way . . ."

Pheasant interrupted—"It's a very good thing for you to see how other fathers do. For my part, I think Renny is perfectly right. Even an infant has frustrations."

"No one worries about mine," said Ernest.

"Yours are the best part of you," returned his brother.

Ernest looked offended.

Augusta smelled her salts but did not utter a word. A mosquito buzzing about the room became fascinated by her curlers, noisily investigating first one and then another of them.

Renny and his daughter were staring at each other. A flicker, as of pain, crossed her face, her eyes darkened. She opened her mouth and laughed. In a moment they were laughing in unison. Even his man's laughter did not drown her shouts. Her voice had become hoarse in her efforts to outdo him.

It was dreadful, Alayne thought. The pair of them looked half mad. Adeline flashed her eyes over her audience and laughed louder than ever. Her hair clung damply to her head.

An audience! thought Alayne. That's what they want. Nothing is too fantastic for them to do, if only they have an audience.... She must interfere, but she dreaded interfering with him in front of the family. One never knew—or, more precisely, she never knew—what he would do. His family had a more profound knowledge of him.

Without warning, Augusta swooped down and took Adeline from his arms.

"Enough of such foolhardiness!" she exclaimed in her deepest tones. "You will make a persistent and incorrigible rogue of her!" She took up the child who went to her, not only without protest but with open arms, clutching Augusta's neck and rolling her eyes accusingly at Renny.

"Naughty Dada!" she said, and repeated the words to her audience.

Alayne looked gratefully at Augusta.

"Say what you like!" exclaimed Renny. "It's done her good. She'll never want to laugh at night again."

"Nor in the daytime either, I should think," said Wakefield. "In effect, I feel tired out."

Renny's face softened. "We'll all go to bed now," he said.

"I shall take the child with me," announced Augusta.

"Good for you, Gussie!" said Nicholas. "You have more courage than I have."

Already little Adeline was relaxed against her great-aunt's shoulder, her mouth drooping in a baby pout.

When Alayne left Augusta's room and the strange spectacle of her and little Adeline bedded together, she returned to her own room to find Renny there, standing by the window, brightly outlined in the moonlight.

The moon had been hidden behind the tree-tops but now it swam clear of them and poured its silver down the sky. The room was full of it; the angles of the furniture sharpened by it. A candle that Alayne had lighted for the sake of the child had sunk into itself, like a dancer into her skirt. Through the open window the provocative scent of late summer drifted in. The house was silent.

She stood in the doorway watching him, herself unseen. He was over by the window, the space of the room was between them, yet it was as though she held him in her arms. He was a part of her, even though their oneness tortured her at times. He was as much a part of her as though she were a tree and he one of her branches thrown out against the moonlight. Yet he was remote. She could not subdue him. All she could do was to hold him in the inexorable bond of her love.

She came into the room, throwing off her dressing-gown that fell with a silken hiss to the floor. It lay in a patch of moonlight, shimmering like the sloughed skin of a snake. He turned and saw her.

"Is she asleep?" he asked.

"Yes," she answered, and, with a gesture, pushed the shadow of the child from between them.

He gave a little laugh. He held out a hand and drew her to the window. They looked down into the garden where the moonlight shone on dewy cobwebs. The locusts had not paused all night in their thin, sweet chorus. Now, in the light of the waning moon, they increased the volume of their song until the pale cobwebs vibrated, shaking dewdrops to the grass, and sleeping birds stirred uneasily and touched wings upon the bough.

She laid her hand against his breast. He bent his head and she looked up into his face from that angle, saw the look in his eyes, his fine carven nostrils, his adroit lips.

He laid his lips on hers.

VII

WAKEFIELD AND PAULINE

WHEN Wakefield was left alone he could not go to sleep. He had been too thoroughly disturbed. Though the house had now become very quiet he was more than ever conscious of the magnetic drawings of the various lives beneath its roof. The vibrations of those secret threads were never so much felt by him as when all doors were closed and the family invisible.

Renny had put out the light before he had gone. No moonlight came in at this window. Yet Wakefield was intensely conscious of the moonlight. It would be coming in at Alayne's window. In the room where Renny and Alayne were.

He lay stretched out, still and dark as the shadow of a statue. It was easy to feel like a child again, a little afraid of the dark, wishing that Renny were there to snuggle against. It would be strange when the time came when he no longer would sleep with Renny. Yet come it must. He was growing into a man. Some night he would stretch out his hand in man's privilege and draw a woman to him. He thought of this dreamily but without longing. He was in no haste. He was willing for a while to remain a boy. He had almost no past. Its few events lay in his remembrance like the fallen petals of a single flower.

Before him stretched a long period of years. If he lived to be as old as Gran he would have eighty-five years ahead of him. Eighty-five Christmases, eighty-five birthdays, eighty-five times three hundred and sixty-five wakings in the morning. . . . A man might do a good deal in that time.

He stretched himself till his toes touched the foot of the bed. He was tall! Renny often said how proud he was to have reared him to such a height and strength, able to do the things that other fellows did. He could ride a horse, swim, play tennis, though he would never be what Renny and Piers were.

He had leaped across a great chasm since the days of childhood. . . . He saw himself being led into the drawing-room to meet strangers, shyly twisting the silken tie of his sailor-suit. He saw himself in a rage, rolling on the floor. He felt the sting of Renny's hard hand on his seat. He remembered the nights when he could not sleep and Renny sat up with him, rubbing his legs, comforting him. He saw himself trailing across the fields to his lessons with Mr. Fennell. He saw himself flying home. Æons ago. The dark chasm, over which he might not return, lay behind him. He was almost a man. Tears filled his eyes at the thought.

He lay wet-eyed in the darkness. . . .

For a while he slept then, but only a half-sleep. He was quite conscious that his dreams were dreams and smiled to himself at their strangeness. A morning breeze blowing in the curtains fanned his face. He could scarcely believe he had slept.

Yet he must have slept, for there lay Renny, stretched out beside him in peaceful slumber, his brown hand curled under his cheek like a child's. Although he looked so peaceful, he wore an air of attentiveness as though listening for the voice of a loved one. The breeze ruffled an upstanding lock on the crown of his head and the first morning sun burnished its redness to fire. . . . How like him little Adeline was, and what a strange pair they had looked, laughing at each other in the lamplight.

All sleep was gone from Wakefield and he found himself, almost without knowing what he was doing, out of bed and searching for his clothes. They were always mixed up with Renny's. The untidiness of their room was a constant annoyance to Alayne.

He drew on a white jersey and grey flannel trousers but he neither washed nor combed his hair. Nothing could teach him to be tidy about his person, yet he always looked better groomed than Finch. He hesitated at the foot of the attic stairs. Should he go up and ask Finch to join him? He turned away—no, he would go alone, he would have this early August morning to himself! He descended the worn carpet of the stairs into the silent hall and let himself out by the side door on to the lawn.

The sun had not yet appeared above the tree-tops but the eastern sky was fantastically streaked with red and gold and purple, and above these hung many bright clouds, some of them no more than rosy flakes, and beyond them a pale-green sky. Every leaf and blade and petal stood out singly, clear-cut, significant, proud. As he reached the open fields the whole world unrolled like a rich-coloured scroll, now signed with a flourish of sunlight. A flock of gulls flew high above his head uttering their plaintive pleasure in the morning.

He stood irresolute, not knowing what to do with himself. The time was past when by running and shouting and waving his arms he could express the feeling that was in him. And yet to move forward on his two legs was not enough—just to look up and down and say what a fine morning this was, would not satisfy him. Even poetic thoughts, which used to come to him so easily, now held aloof.

He looked down at the bright stubble beneath his feet, then up at the gulls circling in their fiery whiteness, and a new and tender longing made his heart ache. He was alone and he longed for the companionship of one who would understand him and rejoice with him. The thought of Pauline Lebraux came to him and he crossed the field and found the path through the birch wood that led toward her home. He wondered why Finch had tried to draw him on to talk of Pauline. Did Finch suspect that he cared for her? And was he, with his artist's instinct, tempting him to expose his soul? But he had not talked of her though he had thought of her a great deal. She had told him one day that she often gathered blackberries on the edge of the wood before the sun grew hot.

60

His feet broke the short golden spears of the stubble, as he moved slowly across the field. The gulls swam, heavy and graceful, nearer and nearer to the ground, waiting only for him to be gone before again taking possession. A field mouse, burnished to bronze by the sun, hesitated for a moment, staring at him astonished, then disappeared in a flurried zigzag. A furry brown caterpillar reared itself on a spear of stubble, thrusting forward its black head, spying out the land for some hazardous expedition. A tiny brown bird scratched in the sandy soil with the energy and composure of a barnyard fowl.

The pines and birches, dark and fair, accepted the persuasive penetration of the path. They held it to them for a space before dismissing it into the sunlight. Then, in the open, it ran alongside a fence which had long been concealed by a dense growth of brambles and wild blackberry bushes. Here the sun slanted his golden gaze, burning to ripen, pressing to mature.

An old apple-tree, its trunk hidden in undergrowth, its branches showing every conceivable distortion, brandished, as it were, three harsh red apples in mockery to the desirous sun.

In among the bushes and the long dry grass the flood of locust song now burst forth, triumphant and yet sounding a tenuous note of despair. A delicious warmth sought even the shady corners, so quick, so filled with energy, was the morning. A milkweed pod having burst, its hoard was released and the silvery particles, detaching themselves one by one from the central mass where the seeds had overlapped like the scales of a fish, swam delicately on the light breeze.

He found her, wearing a yellow cotton dress, pressed in among the thickest growth of brambles where she had worked her way bit by bit. She carried a tin pail and already it was almost full of berries shining as though lacquered.

"Pauline!" he called softly.

She looked over her shoulder and smiled when she saw him.

"May I come and help you?" he asked. But he did not want to go in among the thorns to help her. He wanted her to come out and talk to him.

"I am tired," she answered. "I'll sit down and rest a bit."

But the brambles clung to her so that she could not move. He came and detached her dress thorn by thorn, noticing the pricks and scratches on her arms. He bent down to release a prickly branchlet that embraced her ankle, and looking up saw her eyes slanting above him, and caught her in one of her moments of beauty.

They sat down on the grass together under a birch-tree. She

61

looked little more than a child, and a fragrance, as of the morning, came from her. He was delighted because she was still beautiful, and he decided that it was because she was still smiling. He had never seen anything so gravely sweet as her smile, nothing so young and pure as her forehead beneath the thick dark hair. Yet there was a mocking light in her eyes when she looked at him as though she laughed at him for pretending to be grown up. But there was nothing sharp or cruel about her. She was too gentle, he thought, for her own good and needed someone to care for her. In imagination he touched her cheek with his lips but he could not have brought himself to touch her hand with his.

They ate berries from her pail and she said:

"It's a lovely morning, isn't it? Were you the first one up at Jalna?"

"Yes. There wasn't a soul stirring. Something woke me and I had to come out. I thought I might find you!"

"Finch should have come too. He would have enjoyed it."

"Finch? Why?"

"Well—he's rather poetic, isn't he? He gives one that impression. It's easy to think of him out in the dewy morn."

"And not easy to think of me, Pauline?"

Her eyes looked into his. "Yes, it's very easy. But you seem a part of all this." She made a little foreign gesture, embracing what lay about them. "Finch seems more like someone who looks on. You're a part of it," she repeated.

He loved her for saying that. He had never felt such exquisite companionship with anyone before. The very air seemed tremulously waiting for her next words. Yet if she uttered no word it would be enough that she was near him. He lay down on the grass beside her, his head on his arm, looking up into her face.

"Could we meet sometimes like this?" he asked. "I should like to talk to you when there aren't others by. We've scarcely ever been alone together."

"Yes, we could," she answered simply. "I'd like it too."

"You know, Pauline, I've never really had a friend——"

"Neither have I."

He added shyly—"But I don't exactly want you for a—friend...."

"No?" She looked at him without self-consciousness.

"I don't know how to explain—but—I want to feel that we can meet sometimes like this—perhaps scarcely say a word—keep our meetings secret—and feel nearer to each other, you know, than to any other being."

She listened with gravity. "I think I know what you mean. Something not quite so solid as friendship. Yes—I'd like it."

"I'm so glad, Pauline!" He felt a swift surge of tenderness toward her. He wondered how she could look in his eyes and be unaware of it. Yet she must be unaware or she could not return his gaze with such untroubled sweetness. His long-fringed eyes rested on the magnanimous curve of her lips. A shiver of delight and fear ran over him.

They fell silent, listening to the late summer singing of an oriole. He could remember only half his song of the mating season, and this he pensively repeated, again and again. A chipmunk came near to the pail of berries, flirting his tail and eyeing them covetously. He screwed up the courage to take one, snatched it, sat upright with it beneath his chin, stared hard at the boy and girl, started, dropped the berry, and scampered up the trunk of a young maple, chattering of his exploit and his disappointment.

The two laughed in unison and Wakefield moved a little nearer to her. . . . Would she be frightened if he touched her? Would she draw away? But he could not bring himself to touch her. This meeting was like a bowl of delicate crystal, not to be handled.

But he began to talk to her. He went over his life, drawing out the most colourful of its incidents to dazzle her, as a pedlar the brightest fabrics from his pack. And, with innocent vanity, he embellished his own part in whatever incident he repeated, making a gallant figure of himself.

Pauline listened, enthralled. She had never had companions of her own age. She was so used to this particular loneliness that she seldom gave it a thought, scarcely realised it. Now, to sit under the trees in the bright morning while Wakefield poured out his experiences, opened up unexpected possibilities in life. Even while she drank in all his words, she sought in her own mind for things she might tell him. But she found nothing that she thought would interest him, and gave herself up to listening.

The time passed quickly. The sun beat on the blackberries, making them soft, so that they sank lower in the pail. The heat soon became intense, and the children withdrew farther into the shade. The unseen chorus of locusts became more insistent, more despairing, as though, of the short time left to them, they would let no beat escape unmarked.

Almost before they were aware of the thud of hooves, Renny appeared on the path, riding a highly strung colt. It sidled into view like a self-conscious dancer, turning, curveting, arching its neck to

63

look with scorn at the path. Nothing that the summer morning could produce equalled it for sheer beauty. And its bare-headed rider was as a part of it.

They both saw Wakefield and Pauline. Renny's teeth gleamed, and he made as though to draw rein, but the colt, describing a violent arc that took her among the milkweed and goldenrod, shot fearfully away and, with her rider, disappeared into the darkness of the pine wood. The scent of warm pine needles flung up by their hooves came back to the two peering after.

"Wasn't that splendid?" cried Wakefield.

"Yes." Her voice came in a little gasp and she laid her slender hand against her throat.

"Renny is letting her have her own way. He enjoys that. But he'll pull her up when he wants."

"Yes."

She was looking at him strangely, he thought. With the gallop past of the horse something had come between them.

Wakefield's eyes brooded on her. He muttered—"I must go. . . ." And they parted in a mood of tender melancholy.

But all day he thought of her. From every facet of his mind the reflection of her face looked out, changing the aspect of his world. "I am in love," he thought proudly. He was as a bird whose plumage is burnished in the spring.

Over and over he recaptured her graceful gestures, the changeful colour of her eyes, the sensitive smile that lighted her face to beauty.

"I am in love," he repeated again and again, and wondered that the family could look at him and not see love's sign painted on his forehead.

He followed Finch into the yard behind the house, where he had gone to see the pigeons. Now he would like to talk of Pauline to Finch and yet allow Finch to suspect nothing. He longed to hear his own voice say her name, to feel the form of it on his lips.

But Finch appeared to be engrossed by the pigeons. He stood with one on each shoulder and one swaying on his head. He wore an expression of complete happiness.

The pigeons were Mooey's, and the little boy appeared carrying a basin of corn for them. But they were in no hurry to leave Finch, for there was something about him that they liked.

"They are mine," said Mooey resentfully. "They're not yours."

"I know."

"They're mine," repeated Mooey, scattering more corn. He turned to Wakefield. "Those pigeons are mine."

Wakefield took the empty basin from his hand and turned it upside-down on his head. The little boy, in a rage, dashed it to the ground, kicked it and shouted:

"They're mine! They're mine!"

"If you say that again," said Finch pleasantly, "I'll wring their necks. And yours, too."

Mooey threw himself on the gravel and rolled over, howling. The pigeons, with a stronger flutter of wings, rose to the roof of their cote, and from there peered down with pretty interest on the scene.

"Pauline gave them to me! She did! She did!" came from Mooey's distorted mouth.

"What!" exclaimed Wakefield. "Pauline! I didn't know that!" He turned his face up to them. "Aren't they beauties? I'd not noticed before what beauties."

"I was making friends with them," said Finch sullenly.

One by one the birds dropped to the ground and began to peck at the corn. Mooey sat up and regarded them with possessive, tear-stained eyes.

His young uncles turned away together.

"Pauline gave them to him," said Wakefield.

"Hm-hm."

"I wonder if he feeds them properly?"

"They look all right."

"I hadn't known she gave them to him."

"Hadn't you?"

"I must keep an eye on them and see that he doesn't neglect them."

"Good idea."

"I saw her this morning."

"Did you? Are you going into the house?"

"No—I think I shall go—well, where are you going?"

"Oh, I don't know."

They wandered aimlessly across the lawn.

"What had she to say?" Finch asked politely.

"Well, we talked about a good many things." He cast an oblique look at Finch. "What would you guess we talked about?"

"Not music?"

"No. She doesn't care about music."

"Not care about music? And dance like she does?"

"That's different. Pauline loves the rhythm of motion."

"Music is the soul of motion," said Finch gruffly. "I suppose the truth is that she listened while you talked about yourself."

"Yes," Wakefield answered gaily, "that is exactly what we did."

He pushed his arm through Finch's and hung on it. Should he break down the barriers—tell Finch all? Pour out the story of his love?

A feeling of anger ran through Finch's nerves. He did not want this boy to fall in love with Pauline. He drew away from Wakefield as they reached the sagging tennis-net and they passed it on opposite sides. He said bitterly:

"I suppose you have kissed her?"

His words jarred on Wakefield. He answered in a muffled voice: "No . . . we haven't got that far."

A relief that did not lift his heaviness of soul came to Finch at this admission. They were going toward the rustic bridge, and could already hear the secret August whisper of the stream. Each wished now to be rid of the other, but it was as though Pauline had, with one of her swift gestures, bound them together.

They strained to opposite sides of the bridge. Already the sun touched the topmost boughs, and an earth-scented coolness rose from under every tree and plant. This earthy coolness spread inexorably, silencing the bird-song, except that which came from the exuberant throats of the birds in the highest tree-tops. They still poured out their song to the sunlit arch of the sky, unconscious of the change taking place below.

"It is hard to believe," said Finch, "that I have been home for only two weeks. I feel sometimes as though I had never been away." He must definitely change the subject, he thought, or give himself away.

"Yes. But you've really changed a good deal."

"Have I? Well—of course, I'm older."

"Yes, but . . . Pauline was saying this morning that you seem an outsider. An onlooker, I think she said."

"Did she say that?"

Wake crossed to Finch's side of the bridge.

"Yes. Do you mind?"

Finch answered, in the confusion of sudden hurt:

"Yes. I do mind. I think it was beastly cruel."

"She didn't mean to be cruel. . . . How do you feel about it yourself?"

"I suppose it's true. That's why I mind. But—look here"—his voice broke—"there is not one of you who feels more terribly bound up in Jalna than I do!"

"I'm not going to argue," said Wakefield. "But I think you're wrong."

"You always think I'm wrong! All of you do!"

"Eden thinks you're the best of the bunch."

"He says that only because we have certain things in common."

"But Finch, I——" He laid his hand on Finch's arm. Finch's lank body swayed like the stem of a strange plant.

"Finch, I'd like to tell you something. You said once that we might be friends."

"Yes, yes, I know I did . . . but . . . don't tell me just now, Wake. I'm in the hell of a mood. Just let me get over it first."

"I should say you are! Very well—but perhaps I shan't tell you after all." He turned away and ran lightly, with an air of escape, up the path.

He was half-way to the top, when Finch called:

"I know what you were going to tell me."

"Do you? What then?"

"I can't shout it."

Wakefield stood irresolute a moment, then, turning, leaped the rest of the way up the path and disappeared.

"You're in love with Pauline," muttered Finch, and, leaning against the rail of the bridge, buried his face in his hands.

VIII

DIGGING UP THE ROOT OF ALL EVIL

MONEY had never been so tight at Jalna. It was not only tight. It simply was not there. It was like a river that had sometimes trickled slowly, sometimes rushed in spate, but had now—and without apparent reason—become little more than a moisture in the mud. Even though there were national crises, there must be people who would want horses—if only they could be found! Fruit and grain and stock must still be necessary, but why were the buyers so diffident? Conditions like this might be inevitable in Europe. If the United States were in a mess—well, they had only themselves to blame. But Canada had done nothing to deserve this. She had been good; she had been loyal; she had spilt her blood when there was fighting to be done; and had minded her own business afterwards. Especially the family at Jalna did not deserve it. They had upheld the old traditions in the Province. They had stuck by Jalna and stuck by each other. So they reasoned, and looked at one another baffled.

Alayne lost all patience with them. She tried to talk world politics with them, but they could not see what world politics had to do with Piers not being able to pay his own rent.

In July, Renny, by reason of the unexpected sale of a stallion, had been able to pay Piers the full amount of his feed bill. Piers had seemed glad of this, but not excessively glad. He had been tranquil, as was usual with him when things were going smoothly. Then, when September came, he had calmly told Renny that he could not pay his quarter's rent. He had paid the farm labourers and, after that, there was nothing left.

As was the custom with the Whiteoaks, Renny broke this bad news to the family at the dinner-table. Alayne was shocked at his doing this. It seemed such a dreadfully embarrassing moment for Piers, but she need not have worried. Piers sat stolidly upright, wearing the rather smug expression of one who has developed one of the minor contagious diseases, and is in the act of transmitting it to all those near him. He looked from one to the other of them as though to say—"Well, what are you going to do about it?" And what could they do about it? They could not go to their rooms and open a strong-box and take out sufficient money for current expenses and hand it over to Renny. There were no strong-boxes, and what bank accounts there were were becoming more and more debilitated.

Renny formed the habit of taking out his pass-book and examining his balance at least once every hour in the ingenuous hope that he might have been mistaken in the figures or that by some miracle they might have changed. He would look down at the floor thinking what it would be like to find a pocket-book stuffed with notes. Or he would look at the ceiling imagining a cheque for a thousand dollars plastered on it.

Alayne's heart ached for him when she saw lines of anxiety coming in his face. The lines already there were those of temper, endurance, and pride. She said to him:

"Why don't we dismiss the Wragges? We might easily get less expensive servants. And I know she is extravagant."

"I'd never part with Rags," he said doggedly. "And even if Mrs. Wragge is a bit wasteful we'd never get another such cook." And he added grimly—"Besides they haven't had any wages for six months. How should I pay them off?"

The thought of owing wages to anyone working for her was abhorrent to Alayne. She had always been contemptuous of the Wragges. Now she wondered how she would face them. Rags's impudent little nose, hard jutting chin, and pale eyes that saw everything, rose before her. And so did his wife's ruddy moon face and slow derisive smile.

Well, they must not go unpaid. She could not endure that. She would pay them out of her own income. What her aunt had left her had brought her two thousand dollars a year, but with the cutting of dividends she had no more than a paltry thousand. Out of this she dressed herself and her child and had more than once paid the butcher's bill.

"I will pay their wages," she said, in rather a dead voice, for she did not want him to be grateful yet she wanted him to realise what was forced on her.

He gave her a look of gratitude. "Will you? You *are* a good girl! That will take a load off my mind."

"How much will it come to?" She knew, but she wanted him to realise the importance of the amount.

"Three hundred dollars," he answered quickly.

It would leave her penniless until her next dividends came in. She said:

"What a pity you bought all that Nickel! I suppose it's bringing you almost nothing."

"My distillery stocks are not so bad," he replied, trying to think of pleasant things.

"I had rather *you* paid the Wragges," she said. "I will write you a cheque."

She fetched her cheque-book and wrote a cheque payable to Renny Whiteoak and signed it Alayne Whiteoak. He watched her write their two names there and observed:

"I will give it back to you as soon as I can."

She gave a little weary shrug. Sometimes she felt almost hopeless. As he put the cheque in his note-book he said suddenly:

"I can't think what Eden's going to do. He simply can't get anything. The poor fellow is at his wits' end."

The slow blood rose to her face and head, pricking her cheeks, making her eyes hot. How could he so callously bring up the subject of Eden between them? And call him *poor fellow* in that affectionate tone!

They were in her room. She took the pins from her hair and let it fall about her face. She took up her brush and began brushing the long golden strands which rose with electric energy after each stroke, following the receding bristles.

"I suppose he can go on staying at the Vaughans'," she said coldly.

He frowned. "They're frightfully hard up. Eden says that Maurice seems to think he could get something if only he tried. I'm going into town today to see a man about him. Eden says he will do anything."

She turned and faced him with her hair about her face.

"Do you know what I've been thinking?" she said. "I've been thinking about Sarah Leigh. She attracts me and I know Finch is attracted by her. I am sure that she did not love Arthur Leigh and I am wondering if she and Finch were thrown together—just when she is so lonely—if something would not come of it."

He caught a flying strand of her hair and held it against the arch of his nostril. "How sweet your hair smells. . . . I believe that's a clever thought. We'll invite the girl out to visit us. But perhaps it would be better if it were she and Eden——"

Alayne interrupted impatiently—"We have no reason for thinking she is interested in Eden or he in her. I wish you would not always be dragging Eden into the conversation!"

He threw the strand of hair he was holding back at her. "It's surprising how heartless women are," he said. "You cannot forgive Eden because he was unfaithful to you. And yet if he hadn't been unfaithful, you and I could never have come together."

"I do forgive him," she said, coiling up her hair, "but I do not wish to talk about him."

"No! And you won't let me talk of him! I can tell you he's not at all strong. Even though he's looking so well."

"And yet you'd marry that poor girl to him?"

"Lord, how unreasonable you are!"

"Can't we discuss anything without disagreeing?"

He made a grimace of chagrin. Then, remembering the Wragges' wages, covered the lower part of his face with his hand and appeared to twist it into an expression of amiability. He said:

"You've certainly taken a load off my mind."

She thrust in the last hairpin and gave him a puzzled look in the glass. "A load off your mind . . . oh, that! Well, I'm glad I could do it."

He stood by rather stiffly while she powdered her face, then, as she moistened her finger on her lips and drew it across her eyebrows, he slid his fingers under her collar.

"My rich little wife," he murmured in an embarrassed tone.

"Oh, how I wish I were!" she cried.

He looked interested. "What would you do?"

"So many things!" She looked up at him out of her clear blue eyes. "If you knew how I hate to see you so worried! All this household hanging on your neck. . . ."

He gazed down at her contemplatively.

"What have you left now," he asked, "out of your aunt's legacy?"

Her mind scuttled about like a frightened rabbit. She did not want to tell him. It would seem so much to him in his present hard-up condition. The day might come when they would badly need that money. She hedged:

"Oh, I'm not sure."

"Not sure!" he exclaimed incredulously. "With your precise mind!"

"My mind isn't precise," she said irritably. "It is a perfect jumble nowadays."

That did not interest him.

He sat down and took her on his knee. He laughed rather self-consciously. She looked into his weather-beaten face with suspicion.

"I am not Adeline," she said. "I have no laughing complex."

"Go on," he said coaxingly. "Tell me what you've got left."

"I have nothing left," she returned doggedly, "until my next dividends are paid."

"I'm not talking about dividends. I mean the principal."

She answered in a tight voice, out of the side of her mouth:

"About thirty thousand dollars."

He gave a little whistle and his eyebrows went up. "That's quite a lot. Now I'll tell you what you could do, darling! You could take ten thousand of it and buy that piece of land from Maurice. I'm sure we could get it for that. There would be an end to this sub-division of his. The land would be added to Jalna, and you would own that much of Jalna. Wouldn't that be nice?" He looked at her with his most ingratiating smile.

"No," she returned stonily. "I won't do it, Renny. What good would the land be to us? What is Piers able to make from the land? I feel that it is my duty to keep my money intact to safeguard the future of our child."

"If our child could speak she'd tell you to do it."

"How do you know?"

"I know she would! She would know that you couldn't do a better thing with your money."

"There's no use in talking! I refuse to do it."

He put her from his knee, got up, and with his characteristic glance at his wrist-watch, and his—"Well, I've got to see a man about that mare," he left her.

71

There was a good deal of discussion over Alayne's proposal to invite Sarah to visit Jalna. She confided to the three elderly members of the family what she had in her mind regarding Sarah and Finch. They fell in with the idea with enthusiasm, though neither Nicholas nor Ernest admired the girl. But Piers and Pheasant and, strangely enough, Finch objected to the invitation. It would be an extra expense, Piers and Pheasant declared, and they would be obliged to put on a style for her, accustomed as she was to the Leighs' way of living, which would be a great nuisance. Finch agreed with them.

However, Alayne had her way and, on a glowing September day, Sarah appeared, arriving in her own handsome car with what seemed to the family an extraordinary amount of luggage. From being repressed, having nothing literally to call her own, she had easily acquired the carelessly grand habits of the rich. But she was as simple as ever in her manner—if her low, secretive way of speaking and her rigid movements could be called simple. There was no doubt that with her coming a feeling of strain entered the household.

"I hope to God," said Renny to Nicholas, "that if she's going to get struck on Finch she'll lose no time about.it!"

"She is a queer stick," said Nicholas.

"Have you heard," asked the Master of Jalna, "exactly what has been left her by Leigh?"

"They say," returned his uncle moodily, "that she has a quarter of a million."

"I told her tonight," said Renny, "that Finch is kind-hearted and easy to manage."

"Don't say too much. You may make her suspicious."

"Oh, I just said it casually. I didn't lead up to it in a heavy manner. I simply said it and then changed the subject."

Nicholas regarded him with dubious amusement through the smoke from his pipe. The smoke lost itself in the bluish light that now at evening filled the window of his room. He liked to have Renny sit with him at dusk. Many a good talk they had had in this room.

There was a silence while Nicholas made bubbling noises against the mouthpiece of his pipe. Then Renny remarked:

"There's Eden too. It seems scarcely fair that Finch should have all the luck. But Aunt Augusta says that, in her opinion, Sarah has always been in love with Finch."

Nicholas remembered the faces of Finch and Sarah when he had found them together making music in Augusta's drawing-room. He nodded with his massive grey head.

"Yes. Perhaps she is right. It's hard to tell these days. They're an odd pair. I'm very fond of the lad but I confess that I cannot understand him."

"Nor I."

"If he gets Sarah he'll have his hands full. She's a subtle minx."

Renny raised his brows. "Is she? I should have thought she hadn't two ideas. . . . Now Alayne is what I call subtle."

Nicholas chuckled.

"Poor Alayne," he said.

"Do you know," said Renny, with apparent irrelevancy, "I have not paid the Wragges' wages for six months."

The lines in his uncle's forehead deepened. "By George, that's bad! I was afraid from something Rags said that you were behind but I didn't know it was as bad as that."

"Well, I had the money ready for them but I found that Uncle Ernie was worrying himself sick over his doctor's bill. Gran had never let a doctor's bill stand. It made him horribly afraid of being ill again. There were actually tears in his eyes. I couldn't stand that, so I paid it."

"Hm. . . . Why didn't you just give him something on it and the rest to Rags?"

"That would not have done. I wanted Uncle Ernest's mind put at rest."

"What about your own mind? It hasn't had much peace of late."

Renny laughed. "My mind is a bit easier too. I had enough after the doctor was paid to give the vet something. Now my annual subscription to the church is staring me in the face."

Nicholas shifted uneasily in his chair, which creaked under his growing weight.

"For heaven's sake, don't worry!" exclaimed Renny. "I'm not worrying. Now, look here. Piers and I were talking over things today, and we've decided to have a sale of surplus stock. We think it will do quite a lot to help us."

"But what a time for a sale!"

"It may turn out very well. And it's bound to give us some cash, which we must have."

Nicholas listened rather sombrely to the plans for the sale. But, as he listened, his mind, with the resilience characteristic of the family, became more buoyant. It was filled with interest and hope.

For some weeks little else was talked of in the house or out but the preparations and prospects of the sale. Bills announcing it were fixed to the walls of post offices, hotels and railway stations within a considerable radius. The question of what animals should be sold and what retained was discussed with heat. The three elderly people were dragged to the stables to give their opinions, which indeed were greatly valued, and, once when Nicholas was kept to his room with gout, a young bull and two horses were fetched for his inspection and paraded round the lawn under his window.

Sarah's presence was almost forgotten. Pheasant was as good a man as any of them when it came to interest in the stables. If it had not been for Alayne, Sarah would have felt neglected. Finch fought shy of being alone with her. He wished profoundly that she had not come to Jalna at that time. He did not suspect the motive Alayne had had in asking Sarah to visit them, but he was conscious of something purposeful in the attitude of the family toward Sarah and he felt that she too was conscious of it, for sometimes an expression of childlike mischievousness flitted across her face and she, almost too ingenuously, asked the older members for advice about her future.

"She is a little devil," thought Finch, "and I hate her. I hate her for marrying Arthur without loving him, and I hate her for floating about here in her finery when he is dead."

Nothing in life, he thought, interested him so much at this moment as the development of his feeling for Pauline. Like a close-folded bud it as yet gave no sign of what peculiar form or fragrance it would later reveal.

Augusta had told Meg of their hopes for Sarah and Finch. They did not wish, she said, to rush the girl callously into a new engagement with her tragic widowhood fresh on her, but it was their duty to guard her, to be kind to her, and, when the proper time came, to provide her with a new husband—and him a Whiteoak if possible. There was little doubt that Sarah had cared, and still cared, for Finch.

Meg was heart and soul with the family. Her eyes had glowed, her full bosom swelled with eagerness while her aunt talked. Oh, it was such a good idea and, oh, she wished she could do something to help!

She asked Maurice if he could think of anything they might do to help, but all he could suggest was a picnic, and that was far too commonplace for a girl like Sarah. Then Meg thought of a little dinner—a delightful little dinner of the sort that really smart people gave. It would show Sarah that her relatives could do things just as well as the Leighs and their friends, if they chose. Of course, there would be no guests outside the family.

Maurice thought of their shabby dining-room, their one servant, and looked doubtful. But Meg was sanguine. They had tender young chickens of their own which the maid could cook perfectly. She herself would make the soup and she would order a meringue from town. They would have plenty of sweets and cigarettes and surely Renny ought to supply the wine.

"No, don't ask him to do that. We have some sherry and I'll buy port. I can make a good cocktail." His face brightened as he arranged this part of the entertainment. "How many of them shall you invite?"

"Only Sarah and Finch. Then I must have an extra girl for Eden. Pauline Lebraux is a sweet young thing. I'll ask her."

"Can you leave her mother out?"

"I'll have her over another time. She'll understand that six is quite as many as I can manage."

Meg was exhilarated by the arrangements for the dinner. It gave her a feeling of well-being. She felt almost prosperous when Maurice's evening clothes were returned from the cleaners and laid out on the bed. She herself sponged and pressed her black lace dinner-gown, but she was disconsolate at the amount of plump leg that showed.

"Whatever shall I do with it?" she asked Maurice pathetically.

"Put a frill on it," he suggested.

"A frill! A frill of what?"

"Would passementerie do?" he asked. It was the only material he could think of at the moment.

"No!" She gave him a scornful look. "All I can do is to make my legs as inconspicuous as possible. At dinner-time they'll be under the table and after dinner, in the drawing-room, I'll keep behind the large brass coffee-table."

"Where is that Indian shawl your grandmother left you? You might throw that across your knees."

But she took no interest in this suggestion.

The family at Jalna thought that Meg was admirably doing her part. They looked on the dinner as an event of some import and, for the moment, the coming sale was overshadowed by its significance. The only dissatisfied member of the family was Wakefield. He thought it was unkind of Meggie not to invite him, though he had not been told that Pauline was to be a member of the party.

The midday dinner at Jalna was even better than usual that day, ending with a peach pie smothered in cream. Augusta warned both Sarah and Finch not to over-eat lest they should have no appetite for the delicacies under preparation at Vaughanlands.

"Perhaps I had better not eat my tart, then," Sarah said regretfully. She had had just one bite of it.

"No, I think you had better not."

Finch had already finished his. He was sitting beside Sarah. He said:

"I'll eat it for you. I'm always hungry."

He took it from her abruptly, pushed his plate to one side, and placed hers in front of him.

Sarah regarded him with her sideways, mischievous smile while he devoured it with an air of abstraction.

"I think he's putting flesh on," said Renny, eyeing Finch with an air of approval.

Piers showed his white teeth in a derisive smile. He washed the car for them and himself drove it round to the door at the appointed time. Finch was waiting on the steps. Piers suddenly thought—"Why, the fellow looks distinguished! If I didn't know who he was I'd say he was a remarkable-looking chap." He said:

"The car doesn't look half so bad, does it? I washed it myself and it was in the hell of a mess after the mud yesterday. No one can say that I'm not doing my bit."

Finch looked at him with suspicion but said politely:

"Thanks very much. I'd have done it myself if you had told me."

"Oh, you're too swanky for that sort of thing now."

"What rot!"

"No, no, you are quite right to take care of your hands. They are your fortune now that Gran's money is gone."

Finch hated this sort of talk. He was helpless against it. He climbed gloomily into the seat vacated by Piers and took the wheel in his gloved hands. Piers leaned against the window of the car, looking in at him with his enigmatic smile. Finch could see the pores in the fresh skin of his cheeks, the downy continuance of the line of his eyebrows above his nose, a reddish vein in the clear white of his right eye, a pale scar on his chin, which had once been cut by a kick from a colt. Any defects he had seemed only to increase his look of wholesomeness. After a scrutiny of Finch's tie and waistcoat, he said:

"I admire you. I have a deep respect for you, in fact. You remind me of a lawyer Gran used to tell about. He was a brilliant fellow but he always posed before the jury as a rather dull chap who by a lucky chance was always on the right side."

"Don't see why I should remind you of him," replied Finch heavily.

"Oh yes, you do! It's perfectly obvious. You played Gran like a grand old trout and—you landed her. You're playing Auntie. You're playing Sarah. Yet you always manage to look simple."

"Shut up," growled Finch.

"Yes, I'm just going to. But first I want to tell you that you are quite right in the way you are handling Sarah's case. This he-man stuff—taking the very food out of her mouth—getting into the car and leaving her to clamber in afterward—it's sure to appeal to her after her life with Leigh."

"Oh, hell!" said Finch. "I didn't notice what I was doing." He scrambled quickly out of the car. In his haste he made no allowance for his height and gave the top of his head a cruel knock. He stood dazed, watching Sarah come down the steps from the house. Against the richness of her black cloak, the bands of her black hair, her face looked startlingly white. There was not much colour in her lips and they were folded together with the serene assurance of the lips in a sculptured head. The eyes looked scarcely more alive than the eyes in a statue in that evening light, and she moved down the steps as though without her own volition. She passed the brothers with no more than a flicker of her lashes and entered the car. Piers tucked the rug about her knees, touching her caressingly as though she were something precious.

"Be happy, Sarah," he said. "There are good times coming."

Without looking at him she slid her hand out of her cloak and touched his. He gave a long look into her eyes, trying to sound the depths of her and perhaps coming nearer in his guess than any of the others had done.

Wakefield came around the house. He had not appeared at tea and wore a look of chagrin he did not try to conceal.

"So you're off," he said, in his high-pitched boy's voice. "Well, have a good time! Say—who is going to be there besides you?"

"Pauline," answered Finch, giving him a glance of triumph.

For a second Wakefield scarcely took it in. Pauline invited to dinner at Meggie's and he not! It was impossible! Anger surged through him. There was a plot against him. The family had found out that he loved her and were trying to keep them apart! And he had seen Pauline that very morning and she had said nothing to him of the dinner. He had drawn nearer to her that morning than ever before and yet she had said nothing of the dinner! They had sat under a tree and he had taken her hand in his two hands and had laid first his cheeks and then his lips against it—and she had said nothing to him of the dinner. Was she too in the plot? And what was this hellish plot against him? He looked from one to another of them, baffled. He looked again at Finch and saw the triumph hardening his lips. He turned to Piers.

"Did you know that Pauline was going to be there?" he asked. He could not control the quiver in his voice.

"Why, yes. Didn't you?"

"You know I didn't! Everyone knows I didn't!" He forgot that he was seventeen, that he was almost a man. Tears stung his eyes. "It was contemptible of Meggie!" he exclaimed.

Piers regarded him with amusement and compassion.

"Why don't you hop in," he said, "and go with them? Meg might find a corner for you."

"He can't do that!" shouted Finch. He started the engine.

"I will," said Wakefield fiercely. "I'm not going to be left out of this!"

"You'll not do it," muttered Finch. The car would not start for him.

He pressed the accelerator and set the engine roaring. The car jerked and grunted but would not start. Sarah sat looking straight ahead of her, her hands tucked out of sight beneath her cloak.

"Give her a stronger mixture," suggested Piers.

Wakefield stepped on to the running-board.

"You're not coming," said Finch roughly, but Wakefield held his ground.

Renny came out of the house and he and Piers pushed the car from behind. It started suddenly and, with a violent jerk, sped down the drive.

"Why is the kid on the running-board?" asked Renny of Piers.

"Just for the ride, I suppose."

"There's something more in it than that. He was hurt at not being invited. But he should not have gone. Meggie will be upset."

Meg was upset when her younger brother appeared in the hall with untidy hair and a jersey with a tear on the shoulder through which the white skin gleamed.

"I tried to prevent it," Finch whispered to her, while Maurice shook hands with Sarah. "I don't know what is the matter with him. Except, of course, that he's utterly spoilt."

Wakefield had lighted a cigarette and withdrawn to a corner where he stood gazing in feigned absorption at the painting of a Dutch farm scene.

"He cannot come to the table! It's impossible," said Meg. "As though I hadn't enough to worry me! It's really too bad of him!"

"Shall I go and tell him so?"

"No. You go with Sarah into the drawing-room. Eden and Pauline are already there. I'll attend to Wake." She hurried away and Finch, with chagrin, noticed the shortness of her skirt.

"Darling boy," cooed Meg, propelling Wakefield toward the kitchen, for she did not want him to be harrowed by a sight of the dinner-table, glittering in damask and silver. "Darling boy, don't you understand that we had to have an *even* number? And that you would be an *odd* one? The very next dinner-party I have——"

"Meggie," interrupted Wakefield, opening his eyes wide, "this is the very first dinner-party you have had since I am grown up. And you didn't ask me."

"Listen, pet! I didn't ask Renny or Piers, and they are not complaining."

"They are married men! It's different. And you deceived me. You all hid from me the fact that Pauline was to be here."

"Oh, Wake, you are so silly!" cried Meg in despair. "What if Pauline is here? You're not in love with her, are you?"

"Yes, I am," he replied coldly.

So he made his romantic confession in the heat of the steaming kitchen, with the smell of gravy in his nostrils, with his eyes fixed on a table littered with cooking utensils and the maidservant quarrelling in the pantry with Rags, who had come over to wait at table.

If he had expected to create a sensation by his words he was disappointed. Meg only looked a little more flustered.

The door from the back passage opened and Eden came into the kitchen, closing it noiselessly behind him.

"Can't you come back?" he asked his sister. "We've all had cocktails and Sarah hasn't been taken upstairs yet to leave her cloak. What are you going to do about it?" He leaned against the door, looking at Wakefield with an amused smile.

"What *am* I to do?" exclaimed his sister. "Here is this child looking like a tramp and come over here on purpose to annoy me!"

"Don't worry about me," said Wakefield scornfully. "I'm going! If my family cut themselves off from me they will very quickly find that I cut myself off from them!"

"I think," said Eden, "that Wake looks charming in those rags. Why don't you give him a bite on the kitchen table and have him in the drawing-room afterwards? He'll create a diversion."

"My life has been too full of those sort of diversions," said Meg tragically.

Wakefield was divided between an impulse to fling out of the house for ever, and the desire to spend the evening there. At that moment Katie, the maid, took the roasting-pan from the oven, set it on the table and lifted the cover, disclosing the two round-breasted chickens under their strips of bacon. He discovered that he was very hungry. He raised his accusing eyes to Meg's face.

"Very well," she said. "If you'll have something to eat here, Wake, I'll be glad to have you join us afterward. Dear me, what will those girls think?" She hurried back to the drawing-room followed by Eden.

Sarah Leigh's dress was in the extreme of fashion. She looked like an early Victorian print. As she glided to the dining-room Finch thought he had never seen her look so nearly beautiful. Her immobility of expression added, rather than took from, her power of attraction. For to the subtle observer it spoke of passion repressed, not lacking or spent.

Where had Pauline got the dress, Finch wondered. He had never before seen her in anything but the simplest clothes. Often they were shabby. But this was a lovely golden shade touching the ground and cut low from her thin young shoulders. He leant toward her and whispered his admiration of it.

She looked delighted. "Shall I tell you a secret?" she asked. "No, I won't tell you unless you promise to keep it. Perhaps I shouldn't tell you in any case." She flushed a little and looked as though she would recall her words.

"I'll not tell a soul."

"Well, I'll tell you then. It was a birthday present from Renny! I couldn't have come otherwise."

"I'm glad he gave it to you, then," he said, looking searchingly into her eyes, wondering about Renny and the mother and daughter.

He caught Wakefield's name on Meggie's lips.

"The poor boy," she was saying, "was dreadfully disappointed at not being here tonight. But I told him to drop in later on and I do hope he will."

Pauline too caught the words. She looked at Finch and found his eyes on her. Strange eyes, she thought they were, with their large pupils. Eyes that seemed to look into the depths of hers, searching for something there. She remembered her meeting with Wakefield that morning and how she had not said a word to him of coming here tonight. She had known that he was not to be here and she had felt shy of speaking of the dinner. How foolish that had been, because this very evening she would have to face him, he thinking her a deceitful girl. She felt that Finch was conscious of her distress. Her face burned and she turned back to her dinner but could not enjoy it. Her cheeks grew hot for another reason. She had done wrong in telling Finch that Renny had given her the frock she wore. She had become so used to taking things from him that she found nothing strange in it. But what would Finch think? He might think her a very queer sort of girl.

Finch was thinking of the gift but not of her acceptance of it. Where, he wondered, had Renny's windfall come from? He had paid Uncle Ernest's doctor's bill. He had paid the vet, and now there was this golden foam about the young form of Pauline. . . . Why was she looking unhappy? And just when he had told her that she looked beautiful? Was she angry at him for that? Now, at this moment, she did not look at all beautiful. Only pensive and pathetically young. Her slender hands looked very brown and as though they were used to work; a contrast to the marble whiteness of Sarah's hands, with their delicately rounded fingers. . . . He did not look higher than Sarah's hands. He did not want to look into that pale, closed-in face. Eden was talking to her in a low voice, laughing as he talked, so that nothing of what he said was distinguishable. Maurice had begun to talk to Pauline. Finch turned to Meg.

"Where did he go?" he asked in an undertone.

"He is in the kitchen. I think he is having dinner."

"He must not come in looking as he does."

"How am I to stop him? And Eden suggested it."

"If I had done such a thing at his age I'd have got a wallop on the head."

"Of course you would, dear, but you were so different."

"Hm-hm," he sighed, "I know I was."

Finch could now hear Eden saying—"I know we males are vain, but, after all, we have something to be vain about."

Pauline looked across the table at him with an intense expression. "Oh," she exclaimed, "I think men are wonderful!"

Everyone laughed at her and the talk became general. Eden had the power of drawing Sarah out. She said, as Wragge was bringing in the dessert:

"I have been suggesting to Eden that he should give some readings from modern poetry for a women's club my sister-in-law belongs to. I believe I could arrange it."

"Oh, how good of you!" exclaimed Meg, in a tone too heartfelt. "We should all be so grateful."

"He'd need a lot of courage for that," said Maurice. "I can't think of anything worse than doing things in front of a roomful of women."

"I don't think Eden would find it hard," said Sarah. "They'll simply hang on his words. One of the readings should be from his own poems, and each one of them should buy the book."

They talked eagerly of the project until they left the table. Meg felt that her dinner was a success.

In the meantime a cloth had been laid on the end of the kitchen table for Wakefield, and Rags had, with a flourish, offered him one dish after another as it was brought from the dining-room.

"Do they seem to be enjoying themselves in there?" Wakefield asked of him.

"Well, they're not what you'd call hilarious but they're eating up their victuals. Mr. Eden's the life of the party but little Miss Lebraux looks a bit out of sorts, as if things weren't quite to her taste." He looked meaningly at Wakefield.

"All right, Rags. Don't waste any more time on me." Wake spoke haughtily but he was comforted, as Rags had meant him to be.

When he had finished he went up to the bathroom and looked at himself in the glass. He decided not to brush his hair. If he were to be treated like a tramp he would look the part. When the others came into the drawing-room they found him there, sunk in the corner of a couch under the rose-shaded light of a floor lamp. All Meg's lights were rose-shaded. She was the first to see him and exclaimed gaily:

"Oh, here's little brother! I'm so glad you were able to come, dear! But you look rather—still, it is the fashion to look like an Apache, I hear."

She was quite a good actress and now had the feeling that only she herself was aware that Wakefield had dined in the kitchen. He glanced at her sombrely as he got to his feet.

"Good evening, Pauline," he said, holding out his hand.

"Good evening." She felt his accusing eyes on hers and murmured—"I didn't mention it because I was so sorry you were not coming."

At the sound of her voice and the touch of her hand Wakefield's heart melted. He drew her to the sofa and sat down beside her.

Finch followed Sarah to a seat at a distance and the three who lived in the house found themselves together. Eden thought—"Too much family about this party." His feelings had been hurt by something said that morning by Maurice. He went to the open window

82

and stood looking out into the darkness that was pierced by one star.

He felt lonely. Marked out for loneliness. Set apart. His place was by the black window looking into the night. But no star lighted his way. . . . What was there before him? He was thirty-one and there seemed no open path. Those boys in the room behind had their lives before them. Perhaps they would make something of them. Wakefield at seventeen was in love with Pauline. Eden had been at the door when the boy had coldly and fiercely acknowledged his love. Well, she was a sweet girl to be in love with. That business of first love, how bewildering and beautiful and ridiculous it was. . . . In some ways he felt nearer to Wakefield than to any of the others. And Finch. . . . He liked poor old Finch, who was on his way to becoming a famous pianist or composer, or both . . . if he did not do some idiotic thing that would spoil his chances. Eden looked over his shoulder at Finch and Sarah. . . . He wondered why he hated to see them close together, looking into each other's eyes. Was he jealous? Had he his subconscious eye on her for himself? She was a woman such as one met perhaps once in a lifetime. She was rarer even than that. How had poor Leigh got on with her? He never could understand her—she would never have helped him understand. She looked damned smooth now, for a girl who had lately gone through what she had. But she had never loved Leigh. Eden was sure of that. Probably glad to be rid of him. Looked as though she might have given him a timely push from the boat, just to facilitate his exit. . . . He smiled as he pictured this, and Meg, patting the seat beside her, said:

"Do come and tell me the joke! But first draw the curtains. The sky looks so black."

Eden drew them and came to her side.

"Aren't they a fascinating pair?" she asked, with a flicker of her lashes toward the two he had just been thinking of.

He nodded. "Finch certainly looks absorbed." He decided then that it was this absorption in Sarah that he envied him—not the nearness of the girl herself.

"They're made for each other," she continued.

"Why?"

"Well—they're both artistic and rather odd and don't quite seem to fit in anywhere."

"What a future hell you suggest for them!"

"Not at all. There's nothing like similar tastes for a perfect married life. Maurice and I would often have nothing to talk about

83

only that we're both so fond of pigs. Sometimes when we're quite alone and bored to death or worried he'll begin to grunt like a pig, and I'll simply have to laugh."

"Are you going to ask Finch to play?"

"I don't know. I'd like to, but I hate to break in on their conversation."

"I shouldn't mind that."

When Finch went to the piano Eden took his place beside Sarah. She seemed neither to regret nor to take pleasure in the change.

Finch played with a rapt expression, seeming not to see the keyboard but as though his fingers were directed by an inner vision. Maurice slumped in his chair, smoking and gazing ceilingward, lost in a tranquil reverie induced by the music. For a while Wakefield and Pauline listened dreamily, then he began whispering to her things he would not have dared to say in the sunlit silence of their meeting-place.

"I like your nose. It's a perfectly adorable little nose because it starts off as though it were going to be prim, and then it has an amusing tilt at the tip that exactly corresponds to the tilt of your upper lip. You know, there are tribes that rub noses instead of kissing, and yours is the very first nose I've seen that I'd like to rub with mine! Of course, there's nothing new about kissing but it seems to me there'd be something frightfully new about kissing you."

She listened smiling and, when his hand stole closer and his fingers held hers, she returned the pressure.

When Finch got up he looked about him. He came and sat on the other side of Pauline on the sofa.

"I love your playing," she said. "But I don't know how to make any proper remarks about it."

"You don't care for music, do you?"

"Oh yes, I love it!"

"Wake told me you didn't care for it."

"How could you say that, Wakefield?" She flushed under her olive skin.

"Because you told me so."

"No, I didn't!"

"Yes, you did!"

They began to laugh and Finch laughed with them. He felt happy when he looked into Pauline's laughing face. He wished he might take her home, walk through the darkness of the late summer night with her.

84

When it was time to go he said to his sister:

"I suppose we're to take Pauline home. Still—the road is torn up near her house, isn't it? If Wake would drive the car I could go across the fields with her."

Meg looked worried. "I think you had better drive the car. Sarah would think it very strange if you didn't take her home."

"No, she wouldn't. Sarah never thinks anything is strange."

"Don't you *want* to take her?"

Wakefield strolled up. "I'm going to take Pauline across the fields," he said.

She came, wearing sturdy shoes and carrying her evening slippers in a velvet bag. Maurice and Meg accompanied them to the drive where the car stood. Meg and Pauline had their arms about each other. Maurice and Sarah were finishing what seemed an enthralling conversation. They saw the light from an electric torch moving across an adjoining field.

"I wonder who that is," said Meg, peering into the darkness.

"Whoever it is is looking for something," observed Wakefield.

"Yes. He turns the flash this way and that."

"I do wonder who it is."

"It's Renny," said Pauline suddenly.

"But how do you know?"

"I just know." Instantly she wished she had not said that. She was angry with herself for having so little control over her tongue. They would think she was a very queer girl.

But nothing was said to indicate that they thought her queer. Maurice shouted to the unseen shifter of the light:

"Hullo, there!"

"Hullo!" answered the voice of the master of Jalna.

"What are you looking for?"

The light moved toward them and Renny's voice continued:

"One of Piers' horses that has strayed. The men are out at a concert in the village. Piers and Pheasant are at a show."

"Why should it be in my place?" asked Maurice testily.

"Because all your fences are broken."

"What a black night it is!" exclaimed Meg pacifically.

As he drew nearer to them—he had vaulted the fence—he turned the torch on them and, in its light, they became strangely significant, like a painted group by a master of composition. Meg, with her gleaming shoulders and arms, one of them holding the cloaked figure of the young girl to her. The white face of Sarah, surrounded by the four male forms. They were tensely clear to him, pallid and trance-like in the light he turned on them which, to them, appeared as a long beam emanating from his breast.

At last he stood beside them and they could see his face.

"Pauline said it was you," observed Meg.

"Clever child. Have you had a good evening?"

"Lovely," she answered, in a low voice.

"I like a party," he continued. "I'll give one myself one of these days."

Wakefield said—"I am taking Pauline home." Meg relinquished her and he took her arm possessively in his hand.

Finch looked at the car with shrinking. He did not know what he should say to Sarah in the brief intimacy of the drive home. He felt afraid of her.

Then Sarah said, as though reading his thoughts:

"It is too nice to go indoors. Let us walk to the fox-farm with the others."

"What about your slippers?" asked Finch.

"They're strong enough."

"I'll come too!" exclaimed Renny. "We'll send someone over for the car in the morning."

They set out along the road and, before they had gone far, the horse was discovered grazing in a ditch. He did not start when the light from the torch was turned on him, but raised his head and looked at them with benign approval. He even ambled toward them, a wisp of grass and a trailer of vine hanging from his jaws, green saliva from his underlip. Renny grasped a handful of his mane and they all walked abreast along the road.

Wakefield was disappointed at not having Pauline alone. He pressed her hand and, under cover of the talk of the others, whispered:

"You darling! You darling!"

They said good-night at her gate. When Renny took her hand her fingers clung desperately to his for a moment, then she ran into the house, waving good-bye from the doorstep.

She hesitated outside the open door of her mother's bedroom. A drowsy voice called:

"Is that you, Pauline?"

"Yes, Mummy. Did I wake you?"

She came into the room.

"No. I haven't been asleep yet. I was just dropping off. Come in and tell me if you had a nice time."

Pauline came and sat on the side of the bed. She had turned on the light in the hall and by it she could see, though not clearly, her mother's sunburned face and throat against the pillow, and her tumbled fair hair. Clara Lebraux looked up adoringly at her daughter. The light shone full on her.

"You look awfully nice," she said. "Was your frock admired? I am afraid they would wonder how I could afford it."

"Oh, Mummy, before I thought I told Finch that it was a present from Renny! I shouldn't have done that, should I? But I told him not to tell."

"Let's hope he won't! But after this you mustn't have any more presents from him. You're too big for that now. They might talk."

"If only they knew what he has been to us I'm sure they wouldn't object."

Clara gave a little laugh. "Never mind! Tell me about the party. Did you dance?"

"No. It was very quiet. I suppose because of Mrs. Leigh. I think it is the first time she has been any place. Finch played to us. He's wonderful, Mummy. And we talked and the dinner was delicious. Wakefield came in afterward, and just when we were leaving Renny appeared. He was looking for a horse that had strayed and they all walked home with me."

"Did he find the horse?"

"Yes. He brought it along. It was one of the big farm horses and you should have heard its feet clumping on the road."

Again Clara laughed. She drew her arms from under the bedclothes and stretched them wide across the pillows.

"Pauline," she asked, "which of those boys do you like best?"

Pauline answered evasively—"I like the way you look tonight, Mummy."

"Yes. This sort of light becomes me. My charms are guessed at rather than seen."

"Don't be silly! You never look nicer than you do in the broad sunlight."

"I'm not interested in myself. I want to know which of those three boys you like the best. Eden—Finch—or Wakefield?"

"Wakefield."

"I thought so."

"But I'm interested in Finch. There is something about him—oh, I don't know what it is—but often his face comes before me when I haven't been thinking of him at all."

"And you think a good deal of Wakefield?"

Pauline nodded. "But I don't believe I like Eden very well. He

87

says rather uncomfortable things and he always gives me the feeling that he's hiding something. Something that would make you unhappy if you knew."

"I'm afraid you're too sensitive, Pauline. It's not a good thing. Your father was too much that way. I'm not a bit. I'm made of pretty tough stuff." She put up her arms and drew Pauline's face down to hers. They exchanged a long kiss. "How sweet you smell," murmured Clara. "You're like a bunch of spring flowers. . . . You'll tell me what is in your heart, won't you?—when the time comes?"

Pauline murmured assent but, when she was in her own room, she thought—"How deceitful I am! The time is here and I dare not tell her."

She went and sat by her window, looking out into the blackness that was still pierced by one star as, earlier that night, Eden had done.

"How many girls," she thought, "have sat looking out of their windows, just as I am, not knowing what to do, feeling wicked because they love someone they have no right to love. . . ." The night seemed to her to be full of an aching longing for an unattainable dawn.

As a hyacinth unfolds but still does not give out perfume until a certain moment, so she had unfolded. Now, as a hyacinth gives forth her secret when the time is perfect for her, so Pauline poured out her love, but she dared not speak his name, even to her mother. Over and over she said it to herself—"Renny—Renny—Renny"—as once she had repeated the names of the Saints. . . . Again she felt herself walking beside him in the night. Heard the clip-clop of the farm horse's heavy feet. If only they might have walked on and on through the night together! If only the farm horse might have become a fabulous charger, and they have mounted it and been swept away from the others.

And he was not even aware of her love. She was sure of that. He still looked on her as his little friend. But it seemed to her that she had never loved him as a child loves, from the day her father died. Something passionately unchildlike in the love she had borne her father had that day been transferred to Renny. From that day the heart of a woman beat in her breast.

IX

THE SALE—AND AFTER

THE day of the sale came bright and hot but not so hot as to be ener-
vating. It had been so well advertised that a dense crowd had collected before the appointed time. Renny and Piers had been up
since before six and Wright, the head stableman, looked spruce and
full of importance. The horses to be sold had been groomed until
their coats shone like ripe chestnuts. Their hooves had been washed
and their manes and tails brushed until each separate hair glistened.
The appearance of Piers' Jerseys was equally fastidious. Not a straw
clung to the velvet smoothness of their hides. And their tails
ended in curls. When he looked at the stock to be offered the eyes
of the auctioneer brightened, for such a fine lot had not lately come
under his hammer. The crowd was good-natured and cheery even
though the times were bad. Indeed many of them had come with no
intention of buying but merely because whatever went on at Jalna
was of interest to the country-side.

One after another the stately procession of animals was led forth.
Above arched the golden-blue gulf of the sky, from beneath rose the
smell of trampled earth and the acrid smell of dung. Men jostled
each other to get nearer to the auctioneer, from whose lips came a
stream of anecdotes and ironic jests at their reluctance to bid. Now
and then a cow uttered a moo heavy with boredom or a horse raised
its voice in a clarion neigh. Piers' wire-haired terrier bitterly resented the crowd and barked herself hoarse on its outskirts.

Not one of the brothers was more anxious to make money than
Wakefield. And behind his impulse lay the divine urge of love.
Like Finch, in his boyhood, his pockets were generally empty. It
seemed as much as Renny could do to educate and clothe them. But,
unlike Finch, Wakefield did not in the least mind begging from any
member of the family, and would go all the way to Vaughanlands
to get fifty cents out of Meggie. No amount of money, trifling or
considerable, remained long in his pocket. He liked to buy anything,
if it was only a pair of bootlaces.

Now there was Pauline, whom he loved to buy for. No longer
was he thinking only of himself. He wanted to send her books and
flowers and take her to the theatre. He cast about for something
he himself might offer at the sale.

In a corner of the sitting-room was an old gramophone. It had been a good one but was seldom used now. After some persuasion Renny agreed that it would not be greatly missed and that Wakefield might put it up at the sale. So that day he was in the highest spirits and, pushing a wheelbarrow with the gramophone in it, circled the crowd to find a conspicuous place until the time when the auctioneer should ask for it.

He chose a spot near a young married couple who had come with the object of buying a pig. He thought the young wife had a nice face and the man looked as though he had money in his pocket.

He set down the wheelbarrow and, opening the gramophone, ostentatiously dusted the record inside with his clean silk handkerchief. Ostentatiously he put in a new needle and wound up the machine. Already the young couple and several others turned to watch him.

In a moment the teasing strains of "Sing Something Simple" rose from the bowels of the wheelbarrow. Like an insidious stream it wormed its way among the bystanders. First one and then another turned to look, their attention diverted for the moment from the grand Jersey cow that was under the hammer. After a little, a nasal tenor—just as the auctioneer dramatically paused in his urging—began:

> "Sing something simpul,
> Here's a ditty that's sweet and simpul . . ."

The auctioneer flung an irate glance in the direction of the gramophone and the crowd burst out laughing. The attention of the man who was about to bid was distracted and the beast brought less than she might have done.

Wakefield considerately moved a little farther off, but the jolting of the wheelbarrow did not stop the music and the drone of the tenor came back to the crowd:

> "For God knows it's simpul,
> So get together and let's be simpul. . . ."

The young married couple and several besides followed the wheelbarrow. There was a charm in Wake's aspect, a mysterious light in his eyes, that added to the music, fascinated them. The haunting tenor persisted:

> "Even though you've never sung a song before,
> Even though you stutter and your throat is sore,
> Sing up like a birdie on a perch—
> Like a congregation in a church——"

Another animal had been led out and the auctioneer, deafened by his own voice, did not realise the damage the gramophone was doing to his cause. The horse had been sold and most of the cows. Now he was down to the calves and pigs. He was tired and beginning to sweat. Wakefield turned to the other side of the record. He now had quite a number of people about him. They were hypnotised by the new tune and by the melancholy refrain:

"If I'd only listened to you!"

Piers stepped on to a chair beside the auctioneer and shouted: "Somebody stop that damned machine."

But still the melody, like a narcotic, weakened the purpose of the bidders. They looked at each other and lazily smiled. They were friends—not competitors.

"I might have settled down,
    With little Mary Brown,
    If I'd only listened to you!"

The things they might have done—if they'd only listened to somebody.

Piers' stalwart figure came pushing through the crowd. With a furious look at Wakefield he stopped the music and banged down the lid of the gramophone. "I'll have something to say to you about this later," he said.

The nice young couple decided that they would rather own a gramophone than a pig and, although they had a good many bidders against them, they secured it. It brought twenty dollars.

Wakefield felt elated by the possession of so much money. Ten dollars was the most he had ever had in his life. He saw himself as an engaged man, if only he could find a few more things to sell! Once he had the money in his hand he went over to the Vaughans' and spent the night there in order to avoid Piers. The next day he went into town and bought a dozen long-stemmed pink roses and a two-pound box of chocolates, which he sent to Pauline. He also bought tickets for the newest play, and a white silk evening muffler for himself.

"Well," Nicholas asked of Renny, "how did you make out by the sale?"

"Not so badly. Less than we expected but still—enough to take a load off our minds." He told the amount that had been realised.

"Not a large sum," observed Nicholas, "but better than a poke in the eye with a stick. It will make things easier for a while, eh?"

"Yes. We had reached the point where we couldn't go on."

"Rags said something to me this morning about their wages. I think it would be better if you were to pay them off and let them go."

"No, no, I couldn't do without Rags about me. I'll pay him a little and he'll be satisfied."

Alayne had just come into the room. She stopped and gave him a sudden penetrating look. He reached out his hand and drew her to him.

"Isn't she pretty, Uncle Nick?" he asked gaily. "I think she gets prettier every day." He laid his forehead against her side so that she could not look into his eyes.

Her inherent reserve made such demonstrations before other people distasteful to her. She drew away. She looked down at him suspiciously. What had he done with her cheque?

Nicholas declared—"I agree." But he shrewdly suspected Renny of placating her. And, in truth, she was at that moment looking heavy-eyed and colourless, for she had had a bad night with little Adeline. She went to a table and began searching among papers for a magazine she had mislaid. Could it be possible, she thought, that he had deceived her—done something else with the money? She forgot what she was looking for. A sense of injury rose in her like a tide. She said, with her back to him:

"It is pleasant to think that I can look pretty after such a night as I had."

Nicholas craned his neck to look at her. "Bad night! Well, well. The child again?"

"Yes. Laughing and talking to herself by the hour."

"Tck! You should put her in a room by herself."

"There is nowhere to put her. Besides she is too young to sleep in a room alone. She throws the covers off."

"I'll have to take her in hamd again," said Renny. "She was good for nights after that."

"I think we should all be mental cases," she returned dryly, "if you and she often went on that way."

He did not like her tone. It both hurt and offended him. He thought a moment and then went over to her.

"What are you looking for?" he asked.

"The September number of the *Atlantic Monthly*. I had it here only yesterday. The way things disappear in this house is a mystery to me."

"It is queer, isn't it?" he agreed affably. Then he added, in a whisper—"When you have found it, come up to my room. I want to give you something."

She looked at him puzzled, then continued her search among the pile of papers and farm magazines in a half-hearted way.

It was unseasonably hot. Her feet dragged as she climbed the stairs. She saw every worn spot on them and the dark streak on the wallpaper running parallel with the steps. Today she did not see the walnut newel post carved into clusters of grapes, or the slender spindles of the banister.

He was standing in the doorway of his bedroom. He came to her and pushed a roll of banknotes into her hand.

"What is this for?" she asked, mystified.

He grinned down at her. "I'm paying my debt. Three hundred bucks. You don't forget, do you?"

"No . . . but are you sure you can spare it?"

"Good Lord! I hope so—after the sale! I'm in Easy Street."

"Renny, did you pay the Wragges their wages?"

"Of course I did!"

"What did Uncle Nicholas mean, then? I heard what he said. And you said you must pay them something."

"Well—it's a month since you lent me that money. Another month's wages is due them, d'you see?"

Could she believe him? Yet she must try. "Thank you," she murmured. Then she exclaimed—"How could you say that I looked pretty today? I never looked plainer in my life!"

"You're always pretty to me," he said, and put his arm about her shoulders.

For a moment she relaxed and laid her face against the tweed of his coat. There seemed no air to breathe in the house. She could not endure the smell of stables that came from him, the smell of hot, healthy flesh. She asked petulantly:

"What have you been doing to overheat yourself?"

"Helping to load some apples. Piers is short of a man. The barrels are pretty heavy." He spoke deprecatingly and released her.

She went into her room, laid the banknotes on her desk and, pouring water from the ewer into the basin, began to wash her hands.

He stood just inside the door watching her. "You're always washing, aren't you?" he said.

"Those notes are filthy. It's really not safe to handle them. They actually smell."

"I only wish I could handle more of them!" He came to the desk and picked up the notes and held them to his nose. "I don't smell anything wrong with them. They smell nice to me."

She exclaimed sharply—"Put them down! You don't know where they may have come from!"

He put them down and stood looking at them. He almost wished he had not given them to her. She was drying her hands on a smooth damask towel.

He went to the child's cot and looked down into it. "What a nice crib cover! Did you embroider those forget-me-nots on it?"

"Yes. Baby picks out the embroidery with her fingers and eats the silk. She took out a whole spray this morning before six o'clock."

He gave an embarrassed laugh, for he felt that the child's faults had come from his own body. He said:

"Well, things are looking up. We've had this sale. That will mean considerably less stock to feed. Wake has asked Piers to let him help with the apple-picking, so he will make a little money. Finch has gone to town to make final arrangements for his concert. He's getting a very good soprano to help him out. And, since Sarah has gone home, she has rounded up about a score of women who have agreed to pay Eden ten dollars each for a series of readings from modern poetry. I feel positively high-brow myself, mixed up with this sort of thing. Well, the poor fellow will make two hundred dollars out of it. It will tide him over until something else turns up."

How could he talk to her about Eden! He must realise that she did not want to hear of Eden or his doings—indeed she had told him so. Could he forget, in his anxiety for his brother, that Eden had been her husband, that they had had their secret of the senses together? Could he forget that in this house, while he was still her husband, Eden had made love to Pheasant? No one else in the family forgot it. No one of them spoke of Eden to her—except Renny. She stood, patting almond cream on her hands, her eyes, darkened by pain and reproach, fixed on his.

He saw the shadow in them but only dimly realised the source of it. He said:

"Well, Eden reads poetry damned well. You've said so yourself."

"Yes. He reads poetry beautifully." And she forced herself to add—"I'm very glad this has been arranged for him."

"At one of the meetings he is to read his own poems. That ought to sell some of his books, eh?"

"Yes. I suppose it should sell some of his books." She picked up the money, put it in the small drawer of her desk, and locked the drawer.

He said—"I must be off. I have plenty to do. I must go to Mistwell. What do you say to riding with me?"

94

"I can't. This is Alma's afternoon off. I must look after Baby."

"Get Pheasant to look after her."

"Pheasant can't control her at all. She allows her to eat anything, and Adeline is always pulling Nooky's hair or scratching him."

He exclaimed irritably—"Women have reared half a dozen with no more fuss than you make over this one!"

"I dare say," she said coolly, and she walked past him and went up the attic stairs to the nursery. As she reached the top she exclaimed:

"How stifling it is up here!"

Without answer he turned away and descended to the hall. The rooms on either side of it were now empty and he stood there meditating, thinking how he loved the old house, how irrevocably his own life was bound up in it and in the good land that lay about it. He would go through anything to keep it intact, to protect it from deterioration. He liked to stand here when the house was silent, for then there was a deep and reassuring communion between him and it. He went to the door of his grandmother's bedroom and opened it and stepped inside. There was a quiet coolness there and a beautiful bluish light filtered through the curtains. Sarah Leigh had occupied this room during her visit. It was the first time anyone had slept here since old Adeline's death, but Sarah had seemed an appropriate guest for it and her pale body no desecration to the painted bedstead. Renny felt that the room had not seemed strange to Sarah or Sarah an alien to the room. . . . This had been Gran's fortress. He drew in a deep breath of the air which to anyone else would have seemed close but which to him was freighted with the essence of the stuffs which furnished it, which had been her cherished possessions and worn by the touch of her hands. He passed his own hand over the smooth leather surface of the bed.

He went out then, closing the door behind him.

In the stable—and here was his own fortress—he went from stall to stall with Wright, looking over each horse with complete absorption in its welfare. The stalls left empty by the horses parted with at the sale were not easy to face. Never before had so many gone at one time. There was a two-year-old that he had loved. If he had it to do over again he should not let her go.

A boy brought round his roan and he mounted her. His feet were more at home in the stirrups than on the ground. As he passed the house he looked up at the windows thinking that Alayne and the child might be looking out but they were not. The three old people were, however, sitting outside in the sun and they waved to him.

Something startled the roan, making her rear, and he showed off a bit to make the aunt and uncles smile.

As he rode his mind dwelt on the plans and perplexities of the various members of the family. Wake's education. Its growing expenses and its possible object, what he would make of the boy. A tolerant, amused smile softened his lips when he thought of Wake's attachment to Pauline. Meg had told him of the angry confession of love on the night of her dinner-party. Well, he hoped the attachment would last until Wake was old enough to marry. There was no one he would sooner see him marry than Pauline.

Then there was Finch, a queer unhappy sort of fellow, though he seemed to have a little more character, to be able to stand up for himself a little better than formerly. It was to be hoped that his recital would come off well. For his own part Renny did not like Finch's playing any better for those years of study abroad. His own compositions were queer, shuddering, shameless sorts of things that seemed to express feelings better kept to oneself. But Eden thought they were remarkable and he was probably a good judge.

As for Eden—it was heartening to see how he had improved physically, put on flesh and strength. If only there was someone of influence who would help him to an easy job! Renny went over in his mind the various men of means whom he knew and considered which of them might be likely to help. But he had rarely talked to them about anything except horses. They were business men and Eden knew nothing about business. It was a pity that Alayne was so down on him. He had done no more than many a young fellow would in the same circumstances. Probably Pheasant had inherited a certain looseness from her mother, though, God knew, since that incident her behaviour had been exemplary enough. Now here was Alayne planning a marriage between Sarah and Finch when, whatever way you looked at it, a marriage between Sarah and Eden seemed more desirable. Well, they would just have to work it out for themselves and, whichever got her, he did not envy him his bed.

He loved the roan and he talked to her as they cantered along. "Good old girl. . . . In good fettle today, aren't you? Glad the sale is over and one or two rivals out of the way. . . . Well, and you're a nice old pet, and you move like a rocking-chair. . . . Steady on, now—are you going to shy over a bit of paper at your time of life? Very well, then . . . if you will gallop. . . ." The air was glowing as the sun lowered himself from the zenith. His steady heat warmed the infinitesimal bodies of the hordes of midges that formed quivering patches on the air. As horse and rider passed through one of these patches they whirled into the eyes of the man and the distended nostrils of the beast.

The road was quiet, and from the ditch immense clumps of golden-rod, heavy with pollen, made a playground for butterflies, and the wild asters were a blur of blue and purple to those who sped by swiftly. Now, from a rise of ground, the lake, streaked in bands of green and ultramarine, could be seen and on it the leaning sail of a yacht.

With one hand Renny patted the neck of the roan to reassure her and with the other rubbed his eye, in which a midge was lodged. But he could not get it out and he rode on somewhat subdued and with a sinister gleam in the one open eye. He rode to the house of a farmer who had bought a Clydesdale at the sale and now complained that it had something wrong with it. He had intended to be haughty with the man but he changed his mind and was conciliatory. Certainly if there was a poor horse in the sale this fellow had got it.

Standing outside the barn near an old woman who was plucking the down from the breast of a live goose, the farmer extracted the midge from Renny's eye with the corner of a handkerchief. So they began their interview in a spirit of kindness. And, as they talked in the stall beside the horse, and Renny looked at the farmer out of his reddened weeping eye—the other eye watering in unison—the man thought that Mr. Whiteoak had a real good face—in spite of things he had heard about him—a sad sort of face, not the face of a man who could cheat you. So they talked beside the great-hooved Clydesdale and what the farmer thought was proved to him to be quite wrong, and they parted in great amiability.

Renny turned into the road by the lake and had a cold lunch with a friend named Vale, a widower. He spent the afternoon with him and before he left they had a swim in the lake together.

As he turned his horse's head homeward he thought again of his family. He wished Alayne might have come with him. She would have enjoyed the ride, and it seemed a pity that the care of the child so often kept her at home. He thought that she was needlessly fussy about it, seeming unwilling to leave it to the care of Pheasant or Alma Patch. Yet he did not believe she was as fond of little Adeline as he was. What queer looks she gave him sometimes! He did not understand them, and to make the effort was beyond him. He doubted whether he could hold the complete love and confidence of any woman because of his invincible disinclination to put himself in their place. He felt that if he were to hold a woman to him in any nearness to tranquillity, it would be necessary for him to subdue his inner self without ceasing and to put a continued watch on all he said and did. Yet he could love without asking for complete understanding. It seemed easy for him to arouse love in the other sex, easy to arouse antagonism. These two elements, like a badly matched team, were set to draw the burden of his passions.

His friendship with Clara Lebraux was comforting. There was no strain in it, no puzzlement, no hurt. They reached out to each other as naturally as the boughs of trees intermingle. And if, occasionally, his blood moved a little quicker because of her nearness to him, it was soon over and she knew nothing of it and it did no one any harm. He turned his horse into the side road that led to the fox-farm, thinking that he would like to see her and Pauline before he went home, for he liked to know how things were faring with them and he received a certain peace from the hours spent in their house.

The shabby wooden house lay in cool shade as he went in at the gate. He loosened the roan's bridle and left her to graze on the uncared-for grass plot. She raised her voice in a pleased whinny and, from the stable which he rented from Clara Lebraux, came an answering call, because in it were kept two horses that knew her well. Snatching a mouthful of grass, the roan hastened toward the stable making deep noises of pleasure in her powerful throat.

Renny went to the front door and tapped on it with his riding-crop. In a few minutes it was opened by Pauline.

X

RENNY AND PAULINE

SHE had been at work among the foxes all afternoon, had come in tired out because of the sultriness of the air, and taken a bath in a small tin tub in her bedroom. She had just slipped on a fresh organdie dress with pink flower-sprays scattered over it when she heard the neigh of the roan. She peeped out of the window and saw Renny coming toward the house. For an instant her breath was taken from her and she pressed her hands against her lips with a feeling of terror. Clara had gone into town to do some shopping and Pauline was alone in the house.

First she thought she would not answer the door. She would not risk being alone in the house with him because all of a sudden she doubted if she would be able to hide her love from him. But would he go away if she did not answer the door? He might quite possibly come into the house and wait in the living-room for their return.

His knock sounded abruptly on the door.

She started and a nervous shudder ran through her. "Oh, why am I afraid?" she gasped, and saw her reflection in the glass, pale as though stricken. He was just below, at the very door, and she was alone in the house, and she was shaken by love for him.

Then suddenly her heart leaped toward him. There was this chance to have him to herself. This hour to look back on for ever. She was not afraid. She would answer the door and they would sit talking together quite alone and she would be given the power to hide what was in her heart.

She fastened the neck of her dress, clasped on a string of coral beads given to her by her father, swept the brush hastily across her hair, and went downstairs.

"Hello, Paula!" he exclaimed. This was his pet name for her. "How nice and cool you look! It's getting awfully sultry. I believe we're going to have a storm."

As he talked they were going into the living-room. He dropped into his accustomed chair and fixed his eyes on her admiringly. She had seated herself on an ottoman.

"We're growing up," he said. "Let's see—how old are you?"

"Eighteen," she answered softly, and added—"Some girls are married at that age."

"Pheasant was only seventeen! But you're not that kind. You'll develop much more slowly. You'll be like a young girl at twenty-eight. The chap who gets you will be lucky."

She looked gravely at him. "Do you think so? I am not so sure."

"That's just what I would expect you to say, Paula. . . . But you must have a good opinion of yourself. I don't believe you know how pretty you are—and a great deal more than pretty. . . . Wake thinks so," he added, with a smile.

She did not smile in return, but said, glancing out of the window —"I hope Mummy will not be caught in a storm. She's in town today. She will be coming on the next bus."

"It would be hot in town today. I had business in Mistwell. I had lunch with a friend and we went for a swim in the lake."

"That must have been lovely. I have been working with the foxes."

"All of them well?"

"Oh yes, quite well."

99

"Good. You have a nice lot this year."

A silence came between them. She had a feeling of languor, of disappointment. She had thought that she knew him so well but suddenly she found that she knew nothing of him. All the things she had ever heard of him seemed nothing to go on. She glanced at him furtively, as he sat sunk in his chair, master of himself, sensuous, at ease. He had closed his eyes and was listening to the swish of a newly risen wind and a distant tremor of thunder.

The distant thunder seemed to make their isolation complete. She looked at him out of troubled eyes, and shivered. Though the sun was shining brightly there was a menace in the air. The shadow of a branch was thrown against the wall, every leaf minutely cut, as in a silhouette.

The thunder drew nearer and the sky took on a yellowish tone. She drew a quick deep breath. He opened his eyes and looked at her.

"Are you afraid?" he asked.

"A little," she said, almost in a whisper.

"But this is new, isn't it? You used not to be afraid of a storm."

"It isn't just the storm"—she spoke with difficulty. "I'm just afraid."

"Are you worried about your mother?"

"No. She will go in some place. She is not at all nervous."

He looked at her, a little puzzled. Yet a subtle understanding was coming to him. He could not believe it—it was impossible—yet he had a feeling of apprehension.

Presently a deep peal of thunder broke on their ears. A flash of lightning fell from the yellowish sky.

"Will your horse be all right?" she asked.

He jumped up. "By George! It's a good thing you reminded me. I had better go and put her in."

A second, louder clap followed, and a more vivid flash of lightning. A loud murmur, as of distant rain, came to them and the grass and shrubs began to wave and bend. A few wild drops splashed against the sill.

"Oh, put the window down!" she cried. "I'm afraid!"

He put the window down and went to the door. Then suddenly he turned back and touched her on the shoulder.

"I'll look after the horse," he said. "I'll be right back."

"Don't leave me!" she cried loudly. "I'm afraid—I'm afraid" —and she flung herself into his arms.

"Why—why—poor little Paula." He held her to him, his arms protective and strong about her. He laid his face against her hair.

She clung to him, shaken by sobs.

"Paula—darling little one—tell me what is wrong!"

"Oh, I love you—I love you—I can't help it—but I love you so terribly!"

The thunder now came roll upon roll. The rain dashed fiercely against the pane, making a wall around them. The outside world was lost beyond the blurred, streaming pane. There was a roar like the sea and the house shook on its foundation.

He looked at the lightning trembling along the sill, then down at the girl trembling in his arms. He was aghast. He did not know what to do. A great tenderness for her welled up in his heart, but no passion.

"Darling little Paula—you're unnerved because of the storm. You don't really love me."

She raised her face, her eyes tormented, and said something to him. But he could not make out a word of what she said because of the roaring of the wind. He bent his face close to hers and looked into her eyes.

She took her hands from her breast where they had been clasped tightly together and put her arms about his neck. Still he could not hear what she said but he could see her lips frame the words—"Kiss me."

Her face was blurred before him by the quick moving of the blood through his veins. They were alone—shut in together there—she loved him and wanted him to make love to her. A kiss of passion formed itself on his lips. His hands tightened on her.

She held up her mouth to him like a quivering, storm-beaten flower.

"My God, Paula! You don't know what you are doing!"

He drew himself away from her. He drew to the other side of the room and stood trembling almost as much as she.

She threw herself into the chair where he had been sitting. It was still warm from his body and she huddled her own body into its curve and crouched there, sobbing. Outside the brief storm was lessening. Loud peals of thunder reverberated down the lake but the lightning had ceased and the rain had subsided to a gentle shower.

He threw open the window and an immense, comforting coolness came in at it. He stood there, afraid to look over his shoulder at her. The sound of her sobs cut him to the heart. Little Pauline, to love him like that. . . . His own eyes filled with tears.

She lay exhausted in the chair but her sobs ceased. . . . After a little she said, in a broken voice:

"I am very wicked, I know. . . . But I can't help myself. . . . It's horrible for a young girl to love a married man. . . . But—oh, Renny, you have never seemed like a married man!"

He came then, and stood in front of her. He looked down at her with updrawn, troubled brows. "Haven't I? Why, it seems to me that I am very much married." He tried to force some lightness into his tone. He longed to take her into his arms and comfort her, but he dared not. He continued:

"Look here, Pauline, this sort of thing happens far oftener than you think. . . . Young girls like you . . . well, their emotions are easily stirred. . . ."

"Oh, it hasn't been easy!" she exclaimed piteously. "It's been cruelly hard! I've fought against it—in every way I knew how."

"I know you have," he said gently, and now he seated himself on the ottoman and took her hand. "That isn't what I meant. What I meant was that a young girl—isolated as you have been—is led into feelings for a man she meets constantly——"

"No, no," she interrupted passionately. "It isn't that! It never was that! I have loved you like this—ever since my father died. . . ."

He said eagerly—"Of course. I always tried to take his place. I always——"

"No, no, it's not like that! I loved him one way and you another. A quite, quite different way. But when he died, he—oh, how can I say it so you will understand!—he *gave you to me*. You became mine. I loved you. . . . The way a woman loves. . . ."

She spoke strongly now, and turned her tear-stained face to his. She said—"I never meant to let you know . . . I never should . . . only, being alone . . . and the storm . . . It's getting nice and cool, isn't it?"

She was making an immense effort to be brave. He was filled with pity for her and she was a child to him. He took out a crumpled handkerchief and dried her eyes. But he knew that he must not be too tender with her, for fear that she might again lose control of herself.

She looked into his hard features, thus broken into lines of gentleness, and her mouth quivered.

He said, with a certain metallic quality in his voice:

"You know, Paula . . . I think I ought to tell you that—even if you were older—or I younger—you are not the sort of girl I should love in that way. . . . I love you and always have and always shall—like a darling little sister—but—well, certain women have certain qualities and—I'm no good at explaining this sort of thing—men have certain feelings that only some women draw out. Men will love you—my young Wake loves you now—but I —well—if I were going to love one of the two women in this house—in a passionate way—it would not be you. . . ."

How cruel he was! She stared at him out of tragic eyes. "I see," she said with difficulty, and she took his hand which held the handkerchief and pushed it gently from her.

"It's hell to me to hurt you," he said, "but I thought it would help you if I told you that. If you knew how I hate to see you suffer, and if you knew how truly I believe that you will soon be able to put all this behind you . . ."

A last flash of lightning illuminated the dim room, showing each the face of the other in an intense and sickly light. The noise of a door being sharply shut came from the back of the house, then steps sounded in the kitchen. Pauline sat upright and looked at Renny wildly.

"You look quite all right," he said soothingly. "I shall tell her that I came in and found you a bit upset because of the storm . . . being alone in it. . . ."

He rose and went into the dining-room. He turned on the light there, then went to the door that led into the kitchen. Clara Lebraux had just taken off a streaming coat and hung it across a chair. Her footprints showed wet on the floor. She looked at him without surprise but made a grimace of disgust.

"I'm soaked through," she said, "and I have on my best coat and hat and shoes." She took off her hat and laid it, a sodden lump of straw, on the table. "Look at that!"

He looked from the coat to the hat and from the hat to her. Her hair clung in wet locks against her round boyish head. Even her face was wet and some colouring from the trimming of her hat had made streaks across her forehead. He said:

"Too bad! I don't suppose they'll ever come right again." He picked up the hat and twirled it around on his finger. "I never saw it before," he said disparagingly, "and I don't believe I should have liked it at its best. Anyhow you look better bareheaded. Better go bareheaded after this, eh?"

"That bus," she observed, "was absolutely jammed. I stood most of the way from town. When I got out I stepped right into the storm."

He made a sympathetic sound but his look was abstracted.

"Where is Pauline?" she asked suddenly.

"In the other room." He spoke in a low but casual tone. "She was rather upset—being alone in the storm, I suppose."

"Well, I never! Is she all right now?"

"Yes. But rather sorry for herself. I shouldn't take any notice if I were you."

"I have some new things for her. That will cheer her up. I've never seen such bargains!" She looked at him enthusiastically out of pale-lashed eyes. "You might furnish your home from attic to cellar and dress your family from the skin out for next to nothing—if only you had it!"

She picked up a small suitcase and set it firmly on the table. "I must get the things out of this before the wet soaks through."

He lifted the case and set it down again. "Did you carry this all the way from the bus?"

She nodded, and a damp, tow lock fell across her forehead.

"Why the devil," he exclaimed angrily, "don't you tell me when you are going to do things like that?"

"It was nothing. I am as strong as a horse. You know that."

She began to lay out the things she had bought. Pauline, pale but with a touching air of dignity, came to the door. Clara said, without looking at her:

"Come and see what I have bought you. No—not here. We'll carry them to the dining-room. You'll be surprised."

Pauline looked at Clara with a sudden remorseless scrutiny. She saw her streaked, tow hair, her hot, tired face wet with rain, and the forehead stained by the colouring of her hat, her red, roughened hands, her cheap shoes, oozing wet. So this was the sort of woman Renny—if he had been going to love either of them—would have preferred to her!

She remembered the frequent quarrels between her father and mother, how she had always passionately, in her own mind, taken her father's side, even when she had been too young to understand what the quarrel was about. A wild anger against Clara rose in her, filled her heart to bursting. She hated her in that moment. She said distantly:

"What is that on your forehead? It's all stained."

"My forehead? Oh——" She peered at her reflection in the small glass that hung above the sink. . . . "That's the life-blood of my poor hat. Just see what a wreck it is!" She began to scrub her face with a clean roller towel that hung on the back of the door. Pauline looked at the hat with distaste.

"Is it clean now?" Clara turned and faced them.

"Quite clean," replied Renny. There was a warm, almost protective note in his voice, as though he had been aware of the coldness in Pauline's.

He and Clara carried her purchases into the dining-room and laid them on the table there. Out of doors there was a gleam of watery light from the sinking sun. The windows of the room had remained open during the storm and the curtains hung limp and wet. The roan stood grazing in the long grass; dark patches stained her sides. She raised her head and looked through the window out of melancholy eyes. She uttered a small complaining whinny.

Renny looked at his watch.

"I must be off!" he exclaimed.

Clara said—"Just look at this sweet frock! And I only paid three dollars and ninety-five cents for it!" She carried it, hanging from her hand, toward Pauline. "Let me see if it's the right length, darling."

Pauline backed away. She could not let her mother touch her. She felt disloyal. She hated herself. She would not raise her eyes to Renny's.

"Don't trouble her," he said. "She's unnerved. You shouldn't go off and leave her alone in a storm."

"Good heavens! I could not know it was coming!"

"You should have known. Mothers ought to know those things. Oughtn't they, Paula?"

Pauline, without answering, fled from the room and up the stairs.

Clara made a gesture of despair. "Whatever has come over the girl?"

He gave a short laugh. "Perhaps she's in love."

"But who with? Young Wakefield?"

"Well—he is—with her."

"Has she said anything to make you think so?"

"No."

"It would be a pity. There would be no hope."

"Not for a good many years." Again he looked at his watch. "Now I must be off!" He put his leg over the sill and, in a moment, was on the roan's back.

"That saddle must be drenched!" she exclaimed.

"True for you, woman!" he replied, grinning, and she watched him go splashing through the puddles.

XI

ART AND PROGRESS

EDEN was afraid of the Women's Club before which he was to give talks about modern poetry. He told himself, and it was nearly true, that he disliked women. He had loved Alayne and he looked back on the days of his love for her as the happiest time of his life. Minny Ware had had a sensuous attraction for him but he had never liked her. He loved his sister and his aunt—and had loved his grandmother—because they were inextricably woven into the fabric of his life. Also, he told himself, there were no other women like them. His passing affairs with women in foreign cities had left no mark on him beyond the memory of a parting with dislike. He understood them too well, he thought. He felt a strain of femineity in himself, a careless treachery, a power of appeal, and he hated these qualities. Of one thing he was sure. He was not grasping. A very little money would suffice for him.

Renny had given him money for a new suit to wear at the readings, and Eden had chosen the material with care, had it made by a good tailor, for, if there was anything he hated, it was to appear as an unkempt poet. Renny also had provided him with money to buy copies of the poems of the various authors from whose works he was going to read. Meg had been shocked at the pile of books he had thrown down on the table in the sitting-room.

"But, Eden," she had exclaimed, "couldn't you have got them from the lending library?"

"No," he had answered irritably. "I shall be scribbling in these."

"But I could take out the scribbling with a good eraser when you had done with them."

He had opened one of the books without answering.

"You had quite a lot of poetry books at Jalna, before you went away," she insisted.

"I can't go back there to hunt them up."

"Then there's that huge *Anthology of British Poets*. The book Wakefield always sat on at table when he was a little boy."

He did not reply. He was reading:

"The fatherless children, Colour, Tune, and Rhyme
    (The sweet lad Rhyme), ran all uncomprehending,
    Then, at the way's sad ending,
    Round the raw grave they stayed. Old Wisdom read,
    In mumbling tone, the Service for the Dead."

She continued:

"It seems so much to spend on books. Why, this one is marked two-fifty!"

"My God!" he exclaimed. "Am I never to be out of hearing of the howl of hard times!"

Meggie had been offended, and he had hunched himself, sulkily enough, over his purchases for the rest of the day.

He had spent a good deal of time in reading and preparation for these talks on modern poetry and, now that the day for the first one had come, he was thoroughly depressed. Had he chosen the right poems and the right things to say about them to these women? He longed for the support of another male.

The meeting was at four o'clock, and Sarah had invited him to lunch with her. It was a hot day of Indian summer. The ride into town on the bus had been stifling, the air heavy with dust. He had felt like a captive.

It was the first time he had seen the house which Arthur Leigh had bought and furnished for Sarah. As he noted its luxury he remembered her life with her aunt, and how Mrs. Court had counted every sixpence.

The lunch was perfect and deftly served. Eden was acutely conscious of the intimate and expensive setting as they smoked their cigarettes and drank coffee in the drawing-room. He looked at Sarah speculatively. What was she? Was she shallow? Was she cruel? That mouth of hers looked cruel, though it curved in sly mischief and the voice that came out of it was sweet as honey. Three months had passed since she had gone through that ordeal in the waters of the St. Lawrence, and its shadow had in a degree lifted from her. Something of the brooding look had gone out of her eyes. They laughed back at him, eyes pale and grey beneath their black lashes.

A new spring of happiness, in truth, rose in her today. There were bowls of flowers in her room. A pug dog was sleeping on a velvet cushion near her feet. Eden's smooth fair head, on which there was a greenish sheen, was bent toward her. His large eyes, with their unseeing look, attracted her, while filling her with a strange suspicion. What did he think of her? What was in his mind? What adventures in life lay before her? Arthur Leigh had roused passions in her which he had never been able to satisfy, and now their renewed stirrings filled her with a sensuous elation which she took care to conceal.

A small clock delicately chimed the hour of three. Eden looked at it apprehensively. He said:

"In an hour I shall be there. I shall feel like a dying man in a desert with a flock of vultures sitting around him."

"You'll be all right when the time comes. They'll be charmed with anything you say to them."

"Honestly, Sarah, I'm frightened. If only you were coming! Why don't you belong to this club?"

"It would be too strange," she said. "I could not do it."

"But come with me just for this once! They would not mind, and I could look at you while I talked."

"No, no, Eden. I cannot come. Do you remember how my aunt called me Mouse, and Mole? Those names still suit me—in a sense. I am no good at mixing with other people. Especially other women. But I can't see why you should dread doing this. They will every one feel so friendly toward you—so ready to be pleased with you."

"If only there weren't ten Thursdays ahead of me! An arid waste of Thursdays! There's something sinister in the very word! I feel sure that the world will come to an end on a Thursday."

"Let us hope you will get your ten in first."

When he had gone (she had sent him off in her car and made him promise to return to dinner) she picked up the pug and held him against her cheek. His coat was like fine velvet and his breath came in snuffling gasps. He endured her for a moment, then began to kick and, when she had put him down, returned to his cushion and curled up on it, his black, wrinkled nose pressed into its softness.

She watched him with a small, mischievous smile. She would have liked to torment him but she realised that it would not take much to make him hate her. Her hands lay in her lap, white, small, strong, ringless. She laid the left hand on the palm of the right and examined it with intense interest, as though it were the hand of a stranger whose character she was trying to read from it. Then, one by one, she pressed and pointed the finger-tips which had become slightly blunted from violin-playing. "It looks better so," she murmured. . . . She turned it over, still as the hand of a stranger, and laid a kiss in the palm. Then she closed her fingers and held her own kiss tightly. She sat dreaming for a long while.

In his sleep the pug growled.

Sarah listened for a step in the hall.

The pug woke, rushed barking to the door, its tail curled like a handle above its bouncing behind. Sarah rose and stood rigid, her pale eyes shining, expectant. The maid entered and announced—"Mr. Finch Whiteoak."

"Am I late?" asked Finch, taking her hand.

"I don't know. I haven't been watching the time."

"What have you been doing?"

"Thinking."

"Not unhappy thoughts, I hope?"

"No. I am not unhappy now. I'm in an odd state. Suspended between the past and the future. I feel no responsibility to anyone, for the first time since I was thirteen—when I went to live with my aunt."

Finch bent to pat the pug which pawed against his knees, wholeheartedly approving of him. He noticed Sarah's clenched hand. She saw his look and said:

"You'll never guess what I have here." She held her hand, still closed, out to him.

He felt that she wanted him to take it in his but he would not. Yet he was conscious of its soft strength.

"What then?" he asked, and the pug stood on its hind legs sniffing suspiciously.

"A kiss!" she exclaimed, laughing, and opening her hand as though to let it escape.

He saw it as a pale moth fluttering upward. He saw the quick movement of her breast and the oblique glance at him.

He followed the imaginary flight with his eyes. "Who gave it to you?" he asked.

"Myself," she answered. "An old love."

The maid appeared with tea and Finch asked:

"Did Eden cheer up before he left?"

"A little. He is coming back to dinner and then we shall hear all about it. It is so wonderful to have you and Eden to come and go— as cousins. You can't imagine what it means to me, at this time."

Finch did not answer until they were again alone, then he said:

"Eden may think of you as a cousin. I don't."

She held the green glass jug, on which rings of lemon floated on the iced tea, poised above the tray. "How do you think of me, then?" she asked, giving him a direct and challenging look.

"Well, in the first place," he answered, taking the glass she had filled, "I have never known cousins, so they have no fixed status in my mind, and, in the second, you seem to me much too remote for such a relationship."

"I wonder if I should feel pleased at that speech," she said, with a deliberately musing air.

"I don't attempt to say things to please you, Sarah," he answered boyishly, "for I have no idea of what would give you pleasure."

"Have I changed so?"

He returned sharply—"Did I ever know?" And, as he spoke, a springing emotion, akin to fear, clouded his eyes and he could not see her plainly. He wished he had never consented to spend these hours with her, which he was already beginning perilously to enjoy.

But she answered with gentle composure:

"It is very easy for you to please me. Just by coming to see me as you have been doing, and talking of your work."

She went on then to talk of Eden, affectionately but lightly, and of her present life. But, though she spoke lightly, she kept, without her own volition, it seemed, an air of enchantment about them, as though they two were helpless actors in some magic play.

They heard the hum of the car outside. A melancholy droop depressed her mouth as she realised that their time together was over. Was she playing with him, or was she in earnest? Did he want her play or her earnestness? These questions stabbed Finch as he turned to the door where Eden entered.

He came in smiling, with an air almost radiant.

"It went like a house afire," he said gaily. "They were perfect dears and were game for anything. They sat looking frightfully intelligent and well-groomed and asked me all manner of questions. ... God, I'm thankful it's over! And more tired than you'd believe." He dropped into a chair and smiled at them with the relief of one who has successfully passed through an ordeal. A girl, Finch thought, might have envied Eden the colour in his cheeks, the brightness of his eyes.

Sarah asked—"Shall I send for more tea?"

"No, thanks. I don't want to spoil my appetite for dinner. And I had something there. A bit of pink fluff. An ice ... oh, it was all so tasteful—tea, hostess, guests, and furnishings—and I hated it so, until I began to read. And the scraps of conversation I heard before the show began! 'My dear, you can't buy a well-fitting silk slip in either London or Paris. You can't buy them *at all*. ... I had five teeth out and *every one* of them was abscessed. ... I have four little girls and it's *such fun* seeing that each one gets her proper number of calories.' But they were so nice to me that I couldn't help liking them, even when I gasped in the atmosphere they created."

"I suppose you hate this house of mine," said Sarah.

"I think I should," he replied, looking about, "if you weren't in it." He realised for the first time that Finch was in the room as an accustomed guest. He had accepted his presence without thinking of it. He looked at Finch curiously. What went on in that long head with the mousy fair lock dangling over the troubled brow? He found himself on the point of blurting out—"You're not reviving that affair, I hope!" But he was able to say, instead:

"So, you're here too."

"Yes," agreed Finch, wondering if Eden resented his presence.

"He's going to play to us—something of his own," said Sarah.

Eden said enviously—"They were all asking about your recital. They all seem to be going. I suppose you will make three times as much out of that concert as I shall out of my ten Thursdays."

"Well," answered Finch, "perhaps I shall. I don't know. I wish it were over." He became silent and fell into thought, his eyes fixed on Sarah.

All three were silent, and the pug, rising from its cushion, sniffed at each of them in turn with an air of polite contempt. It was almost dark now. The faint light that there was rested with a tentative caress on Sarah's profile, on Finch's drooping hands, on Eden's shining hair. Sarah still held Finch in that circle of enchantment, that feeling of being moved by a power outside himself. But she could not, nor did she make the effort to, draw Eden into it. He did not give himself, for freedom was necessary to his spirit. In his isolation he had a solitary pleasure in the delicate game of love being played before him. Yet he honestly trembled for Finch, for whom he thought marriage would be a snare and an imprisonment.

They were quiet all through dinner, each repelling any advance toward intimacy from one of the others. Yet each felt a deeper peace than was usual and a desire to prolong this hour.

Three thin trails of cigarette smoke followed them back into the drawing-room. Like these fragrant trails of smoke, formless and cloudy thoughts rose from the mind of each. Freedom, thought Sarah, to be passively free like this, without effort and without movement. . . . This perfumed, flowery room we go into. . . . The delicious bond between me and Finch. . . . She went to a bowl of yellow roses and pressed her face, in which there was no softness, against their petals.

If only the time did not go so fast, thought Eden. If only I could be here and yet not be seen, not be expected to make any effort. Yet no woman could ask less of me than Sarah, because her mind is centred on herself and Finch. . . . I shall make straight for the chair I had before. . . . It is the most comfortable and stands back from the centre of the room.

Finch thought: If only I were not tormented by memory. . . . If only I could forget that I loved her in England. . . . And hated her in England. . . . If I could forget Arthur. . . . If I could love his memory. This is one of the nights when the piano is friendly to me. . . . If I can play as well on the night of my recital as I shall play tonight . . .

Sarah said—"Where shall we sit? Oh, you're taking that chair, are you, Eden? We'll sit on the couch, then, Finch, and we'll share this little table between us."

The light touched the *crème de menthe* as they raised the small glasses to their lips; there was an air of worship in the attitude of both men toward Sarah. But in both cases it was a cloak to hide other feelings. In Eden's, a lassitude of body and mind that was not unpleasant, and a preoccupation with his own thoughts. In Finch's, a shrinking from the passion that was already assailing him.

They still talked little, throwing out scraps of conversation that were no more real than paper flowers but, like paper flowers, served their purpose of imparting a surface gaiety.

After a while Finch played, and Sarah and Eden relaxed in their separate shadows, he to the contemplative state he desired, and she to the desirous contemplation of Finch's reflection in a long mirror that hung behind the piano.

They scarcely noticed what he played. They only knew that the room was filled with harmonies as true as their conversation had been false. They knew that now Finch talked to them out of the integrity of his soul and that truth moved from their souls in answer. He was aware of Eden's loneliness, of Sarah's desire, but they were necessary notes in his music.

He played, at the last, a composition of his own, in which two voices appeared to follow each other in questioning and again questioning, but receiving no answer, sometimes seeming to have no relation to one another. There were few full harmonies, but always the lonely and passionate repetition of the question.

"What is it?" asked Eden, rather irritably, when Finch's hands lay quiet on the keyboard.

Sarah answered for him—"It's his own. He calls it 'Body and Soul.'"

"'Body and Soul,'" repeated Eden, and added, with a touch of malice—"He seems to have trouble in keeping them together."

XII

THE CONCERT—AND AFTER

FINCH's concert was a success. Not the triumph that, in moments of exhilaration, he had sometimes pictured it. But still an undoubted success. His audience seemed rather cold, he thought, but it became more responsive as the programme proceeded, and he was elated when his own compositions were well received. The soprano who had joined with him was an accomplished singer, though personally he hated her voice.

He felt that he might have played with less sense of strain had the family not come to hear him. His first impulse had been to beg them to let him succeed or fail without their possessive eyes on him, but, when he saw what preparations his aunt and uncles were making, what importance the entire clan placed on their support of him, he hid his misgivings and nerved himself to withstand the electric force of their united presence. "But for heaven's sake, don't clap!" he had exclaimed. "If you do, I'll know it, and it will throw me off."

But not to clap was impossible to them. In truth, the increased responsiveness of the audience was in part due to their passionate applause. They were proud of him and they did not care who knew it. Whether Finch achieved a strong crescendo that made the drums of their ears vibrate or produced no more than a tentative trickle of sound, they gave him their undivided support. When Finch was recalled and bowed with outward composure he threw a long glance of indignant appeal toward his family which was perceived only by Piers, and answered by an enigmatic grin.

In the interval the soprano, who had just had a success in *Orpheus with his Lute,* observed to Finch:

"It's strange how always there is one person in an audience who understands me. Who, as it were, sings with me, gives magnetism out to me. I know I'm funny that way, but if there is a single person of that sort in the audience, I am able to locate them."

"What if he is at the back of the gallery?" asked Finch genially.

"It would be just the same. But he is usually in one of the front rows. Tonight it is a man with a handsome fair face. He is sitting between an old lady and a girl in green. There is a red-haired man at the end of the seat."

Piers! Finch was delighted. Here was a joke for the family!

The three elders, Renny, Alayne, Piers, Pheasant, and Mooey sat together. It was Ernest's first dissipation since his illness, and his eager nature, not yet subjugated by age, drank in all of brightness and colour that the evening offered. It was Mooey's first night out. When Pheasant had suggested taking the little boy, it had seemed a ridiculous proposal. But she had insisted, urging that she wanted him to be able to say, in later years, that he had heard his famous uncle's first concert in his own country. Then, too, the ticket would cost them nothing, so Mooey might as well have the benefit of it, if benefit there was.   And she had had her way and Mooey had behaved with the nonchalance of the habitual concert-goer.   His clothes had been a problem until Augusta had produced a dark-blue velvet suit that had been Wakefield's at the same age.

Wakefield himself sat with the Vaughans and Clara and Pauline Lebraux, on the other side of the hall.   Eden and Sarah had seats in the top gallery where, as Eden said, they would hear comments from those who knew something about music.

A result of the concert was that Finch was able to make engagements to play in several of the American and Canadian cities.   An agent was arranging a tour for him during the winter.

Renny carried off the newspapers which he found next day in the sitting-room to his office in the stables, and there sat pouring over them with his knitted brow.   On the whole, he thought the notices of the concert were very good, though a strange jumble of adjectives was used to describe the boy's playing.   Well, the hall had been three-quarters filled, and the takings respectable, and that was a good thing.

He lighted his pipe and leant back puffing at it.   His mind revolved round his affairs, with Maurice's subdividing of the property adjoining Jalna, as its pivot.   That was what he could not forget, and that was what he seemingly could not prevent. - For the thousandth time he pictured the appearance of the fields when jerry-built bungalows dotted them, when clothes-lines hung from fence to fence, and mongrels and screaming children ran through his own woods, tearing up the flowers, tearing the beautiful bark from the birch-trees, throwing stones at the birds.   It gave him a gloomy pleasure to imagine the worst.   If only Maurice had not had the land divided into small lots there would have been hope of a tolerable neighbour, but he had been set in his own way as offering him the best chance of a large profit.

He could scarcely be angry with Maurice.   He was having a rough time of it.   With the help of a boy he was doing the work of the place, coming in at dark, tired out, and depressed with the sense of approaching failure.   All that kept up his spirits was the hope of selling his lots.

Well, if things kept on as they were, on a steady decline, it would not be long before he was in the same pass as Maurice, selling off Jalna in paltry lots until the house would stand like a leaky old battleship surrounded by the small craft of a summer resort. . . .   At the thought a voice from the house seemed to cry out to him to save it from such ignominy.   Without knowing what he did he sprang from his chair, strode to the windows and looked with passionate and possessive pride at the red brick walls, hung with a rich tapestry of autumn-tinted Virginia creeper, at the chimneys from which wood-smoke from his own logs curled.

A quiver passed over his face and it was with an effort that he turned it into a humorous grimace. His pipe had gone out. He relighted it and stood puffing steadily, for it was drawing badly, and he received from this simple act and the benign bulk of the house surrounded by trees a sense of direct comfort. Things would get better. They would get better. It could not go on like this. He pushed his hands into his pockets and his fingers closed on a penknife given him by his father when he was a boy.

There was a tap at the door. It opened at almost the same moment and Piers came in. He extracted a large, perfectly shaped MacIntosh Red from his pocket and laid it on Renny's desk. He said:

"There should be no complaint against the apples this year. Just look at that fellow! And there's not such a crop as to glut the market."

They stood in the stark bareness of the room, whose only distinguishing feature was the array of photographs and coloured lithographs of horses on the walls, staring at the apple whose glowing colour, satin skin, and spicy perfume made it the perfect symbol for the temptation of Eve.

"The Northern Spies and greenings and russets and pippins," went on Piers, "are just as good. I should have a first-rate profit from them if they're handled properly. The shortage of packers is the trouble just now."

"What about selling the orchards as they stand?"

Piers pushed out his lips. "No. I can do better with them if I handle them myself. I guess I'll have to engage a packer."

Renny looked at him speculatively.

"I don't suppose," he said slowly, "that you would tolerate the thought of engaging Eden. All of us know something about packing apples."

A suffused look clouded Piers' full eyes. "What do you take me for?" he growled. "Now I'll tell you what. I'd rather let all the apples rot on the trees. . . . I'd rather cut the trees down with my own hands . . ."

"Keep your shirt on! I'm not going to ask you to do it. I only thought that he might work in one orchard while you were in another. . . ."

Piers spoke more quietly but with an intensity that was sufficient emphasis. "Jalna is not large enough for that swine and me."

"Well, well," Renny spoke as though to a rearing horse, "I

suppose I shouldn't have suggested it. But he wants work so badly, and out-of-door work is what he should have."

"Let him help Maurice then! Maurice is wearing himself out. I saw him this morning and he's hobbling about with lumbago. He tells me that Eden is sitting on the veranda writing poetry, or reading up for his lectures."

"Eden is not fit to do ordinary farm work."

"He is looking a damned sight more fit than Maurice. And Maurice was never brought up to work. He's always led an easy life."

"He has no weakness such as Eden has."

"What about his hand? He showed me this morning how the wrist is swollen. The leather bandage he wears has got too tight. He says that there are dozens of things Eden could do—if he would. He could look after the stock mornings and evenings, for instance. The boy doesn't do it properly. He stuffs the beasts on hay till their bellies are fit to burst. And the horses are lying down resting when Maurice wants them for work. He won't ask Eden to help—not if he drops down himself. For my part"—an almost hearty ring came into Piers' voice.—"I think it's up to you to tell Eden what a sponge he is."

Renny picked up the apple, sniffed it, and laid it down again.

He said—"I'll go over and have a talk with him."

"Well, if you do, don't let him persuade you that he isn't strong enough to work. Maurice says he eats twice what he does."

"God!" exclaimed Renny. "He grudges him what he eats, eh?" He spoke with bitter chagrin and turned about in the narrow room with the restive movements of a wild animal made captive. He said:

"I won't stand this! I'll insist on paying Maurice for his board."

Piers, in his turn, spoke soothingly. "No, no, don't do that! Maurice would be frightfully cut up. All you have to do is to make Eden see things as they are. I suppose he goes about with his head in the clouds."

"Maurice made a mistake," said Renny, "in trying to work his farm-lands himself. He had a good tenant in Kyle."

"If you call a tenant good who can't pay his rent. You don't want that sort yourself."

"Where has Kyle gone?"

"Into the city. Got a job in a warehouse."

"Poor devil!"

Renny sat down in front of his desk. He touched his newspapers with the stem of his pipe. "Finch didn't do so badly, eh? They've given him good notices."

"He's all right. Got a good head on his shoulders, too. You'll see, he'll marry Sarah."

A quick step sounded on the floor of the passage. Without a warning knock the door was thrown open and Wakefield appeared in an old jersey and baggy trousers, as was his habit on Saturday mornings. He wore an expression of being worked up to the point of making a breath-taking statement, and, when he saw that Piers was in the office, he exhaled, in a gasp of disappointment.

His brothers regarded him with amused smiles.

"You seem pressed for time," said Piers.

"Perhaps he's come to apply for a job," Renny said, grinning.

Wakefield gave an excited laugh.

"That's just what I have come for!" he exclaimed.

His elders looked at him tolerantly. What foolery had the youngster in his mind?

"That is exactly what I have come for," he repeated. "I may as well say it in front of you—since you're here, Piers. Though I had intended talking it over quietly with Renny first." He took out a ball of a handkerchief and wiped his forehead.

"Sorry to be in the way," said Piers.

"No, no. It's all right. It concerns you. So you had better be here."

"What have you been up to?" asked Renny with a frown.

Wakefield thrust his hands into the pockets of his trousers. He said defiantly:

"Nothing. . . . But I want to go to work!"

"What do you mean, go to work?" demanded Renny.

"I want to leave school and work with you fellows at Jalna."

They stared at him disbelievingly.

"I'm in dead earnest, I tell you! I was never so much in earnest in my life before. I want a job. I will work for either or both of you, and you'll see that I can do as good a day's work as any man."

As any man! They looked at his slender neck and wrists, the delicate modelling of his face, and grinned.

Renny said—"I can't let you leave school, Wake. In the first place, you must have an education. In the second, you're not strong enough. You might strain your heart."

Wakefield answered passionately:

"As for education—I say to hell with it! Can you tell me what good your education has done you? Can either of you remember the things you swotted over for exams?"

"Of course we can," answered Renny.

"Then why are you always stuck when I ask you to help me out?"

"When I said we remembered things, I didn't mean it in an exact sense. I meant that study broadens the mind and teaches you to think."

"Come now, Renny, be honest! Has your education helped you in the stables?" He turned to Piers. "Would a University education have helped you on the farm?"

"Not a bit."

"Then look at Finch! What would have become of his music if he had been studying for exams?"

Renny answered—"You have no special talent like Finch. But you're clever, and I've always promised myself that I'd put you through 'Varsity. By that time things will be better."

Wakefield fixed his brilliant eyes on Renny's face. He said:

"Once you asked me, Renny, whether I wanted to be like Eden and Finch—go in for art, and all that—or be an outdoor man like you and Piers. Now I can answer you. I want to be like you and Piers. I want to work for you. And if you won't let me—if you force me to go to school—I'll run away and find work somewhere else!"

"Look here," said Renny quietly, "stick it out till next spring, when you'll matriculate. Then I'll see what can be done."

"But I don't want to matriculate! I don't want to be wasting my life. I have—things I want to do."

Piers said to Renny—"It would cut down your expenses considerably."

"Of course it would!" cried Wakefield. "I'm a frightful expense. I feel mean every time I ask for half a dollar——"

"Oh, come, come, come!" interrupted Renny, flushing red.

Wakefield answered—"It's not your fault that I feel that way, Renny. You're too generous, that's your only fault! But I know how tight money is. I can see that on every hand. All I ask is for you to let me be a man and to cease being a burden on you."

Cease being a burden on him? Renny gave an abrupt laugh and threw his arm about the boy's shoulders. "You're a little fool," he said.

"At the same time," said Piers, "there's a good deal of sense in what he says. Now this is my suggestion. Let him cut out school for a year. Let him work, seeing that he wants to. He can do a bit of reading at home. He'll gain a lot of physical strength—perhaps be stronger for the rest of his life because of it. Then, if he's tired of work and wants to go to his books, he can."

Renny was weakening. Wakefield saw it and his face lighted.

"I think that's a very good suggestion," he said. "Just give me a year—on trial! If I don't do a man's work you can fire me, and I'll go back to school."

"The question is," said Renny, looking at Piers, "will you overwork him?"

"No. I know what he's capable of. And I'll pay him what he's worth to me. You can do the same when he works for you."

"Why, yes," exclaimed Wake excitedly. "You can let one of your men go! We could get along quite well."

"His strength is as the strength of ten because his heart is pure," said Renny, and he smiled grimly to cover his tenderness.

He and Wakefield were alone now. He had sat down at his desk and he looked up rather shyly at the boy.

"Is it Pauline?" he asked in a low voice.

"Yes—it's Pauline."

"I thought so." He picked up a pen, dipped it in the ink and made a pretence of jotting down some memoranda. He was thinking: "What ought I to do? With a word I might break up all this and send him back to school. But how can I bring myself to do it? To tell him that she loves me . . . it would be enough to make him hate me . . . the man he has looked on as a father . . . and old enough to be her father. . . ."

Wakefield stood by the door looking down on Renny's bent head. Renny appeared to him invulnerable, cast in an invincible mould. Nevertheless, tender-hearted toward him. He said, with a tremor in his voice:

"I ought to be frank with you, Renny. If I'm not, you'll not realise how desperately in earnest I am. . . . She has not said she loves me, and I don't feel that I have any right to press her to say so. But, in these last weeks she has changed. There's a seriousness about her, and she has the gentlest way of looking at me. She likes to be with me, and she's even said that she's happier alone with me than at any other time. That's something to go on, eh?"

"A good deal, I should say."

"Renny, do you think that that mother of hers is kind to her?"

Renny raised his head with a jerk. "I think she's tremendously kind."

"Well, I am glad of that because sometimes I've doubted it. Pauline speaks of her in an odd sort of way, as if her mother had hurt her. Then again she'll say—'Oh, Mummy is so good to me!' As though she forced herself to acknowledge it."

"You may take it from me that Mummy *is* good to her."

There was a short silence in which the stamping of hooves and the jangle of harness could be heard, then Renny said:

"It is a serious thing you're proposing, Wake. You're proposing to dedicate yourself to a girl who may have quite different ideas for her future in her head."

Wakefield answered eagerly—"But our ideas are the same on almost every subject. I've purposely brought up different test questions, and it's amazing how our ideas fit in."

"But don't you think you could offer her more if you went in for a profession?"

"There you're wrong!" cried Wakefield. "Pauline hates city life. She'd pine away without her foxes and her fields. She is far more suited to the life we lead than—well, Alayne, for instance."

Renny got to his feet, and the spaniels who had been waiting outside the door for him began to scratch on it and whine. He said:

"Very well. Take your year. But remember, you must do some reading when you have the time. And remember, too, that you're only seventeen and that there are a good many girls in the world."

"But only one for me!" He gripped Renny's arm. "Look here, you won't let anyone know about Pauline, will you?"

"Not a soul."

There was strong opposition from the older members of the family when that evening they were told that Wakefield was leaving school for a year. There was all the more opposition as there had been no conclave to discuss the proposal. Renny announced his decision in a matter-of-fact tone, just as Augusta, Nicholas, Ernest, and Piers were settling down to a game of cards. Alayne was buried in a book of essays and Pheasant had Mooey on her knee, reading him the story of Bluebeard. Wake was at the fox-farm, and Finch had gone into town to consult his agent about the proposed tour. The parrot Boney was sitting muffled on his perch. The lamps were lit. It was the first cold evening and the crackling fire was agreeable, as was that sense of shut-in-ness, even imperviousness, which the Whiteoaks had the power of creating, as though by the united beating of their hearts they built a wall around them.

Augusta, Nicholas, and Ernest laid down their cards with one accord: Piers, on the other hand, examined those he held with apparent concentration.

"It is nothing short of ridiculous," boomed Augusta, "for that child to be allowed to say whether or no he will go to University."

"Egad! It's not the way we were brought up," said Nicholas.

"Mamma," declared Ernest, "would have taken a stick to one of us if we had ventured such a proposal. 'A whelp like you!' she would have shouted, and as like as not, drawn blood from us. And serve us right!"

At his words a vision of the old woman came to them as they sat close together in the room where, for seventy-five years, she had played cards, supped tea, gossiped, wrangled, and domineered over her descendants. They saw her, in her beribboned cap, her purple velvet tea-gown, her shapely old hands flashing with rings, her teeth prominent in a grin or getting out of her control and being noisily sucked back into position, her eyes bright with the desire to draw the full savour from life. And, as though their vision of her had produced the sound of her harsh old voice in Boney's ears, he reared himself on his perch, flapped his wings and screamed:

"Shaitan! Shaitan ka batka! Chore! Chore!"

As his wings sank to his sides, feathers fell from beneath them and settled slowly to the floor.

"It beats all," said Nicholas, "how he understands. He knew we were talking of her——"

"And it made him swear," added Piers, throwing down his cards. "Now, if you don't mind my saying so, I think you're quite wrong about Gran's attitude toward Wake's leaving school. I think she'd look on it as a good idea to let him develop physically, and not rush him through 'Varsity."

Alayne spoke for the first time. "Wakefield never grew out of his delicacy until he went to school," she said, in her cool voice.

"And—mark my words," said Nicholas, "if he leaves it for a year he'll never go back. That's just what you did, Piers."

"Have I ever regretted it?" asked Piers.

"That's quite beside the mark. You are an outdoor fellow. Wakefield would repay a classical education. I have had dreams of sending him to Oxford, though that seems hopeless now."

"Oxford would unfit him for life here," said Piers.

"Did it unfit my brother and me?" demanded Ernest truculently.

Piers' only answer was a grin.

Renny said—"Well, I have promised him a year off, and I can't see that it will do him any harm. If I forced him to go back now he would only be dissatisfied and unhappy."

"In my opinion it's a great, great pity," said Alayne.

Renny looked at her without seeming to see her, but he added:

"It may be a pity in one way, but in another it will be quite a relief. I mean, in regard to expense."

Ernest said, irritably—"How different things are from when we were young! Why, there seemed to be money for everything. I really can't see where it's all gone to."

"My father's brother," put in Nicholas, "spent many years in India, and I've often heard my father tell how, when he went back to England, he used to send his linen to India to be laundered, for they could not do it in England to please him."

"There's a very different spirit nowadays," said Ernest.

"All the way to India! How ridiculous!" said Alayne.

"There was nothing ridiculous about it," answered Nicholas. "My uncle wanted his washing properly done, and he did not mind trouble or expense."

"That's what I say," added Ernest. "It's the spirit of thoroughness."

Augusta observed—"One must accommodate oneself to different times. I economise in every possible way. I used to keep two gardeners, now I keep one—and him on half time. I do a good deal myself, and it's not easy for a woman of my years. I spend my evenings gathering snails and slugs. I peer about the garden with an electric torch. One night I had a flower-pot filled with them and I covered it with a saucer and set it in the conservatory for the maid to get in the morning, as I always do. But I quite forgot to salt them down and the consequence was that they pushed the saucer aside and, when I came down in the morning, there was not a plant or a pane of glass without its snail or slug."

"I don't see what that has to do with the point we are discussing," observed Nicholas.

"It has just as much as sending laundry to India has," returned Augusta.

"I should like to know," asked Ernest, "how I should have done my Annotation of Shakespeare if I had not been to University?"

Alayne shut her book sharply and rose to her feet. This was one of the moments when she could not endure them. They had no reason in them—only a devouring instinct.

"I hear Baby crying," she said. "I must go up to her."

"I'll go," offered Pheasant. "I must take Mooey to bed."

Mooey wriggled on to his backbone. "No, no, I don't want to go to bed! I want to hear another story!"

"Bluebeard is quite enough for tonight, darling."

"But it frightens me," objected the little boy. "I don't like all those bloody heads hanging in a row."

"But you said, just a few minutes ago, that you loved them!"

"I know, but that wasn't bedtime. I don't like to think of them hanging in the cupboard in a row."

Piers said—"I'll hang yours up beside them if you don't go along!"

Mooey reluctantly slid to his feet, his picture-book in his hand. He gazed fascinated at the heads of Bluebeard's wives for a moment before he resignedly began the round of kissing everyone good-night.

Alayne said to Pheasant—"Thanks so much. But I think I had better go."

When the two young women and the child were gone, Piers asked: "Can't we get on with the game now? It's all settled about Wake, isn't it, Renny?"

Renny nodded, with a sombre look at the faces surrounding him.

"You don't look any too well pleased about it yourself," observed Nicholas.

"I don't pretend to be pleased, but I agree that he's doing the right thing."

Nicholas picked up his cards. "Have it your own way," he said, "but, mark my words, you'll live to hear Wakefield reproach you for it."

Ernest also took up his cards. "In any case," he muttered, "we weren't consulted about it."

Augusta arranged hers into the different suits. She gave a preliminary offended look at her opponents, a preliminary admonishing look at Piers, her partner, and, in a deep voice, made her bid.

Renny sat motionless, his long legs, encased in grey woollen stockings, stretched toward the fire. On its glowing bed he saw changeful pictures. They formed themselves, evoked by subconscious thought, into shapes delightful, sensual, repellent, flowing one upon another in fiery intimacy. He was in a state independent of happiness or unhappiness, isolated, aloof, acquiescent.

The reflection of his head and shoulders, coloured by firelight, was thrown on the polished door of a mahogany cabinet. The parrot sat gazing for a long time at this reflection, then, spreading its wings, flew against the door and sought to cling there, scratching with its claws and giving angry cries.

"Whatever is exciting Boney?" asked Augusta, looking over her shoulder.

"He knows there is sugar for him in the cabinet," said Ernest.

Renny bent and picked up the bird, which now panted, with outstretched wings, on the floor, and lifted it to his shoulder. He stroked its bright plumage and, after an angry cry of "*Shaitan! Shaita ka batka!*" it nestled against his cheek, stretching its ruffled neck to peer into his features, with an air of almost sinister sagacity.

123

XIII

CARE FLIES FROM THE LAD THAT IS MERRY

STRENGTH and happiness flowed in on Wakefield in the days that followed. Sunny noon succeeded frosty morning. The sunny hours surrendered themselves to dusk and moonlit night. In the evenings, tired out from his work, he changed into flannels and went through the wood to the fox-farm. Sometimes he heard the foxes barking as he neared the house. The feeble electric light burning in the hall beckoned him. When he was inside, sitting close to Pauline in the living-room, his eyes laughed into hers. He told her of all he had been doing that day, of how he had made a suggestion to Piers that Piers had been glad to follow, of how Renny had said that he was getting to be a good judge of a horse.

Sometimes Clara Lebraux came in and sat with them but she never stayed long. She went back to her book in the dining-room and thought with astonishment—"My little girl has grown up. That boy loves her." The thought of a connection with the Whiteoaks by a possible marriage of Pauline and Wakefield pleased her.

Pauline looked forward all day to her evenings with Wakefield. The thought of his coming, the comfort of his presence, helped to ease the pain of her longing for Renny. She scarcely saw him now, for she hid when she heard his voice, and once, when he came while her mother was out, she did not answer the door. A more subtle woman than Clara would have noticed that Pauline paled or flushed when Renny's name was mentioned, that she shrank from talking about him. Clara saw only life as it came to her hour by hour.

Sometimes when Wakefield's profile was turned toward Pauline and she saw, not his large luminous eyes or his sensitive mouth, but the curve of his nose, the sweep of his nostril and jaw becoming accentuated as he developed, she saw in him a resemblance to Renny that stirred her to her depths. Then when he turned his face to her he found her looking at him so intently that he was filled with a sudden exhilaration. He longed to say something that would charm her, fill her with wonder, but all his glibness had left him.

Piers paid him at noon on Saturdays, like any other of the labourers, and Renny paid him when he remembered to. He went from one to the other of them, sometimes so tired that he could hardly walk, but determined to prove himself as good a man as any.

On Saturday afternoon was his reward. Then he took the old car and drove into town. He was incorrigibly extravagant and spent like water what he had earned by the sweat of his brow. He bought ties to make himself look handsome. Ordinary chocolates were not good enough to take Pauline. He must search the shops for the most gay and beribboned. If roses were on sale at a special price, he would have none of them but bought tight little made-up nosegays that wilted the next day. He was so gay and happy in the house that everyone loved him. The children laughed in anticipation when they saw him coming.

One evening he and Pauline took their tea in a picnic basket to a quiet spot on the lake shore. Wakefield built a fire and boiled their kettle over it. While he gathered the driftwood Pauline spread the cloth and set out the sandwiches and cakes. The lake lay quiet except for an occasional ruffling. It spread silken to the blue horizon. The sun was slipping down among a cluster of tulip-tinted clouds which the tranquil surface of the water reflected in duskier tones.

As Wakefield bent to collect the driftwood he longed to be alone with Pauline on some tropic island where he might work for her with no thought but to provide them with food and shelter. Where they would lie at night in their hut of reeds, listening to the sweep of the surf. . . . Now they had this hour of love and isolation, but how soon would it be over! How soon they would be apart in the darkness!

He lighted the fire on the stones. The flames slyly licked the sides of the kettle. Pauline put a sandwich into his hand.

"How happy you look!" she exclaimed.

"I am happy—but I am unhappy too."

"I am the same."

"Isn't it wonderful that we should feel alike?"

He was on the watch for an answer in her eyes, but she lay looking out across the lake, only now and again giving him a swift, half-pleading glance.

He thought to himself—"I am a man in love. At first there was my grandmother at one end of the family, and me at the extreme other end. An old, old woman and a delicate little boy. And now Gran is in her grave and there are new little boys in the family and I am a man—as good as any of them—and I am in love. My love is as wide and deep as this lake. Nothing can ever change it."

Pauline was sifting the sand through her fingers. He took them in his and kissed them one by one. He thought that his love was as deep and wide as the sea. Nothing could change it.

Just as the sun sank, a flock of wild ducks appeared skimming above the surface of the water with outstretched necks and beating wings. There was a metallic sheen on their heads. They moved in swift, unpremeditated unity.

"Look! Aren't they adorable things?" cried Pauline.

He held her hand close. He wished that he and Pauline were as free as these wild birds flying with their mates. But while they watched, the explosion of a gun startled them. The V-shaped formation of the ducks was broken. They were scattered like flying leaves. Another shot was fired, and those of the flock that were left strained forward with a frantic beating of the wings, striving, as they did so, to form once more the pattern of their flight.

The rosy surface of the lake was broken by the fluttering of those which were dying. Renny's spaniels rushed from the undergrowth and swam out into the lake. He followed them, gun in hand, to the shore.

Pauline stood tense as the dogs carried the ducks to his feet and laid there—what, a moment before, had moved so free and strong. She saw Renny as cruel and relentless, and, when he came toward her with a triumphant smile, she turned to Wakefield, a look of pain in her eyes.

XIV

WAKEFIELD AND PIERS

It was November but the sun had a beneficent warmth in it. Piers and Wakefield, heading in barrels of apples in front of the stone apple-house where they had been stored, had thrown off their coats and were working in the jerseys which revealed Piers' muscular shoulders and Wakefield's slender body. The trees were leafless, so that they had the full benefit of the sun, and from a large heap of discarded apples a scent delicious and spicy rose to their nostrils. Some white pullets hovered about the apples, now and then leaving a mark of a sharp beak in a Northern Spy or pippin, while a guinea-fowl circled nervously about the group.

"Are these all right, Piers?" asked Wakefield, indicating some barrels he was going to head in.

Piers came and looked them over. "They'll do," he said approvingly.

Wakefield took up his hammer and began vigorously to hammer

126

down the top. Piers looked at him curiously, wondering how his transparent affair with Pauline was progressing.

"You'll be a young ass," he said, not unkindly, "if you get tangled up with a girl at this stage of your life."

Wakefield looked up at him innocently.

"What do you mean—tangled up?" he asked.

"Well, any silly boy-and-girl engagement."

"I suppose you didn't consider your engagement to Pheasant a silly boy-and-girl affair."

"She was seventeen and I was twenty. I was a man. Times were different."

"Don't worry about me," returned Wakefield nonchalantly.

"But you are fond of Pauline, aren't you?"

"Oh, I like her very well." What would Piers say if he knew that Pauline had promised to wear a ring—when he could get one for her!

Piers said—"It would be a good idea, Wake, if you would leave your wages with me and I would save them for you. You're not used to handling much money, you know, and I have an idea that you're frittering it away."

"No, I'm not," said Wakefield earnestly. "I pinch every penny before I spend it, I assure you."

Young liar, thought Piers, but he returned to his own barrel.

After a little he asked carelessly—"Do you often see Renny at the fox-farm?"

"Very seldom. I don't think he goes there often."

"Well, it's a good thing if he doesn't. There was gossip about him and Mrs. Lebraux."

"What would the gossips do without us?"

"Renny doesn't like being gossiped about, though."

Finch strolled up to them from the direction of the house. He had been practising for three hours and felt stiff and cold. These fellows out in the sun, he thought, what a pleasant time they had! It was hard luck when one's work kept one cooped up indoors. Yes, it was the work he loved—exacting, even cruel, though it might be, he would have no other. He realised, as his eyes took in the scene before him, so full of life and colour, as his nostrils drank the pungent smell of the apples, that he wanted all things from life—music, study, travel, a simple muscular outdoor life, women, the bondage of love, and complete freedom. He threw back his head and drew in the morning air in a great gulp.

Piers ceased his loud hammering on a barrel and threw Finch a look. "The next movement," he said, "is *allegro,* developing into *minuetto.*"

"Don't be an ass!"

"I'll try not to be," returned Piers good-humouredly, "but you do give one a turn, the way you look."

"He feels proud," said Wakefield, "and no wonder. I should, myself, if I were going on a tour."

Finch, to cover his embarrassment, caught hold of Wakefield and tried to bend him across a barrel. But he misjudged his man. Wakefield not only fought free but it seemed possible that he might succeed in his struggle to place Finch himself in the ignominious position.

"Good boy! Good boy!" encouraged Piers. "Hook your arm round his neck!"

Just then Wright came running up. "The horses that were in the field next to Mr. Vaughan's have broken into his place," he announced. "Shall I take men off their work to fetch 'em, sir? Or try to round 'em up myself?"

"My God!" exclaimed Piers in a rage, hurling his hammer to the ground. "Will Maurice never mend his fences?" He said to Wright—"I'll help you. . . . And, Wake, you go on with this work. I'll probably not be long. . . . Come along, Finch—you may as well make yourself useful."

It was a job after Finch's heart. Running helter-skelter over the fields in the morning air, chasing wild horses, flinging up his arms and shouting. He was soon in advance of the other two.

Wakefield, left to himself, picked up an apple, polished it on his sleeve, and, sitting down on a barrel, began to eat with great relish. From a pocket he took a rather shabby piece of toffee and ate it, bite about, with the apple. He felt tired from wrestling and he was hungry.

He kicked his heel against the side of the barrel and thought of the scores of sound and beautiful apples inside. Life was very pleasant.

Then his thoughts, as their habit had become, turned to Pauline. He pictured her coming toward him through the pine wood, along the path that bordered the fields, and through the orchard to his side. She had done this once or twice before she went on to the house on a message. Renny and Piers were leaving in a few days for their annual duck-shooting, and he would persuade her to come and stay with him while he worked as he had seen Pheasant stay beside Piers. He lost himself in dreams of the time when they would no longer be separated. He considered, with a little anxiety, the possibility of making room for her in the house. Either they, as a married couple, would have to take the spare room, now occupied by Aunt Augusta, or Renny would have to sleep with his own wife, as indeed he should, and leave his place vacant for Pauline. There was a third alternative, and in some ways it seemed to him the most appropriate. It was that he and Pauline should occupy his grandmother's room, sleep in the old painted bed, with Boney perching on its head. But any of these arrangements would, of course, be temporary. In time, and not too long a time, he would build Pauline a house for herself. . . . Renny would give him the land—with birch-trees standing about.

He had smoked a couple of cigarettes and considerable time had passed before he decided to begin work again. He had had a hard day the day before and he had been up since six, so he felt that a respite was due him. He went into the apple-house and began to carry out crates for the filling of a particularly nice order Piers had got that morning. Piers was doing well with the orchards this fall That last cheque from Montreal had pleased him mightily. As Wakefield carried out the last of the crates he noticed Piers' coat hanging on the door of the apple-house, and he wondered if Piers were so careless as to leave his coat there with his pocket-book in it. It had been in it when they had begun work that morning, for Piers had laughingly drawn his attention to its bulk and had said—"That will soon be flattened out when I have paid you and the other blighters who pretend to work for me."

Wakefield regarded the coat dreamily, then, as it seemed to him, without volition on his part, he put out his hand and turned the coat inside out. Yes, there was the edge of the pocket-book projecting above the worn lining of the pocket! Well, he might as well see how much old Piers had in it. No harm in that.

He took it hesitatingly from the pocket and opened it. There were what seemed to Wakefield a great many banknotes in it. Ten-dollar bills laid flat one upon another. No fives—no twenties—just tens and tens and tens. No wonder it had looked bulky! Nice clean notes they were, too, fresh from the bank, clean, crisp, powerful.

Then between him and the pocket-book he saw Pauline's hand, and the third finger of her left hand. He saw on it a half-hoop of pearls and diamonds, such as his heart was set on buying for her. Never till that ring was on her finger would she be properly bound to him. One of these notes, two of them, even three of them, would scarcely be missed. In fact they were really due him, considering the way he worked. And it was so terribly difficult for him to save money. A real start like this would give him courage.

He fluttered the notes under his thumb. Would he? No, no!

Would he? Yes—something drove him to it. He grew hot all over. His skin pricked. He shut the pocket-book with a snap—opened it again and looked straight into Piers' face as he advanced toward the door of the apple-house!

In a frenzy of self-preservation Wakefield slammed the door in his brother's face, hurled the pocket-book into the darkest corner of the apple-house and fled through the door at the other end, slamming it also behind him. By this time he heard Piers' feet spurning the cement within. Outside he looked wildly about, hoping Renny might be near to protect him, but no one was about except old Noah Binns, wheeling a barrow of decaying apples in the direction of the piggery.

Wakefield shot past him like an arrow. Without looking back he kept toward the house.

Noah set down the barrow, rubbed his hands in glee, and cried: "He's right after ye, sure enough!" and added to himself—"Dang both on 'em!"

Wakefield's feet seemed scarcely to touch the ground, yet nearer and nearer, he could hear Piers' in pursuit. He ran behind a small wood-house and from that dodged into the shelter of a battalion of sheets waving on the line. Terror-stricken, he glanced over his shoulder and saw Piers' face fiery red bearing down upon him.

He could not reach the house. Piers would be able to head him off and perhaps drag him back into the wood-shed. But, nearer than the house, was the old carriage-house where the carriage in which his grandmother had always driven to church still stood. If only he could gain it and lock the door! But, when he got to it, the door was shut. A ladder stood against the wall and, without further consideration, he dashed up it and ran across the roof.

There was a skylight in the carriage-house and he noticed that it was open. He had a mind to fling himself into it, for a broken neck seemed preferable to being caught by Piers. But, after one glance at the rearing shafts of the carriage below and its glass lamps, he flew on and was just about to jump off the roof to the grass on the other side, when he heard Piers' footsteps springing from the top of the ladder. He felt paralysed by terror. He could not force his legs to move in any direction. Then he heard a slithering sound, a bump, a groan, and looked round to see Piers' muscular hands showing above the edge of the skylight.

A sweet feeling of relief welled up in him. It seemed too good to be true. His lungs, which had been cramped with pain, expanded. He crept on tiptoe to the skylight and looked into the aperture.

Piers was clinging desperately to the edge, his legs dangling in space, and underneath him the lamps, the dashboard, and the rearing shafts of the old carriage.

Wakefield tiptoed to the top of the ladder and placed his foot on the nearest rung. He would send help back to Piers. Rather an heroic thing to do, for to leave him to die would be to save himself.

However, Piers heard him and shouted:

"Are you going to leave me here, you filthy young thief?"

Wakefield stood hesitant at the top of the ladder, looking at the beautiful world about him to which he had been so miraculously restored.

"Wake!" came Piers' voice, with a note of anguish in it, "you little swine, come here!"

Wakefield left the ladder and came slowly toward the skylight. "Were you wanting me?" he asked.

"Of course I want you! How long do you think I can hang here without falling?"

"Well, I was going for help."

"Don't leave me!" shouted Piers. "My arms are almost broken! Come and help me out!"

Wakefield approached him gingerly. He saw that Piers was in a bad way, that the projection offered him the slenderest hold, that, if he left him, he would probably go down to his death on the wheels of Gran's chariot. He squatted beside the skylight and placed his hands under Piers' armpits.

Piers uttered a grunt of relief. "Lift!" he ejaculated.

Wakefield heaved at him without avail.

"Lift, can't you! Have you no more strength than a kitten?"

"Are you under the impression that you have no more weight than one?" asked Wakefield severely.

"Shout for help, then!"

But their voices had already attracted Finch, who was returning to the house.

"Anything wrong?" he called from the bottom of the ladder.

"Come quick!" cried Wakefield, "and help me to save Piers!"

Finch's long face appeared so speedily that he seemed to have ascended the ladder in one bound.

"Thank God!" groaned Piers, as he felt the bony arms grip him.

"Now then," gasped Finch, "both at once! Heave. . . ."

Up he came, and the three lay in a dishevelled heap on the roof. Finch was the first to sit up and look at the faces of the other two. He began to laugh hysterically.

"You wouldn't laugh," said Piers, nursing his arm, "if you were in my place."

"Or mine," chimed in Wakefield.

Piers growled—"I've not finished with you."

"What's it all about?" asked Finch.

"I'll not tell you. It's a disgrace to the family. One thing I will say, and that is that this young man is going to land in gaol some day."

Wakefield rose. He said, with an attempt at airiness:

"Well, I'm off!"

"No, you're not," returned Piers, catching him by the leg. Wakefield struggled.

"Look out!" shouted Finch. "You'll be off the roof in another minute!" He moved to a safe distance from them.

"If I hadn't hurt my arm," said Piers, "he'd get the best hiding of his life!" He jerked Wakefield's leg from under him and he fell with a crash.

"Be careful what you do!" shouted the boy. "Or I'll set fire to your old barn."

Piers gave Finch a horrified look across the prostrate body.

"He's a downright criminal," he said. "I always felt that he had it in him."

"He doesn't mean it," said Finch, feeling sorry for Wakefield.

"Doesn't he? Well, now, I'll tell you what I caught him doing!" The culprit threw an arm across his eyes and lay still.

"I caught him in the act," went on Piers slowly, "of stealing money out of my pocket-book."

"You did! Well—he's a nice one."

A thought struck Piers and he exclaimed—"What did you do with the pocket-book?"

"It's in the apple-house," muttered Wakefield. "And all I was doing was looking to see what you had. . . . You're always crying poverty."

"Young liar! You were stealing."

"Well, after all," said Finch, "he kept you from falling through the skylight."

Wakefield began to cry. "I saved his life," he sobbed, "and this is the thanks I get."

"What rot!" retorted Piers. "I shouldn't have been much hurt."

Finch was suddenly on Wakefield's side.

"You'd have broken your leg, at the least," he said. "Come along, kid. We'll go and find the pocket-book. You'd better put some liniment on that arm, Piers."

With one accord they gathered themselves up and descended the ladder.

But Wakefield spent the week-end at Meggie's.

XV

THE TENTH THURSDAY

ACCEPTANCE of life, and of himself as a frail vessel tossed on its surface, came to Eden on these sharp November mornings while he was in the stable. The mist that always seemed to linger about Vaughan-lands, for it lay in a hollow, was chill and penetrating as he crossed the yard, making him shiver, but in the stable there was a comforting animal warmth, there was calm breathing from the massive, barrel-like bodies, a glad glow in the great eyes of the beasts. They reached eagerly toward the hay with which he filled their mangers, plunged their lips into the ice-cold water he offered in the bucket, and made way with decent civility when he cleaned their stalls.

The hard work made him sweat. Drops fell from his forehead on to the straw. He could feel sweat running down his back and his chest.

He did not mind the work. He wondered if perhaps, after all, tranquillity came only with labour. He looked with satisfaction at the barrow mounded with dung which he had shovelled from the stalls. He trundled it along the uneven floor and dumped it on to the great heap in the stable-yard. He groomed the hard flanks of the farm horses and, the dust making him cough, he thought of the pot of tea he had set brewing in the kitchen before he came out.

When all else was done he fed the poultry and flung open the door of the poultry-house. He stood leaning against the door watching the squawking, pecking crew while the red sun beamed on the up-kicked straw and the dangling comb of the cock.

Morning after morning he stood so, for a little, resting before he returned to the house to bathe and breakfast. He was happier, now that he was helping Maurice. Renny had been surprised and re-lieved by his eager acceptance of the suggested farm-work. Maurice was innately indolent and, once that he was no longer driven by necessity, he drifted more completely into his plans for subdividing his land.

He had actually sold two lots. One was being held, but on the other a flimsy erection was already being put up by a retired grocer. Maurice took a sincere interest in its progress and spent a part of each day agreeably in aiding and advising the builder, and occasionally showing prospective purchasers over the property.

The weather was heavy. Eden felt the strain of going into town to give his Thursday readings. His dinner afterward with Sarah and the remote calm of her presence was a deep relief to him. They would sit without talking because his voice was husky after the strain. On the ninth Thursday he had difficulty in restraining a cough which threatened to spoil the effect of his reading. He went to Sarah profoundly depressed. They scarcely spoke during dinner, but, afterward in the drawing-room, she talked quickly and lightly without waiting for an answer. Watching her, he noticed that a change had come over her face in the past few months. Her eyes had a burning look, and a faint colour warmed the marble of her cheeks. But any changes in her were of only momentary interest to him.

"I am wondering," he interrupted her at last, "whether I can keep up until next Thursday. I feel frightfully tired."

"Don't you think," she suggested, "that it is the farm-work? You are not used to anything of that sort. For my part I think it is cruel of them to ask you. But then—relations are cruel."

"I don't think it is cruel," he returned. "I look so fit. . . . They don't realise . . . . Besides, I like the work."

"What don't they realise?" She looked a little startled.

"Well, that I'm not so fit as I look. I've a temperature all the time."

"But that is terrible! You must see a doctor."

"I've been under our old doctor's care ever since I came home. He helped me into the world."

"And will help you out!" she cried scornfully.

"He is satisfied with me, he says."

"I don't believe this part of the country—it's low and damp—is healthful for you. Will you see a good doctor—to please Finch and me? We're both so fond of you!"

"I cannot afford it," he muttered.

"Let me pay! You must."

He got up immediately and began to walk about the room.

"I shall be all right—once these Thursdays are over. The next one—the last, thank God!—is my own poetry. I must do that well." He stopped in front of her. "Do you know, Sarah, I still have a hundred and seventy dollars of the money I got from those women! I have only spent thirty dollars in nine weeks!"

"I used to spend less than that," she returned.

"Yes—I suppose you did. But I guess you spend a good deal

more than that now." He looked at her appraisingly, again noticing the recent change in her.

"You look different, Sarah," he said. "I wonder what is going on in that sleek black head of yours?"

"Why should I not look different?" she asked. "I'm a different woman. When I look back on my old life I can't believe in it. I tell myself that that was I, but I don't really believe in it."

"You're so much happier now?"

"I don't know what it is to be happy," she answered with meaning.

"But you will yet. I am sure you will."

"I wish I were sure of it."

A veiled smile passed across Eden's face. "Sure of *him*, you mean!" he said teasingly.

"He hates me," she said.

"No, no, Sarah. He is afraid of you. That's all."

She asked ingenuously as a child—"How can I stop that?"

He sat down beside her. "By pretending that you are afraid of him."

"It would be no pretence! I'm terrified of him." She gave a little nervous laugh, then pushed a box of cigarettes toward him. "Here are some of your favourite Russians," she said.

He shook his head. "I've given up smoking," he said. "It makes me cough."

"Hard luck! I shan't take one either."

"Please do. I'll like to watch you smoke. We'll talk about young Finch."

They talked, and Eden wondered if perhaps, after all, a marriage with Sarah might bring Finch happiness. But he could not bring himself to believe that. She would entrap him, and Finch should be free. Still, he was sorry for her, even while he distrusted her. She fascinated him.

In the days that followed Eden amused himself, kept his mind off his own troubles by thinking of Sarah and Finch. He had an odd feeling that it was for him to bring them together or keep them apart. He felt that he had a certain power over Finch, who was at this time away on the tour that had been arranged for him.

But, by the end of the week, his thoughts were occupied only with his own condition. His cough had become so much worse that Meg was concerned and dosed him with rum and honey, flaxseed tea, and patent cough medicines. He was drenched with sweat after his early morning work in the stable, but his pride kept him from complaining to Maurice. He would drag himself back to his bed and throw himself on it where still was the shape of his body in moisture from his sweat of the night. Much of the day he spent bent over his desk. His feverish brain found its solace in a new dramatic poem. "Thank God!" he said aloud, as he drove Maurice's car through the bitter cold streets, whirling dust half choking him, "this will soon be over!" It was his tenth Thursday.

Renny was in his office the next morning, as was his custom after breakfast. He was reading his mail, which consisted mostly of bills and circulars. The morning paper lay open on the desk, its back page uppermost, showing a large advertisement of Christmas goods by a department store. He laid down his last letter and his eyes fell on the advertisement. Was it possible that Christmas was so near? He smiled as he thought that little Adeline would be old enough to enjoy it this year.

He rubbed his eyes, which were smarting from the smoke of the small stove, which always refused to draw when the wind was off the lake. Yet he must have the fire for there was a raw, penetrating chill in the air. Outside lay several inches of wet snow. He had been walking in that and, as it had melted from his boots, it had formed a small puddle on the floor beneath them.

A quick rap sounded on the door and, when he said "Come in," it opened half-way and Eden was revealed standing back from it.

"Are you alone?" he asked.

"Yes," Renny answered, startled at seeing him there.

Eden entered and closed the door behind him. He looked dishevelled, desperate, and wild.

Renny sprang up and went to him.

"What's wrong?" he demanded.

Eden tried to answer but he could make no sound at first. Then his voice came loud and harsh.

"I'm ill . . . I've been to see a doctor. . . . My God, Renny, I'm going to die!"

Renny looked at him horrified, yet unbelieving.

"What are you saying?" he said roughly. "I don't think you know. You've been drinking!"

Eden gave a despairing laugh. "No such luck! It's true, I tell you. . . . I saw a specialist yesterday. He was a cold-blooded fellow. Well—I asked him for the truth! I've been suspecting it but, by God, I didn't want to hear it!"

"What did he say?"

"I've about three months. He couldn't do anything for me. No one can!" His face cleared for a moment and he added: "No wonder you look staggered. I was staggered myself."

Renny took him by the arm. "Sit down and tell me about it." He put Eden into his chair.

Eden wrung his hands together under the desk. He raised his stricken eyes to Renny's face. He spoke in jerky sentences in a broken voice.

"I've been feeling rotten for a month. . . . But this week has been the limit. . . . I made up my mind to see a specialist. . . . Sarah told me she didn't think old Harding much good. . . . Anyhow he hadn't seen me lately. I've been getting worse, I tell you—for some time."

"Yes." Renny spoke quietly. "Go on."

"Well—I went into town early. . . . It was bad going through the wet snow. . . . I was exhausted when I got to the doctor's. . . . He examined me. Told me—that. . . . I was dazed when I left his office. . . ." His wide-open eyes looked intensely blue. Renny thought, as though it were a discovery—"How blue his eyes are. . . ." He asked gently:

"Where did you go then?"

"Then? Why, I drove the car into a side street and I stopped there. I must have sat a long time. . . . I don't remember . . . I don't remember . . . I don't remember. . . ." He kept repeating the words while he stared straight ahead, as though at something horrible.

Renny opened a cupboard and took out a flask of brandy. He poured some into a glass and gave it to Eden. He seemed clearer in his head after that. He said, in a voice that was almost natural:

"Well, it was a great shock, you know. It took me a bit to get over it. And it was a vile day—blackness and slush—like the end of the world."

"Did you go to Sarah's?"

"No. I couldn't face that! But I gave my reading! All the nice ladies were there, armed with my poems. I read—and I read horribly, but somehow I got through. . . . They said they'd *loved* the readings and they kept inviting me to their houses and I accepted every invitation. It was amusing—knowing that I was going home to die. . . ."

"If you're willing to accept that man's word for it, I'm not. I'll take you to the best doctors in the country."

Eden shook his head. "No use, old fellow. He's right. I'm done for. I've no lungs left to cure."

The lines in Renny's face were as though they had been cut there with a knife. "Have you told Meg or Maurice about this?" he asked.

"No. I've left that for you to do. I said I was tired when I got back and went to bed. I was actually too tired to put the car in. I left that for Maurice. He was rather crusty about it. . . . I don't believe I slept two hours. But I did the work this morning. We've let the boy go. He wasn't any good, and there's not much to do now."

"Why the hell," exclaimed Renny, "did Maurice leave it to you? Couldn't he see that you weren't able?"

"Oh, he'd never notice!"

Renny saw that Eden had lost flesh since he had last seen him. He saw that there was dust and chaff on his clothes, that his hands were dirty.

"I suppose," he said, "that this work hasn't been good for you."

"The worst thing possible. Early morning exertion. The dust . . . But the climate's been bad too. The doctor said I should have been up north."

"You could have gone—if we'd known!"

"Yes—I suppose I could."

A silence fell between them. Through it came the pleasant sounds of the stable. . . . The sound of a pump, a man's deep voice singing, the contented neigh of a horse.

Another sound was added to these—steady footsteps coming toward the office. Eden started up. He knew the step.

Renny moved to the door to lock it, then stopped. An idea had come into his mind. Perhaps a reconciliation might be possible between these two—in such a case. He fixed his eyes on the door, and on Piers' face, when he opened it and came in.

That face was a study. For a moment its habitual bold, firm expression was broken into a look of positive dismay. Then it hardened into grey iciness and he turned to go away. But Renny stopped him.

"Look here, Piers," he said. "Shut that door. I want you two——"

Piers saw his purpose. "Let me out!" he said fiercely. "Do you think I'll do that? Do you take me for a fool?"

Renny reached out and shut the door. Eden had risen and was standing with his hands on the desk.

Piers looked at him again and was struck by his strange appearance. His eyes turned questioningly to Renny.

"He's a sick man," said Renny. "A specialist told him yesterday that—he's not going to get better."

Piers frowned. His mouth was drawn to one side in an expression of disgust.

"You fellows," Renny went on, "had the same mother. . . ."

"I'm sorry for that," muttered Piers.

"If you can't be decent to him—after what I've told you—get out and leave us alone!"

"I'm going!" He swung round and put his hand on the door-knob. He hesitated, then looked over his shoulder, as though unwillingly, at Eden.

Eden said—"I don't give a damn for your forgiveness."

"I've said to myself," said Piers, "that if ever I met you face to face I'd bash yours in. But you take care never to come about unless you're down and out. It seems to me that I've been hearing for years that you are dangerously ill."

"It has taken rather a long while," returned Eden bitterly.

"If you had lived a decent life you wouldn't have come to this!" Renny exclaimed—"Get out of here!"

Piers turned on him—"Oh, I know what you'd like! You'd like me to say, 'Dear brother, I want to be friends! If I can do anything for you, just let me know.' But I'm not that sort. Neither would you be if you were in my place. By God, I'd like to know what you'd have done if you had been in my place! Put a bullet through him, I'll bet!"

Eden said—"You fellows embarrass me. I feel as though I were overhearing a private conversation." He gave a rasping laugh. "Don't you think you'd better postpone this post-mortem for a little?" The brandy had given him heart. He threw them one of his old mocking looks. . . . Well—he had lain with both their women. . . .

Again Piers made as though to go, but he hesitated once more and said to Eden, without looking at him:

"I'll send one of my men over to help Maurice. Don't worry about the work." It cost him an effort to say this.

"Oh, I'm not worrying about the work—now," answered Eden. He watched Piers go out. He held himself together until the door had shut on the stalwart figure, then he dropped with an air of unutterable fatigue into Renny's chair and buried his face in his arms.

"I feel," he said, "as though I never want to move again."

The old people definitely felt that winter had come that day—a mean, shuffling, down-at-heel approach, with nothing grand about it, but nevertheless as certain as death. After dinner the three gathered about the fire in the drawing-room, which huddled sputtering under the smoke that the east wind was driving down the chimney.

Now and then it thrust out an angry tongue of flame, but more often sent a puff of smoke into the room.

Ernest sat, with hands outstretched, getting more than his share of what heat the fire gave out, his expression verging toward peevishness. He wore a woollen dressing-gown over his suit, and he had lighted a cigar, an unusual indiscretion for him.

Nicholas had been having a spell of gout, and from his afflicted leg, that was propped on one of the beaded ottomans, there rose a strong smell of liniment. His pipe hung slackly from the corner of his mouth, and he kept noisily rubbing his large shapely hands together. His Yorkshire terrier, Nip, lay curled up tightly on the ottoman beside his leg and, either from nerves or cold, kept up a continuous shivering.

Augusta sat upright in front of the cabinet of Indian curios, a small purple shawl around her shoulders, her knitting, a grey sock for her gardener in England, twitching under her quick needles. Being accustomed to English houses she did not find the room nearly so uncomfortable as her brothers did. She looked over her spectacles at the terrier with a disapproving expression.

"Nip takes up too much of the ottoman," she observed. "He has your leg pushed almost off. It is a good thing you never had a child, Nicholas. You would have ruined it."

"He likes the smell of the liniment," returned Nicholas.

"I've never heard of such a thing," Ernest declared. "Animals invariably hate such smells. And I must say I sympathise with them. That liniment of yours is particularly objectionable. It's making me feel quite squeamish."

"Blame your cigar, not my liniment. Gad, it smells like what Mrs. Wragge calls a 'heap of refuge' burning."

Ernest stared at him indignantly through the smoke.

"It's an excellent cigar," he said.

"I agree," put in Augusta. "It has a very pleasant aroma. . . . As for the dog's snuggling up to Nicholas, he probably feels the cold. It's a wretched day."

"And there is a wretched fire in the furnace," said Nicholas. "I felt the radiator when I came into the room and it's scarcely warm."

"We seldom have a really good fire now," agreed Ernest, his mind taken off his cigar. "I spoke to Wragge about it yesterday and he said—'We must make the coals last as long as we can, sir.' I thought it was distinctly cheeky on his part."

"Sometimes I think that Renny is getting a little more than close-fisted," said Nicholas.

Augusta took off her spectacles and looked solemnly at her brothers. "There is no doubt about it," she said. "He is. More than a little."

"Well, of course—of course," said Ernest nervously, "he has a good many—quite a good many demands on him."

"I sympathise," Augusta went on, "with frugality in times like these, but it should be used consistently. Renny will still cut slices off the hot joint for his spaniels but he will not mend the roof, which leaks in half a dozen places. It hurts me to see the place going to rack."

"*And* ruin," added Nicholas.

"Speaking of joints," said Ernest. "That last was as tough as leather."

"Nothing better than a boiling piece," boomed Augusta.

Nicholas scowled, sucking at his pipe. Then he said:

"Every mattress in the house needs doing over."

"Very true," agreed Ernest. "And every carpet needs cleaning. Just look at this one!"

All three peered at the carpet.

"The pattern is scarcely visible," said Augusta.

"What we need," said Ernest, "is one of those electric suction cleaners. Alayne tells me that her aunt has one. It's quite wonderful, she says."

"A good broom and some elbow-grease is all it needs," rumbled Nicholas.

The door opened and Renny came in.

"Well," he said, "and what are you looking for?"

"We were just remarking," said Augusta, "how well the carpet wears."

"We were wondering," added Ernest, "if perhaps it should be sent to the cleaners."

"Your fire seems to be smoking," observed Renny. He advanced into the room, picked up the poker, and beat a large piece of coal into fragments. Dusky flames shot through the crevices. He said:

"It's a devil of a day. I've just been over at the Vaughans'."

"We heard you were there," said Augusta. "We waited dinner some little time for you."

"You shouldn't have done that." He added, apologetically—"I didn't know that I was going to be there for dinner but they would have me stay."

"How are they all?" asked Ernest.

"Oh—Patience had a stomach-ache last night but it's better today."

Augusta said—"Children are given too much variety nowadays. They're spoiled and they're none the happier for it. Pheasant was saying to me this morning that her children are bored by this weather and that it bores her too. Fancy being bored by the weather! I remember being bored only once in my life and that was when I was five years old. My Mamma had taken the three of us for a picnic on the lake-shore and she'd forgotten to take my sewing along. I watched my brothers gambol about but I was bored because I had no sewing with me." She put on her glasses and resumed her knitting with an offended expression.

Renny sat down beside her on the sofa.

He touched her knitting. "Socks as usual," he said. For some moments he watched the needles as though they fascinated him. The fire had begun to crackle and burn brightly. Nicholas said:

"It's burning quite well now. Perhaps the east wind has fallen."

"I find east wind very trying," observed Ernest. "I wonder how it affects Eden. How is he, Renny?"

Renny still stared at the knitting-needles. "Eden? Oh—well, he's not very well, to tell the truth."

"No wonder," said Nicholas. "It's a miserable day."

"It would have been well for both Eden and me," said Ernest, "if we could have gone south this winter."

Renny drew a deep breath. He pressed his fingers between his brows and closed his eyes. The elderly people felt something odd about him and were silent. The flames made small flapping noises.

"I don't know," said Renny, "how I'm going to tell you something I heard this morning. But I feel that I must."

His uncles looked at him with shrinking in their eyes. They felt that they had endured enough worry and unpleasantness that year. But Augusta once more removed her spectacles and turned her full gaze upon him.

"Yes," she said, her deep voice sympathetic, "you had better tell us. It's easier to face things together."

Renny tried to smile at her but his smile contracted into a miserable look of pain. "It's Eden," he said, in a husky voice. "I'm afraid he's not going to get better."

Nicholas had not taken in the words.

"What's that?" he demanded sharply. And, as Renny did not answer him, he turned to Ernest. "What's he say? I don't see why he should mumble like that."

Ernest looked at him pathetically. "It's Eden. Renny says he's not going to get better. Why, I don't see how that can be! I understood all along that he was getting better. Dr. Harding told me so himself."

"Harding's an old fool!" exclaimed Renny.

Augusta laid aside the sock she was knitting and folded her hands together in her lap.

"I hope you have considered well before you have spoken, Renny," she said. "Because this is a terrible blow you have given us."

"Why—why—I can't believe it," stammered Nicholas. "Why, I saw him just three weeks ago and he'd a splendid colour. His eyes were as clear and bright as a child's."

"He saw a doctor in town yesterday," said Renny. "He came to my office this morning and told me about it. He was badly upset. I took him back to Meg's. And I called up the doctor. There isn't an atom of hope. The doctor said it was a miracle that he'd kept up so long. He's made of good stuff, that boy, I can tell you!"

"This is too much! It's too much!" Tears ran down Ernest's cheeks.

"That young life," mumbled Nicholas, as though to himself, "that young life . . . ."

"I must go to him at once," said Augusta.

"Why, it seems only yesterday that he was a little boy," said Nicholas. "Pretty as a picture. And now, to think of this happening to him. . . ." He covered his mouth with his hand to hide its trembling. Pictures of Eden's mother, of Eden as a child, came before his eyes, and were blotted out by the picture of Eden dying.

To Ernest the shock of finding all he had held so important—his illness, his recovery, his comfort, the intimate doings of the family —overshadowed into nothingness by the terror of the approaching event was almost more than he could bear. He looked pitifully into the faces about him for comfort, but found in Nicholas's face only a bleak dismay, in Augusta's a sorrowful dignity, and in Renny's a bitter resignation.

"It is a blessing," said Augusta, "that I did not go home this winter. Now I can be of some use to the boy. And to Meggie. How did she take the news?"

Renny drew down his brows. "She took it very hard. After I had told her, she ran straight upstairs to his room and knelt down by the bed—I'd got him into bed—and they cried together. He tried to comfort her. Eden's made of good stuff."

"How old is he?" asked Nicholas.

"Thirty-one."

"My God! And I'm eighty!"

"That is quite beside the point," said Augusta.

"Auntie's right," said Renny. "What we've got to do is to face

143

this thing together. There is no use in harrowing ourselves any more than we can help. I suppose that each one of us could find something. . . . I'd give a good deal, for instance, if I hadn't pushed him into working for Maurice. It's done him harm."

"It's shocking," said Augusta, "to think of a Whiteoak doing the work of a stable-boy. I wonder at Maurice."

The sound of little Adeline's screaming came from above. Renny got up. "I think I'll go up and tell Alayne," he said.

Augusta took his hand and gave it a quick squeeze. "Break it to her gently," she said. "It will hurt her more than you think, for she worries greatly over the child and that keeps her in a strung-up state."

"I know it does. And it's very foolish of her."

Nicholas was moving restlessly in his chair.

"Give me an arm, Renny," he growled. "I'm a stiff old fellow today."

It was with difficulty that Renny heaved him out of the chair. When he was on his feet he stood rigid for a space, as though he had lost the use of his legs, staring from under his beetling brows like an old lion at bay.

"Where are you going?" Renny asked him.

"Nowhere. Nowhere," he answered testily. "But I can't sit in one spot for ever!" He began to walk unevenly up and down the room. When he came opposite the bow window he stopped and stared out at the draggled, unimpressive day. "Thirty-one," he muttered. "Well, I declare, it's enough to break a man up to live to see this! It's just enough to break a man to pieces."

"I wish you would help me up too, Renny," said Ernest, who had, in addition to his grief, a sense of deep personal injury. "I feel very weak. I think I must go and lie down."

"Wait a moment," said Renny. "I'm going to fetch you a drink." He went into the dining-room and returned with brandy and soda.

As usual the spirits went to Ernest's head. He turned quite dizzy as he ascended the stairs, clutching the banister on one side while Renny supported him on the other. Again and again he tripped on the dangling cord of his dressing-gown until Renny gathered it up and carried it.

"You'd better lie down at once," he said, "and I'll cover you up."

But Ernest detached himself and, going to the radiator, put his hand on it. He said complainingly:

"It's almost cold. There has been little or no fire all day."

Renny's face shadowed. He said—"You'll be warm enough

when you're under the eiderdown." Rather brusquely he led him to the bed and covered him up.

When he had closed the door behind him he stood motionless outside it listening. He wondered whether Alayne were in her room or above in the nursery. As he hesitated he saw Pheasant cross the passage and enter her room. For a moment her figure was darkly silhouetted against a window. She had raised her hands to touch her hair and he perceived that she was with child. A swift emotion made his heart swell—pride that another Whiteoak was on the way and, mingled with the pride, a kind of anger at the intruding of this new life when Eden's was passing away.

Pheasant disappeared into the room. He went toward the door and asked:

"Where is Alayne?"

She came and looked out at him, her eyes dark and wistful in her pale face.

"She's upstairs giving Adeline her tea. You'd better not go up. Alayne has trouble enough in getting her to eat properly."

He stood for a moment rebuffed. Then he said—"I must see her."

"Well, then, I'll go up and stay with Adeline."

She looked tired, he thought. Almost ill.

"What nonsense," he said, and sprang up the stairs.

The door of the nursery was shut but his step had been heard, and Mooey flung it open, delighted with this unexpected diversion. He was eating an apple and, with a mouthful distending his cheek, he exclaimed:

"Hullo, Uncle Renny!"

His small brother, slavish imitator in all he did, came running too.

"Hullo, Uncle Wenny!" he cried.

Adeline alone remained at the children's table. She had been perversely refusing to eat and Alayne had been painstakingly explaining to her that, when she had finished her milk, she would see the pretty picture on the bottom of her mug. Bits of bread were scattered on the floor about her and, when she had the chance, she thrust other bits into the proffered milk.

"Swing me up, please," shouted Mooey.

"Me too, me too," clamoured Nooky.

Little Adeline, seeing her father, kicked her heels on her high chair in joy and, snatching the mug from her mother's hand, began greedily to drink the milk. Her eyes beamed at Renny over the rim of the mug.

"How jolly you all look here," he said, taking up Nooky.

Alayne gave a faint smile. "I have been sitting here an hour trying to induce her to eat her tea."

Adeline set down the empty mug. Milk and crumbs trickled down her chin. She was enraged by the sight of Nooky in her father's arms. To show it she began to throw the cutlery to the floor. Alayne caught her hands and held them.

"She wants you to put Nooky down," explained Mooey.

Renny set him down.

Adeline showed a double row of pearls and held out her arms. "Up, up, Dadda!"

Renny snatched her up and pressed his cheek against her damask one.

"Could you come downstairs?" he asked. "I want to talk to you."

"I suppose so," she said doubtfully, "but we'll have to take Baby too. Alma is having her tea in the kitchen."

The three descended the stairs followed by the two little boys. Alayne closed her door before Mooey and Nooky had time to enter.

She could hear Pheasant intercept them in the passage, driving them back up the stairs with mingled threats and promises. "Children, you shall each have a chocolate bar if you'll go back upstairs and be good till Alma comes. Mooey, if you climb on the banister, I'll tell Daddy! Nooky dear, *don't* lick the wallpaper! Take his hand, Mooey. . . . If I have to go up after you, my lads, you'll be sorry!"

Renny set his daughter on her feet. Like a small automaton she started off immediately toward the cupboard. She flung open the door, took out a hot-water bottle and returned with it to him.

"For you," she lisped with an ingratiating smile.

Alayne wrenched it from her. "Did you ever see such a child!" she exclaimed. "She's into mischief the instant she's put down." She took a sponge and wet it in the ewer. "I must wipe her face and hands before we talk. Really, it's hopeless teaching her to eat properly."

Adeline turned up a rosy face resignedly puckered against the sponge. Renny watched mother and child, feeling suddenly tired in body and mind. The shock, the grief he had undergone, assumed an unreal aspect. He wished he had gone away by himself for a while. He felt unequal to telling Alayne of what had happened. He dreaded her reception of the news. He had a mind not to tell her but to leave her to hear it from the old people.

She had finished washing the child and said:

146

"Now, go and show your clean hands."

Adeline marched up to him, holding out two moist pink palms.

"Yes," he approved. "Nice and clean."

For the first time since he had come in Alayne looked at him consciously. Something in his voice had penetrated her irritability.

"What is wrong?" she asked quickly.

He frowned but did not answer.

"Renny!" She came to him and put her hand on his arm.

Adeline, sensitive to a situation beyond her understanding, stood motionless staring up at them.

"I can't tell you," he muttered, and turned away.

"Renny, you must tell me. You're frightening me." She had turned pale. She looked at him pleadingly.

"No, no. Someone else had better tell you. I can't." He stood rigid, his fount of tenderness sterile. He looked at her as a man might look at a woman who superficially resembled a woman he had loved.

"You are being very cruel," she said. Her pride forced her to withdraw her hand from him. She was deeply hurt.

"I can't tell you," he repeated. "You must ask the others."

"Very well. I shall." She turned in one of her swift graceful movements and went from the room.

He listened to the sound of her steps descending the stair. When he heard the door of the drawing-room open and close behind her, he went into the passage and stood listening but he could distinguish no voices. He could hear nothing but Jock's elbow knocking on the floor as he scratched himself beside the stove in the hall below.

Little Adeline had followed him and now clasped her arms about one of his legs, which appeared to her as a towering pillar. And so they stood thus united.

XVI

THE FESTIVE SEASON

RENNY, followed by his spaniels, Piers' terrier, and Jock, the sheep dog, was prowling through the snowy winter woods in search of a Christmas-tree. Among the bare-limbed oaks and maples the vigorous green of the young spruces invited him. They thrust out their boughs, tier upon tier, their central peaks seeming designed to support a gilded star. The snow lay feathery on them and still fell in a sunlit mist. The sun, silver and rayless, showed himself less grand this morning, but gently cognisant of the earth's approach.

Renny desired a specially fine tree this Christmas, for little Adeline was now old enough to appreciate it. He had another reason too, perhaps rather a glimmering instinct in the troubled depths of his mind than a definite thought. The finer the tree the more freely might the spirit of Christmas radiate from it. He would choose a tree with boughs to hold a hundred candles.

The dogs hurried here and there snuffing and scratching at the snow-hidden burrows of rabbit and groundhog, the spaniels leaving ruffled trails behind their feathered feet, pretty young Biddy covering as much ground as the other three put together.

He chose his tree and, when he struck it the first blow with his axe, a rabbit darted from under the broad shelter of its boughs and scurried away with the dogs in pursuit.

The tree fell, shaking off its frail burden of snow, and stretched its length where its growing shadow had long been cast. The clean-cut stump it left looked insignificant to have been the support of so broad a stretch of boughs. A delicious scent rose from the bruised needles, a scent reminiscent to Renny of two-score past Christmases and their festivities.

He followed a distant clamour from the dogs and found them circled about a grizzly groundhog at bay with its back against a tree. It showed its yellow teeth, never taking its eyes from its assailants. The spaniels and Jock were obedient when whistled off, but Biddy had to be caught and cuffed and, on the way back, her hackle bristled and she whined distractedly.

Renny laid down the tree behind the carriage-house, for he heard the children's voices from the snow-covered lawn. He began to hack off a few of the lowest branches to make the contour of the tree more seemly for its high destiny. He did not hear steps in the snow but a shadow was thrown beside the prostrate tree and, looking up, he saw Finch. He had just returned that morning from his tour. One glance at his face discovered that he had heard the news about Eden.

"Hullo!" said Renny, straightening himself. "You back?"

"Yes. Just an hour ago."

"Have a good tour?"

"Pretty good."

Renny raised the tree and held it upright.

"What do you think of that for a Christmas-tree?"

"Splendid. We haven't had so big a one in a long time." Finch tried to speak cheerfully, but he had a sense of shock in finding Renny preoccupied with so trivial a matter. How could he think of a

Christmas-tree at a time like this? Why, he looked as absorbed in what he was doing as though no blackness shadowed them.

"I suppose," observed Renny, "that you've done rather well financially. How much did you make?"

"I shan't know until things are settled up." He spoke tersely. He had dreaded meeting Renny, now he shrank from his apparent materialism. Yet he was relieved. He drew a deep breath of the tingling air. The poignant scent of the tree stabbed him. Seeing it stricken so, he thought of Eden. He broke out:

"This is terrible, Renny! They've been telling me. I can hardly believe it."

"You'll believe it all right when you see him," replied Renny. "He's gone down quickly in the last fortnight. He's had haemorrhage."

Finch wrung his fingers together. His mouth was contorted as though he were about to cry.

"It's too horrible," he said. "I don't see how you can bear to think about Christmas, Renny."

Renny stood facing him, grasping the tree. He looked splendid, Finch thought bitterly, the picture of strength and vigour. Renny said:

"Well, there are the kids. There's no use in making them miserable. And we can't do Eden any good by mourning. I like Christmas myself, and I mean to have as good a one as possible—under the circumstances."

Fat, red-faced Mrs. Wragge appeared from the scullery, carrying a dish-pan heaped with tea-towels she had been washing.

"Now then, cook!" said Renny, "just have a look at this tree! Room for presents for everyone on that, eh?"

"Lord bless you, sir, it is a grand one! It'll tike some trimming, and I'd like nothing better than to 'ave a 'and in it myself, if 'tweren't that I'm so bad on me legs along o' me varicose veins."

"So they're troubling you?"

"Troubling me! I've got three ulsters the size of pennies on me left leg and me right one is not what you'd call perfect. But I do admire that tree, and if I 'ad coloured paper I'd make some pretty decorations for it, which I could sitting in comfort."

Finch left them and went toward the house. He was without coat or hat. He buttoned his jacket and shivered. The children saw him and began to shout:

"Hullo, Uncle Finch! Hullo! Hullo!"

Mooey and Patience were making snowballs. They ran nearer,

holding them aloft, ready to throw. As they ran they jostled Nooky and he fell, plunging his little red hands into the snow. Adeline came last, marching steadily, the picture of infantile triumph.

"Snow—snow—snow," she chanted.

"Why are you here?" Finch asked of Patience.

She answered—"I live here now. Uncle Eden's at our house. Mummy's nursing him. I've lost a tooth. Look!" She held up her round face and displayed a gap in the milk-white row of her teeth.

Finch rescued Nooky and dried his hands on his handkerchief. He had a tender feeling for the tiny boy.

"Love Uncle Finch?" he mumbled against his cheek.

"Ah," replied Nooky, and clasped his neck.

Finch thought—"If only I could be like the children and not be forced to face things! They don't see what goes on so long as they are fed and cared for. Their very hair sticks out with egotism. Their eyes are as bright as the eyes of animals. And Eden is dying. . . . I think it might have been broken to me carefully and not blurted out by Uncle Nick, while Uncle Ernie and Alayne and Wakefield were all staring at me."

The words had been more terrible, uttered in Nicholas's sonorous, broken tones. Ernest had seemed a bundle of nerves, fingering his chin, biting his nails. Alayne had sat rigid, as though she did not know what it was to relax. Wakefield had appeared to be more interested in Finch's reaction to the news than in the news itself. Augusta was not there. She had gone to stay at Vaughanlands. Pheasant had slipped out of the room soon after Finch's arrival. She knew that the family were waiting for her to leave so that they might be free to talk. . . .

A snowball shot past and hit Mooey on the head. Finch turned and saw Renny. At the same instant one caught him on the ear. Rage overwhelmed him. He set Nooky down and fled from the scene of romping.

"The brute!" he muttered, digging the snow from his ear. "He doesn't care! He doesn't care! He and Piers and Maurice have killed Eden among them—making him work like a labourer—curse them!"

He had dreaded going to Vaughanlands but now he hastened in that direction, as if there were no time to spare.

He found his sister in the pantry stirring an egg-nog for Eden. She looked reassuringly natural. He held her plump body close to his, kissing her.

"Oh, Meggie," he groaned, "this is a terrible blow! How are we going to go through with it? Can I help you? Tell me something I can do!"

Meg put him from her gently.

"We'll not talk now. I must get this egg-nog ready."

"May I see him?"

"Of course. He was speaking of you only this morning. Here, you may take him this. That will be helping. Be careful not to slop it." She gave it to him cautiously, for she had filled it to the brim, as was her way.

He mounted the stairs, his eyes riveted on the glass. His hand shook so that the liquid overflowed and dripped on to the carpet.

"God!" he exclaimed between set teeth, "to think that I can't carry this up without spilling it!"

He stood wondering what to do, then he put his lips to the glass and drank a mouthful or two so that he was able to carry it.

He tapped on the door of Eden's room and Augusta's voice said "Come in."

He entered and found her alone in the room. The windows were wide open, the fine snow sifting in on the air. She was making the bed. The bedclothes were heaped on a chair and she was shaking a mattress.

"Well, my dear," she said, "so you've come back to us! And you look very well. The tour did not tire you greatly?"

"I'm all right," he said. He went to her and kissed her, holding the glass gingerly. "Look here," he added, "you shouldn't be doing this alone. It's far too heavy for you."

He set down the glass, took the mattress from her and turned it over, shaking it vigorously.

They made the bed together, smoothing the sheets so there should be no wrinkles, and Finch asked:

"Do you think it's a good bed?"

"I think it's a very good bed." She talked to him calmly all the while, by her dignified restraint helping him to control himself.

When the bed lay smooth and white he stood looking down at it for a moment and his heart turned with pity in his breast. His eyes sought Augusta's and he made a quick gesture with his hand toward the bed. She came to him and patted his shoulder. "You must be a good brave boy," she said.

"Where is he?"

"In Meg's sitting-room. He's reading or writing—something to pass the time."

Finch stood outside the door of the sitting-room. His tongue was dry and clung to the roof of his mouth. He did not know how to face Eden. He pictured himself in Eden's position—how he would have risen to face the brother who entered, his eyes wide with horror, his body shaken by sobs. He could not muster the courage to go in. But Eden's voice, with the old note of irritability, called from the room:

"Who's that? Why don't you come in if you're coming?"

Finch went in hesitatingly, the glass of egg-nog in his hand.

"Meggie sent you this," he managed to get out in a trembling voice.

"She's half an hour late with it," observed Eden. He took the glass and began to drink, avoiding Finch's eyes.

Finch had been prepared for a change in him but he was not prepared to see him so etherealised, so transparent, with such hollow, shining eyes and feverish cheeks. He wore a light-blue dressing-gown and was sitting by the table with writing things in front of him.

When he had finished the egg-nog he turned and looked at Finch, as though it had given him strength.

"Good old Meggie," he said. "She's put lots of brandy in it."

Finch looked at him, filled with an immense pity. He longed to give out strength to him.

Eden said—"Sit down and tell me how you got on."

In a voice he could hardly recognise as his own Finch recalled what he could. Eden listened eagerly. "You're doing well," he said, and added significantly—"Stick to it. Don't let yourself worry. Don't be too sympathetic. That's the only way for an artist."

"Have you been doing anything? Any writing, I mean?"

Eden frowned. "Well—I do what I can. I'm trying to finish that long poem. I've been at it for months but I don't seem to get much forrarder."

"May I read what you've written—some day?"

"Yes." Eden spoke in a business-like tone. "Now I'll tell you what I have in mind to do." He began to talk very practically of the publishing of his poems, those he wanted to include and the form he desired. He ended—"I should like to have it brought out by the 1st of March. I think I'll last till then."

Finch reached out and grasped his hand.

"Don't give up hope, old fellow. You've been through a hard time. But rest and care will put you on your feet again." Before he had finished speaking his voice became flat and toneless from the effort of uttering the futile words.

Eden answered—"I was done for when I came home." He looked

152

at Finch with wide-open eyes but he had the appearance of one who does not see. His fingers played with the collar of his dressing-gown, drawing it close about his throat.

After a little he said—"I hear that Sarah is coming to Jalna for Christmas."

"I have not been told. Why should they ask her?"

"Why not?"

"You are ill. We don't want company." Finch spoke fiercely. The thought of Sarah was repellent to him.

"I am becoming a shadow. And Sarah is as real as the sun and wind. God—how I've loved the sun and wind!"

"Eden, will you promise me to try to live?"

"Yes, yes, of course! But don't bother me. It's irritating. Now, put yourself in my place. You'd hate that sort of talk."

"But, Eden—you want to live, don't you?"

"Of course I do! That's just why the things you say irritate me. . . . I'm standing on a lonely shore. A great wave has just broken at my feet. I'm looking into its depths. And you come along and begin to throw little sharp pebbles at me to divert my attention."

Augusta came into the room.

"Are you comfortable?" she asked Eden.

"This fellow," he answered, "is boring me. He's not nearly such good company as Renny or Wake."

"Should you like to lie down?" she asked.

"Mm. . ." He looked at her petulantly, not knowing what he wanted.

She laid his head against her and stroked his hair. He began to cough. Finch had never heard such coughing. When it was over and they had got him into his bed, Finch slipped out of the house and went back across the snowy fields to Jalna.

He went in at the side door. He could not face the others, answer their questions about Eden. He must escape to his own room. He was tired out for he had been travelling most of the night, eager to be home, eager for the Christmas festivities at Jalna, from which he had been absent for two years.

The smell of the Christmas-tree followed him all the way up the stairs. Even to his own room its resinous smell had penetrated. It must be locked in the sitting-room now, for four days to be guarded from prying young eyes. In the passage he had seen a mound of club moss to be used for wreathing. He had no place here! No place but his own room where he could shut himself in—refuse to give himself to this farce of merrymaking.

There was ice on the pane. Inside it had melted, trickled down and formed a puddle on the sill and frozen again. The tooting of a toy horn came from the nursery.

"Little brutes," he said savagely. "Let them do without their Christmas this year! If I had my way there'd be no Christmas in this house." He strode up and down the worn carpet. He looked wildly at his boyhood's belongings.

"I've prayed in this room," he thought. "I've prayed and not been answered. But no more prayer for me! I'll tear prayer out of my heart by the roots. It's no use. It's like the smell of that tree. It drugs you. It's religion, and it's no use in this world. . . . Oh, God—no, I won't! I'm a fool! Who would be such a fool as to pray for Eden—after what I saw this morning." He fell on his knees beside the bed, gripping the coverlet. "Oh, God, save him—save him—make him well."

XVII

CHRISTMAS DAY

A FRESH fall of snow was spread across the land on Christmas Eve—an immaculate cloth for the altar of the world. The air was very clear, so that the stars, faint as candles, lingered into the morning. The vigorous green of the evergreens was the only colour in the pallid landscape. The only sound was the distant roaring of the lake, still troubled by a gale now fallen.

The first person to awake in the house was young Maurice, whose heart, the moment he opened his eyes, began to beat quickly in anticipation of the day. He sat up in his cot and looked across the room to where his cousin Patience was fast asleep. He could see her round face framed in her hair like a closed flower-bud in curling leaves. He gave an excited laugh. Where was Santa Claus now, he wondered, and pictured him speeding back across snowy wastes to the north. The swift reindeer, they needed no urging. Faster than any horse in the stables they flew through the frosty air, and Santa Claus' white beard flapped on his great chest.

The tree! The tree! How could he wait to see the tree! Not until late afternoon would its splendours be visible. Unless (the thought made him dive under the covers in fear and ecstasy), unless he stole down and peeped through the keyhole at it!

His legs, clad in a flannel sleeping-suit, dangled over the side of the cot. He found the floor and put on his slippers and dressing-gown.

Should he wake Patience and enjoy the pride of power of escorting her through the twilit stairways to the forbidden sight of the tree? He decided that he would not. At any moment she would be likely to give one of her sudden peals of laughter and they would be discovered.

He had one eye pressed to the keyhole of the library door, trying to distinguish the pale shapes on the dark mass in the corner, feeling a little frightened, for the way had been long and the growling, rumbling noises that had come from Uncle Nick's room rather terrible, when Rags had crept up behind him and caught him by the seat of the pyjamas with:

"'Ello, naow, Master Mooey, and w'at do you think you'll get for spying on Father Christmas? He'll tike aw'y yer toys and leave you a bundle of birches, see!"

Mooey began to cry bitterly, and Rags, not wishing to have the household disturbed, carried him down to the basement where Mrs. Wragge gave him a breakfast of sausages and fried potatoes from a corner of the kitchen table.

She had the kitchen in that delicious state of flurry which she always achieved on a special occasion. She could not keep her head, yet her dishes almost always turned out well and she got more work out of her husband and Bessie than could any other human being. She showed Mooey the mince-pies, the enormous plum-pudding, and the colossal turkey. She showed him the moulds of cranberry jelly and the plum-cake covered with marzipan to be cut for tea. The thought of Santa Claus and the tree was for the time being driven from his mind.

"And w'at would you s'y," she asked, cuddling him, "to 'aving a nice noo little brother along o' springtime?"

"I have a little brother," answered Mooey without enthusiasm. "He's enough."

"A baby sister, then? With big blue eyes."

"No. Don't want no more babies."

"Bless yer 'eart," and Mrs. Wragge kissed him on the mouth. "You'll love 'er all right w'en the time comes!"

Rags addressed his wife. "There'll be some cursin' upstairs this morning. The snow's too deep for the car and they've got to walk to early communion. And a bitter walk it'll be!"

Bessie lifted her face from a saucer of tea.

"Well," she said, "I don't call that Christian, anyhow."

Mrs. Wragge observed—"If the boss would give less to the Church and more to me for pots and pans it would be Christianer. As for the missus—she's gettin' more penoorious every day. Thank goodness I've got her pretty well broke of comin' down here to interfere."

"Which of them are going?" asked Bessie.

"The master and the three young fellers," answered Rags. "I could hear Mr. Wake complaining how tired he is and how cold it is, and w'en the master called up to Mr. Finch I 'eard 'im call back that 'e wasn't goin', that 'e didn't feel like it, some'ow. 'Feel like it or no,' says the master, 'you'll come to early communion on Christmas morning. You were brought up to it and you'll do it.' And you'll see that 'e will!"

There was a sharp crunching on the snow outside the window. Four pairs of legs strode past, one pair well in advance of the others. Mrs. Wragge regarded this pair with disapproval. She said:

"I don't think it looks respectful goin' off to service in them plush-fours."

"Early communion ain't real church," said Rags. "Mr. Finch 'as got a thin pair of shanks. And it ain't because 'e daon't eat." He added with satisfaction—"There's not many 'ouses that can send out four fine-lookin' young men to the 'early service and two 'andsome old ones to the late."

"Lor', w'at a pity it is about Mr. Eden," sighed Mrs. Wragge. A gloom fell over the kitchen. With a shadowed face Rags carried a tray laden with breakfast things up the stairs.

When he returned he said:

"Madam's down. She wants 'er coffee and a soft-boiled egg. She seemed surprised that there weren't no gripe fruit."

"I should think," said his wife, "that she'd 'ave got over surprises. W'y couldn't she 'ave stopped in bed till the men-folk came back?"

Alma Patch appeared at the door which led into the yard. She was late and divested herself of her outer garments as she entered.

"You'd better tike this young man up with you," said Mrs. Wragge to the girl, "and dress 'im. 'E's 'ad 'is breakfast."

Alma looked at them blankly and took Mooey by the hand.

Rags came hurrying down the stairs. "She says she's cold," he announced. "Do go along, Bessie, and open up the draughts of the furnace. You can clean out the ashes, but just put two small shovels of coal on. This last lot must do us to the New Year."

"I don't see why I should do the furnace," grumbled the girl.

"There's some in the 'ouse," said Rags meaningly, "as don't see w'y you should be 'ere at all. Economise we must, and I've 'eard more than one 'int that you may be the next item dropped from the list of luxuries."

Bessie began to blubber and hurried toward the furnace-room. Mrs. Wragge looked smug. Alma trailed up the stairs leading Mooey. Before long she reappeared and said:

"Mrs. Piers asked me would I take her up a tray with a little toast and tea. She's not feeling too bright this morning. She looks as white as a sheet."

"Pore little thing," said the cook. "I'll make 'er a nice breakfast and you carry it up without slopping, mind you."

Again Rags appeared from above. "Both old gentlemen are down," he said, "an' look a little cheerier than they 'ave lately."

Mrs. Wragge said to him out of the side of her mouth:

"Any Christmas presents yet?"

Rags grinned and tapped his breast pocket. "Sime as usual. They'll not let *me* daown!"

While the dishes from the first breakfast were being washed, four pairs of snowy legs again passed the basement windows and soon there was a steady march of feet into the dining-room. The brothers had knelt in a row on the step before the altar. They had held up four strong hands for the Bread. They had bent four heads, emptied of thought, above the Goblet. Now, with clamorous stomachs, they sought to break their fast.

Sarah had shivered upstairs in her room till she heard them return. Her entry into the dining-room was timed with theirs.

"I could not wake," she said in her honey-sweet voice, "or I should have gone to church with you." She slid into a chair beside Finch.

He thought—"Now I must talk to her instead of eating in peace! Damn her, why didn't she have breakfast with the others?"

Renny gave her an arch look.

"You may come with us at eleven. We go again then."

"Leave me out," said Piers.

Finch said nothing, but he intended spending the morning with Eden.

"There is a collection," Renny proceeded, "for church expenses. Mr. Fennel was in favour of one for the Eastern Missions, but I stood out for home charities and I got my way. I hope you'll contribute generously, Sarah."

Sarah smiled enigmatically. She did not want to go to church. She hated church.

"Are you going again?" she whispered to Finch, under cover of Renny's going to the top of the basement stairs and shouting for Rags.

"I'm going to see Eden," he answered.

"Of course, you must! I'll go too. I'll send my contribution by Wakefield."

Renny returned to the table. Mooey came in at his heels. He went to his father and, standing on the rung of his chair, whispered in his ear:

"Daddy, when are we going to have the tree?"

Piers stared at him, with eyes prominent.

"What tree?"

"Why, you know—the Christmas-tree!"

Piers looked stupid.

"I have heard nothing about a tree."

Mooey thumped his sire's hard body with his fists.

"You have! You have! It's the tree what Santa Claus——" He was between laughter and tears.

The remainder of breakfast was enlivened by the baiting of Mooey.

In the hall Renny was met by his small daughter and her mother. Adeline importantly carried a package wrapped in tissue paper and tied with silver ribbon.

"Me'y K'ismus," she shouted again and again.

Alayne had spent some time in teaching her the festive greeting. She said:

"It's her first Christmas present to you."

He hugged them both and examined the grey suède gloves with expressions of delight.

Alayne stroked his lean, freshly shaven cheek. "Can't we be alone together for a little?" she asked.

He looked at his wrist-watch. "Ten o'clock. I have just time to go to the stables before eleven o'clock service. The snow is too deep for the car. We must walk."

"I don't think I'll go," she said. "It's very cold. The walk through the snow will be tiring."

"But it's Christmas Day!" he exclaimed.

"You know that I am not orthodox," she returned.

He reached for his cap from the rack, from the top of which the carved muzzle of a fox looked down. She continued:

"And I don't think the uncles should attempt the walk."

"Oh, a little snow won't discourage *them*." He put the child into her arms and went out.

She stood looking after him. The ghosts of four-score Christmases celebrated by Whiteoaks under this roof pressed in upon her. She could feel the Christmas spirit palpitating through the house.

Four-score hoary heads of Santa Claus peered at her from the walls. A procession of eighty turkeys passed by her gobbling in despair. Eighty round Christmas puddings flamed and sputtered like eighty burnt-out worlds. From the drawing-room came the voice of the parrot declaiming, for the benefit of Sarah:

"*Kutni! Kutni! Kutni! Paji! Paji! Shaitan-ka-bacha!*"

She pictured Augusta, a child of two, offering her first Christmas present to Captain Whiteoak on this very spot. It took the individuality out of one, she thought; one could put up only a losing fight against the power of the Whiteoaks.

Pheasant came slowly down the stairs. She was dressed for going out and had Mooey by the hand.

"Pheasant!" cried Alayne, "surely you're not attempting to go to church through the snow!"

"Oh yes. We always do, don't we? Mooey and I are starting early because we can't walk very fast."

"You're not well. I don't see any sense in it. Anyhow, I'm not going."

She opened the door for Pheasant, and a wind, fresh and wild as though it had just swept the Pole, leaped in on her. She stood for a moment, letting it have its way, smiling ironically as it slammed doors throughout the house. She could hear Nicholas grumbling and Ernest complaining. She and the child laughed at each other as the sparkling snow drove in on them.

She watched them set out in pairs and trios. Pheasant and Mooey. Sarah and Finch, in the direction of Vaughanlands. Nicholas and Ernest, the first leaning on Renny, the second on his mother's ebony stick. Wakefield dashing off late, with Sarah's offering in his pocket. She had the house to herself! Adeline was as good as gold this morning. They were gay together. Alayne found the key of the sitting-room and had the pleasure of seeing Adeline's eyes dance at the first sight of the bedizened tree.

Sarah had casually given Wakefield ten dollars as her contribution to church charities. He had managed, with difficulty, to conceal his amazement at such largesse. He was poverty-stricken after the buying of Christmas presents and he was stirred to exhilaration by this unexpected wealth in his pocket. But for how short a time it would be there! For no longer than it took him to dash across the snowy fields to church. To him there was something showy in placing such an amount in the alms dish. It would be an embarrassing moment for him. It might be better, he thought, hurrying through the unmarked snow, for he had taken a short cut, to poke it into the poor-box in the vestibule. Still, that would scarcely be fair to Sarah, who had designed her gift for the offertory.

He skirted the pews at the back of the church and entered the family pew from a side aisle, for he knew that Nicholas would not budge from his place at the end. He found himself next Pheasant and beyond he saw the profiles of Ernest, Renny, and Nicholas, and the round face of Mooey peering at him like a flower-bud among tall stalks. Across the aisle he saw Maurice and Augusta. It was strange to see her in the Vaughans' pew.

Wakefield sniffed the spicy scent of the Christmas decorations. He was pleased with the effect of the club moss and holly with which he himself had enriched the window. As long as he could remember he had taken part in the Christmas decorating. When he was three Meg had held him up so that he might place a flower in a vase on the altar. Though he considered himself an agnostic he loved this church that his grandfather had built, and to him the scattered congregation was an imposing gathering. Certainly Mr. Fennel could not complain of thin feminine singing when there was always a male quartette of Whiteoaks to bulwark the responses and keep Miss Pink, the organist, from lagging.

Wandering in and out of the pattern of the Christmas service was the shining thread of the thought of Pauline. In a few hours they would be together again. Together! Lovely word! It had the sweetness of the evergreens and the brightness of the stained-glass windows in it. . . . If only he might have given her the hoop of pearls and diamonds today! God only knew when he should be able to afford it. . . . "I must be adamant. I must be steel. Deny myself everything in order to afford it."

Renny, casting a look sideways at him, thought—"He still has the look of a child. I'm glad of that."

The offertory plate was now moving from pew to pew, carried by old Chalk, the blacksmith, whose son now had a petrol station. Chalk watched with discreet interest to see what the Whiteoaks' offerings would be, and his Christian spirit wavered for an instant in the direction of unpaid bills for horseshoeing and motor repairs.

Regretfully Wakefield laid Sarah's banknote on the alms dish. His eyes slanted toward the faces beside him to observe its effect on them. He saw Pheasant start, heard her amazed intake of breath. He saw Uncle Ernest lean forward blinking unbelievingly at its crisp surface. Mooey stretched out his small chapped hand and pointed at it, his mouth forming to an "oo" of wonder. Nicholas glared at it over his glasses, but it was Renny who nipped it up and held it suspended while he scanned, with desperate inquiry, the faces beside him.

Wakefield nodded a resigned affirmation of the offering. Pheasant began to quiver with laughter. Ernest made futile faces of protest. Nicholas blew out his cheeks, while Mooey's "oo" became articulate.

Renny replaced the note on the plate, grinned affably at Chalk, who, very red in the face, clumped on down the aisle. From across the way Maurice and Augusta scented something strange. They too stopped singing and gazed at their kinsfolk. The Misses Lacey whispered together. The infection spread to Miss Pink and she fumbled for the keys. The congregation wavered. The hymn all but expired. Mr. Fennel mounted the pulpit and covered his face with his hands. . . .

The family progressed slowly along the icy slope from the church. Augusta, leaning on Maurice's arm, was joined by Nicholas, who supported himself on Wakefield. They were followed by Renny, who assisted Ernest. Mooey slid alongside on the ice. Pheasant came last bearing her unborn child, whose weight, on a morning like this, was something of a burden to her.

Nicholas said to his sister—"I can't wish you a Merry Christmas, Gussie! Not at a time like this. But I can and do wish you many happier ones. How's the boy?"

"Not improving, Nicholas. But he had a quieter sleep last night and seems quite bright today."

"Are you coming to Jalna for dinner?"

"No. I shall stay with Eden and let Maurice and Meg go. I'll go over later in the day."

The elder Miss Lacey, who had set her cap at Nicholas in her youth, now shuffled up to him across the icy path and they shook hands warmly. She was a pretty old lady, he thought, and he might have done worse than get spliced up with her.

"Real Christmas weather, isn't it?" she said.

"Yes," he agreed sombrely. "A sad Christmas for us. But we make the best of it for the sake of the young people."

"How time does fly," she sighed. "It seems just yesterday when they were children and we were—not so old. And not so very long ago since we ourselves were young. What sleigh rides we used to have on Christmas Day!"

"Yes, yes," he returned abruptly, and held Wakefield back and let her shuffle on alone. He cast a bleak look over the family plot, at the granite plinth pointing upward from the snow, the low iron fence, the ornamental chains and balls of which each bore its fragile mound of whiteness, the graves levelled and indistinguishable.

Wakefield gave his arm a little tug. "Come along, Uncle Nick, I see Piers down there with the car. He's managed to get it here through the snow."

Nicholas hastened to join the others. "Good boy, good boy, I'm very glad of that! The walk here was quite enough. Well, I'm very glad he's brought the car. I hope you'll have a Merry Christmas, Wake. If we elders are a bit quiet—well, you must try to keep your spirits up."

"Thanks, Uncle Nick."

Piers accepted their gratitude for bringing the car but, in truth, he had had his young wife and her burden in mind and not the fatigue of the old people. She and Mooey sat in front with him while Augusta and her brothers squeezed themselves into the back seat. Renny, Maurice, and Wakefield, relieved of responsibility, strode homeward together.

Surely, thought Mooey, when the heavy two o'clock dinner was over and the grown-ups were established in the drawing-room about a blazing fire, surely Santa Claus will come now! He stood, shivering with excitement, outside the locked door of the sitting-room. The other children were being dressed for the occasion, but he had been dressed ready and waiting all day for the coming of Santa Claus and the glory of the tree. The clock in the hall struck four. The wintry twilight was already drawing in.

Jock, sitting by the stove, gave a wide yawn.

"You're tired of waiting too, aren't you?" said Mooey.

Jock looked at him quizzically.

"But you won't get anything off the tree, will you?"

Jock closed his eyes.

"Rags," said Mooey, as the ever-busy houseman flitted by, "is Santa Claus back in his own house now?"

Rags almost dropped the tray he was carrying. "In 'is own 'ouse? Not a bit of it! 'E's in this 'ouse 'ere, that's w'ere 'e is. Right in Jalner!"

Mooey's heart gave a leap of joy and terror. He caught Rags by the coat-tails and held him fast.

"Don't go! Tell me—how did he get in? Where is he?"

Rags pointed a thin, greyish-white forefinger at the door of the library. He compressed his lips. His eyes were two gimlets boring into the door.

Mooey dropped Rags's coat-tail. His scalp pricked and his hair looked suddenly very lively.

Jock rose, went to the door of the library, sniffed it and whined. "Rags! Rags!" cried Mooey, "don't go! Stay with me!"

His knees shook when he found himself alone with Jock still sniffing at the door. He had had a glimpse of the grown people sitting about the drawing-room but he could not go in to them, frightened though he was. He must stay here, waiting for Santa Claus.

Without warning the front door opened and Augusta, followed by Finch and Sarah, stood on the threshold. Behind them Mooey saw the great dark-blue sky splashed with bronze and scarlet, the black shapes of the evergreens. He found himself enveloped in his great-aunt's embrace.

"I hope we have not kept the children waiting," said Augusta over the little boy's head to Alayne, who had just come into the hall.

"Not very long, I think," answered Alayne, and added in a whisper —"How is he?"

"Much better than we could have hoped for. Just his old gay self —but weak."

Finch put icy fingers down Mooey's collar. He laughed excitedly and wriggled.

Finch said to Sarah—"He's a nice little fellow, isn't he? He's funny and wistful—rather like Pheasant."

Sarah stood with hands folded in her muff and looked coldly down at the child.

"I don't care for them," she said, in her velvety voice. "They make me uncomfortable."

Finch laughed. "Just what I should expect of you, Sarah. I can't picture you with a child."

Pheasant was descending the stairs with Nooky by the hand. They looked up and saw her. The change in her figure was noticeable.

Sarah said—"I can picture myself with my own child. I should love it like a tigress."

"Those poor babes," said Pheasant, "are at the end of all patience. Mooey's been waiting outside this door for hours."

As she spoke, a deep voice called from within:

"Mooey! Mooey! Bring young Mooey here!"

Mooey rushed in terror to his mother.

"It's Santa Claus," she said. "He's calling for you!"

"Mooey! Mooey!" boomed the voice.

The drawing-room emptied itself into the hall. It became crowded.

Mooey thrust his head against Pheasant's side and burrowed there as though he would harry the unborn from her womb and re-establish himself in that dark security.

"Mooey! Mooey!" roared the voice.

He could not help himself. He was swept into the library by strong avuncular hands. The tree blazed above him. The air was heavy with the scent of evergreens, candlewax, and oranges. Santa Claus, enormous, red of coat and breeches, pink of face, white of beard, blue of eye, demanded in terrible accents if he had been a good boy all the year.

Mooey's chin rested on his heaving breast. Wakefield propelled him toward the saint. Every eye was on him when—"Me too," cried Nooky, and ran forward without shame.

"Splendid!" said Santa Claus, and placed a Noah's ark in Nooky's arms.

"Speak up," urged Wakefield, in Mooey's ear. "Tell him you've been good!"

Mooey's eye was drawn by a toy train. He gathered all his force and said huskily:

"I've been good!"

"What!" roared Santa Claus. "Good all the year? Every single day?" His gaze was all the more terrible because it was so strangely familiar. Now it searched the faces of the collected family. "Has he really been good or is this just bluff?"

"He's been angelic," growled Nicholas. "Give him that puff-puff or I'll pull your beard off!"

Mooey hugged the train to his breast and dived behind the towering forms of his uncles.

"Now," said Santa Claus, in a gentler tone, "who's this I see?"

It was Patience. She pointed, bright-eyed, to a doll's perambulator. Santa Claus placed a blue rabbit in it and trundled it toward her. She grasped the handle and, breaking into a loud song of triumph, wheeled it between Ernest's legs and almost upset him.

Renny, who had been holding Adeline on his shoulder, now set her down and she started off like a small automaton toward Santa Claus. He glared at her.

"Have you been good?"

Adeline stood intrepid. Then, as Santa Claus did not offer her a present, she marched to the tree and pulled the lowest candle from its place.

"You have exasperated the child," said Augusta. "She must be pacified".

164

Santa Claus extinguished the candle and gave Adeline a flamboyant doll chosen by Renny.

The jovial saint must be embraced for that, and Adeline liked the feel of his smooth lips and woolly beard so well that nothing less than a score of kisses would satisfy her.

"She's Mamma all over again," said Nicholas.

"What a pity Gran couldn't have seen her," said Renny.

Present by present the tree was stripped and Santa Claus offered a pungent remark with each gift. The presents had never been so inexpensive but there had never been so many candles.

When the library was again in darkness and the children had been put to bed, the spirits that had upheld the older folk failed. They talked, in low desultory tones, about the fire. Piers demanded to have a window open to cool his head after the heat of the wig and beard.

"Open that window," he tersely ordered Wakefield. "I'm as hot as blazes!"

"What about me?" demanded Ernest. "D'you think I can stand the cold night air?"

"Why, Uncle Ernest, the air can't touch you where you're sitting," said Pheasant, "and Piers is frightfully overheated."

"Let him go out and stick his head in a snow-bank," said Nicholas.

"Will someone play bridge, then?" asked Piers, without resentment.

Augusta and Meg looked at each other. They said:

"We must go. We've been away too long as it is."

Piers brought out the card-table and seated himself before it. He began to shuffle the cards.

Maurice said—"I'd like to play, but I suppose I must go."

"I'll drive them over," said Renny. "I'd like to see him."

Pheasant's gaze was fixed timidly on Piers' downcast eyes.

Alayne thought—"Oh, I wish it were over! I wish it were over!"

Nicholas turned his grey head from side to side on the back of his chair. He stretched out his hand and took his sister's.

"Yes. You must go to him, Gussie. He should not be left too long."

Meg said—"The maid is there, Uncle Nick, and she is very kind."

"But it's not the same. It's not the same. Tell him I'll be over tomorrow."

"Tell him that I'll go too," said Ernest, "just as soon as it thaws. Give him my love."

Piers tapped the pack of cards sharply on the table. "Who is going to play?" he asked.

Meg bent over him to kiss him good-bye. She took the opportunity of whispering:

"You might show a little sympathy when all the rest of us are feeling so badly."

He wrenched his shoulder free of her embrace.

"The hell I will!" he said stubbornly.

Renny said—"Hurry up, Meggie! Get your things on."

She and Augusta went upstairs. Alayne never knew whether or not to treat Meg as a guest. She always felt that Meg resented whichever attitude she took. She stood hesitant, wondering whether she were expected to accompany her upstairs.

Pheasant went to Piers. "Shall I play?" she asked.

He looked at her sullenly, without replying.

"Now, Sarah," said Maurice, cheerful at being left behind, "you and I will play Piers and Alayne. Pheasant looks tired. Bed is the place for her."

Alayne suffered herself to be drawn into the game of bridge though she did not care for cards, and Piers as a partner was exacting. Throughout the game he was too attentive to Sarah to please Pheasant, who, from the corner of the sofa, kept jealous eyes on them.

Ernest leaned toward his brother.

"We could arrange another table," he said.

Nicholas shook his head. He took out his pipe. "Not tonight. I'm tired. That was a hard walk to church."

Ernest pulled at his lip. He considered what possibilities were left. Finch, Wakefield, Pheasant (she was looking rather mopy), and himself.

"Fetch the other card-table, Wakefield," he said, authoritatively. "There is no reason why we shouldn't have a game."

Pheasant was glad of the distraction. Finch sat where he could watch Sarah unobserved. Wakefield's thoughts were on Pauline, who, with her mother, had gone to spend the day with Clara Lebraux's brother.

Finch suddenly remembered something. He said, in an undertone to Wakefield, while the others were discussing a hand:

"Eden gave me something for you. A present, I think. It went completely out of my mind." He slid an envelope under the table on to Wakefield's knee.

Wakefield fingered the bulky packet wondering what it might contain, excited by the possibilities of the belated present. Still keeping it concealed, he tore open one end and looked into it. Saying nothing, he continued the game. But it did not last long.

Pheasant became faint, all but keeled over, and had to be half carried upstairs. Wakefield retreated into the dining-room. A few minutes later he called out to Finch.

"Hullo!" said Finch. "What was it?"

Wakefield stammered with excitement.

"Why—why—I could hardly believe my eyes! It's a secret, but I'll tell you, Finch! He has sent me practically all he made from his readings. He didn't spend it and now he says he doesn't need it. It's to buy the engagement ring for Pauline! He says he'd rather do that with it than anything, so I'm not to feel too grateful. God, how excited I am!"

A dramatic gesture, Finch thought, and how Eden loved to make them! He looked enviously into Wakefield's happy face. To be able to love like that. . . . To be able to give oneself without reserve. . . . He himself might have felt so about Pauline. . . . If only Wake had given him the chance. . . . A kid like that—why, he couldn't marry for years! The affair was ridiculous and Eden should not have encouraged it. He said:

"Well, it was generous of Eden and I suppose it's true—what he says about not needing it himself. But when I think how he worked —for that paltry sum——" His eyes darkened and he saw, not Wakefield's happy face, but Eden's sunken cheeks, his too brilliant eyes.

"Don't think I'm not appreciating it! I'll never forget it as long as I live. You see, I was so young when Eden left home that I've never known him very well. And I've always heard Piers saying things against him. The thought that he's not going to get better hasn't meant so much to me as it has to you and Renny. But now —if he wasn't so ill I'd go straight to him this minute and thank him."

Finch could not bear to hear this child babbling about Eden. He said gruffly:

"I suppose Pauline will be pleased."

"Pleased! She'll be overjoyed! I'll not tell her a thing about it until I put the ring on her finger. Have you ever noticed her hands?"

"Yes—I've noticed them. Look here, Wake, don't tell Pauline how you got the ring."

"But why? I think she ought to know."

"I think it would be better for her to think you had saved up for it." He could not bear to think of those two babbling together over Eden's generosity.

"I believe you're right. She'll have all the more confidence in me if she thinks I saved up for it. She looks on me as rather extravagant, you know. But, on the whole, we're perfect in each other's eyes!"

"Oh, Lord——" Finch turned away.

"You won't tell anyone," said Wakefield to his back, "because Eden says he'd rather they didn't know."

"Of course I won't."

Going moodily through the hall he met Renny returning from Vaughanlands. He said:

"I suppose he's just the same?"

Renny nodded, frowning.

Sarah appeared in the doorway of the drawing-room.

"They want us to make some music, Finch," she said.

He looked at her sombrely.

"I wish you would," said Renny. "I'd like it."

The two had never before played together with such sympathy. They were released from all the conflicting emotions about them. They found themselves so happy in their music that they forgot the presence of the others and played each to each.

Wakefield sat, shading his eyes with his hand, his heart going out through the night to Pauline. Renny's hand slid along the sofa to Alayne's.

They two were the last to go upstairs. She stood on the bottom step and so could look levelly into his eyes. She touched her finger to his forehead between the brows.

"Those lines are getting deep, poor darling," she said.

"Kiss them away." He bent his head toward her.

She kissed his forehead tenderly, then his cheeks, then his lips, and clung to him.

"See what I have," he said. He showed her the corner of one of the silk handkerchiefs she had given him, projecting from his pocket.

"Do you like them?"

"Do I? Do I like you?" He took the handkerchief from his pocket, shook it out, and, with a short laugh, laid it over their two heads.

"Now," he said, "you have me alone."

Under this silken tent his eyes looked black and mysterious, but the harsh contours of his face were obscured. He did these childish things, she thought, and calculatingly increased his power over her. Each fragment of experience with him was laid upon the preceding one, and so was being built up the edifice of their inner life. By his most trivial act he was unconsciously making more concrete her imagining of him. While she craved his gentleness she feared it, as though by it he would transmute her into the passive creature of his need.

He, on his part, thought only of a moment's sweet escape from the thoughts that harassed him.

XVIII

DEATH OF A POET

IN the weeks following Christmas Eden's decline was rapid. In the New Year he had a second haemorrhage and, after that, it was apparent to all about him that his time was short. Yet, toward the end of January, his strength rallied. He was up every day for a while, sitting, in his light-blue dressing-gown, at the table where his manuscripts were littered. His interest and pleasure in this last book of poems gave him strength. He felt a certain enchantment in his isolation, his lack of responsibility. He had only one thing to do and that was to get the proofs ready for the publishers. He hoped to live to see his book between covers, and he had a yearning to read one or two good reviews.

Finch spent several hours each day with him. He was constantly amazed by Eden's matter-of-factness, his cool acceptance of his fate. It was rather shocking to see him so detached, to hear his callous, and often ribald and blasphemous remarks. Eden was pleased when he could startle Finch into laughter. The unexpected laughter would make Finch lose control of his nerves. He would laugh until he croaked and the tears would run down his cheeks and his breath come with a sob.

Augusta would say, looking into the room:

"You boys seem to be having a good time. I think you feel a little better today, Eden."

And he would look up at her with his mocking smile, and say:

"This fellow is an awful ass, Auntie. It takes nothing to set him off."

The one thing that Eden was bitter about was the weather. It was a cold snowy winter and he grew sick of the sight of all the whiteness. More than anything he loved the colours of the earth and now it was drained of all but black and white. Out of the cold sky came the weary drift of snowflakes, muffling all sound, blurring all contours, making mounds that softened and sank, only to be wearily replenished. He longed for spring, even while he scarcely hoped to live till spring.

He showed decided preferences for certain members of the family. He liked to have Wakefield come to see him but this was not encouraged, because of the boy's delicacy. Gentle Ernest, for some unknown reason, tired him, while Nicholas, big-bodied and sonorous-voiced, made him more tranquil. He could not bear to have Meg about him for long but yearned toward Augusta, whose rather stuffy style of dress and long gold ear-rings hardly seemed suited to a sickroom. Renny, in his lean strength, his look of outdoors, his troubled, compassionate eyes, his forced cheerfulness, cast down Eden's spirits more than any of the others. It was to Finch he clung, Finch whom he could move to wild laughter or—by a tone of the voice or a gesture—to scarcely concealed tears. He liked to watch Finch's face as Finch read aloud to him—his large flexible mouth; his long, actor's upper lip; the sensitive structure of his face. When he chose he could send Finch down to the piano to play for him.

The new book was a bond between them. They discussed phrases and rhythm together, Eden placing dependence on Finch's ear for music. Finch thought that these poems were the best Eden had written. He wrote to the New York publishers urging them to hasten the publication.

As the snowy weeks moved on, with dragging days but terrifying swiftness, the burden of apprehension pressed more and more cruelly on the family. Even Piers had less vitality and would often sit silent, buried in thought.

For the first time in his life Finch's appetite failed him. He grew to hate the sight of food. The dish of California grapes in Eden's room became abhorrent to him. Their opaque, sickly greenness, through which he could discern the seeds, was repugnant. The watching of Eden's swift decline in substance wrung his breast. He had a continual nervous pressure there. And when Eden coughed, with a low rattling sound, as though there were nothing left to cough with, the pressure became a pain.

It would not have been so bad, he thought, if Eden had not got up. But to help him half dress his emaciated body, that had once been so beautiful, to see him move about the room in the light-blue, slack-hanging dressing-gown, to see him looking out of the frosted window at the snow, was almost beyond bearing.

Yet when, in late February, Eden had a third haemorrhage and did not get up from his bed again, what would Finch have not given to have seen him once more at the window!

Now Eden was a different being. His face was ravished to a sunken semblance of what it had been. He lay with his great eyes full of pleading, his sallow cheeks sunken, his mouth and teeth prominent.

He no longer wanted music or reading, and his preferences in the family were reversed. The presence of Augusta now worried him, while Meg's warm arms comforted. Augusta now assisted in the work of the house, and this was a relief to her, for she was worn out with nursing and she was eighty-one.

He no longer liked to have Nicholas sit with him. His heavy body loomed too large. He was always heaving himself about in his chair. When he gave Eden a drink he spilled half of it. But Ernest was deft, gentle, and soothing.

But most of all he turned now to Renny. Here was the one he wanted. Here was the hand and the voice and the support he craved always to be at his side. It was Renny who sat up with him night after winter night.

So the clan helped him with the best that was in them. They went with him to the very gates through which he must pass alone.

The second week in March an advance copy of *Last Poems* was sent from the publisher. Finch carried the book to Eden. It had come on the morning post. Renny had just gone to lie down. Ernest was in the room.

Finch put the book, delicate, spring-like in colouring, into Eden's hand. He took it meekly as he would take what was offered him. But he scarcely seemed to see it. A smell of sickness rose from the bed. Finch saw a basin underneath it stained with blood.

"It's your book, Eden," he said. "Do you like the way they've done it?"

Eden opened the book but he could not read.

Ernest came forward.

"How very nice," he said, in a quavering voice. "How very nice."

Eden closed the book and turned it over. He handed it back to Finch.

Then he looked with widening eyes at the two faces above him.

"Don't leave me alone!" he said loudly, almost chanting the words. "I don't want to be alone."

But it was a week before he died.

Then one morning Renny came down to the dining-room where Augusta and Meg and Finch were seated about the table. It was half-past seven and they were expecting him, for he had been with Eden since midnight.

He looked ghastly in the early morning light, and a stubble of red beard gave him a ruffianly appearance.

He stood inside the door and looked at them.

Finch started up. Meg put her hand to her mouth as though to stifle a cry. Augusta sat bolt upright.

"He's gone," said Renny hoarsely.

Meg threw herself on Finch's breast, sobbing.

"Was there no warning?" asked Augusta. "Couldn't you have called us?"

"No. I knew he was worse. But he went suddenly—just like that!" He made a decisive, sweeping gesture with his hand.

"Thank God!" said Augusta. "Poor boy! Poor boy!"

Meg loosed Finch's arms from her. "I must go to him," she sobbed.

But Finch caught at her skirt. "No, no," he cried. "You mustn't, Meggie!"

"Let her come," said Renny. "I'll take her."

He put his arm about her and led her up the stairs.

XIX

WINTER IN SPRINGTIME

THE cold did not abate in the following days. Rather, the wintry rigour increased. The hard round granules of snow were whipped by the north wind, as though in spite, against the cheeks of those who faced it. Miniature ponds of ice were uncovered by the wind, and others were concealed by it under the light snow.

Piers had faced the wind for some time, his fresh skin whipped to bright pink. The flesh of his cheeks was as firm and cold as a winter apple. His full red lips were compressed into an expression of stubborn reserve. He had walked into the village and was now walking back, in the direction of Vaughanlands, in response to a message from Renny.

What did Renny want with him, he wondered, as he approached the house. Something, he felt sure, that would be unpleasant, probably impossible, for him to do. He stood on the drive, determined not to go into the house, but to wait there until he was seen. The sight of the house, with its drawn blinds, the crêpe fluttering on the door, made him withdraw still more into himself. He turned up the collar of his coat and stood motionless in the snow.

He had not long to wait. He saw a movement of one of the blinds, and, in a moment, Renny came from the back of the house. Against the purity of the snow his unkempt appearance was startling. The short dense growth of red beard gave his face a look both ruffianly and wan.

Piers looked at him inquiringly. It was not the first time he had seen him since Eden's death yesterday morning, for it was Renny who had carried the news to Jalna. But surely he might have found an opportunity to make himself decent—not go about looking like the end of the world.

They looked steadily into each other's eyes, like antagonists marking each other's armour, then Renny said:

"I want you to come in to see him."

Piers drew back.

"See him!" he repeated. "See him! You must have lost your reason!"

"No, I haven't. I want you to come in to see him."

"But, good God! Why should I see him now—when I did not come while he was living?"

"It's different now."

"If you think my feelings are different, you're mistaken!"

Renny took him by the sleeve and said, in a tone almost cajoling: "Come along. Come along—to please me!"

Piers shook himself free.

"I don't know why you are urging me to do this," he said. "But I tell you, it's useless. I won't do it!"

A car turned in at the gate. Two people alighted and went to the door. The brothers drew out of sight behind the hedge.

"They won't be long," said Renny. "We'll go in then."

Piers kept his temper with an effort. He said, in a hard voice: "I refuse to go into that house while he is there. Why do you ask me?"

"Because," answered Renny, "I want you to be one of the pall-bearers."

This was what Piers had dreaded. He said at once:

"I can't do it!"

Renny returned—"If you saw him you couldn't refuse."

Piers burst out—"I think it's damned hard luck to be asked to do this! I'd never ask it of you—if you were in my place."

Renny broke a clear, bright icicle from a snow-laden bough of spruce and bit a piece from it, holding it in his parched mouth until it dissolved. He did not speak.

Piers continued—"I see now what you're thinking. You're thinking what people will say—if I don't help to carry him."

"Well, it's partly that but there's another reason. As to what people will say—you don't want to give them a chance to gossip, do you? They'd say you were bitter against Eden. They'd be certain why. They'd be certain it was jealousy. Very well—don't give them the opening. Then the other reason: I've always tried to keep the family together. I've liked to feel that those gone on ahead knew I was doing it. It's been my religion—all I've had—I guess. You boys—one of you is gone now—have been a part of my love for Jalna. I can't bear to think that one of you could hate another so that he wouldn't touch his dead body. . . . That's why I want you to see Eden. You'll feel quite different when you do."

Piers looked at him standing there bareheaded, unprotected from the weather. He remembered all he had been through, the harassment, the loss of sleep, the agonising sights of which he must have been the witness. He recognised in him a formidable power, almost a menace. He drew from Piers a kind of angry compassion.

Piers said—"I'll go into the house with you. You'll get a chill out here. But I won't promise anything."

"Good boy," said Renny, and gave his arm a squeeze.

Piers pushed out his lips. He said:

"Isn't it time you had a shave? And you need sleep, too, by the look of your eyes. Can't Maurice and Finch attend to things?"

They found Finch in the dining-room drinking a glass of whisky and soda. The glass shook against his teeth. The remains of a meal lay on the table.

Renny gave him a sharp look.

"Another!" he exclaimed. "Let that be the last."

"I know when I've had enough," said Finch truculently, "without being told by anyone. I can't eat, and I've got to keep up, haven't I?"

Renny took the glass from his hand and set it on the sideboard. "You ought to be ashamed of yourself," he said.

Meg came into the room. She had on a new black dress which accentuated the pallor of her round face and the blueness of her eyes. The strands of grey hair springing from either temple gave her a maternal dignity. She carried a wreath of red and white roses. When she saw Piers her eyes, which she had just dried, again filled with tears.

He went to her and kissed her.

"I've been expecting you," she said, and there was reproach in her voice. "But better late than never, Piers."

Renny asked—"Have those people gone?"

"Yes. It was Mrs. Page and her son. These flowers just came from the Miss Laceys. What do you think of the red roses? Red seems rather strange in a wreath, doesn't it?"

"Red is beautiful in a wreath," said Finch heavily. "Red is a beautiful colour. A beautiful and terrible colour. It's a tragic colour. Why"—he looked wildly at his sister and brothers—"I'd cover his coffin with red roses."

"Sh," said Meg. "Don't speak so loudly."

"Why not? We won't disturb Eden."

Renny said in an undertone to Meg:

"Finch has been drinking."

"But how disgraceful! Oh, Finch, how could you?"

"Don't talk to me," he returned. "I've done my part. I've been here through the thick of it! I'm not like that cold-eyed brute"—he raised his hand toward Piers—"that cold-eyed brute——"

Piers turned white. "Now I've seen you, Meg, I'll go."

Renny led Finch to the door and pushed him through it.

Meg cried—"Go, Piers? Go? And not see our poor darling? Oh, Piers, you couldn't be so cruel!"

"Why should I see him?" he demanded. "What good can it do? I wish to God I'd never come here!"

She clasped Piers' arm in her hands.

"No, no, don't say that! I say that a Will stronger than yours led you here. There is Someone, you know, Piers, Who watches all our doings. . . ."

Piers stared at the floor.

Renny stood, with his back to the door, watching them. Then he saw that there was danger of the flowers being crushed, and came and took the wreath from Meg's arms and laid it on the table. He replaced one of the roses which had been disarranged. He did not speak but waited to see what Piers would do.

Meg rested her pale cheek against Piers' shoulder. Her fingers held his tightly. He felt trapped. He ceased to think clearly, and stood looking stupidly at the carpet. After a little he drew a deep breath and said:

"Very well, I'll go."

Meg turned to Renny. "Will you go with him?"

He nodded. He picked up the wreath. "We may as well take this with us," he said.

In the parlour the blinds were drawn but a shaft of flickering wintry sunlight fell across the room. Renny laid the flowers on the foot of the coffin. He turned away then, and Piers heard the door close behind him.

He stood alone looking at the shaft of sunlight. He thought how cold the room was and noticed that one of the windows was raised a little and that snow had sifted beneath it and lay in a slender ridge along the sill.

If he chose, he thought, he could stand where he was for a few moments, then go out without having seen Eden. No one would know. He stood hesitating.

But he was spurred by a sudden curiosity. He advanced steadily to the coffin and looked down on to his brother's face. . . . All else in the room dissolved as in a mist. Only Eden was real, holding Piers' gaze with a terrible fascination. But—was this Eden? Was this man Eden? Was it possible that this was Eden? Why, he said to himself, looking at all that was real in the room, this is Eden! I can't believe it. . . . But this is Eden. This is the one I played with as a boy. . . . This is the one I grew up with. . . . Who seduced my wife. . . . But was it possible that the cold, aloof, bitterly smiling lips had ever softened in desire for a woman? Gran had looked peaceful in her coffin. Haughty—but at peace. There was no peace here—only cold, aloof rigidity. The personification of disdainful suffering. If the salt of the sea had chosen to solidify itself into the semblance of a man surely it would have stretched itself on the rock in just such bitter composure. . . . And those hands. . . . Piers stretched out his own strong warm hand and touched them timidly. Those hands had gripped him in play when they were boys. Those hands had done Eden's bidding all his life long. Those hands had—Piers set his teeth and turned away. . . . The scent of the flowers was stifling.

Meg's cat, which was accustomed to take her ease in this room, leaped to the window-sill. Piers saw her eyes staring anxiously at him through the open crack. He put up the blind a little and she reared herself on her hind legs, pawing on the frosty pane, showing her furry white belly. She opened her mouth slightly and uttered an imploring mew.

The door opened and Renny came in again. He went to the window, put it down sharply. He struck the glass with his knuckles, frightening the cat away. He threw down the blind. He kept his eyes turned from Piers' face. He asked:

"Does he look at all natural to you?"

"No," answered Piers. "I should not have known him."

Renny went to the coffin. "Did you see this?" he asked.

Piers followed him. "No. What?"

"This." Renny pointed where, secure between Eden's arm and ide, was the volume of *Last Poems*.

"Finch did that," Renny said. "He's a strange fellow."

"Yes," agreed Piers, "it was a queer thing to do."

They stood looking down at Eden together.

At length Renny asked—"Well—will you do what I want?"

"Yes," said Piers. "I don't think I shall mind doing it, after all."

XX

"NO MORE SEEN"

RENNY stood in the drawing-room at Jalna waiting for his brothers. He stood as though listening intently. In truth he was listening to what the house had to say to him, for it spoke to him as to no other. Now it spoke to him in a low but distinct murmur of sorrow. It craved something that it had not got, something that for ever it would mourn—the body of Eden who had been born here, who should have lain dead here for a little before he went to his place beside the other dead. The roof bent desolate above the living.

Renny's eyes were fixed on the spot where Eden should now be lying. He pictured himself and Piers and Finch and Wakefield raising him to their shoulders and bearing him forth. Though shortly they would be doing that very service for him, no reality could be as vivid as the picture he now saw.

Wakefield was beside him before he was aware of his approach. The boy looked tall and strangely handsome in his black clothes. Renny gave him an abstracted look and then said:

"It was a great disappointment to me not to bring Eden's body home."

Wakefield was startled. "Home? Here? Oh, yes—I hadn't thought of that. But it would have been the right thing, I suppose."

Renny continued—"I could not do it because of—well, I suppose you understand."

"Of course. It would have been rather hard on Pheasant and Piers. And on Alayne, too." His young mind hovered over the situation like an inquisitive bird.

Renny looked at the clock.

"What is keeping the others? We'll be late."

"They're coming now. I think they've had to help the uncles dress. They seem sort of confused. Uncle Ernest tried to tell me something three times this morning but he never really got it out. Alayne says she doesn't think he's fit to go to the churchyard on such a day."

"It won't hurt him. He has a good warm coat." He turned to the four who now entered. "Well—there's no time to spare. We should be at the house now."

"Dear me," said Ernest, "I'm afraid it is my fault we're late. I don't know how I should have dressed if Piers had not helped me. I mislaid one thing after another. First it was my studs and then it was my—what was it I mislaid next, Piers?"

"Gloves," replied Piers briefly, and took his arm. Ernest seemed unsteady on his legs. The smell of brandy was on his breath.

Renny said in an undertone to Piers:

"You've done this!"

"You don't want him to take his death of cold, do you?" answered Piers hotly.

Fresh snow had fallen and they must drive slowly. The Vaughans' house seemed full of people when they arrived. Meg was excited, deeply touched by a wreath of roses, orchids and lilies from the women's club for which Eden had given his Thursdays. It lay in sumptuous beauty at the foot of the coffin, making the other floral offerings appear almost insignificant.

Wakefield was proud of the flowers. He hung over them, reading the cards attached. On a cross of white roses and lilies of the valley he read: "To our dear boy, from his ever-loving Aunt and Uncles," in Augusta's long, slanting hand. But what pleased him most was the wreath of spring flowers bearing a card with the words: "In abiding gratitude from Wakefield and Pauline."

He could see her across the room, her dark serious face in contrast to her mother's blonde bold one. He dared not give her more than a glance for fear that his lips would part in a smile. Her mere presence in that sorrowful room lightened his heart.

A sombre pride made his heart swell as he took his part in carrying the heavy coffin out of the house. He stood tall and straight among his brothers beside the hearse while the coffin was established in its place and the flowers arranged about it. There had been no prayers in the house because Mr. Fennel had gone on an urgent call to a sick-bed. He would be waiting at the church.

Though the house had seemed full, the funeral was a very small one as compared to old Adeline's. That cortège had swept its imposing length in fitting tribute to her great age and her position in the country-side. Her sudden death had come as a shock and as the dramatic obliterating of a landmark. During Eden's long illness the family had drawn into themselves and only friends of long standing had been notified of the hour of burial.

On the incline toward the church the snow lay deep and scarcely broken. The motors made the ascent with difficulty. The heavy hearse scarcely moved, and it seemed grotesque that this cumbersome vehicle should be taxed to its utmost to carry the fragile body which a single man might have borne without pain.

But at last it lay within the church, where the air smelt of the freshly lighted fire. It lay at the chancel steps and the mourners gathered in the near-by pews. The bearers breathed quickly, for the ascent to the church door was both steep and slippery. Clots of snow had been carried in by the feet of those who entered, and these lay scattered on the aisle like trampled petals of flowers.

There had been surprise when Mr. Fennel had not met them at the gate. The surprise deepened to anxiety when the sexton tiptoed to Renny's side and whispered that the rector had been delayed, probably because of the condition of the roads, and that Mrs. Fennel was much worried.

The long minutes dragged by, while Renny's face grew dark. Nicholas and Ernest whispered together, and the rest of the family tried to hear what they were saying. Augusta and Meg had come also, the first sallow and composed, the second pale and slightly weeping.

Little Miss Pink, the organist, came to Renny.

"Do you think we had better sing a hymn?" she whispered, looking up into his face.

"Very well," he agreed, frowning.

"Have you a preference?" she asked timidly.

"'Day of Wrath,'" he answered.

She hesitated. "But we are having that at the service."

"Well, then, 'When our heads are bowed with woe.'" This hymn had been sung at his grandmother's funeral.

She tiptoed back into the chancel.

The organ sounded the preliminary notes. The voices rose:

> "When our heads are bowed with woe,
>   When our bitter tears o'erflow,
>   When we mourn the lost, the dear,
>   Jesu, Son of Mary, hear.

> "When the solemn death-bell tolls
>   For our own departed souls,
>   When our final doom is near,
>   Jesu, Son of Mary, hear."

Nicholas had sung through the first verse but now his voice failed him. He stood, looking on the same hymn-book with Ernest, painfully aware of Meg's weeping and his brother's trembling hand.

After the hymn another time of waiting elapsed which seemed only emphasised by nervous fragments played on the organ.

Renny said to Finch—"I'm going to find out what is wrong."

"Let me go."

"No, no. Stay where you are." He left the church by the side door and crossed the churchyard to the Rectory.

The snow had ceased, and out of the hard blue sky the sun, brilliant, but without warmth, searched out every smallest object, a twig, the dead body of a mouse, and cast its shadow with relentless exactitude on the snow. An icy wind blew without wavering from the north, sometimes bearing on it snowy particles that shone with a cold fire.

Renny's eyes were drawn by his own family plot, its whiteness disfigured by the thrown-up earth from the freshly dug grave. The yellowish brown of the frozen earth was hideous, the cavity discovered an abomination for the body of a loved one.

He stood looking into it with horror. A feeling of panic rose in him. He had a wild wish to escape from all that was to follow—to escape and leave the others to bury Eden. He raised his face to the north wind, welcoming its sting. He longed to struggle in the wind, to free himself from all that held him.

A feeble singing from inside the church penetrated his mind and he was now filled with anger against the rector for causing one of his family to wait so long for burial. He hurried on, almost running along the slippery walk that led to the house.

Just as he reached the steps before the porch, he slipped and fell heavily, striking his head against the top step. He rose quickly and stood dazed a moment, then sprang up the steps and rang the bell.

The door was opened by George Fennel. He looked frightened and exclaimed:

"Why, Renny, what's the matter?"

"Where is your father? What the hell is he keeping us waiting for?"

"I thought you knew. Mother is in the church. She told the sexton to explain, didn't she? His car broke down. He telephoned us. But he's on his way. He'll be here any minute. I'm waiting for him. But—I'm worried about you—you've hurt yourself—you're bleeding."

Renny put his hand to his head and felt the blood trickling warmly from a cut above his brow.

"I fell," he explained. "But it's nothing." He took out his

handkerchief and held it to his forehead. "What is important is that your father went off this morning knowing—yes, knowing—the condition of the roads and left us with no one to conduct the service."

"But the woman was dying!"

"My brother is dead. He's waiting in the church there. We have waited an hour—an hour——"

"I know," said George Fennel. "I'm frightfully sorry. . . ."

"By God!" interrupted Renny, "if your father is not here soon I'll read the burial service myself and we'll have Eden in his grave without help from anyone."

George Fennel regarded him with something of the same anger and compassion which he had evoked from Piers the morning before. He also felt his formidable power and menace. He said quietly, though:

"I wish you'd come and let me put some plaster on your head."

"No, no, I won't let anyone touch my head."

But he went with George into the house.

They were scarcely in when they heard the sound of the rector's car. Soon he came hurriedly into the room where they were.

"This has been most unfortunate," he said. "I hope I haven't kept you waiting long."

Renny stared at him in savage silence. He held his handkerchief pressed against his head. His eyes, wide open, were dark and opaque.

George gave his father a meaning glance. He said:

"Here is your surplice, Dad. It will save time to put it on here." He helped his father to remove his coat and put on his cassock and surplice.

Mr. Fennel passed his hand over his hair and stroked his beard into order. He moved quickly but without undignified haste. He bent his head and murmured a few words of prayer.

"Now," he said composedly, "we are ready."

The three proceeded along the snowy walk to the church, Mr. Fennel's surplice, bellying about him like a sail, threw a volatile moving shadow on the snow.

His voice echoed through the church:

"'I held my tongue, and spake nothing: I kept silence, yea, even from good words; but it was pain and grief to me. . . . Lord, let me know mine end, and the number of my days: that I may be certified how long I have to live. . . . For man walketh in a vain shadow and disquieteth himself in vain. . . . When Thou with rebukes dost chasten man for sin, Thou makest his beauty to consume away, like as it were a moth fretting a garment.'"

Finch crouched, with bent head, his fingers pressed against his eyeballs, between Renny and Piers. He was conscious of their bodies pressed close to him, of their statuesque immobility that could be so easily transformed into movement. He was above all conscious of Eden's static pose that would at last be fretted away. But though his body was conscious of his living brothers, his spirit crouched in the coffin with Eden. His own voice rang in his ears—"'Turn Thee again, O Lord, at the last!'"

When it was time to rise and again shoulder the burden, he did not move until Piers had grasped his shoulder and pushed him toward the aisle. As they moved to the chancel steps his face looked ravished, ugly. Still he felt himself in Eden's place. He heard his faint voice call—"O spare me a little that I may recover my strength: before I go hence, and be no more seen!"

Down the slippery steps, through the snow, the four brothers strove under their burden to the family plot, followed by Maurice and Meg, and their aunt and uncles. They grouped themselves about the grave, the bitter wind ruffling the uncovered heads of the men, and fluttering the scarves of the women. Ernest stood with closed eyes. Nicholas stared bleakly at the granite plinth bearing the name Whiteoak. But Augusta looked steadfastly into the grave.

The wind separated Mr. Fennel's beard into two parts, resolutely blowing a half over each shoulder. From his mouth came the words:

"'Man that is born of woman hath but a short time to live, and is full of misery. He cometh up, and is cut down, like a flower; he fleeth as it were a shadow, and never continueth in one stay.'"

Finch, for the first time, saw the blood trickling down Renny's forehead, which he continuously wiped with a reddened handkerchief. Finch turned dizzy and caught Piers' arm to steady himself.

The rector's voice went on—"'Forasmuch as it has pleased Almighty God of His great mercy to take unto Himself the soul of our dear brother here departed, we therefore commit his body to the ground. . . .'" Frozen earth had been cast upon the body.

Finch whispered to Piers—"Let me hold on to you. I'm dizzy."

"All right," answered Piers. "It will soon be over."

The prayer continued—"'I heard a voice from Heaven, saying unto me, Write. From henceforth blessed are the dead . . . for they have rested from their labours.'"

Renny's mind was on his grandmother. He could fancy her saying, if she knew that Eden's body was being laid beside hers:

"What! One of the whelps come to join me! Well, well, I'm glad of that. I like the young folk about me."

XXI

SPRING AT LAST

THE spring that Eden did not live to see, refused itself only till he was in his grave, then gave forth its sun and its running sap without stint. The snowdrifts sank and were transferred to lively runnels of water. The air cast off its cold impersonal purity and smelled of wet earth. Black wings of crows beat across the pale-blue sky.

The effect on the family at Jalna of Eden's death was revealed as more depressing than the death of old Adeline had been. She had died in late summer when all the windows of the house were open, when all the activities of stable and farm were manifest. Wagons loaded with oats or wheat lumbered from Piers' fields to the barn. The harvest apples were being picked when she, ripe in years, was garnered in. But Eden died at the end of a long winter, when the elderly people were enervated by confinement. In other winters they had absorbed vitality from their nephews, but, in this winter, Renny and Finch had none to spare for them and Piers was often silent and even morose. Alayne too was preoccupied with her own thoughts, and it was with a visible effort that she roused herself to cheer Nicholas and Ernest. Wakefield spent more and more time at the fox-farm.

After Adeline's sudden death (in which no hearts were wrung by the sight of suffering) excitement was maintained by the reading of her will and the fierce discussion following it. But Eden had nothing to bequeath but the memory of his cruel decline, which, at this time, blotted out remembrance of his happy youth.

It was appalling to Nicholas to think of this young life being cut off, while his own, almost fifty years in excess of it, lingered on. He became possessed by this thought, brooding on it by day, and pressing it against his aching heart when he lay awake at night. He lay awake so often that his haggard eyes told their own tale though he made no complaint. He and Ernest took to reviewing their own lives, recalling the mistakes, the false moves they had made, and speculating on what they might have made of them if they had done differently; deriving sometimes a forlorn exhilaration in the triumphs thus imagined. They would raise their peevish voices, each eager to give his own version of the bygone tale, talking each other down until they were tired out and the fire was low. Then Nicholas would stump off to his own room,

Nip trotting at his heels, and stand in the middle of it with a dazed expression. Once, thus alone, he broke down and, raising his arms in a gesture of appeal, sobbed out—"Oh, God, give me another chance! Make me a boy again!"

But Augusta, though she looked thin and old, was admirable in her calm. She felt a deep relief at Eden's going, for she had seen all his suffering. Her own affairs in Devon demanded her attention and she began her preparations for departure. The bitter thought in her mind was the unlikelihood that she would ever see her brothers again. She felt that she could never return to Canada. Even if she were able to let her house, the effort to get it ready for a tenant was too great, the journey too long for a woman of her years. Ernest and Nicholas could not afford to go to see her, and they were getting too old for travel. So it was with a strange sense of finality that she turned her thoughts toward England.

Pheasant, her young face growing thinner as her body increased in bulk, progressed through her pregnancy without attracting much sympathy or even notice. She felt Eden's shadow between herself and Piers in the months before his death, but afterward her spirits lightened a little and, in the early part of April, she gave birth to a third son.

For Finch the ordeal had been greater than for anyone. His strength had been too lately acquired to stand the strain. He grew hollow-cheeked and his nerves, always ready to betray him, once more became a torture. He took a severe cold which lingered in a bronchial cough, and after each bout of this he found himself overcome by a charged melancholy—he was going the way Eden had gone, he told himself. But he coughed mostly at night and, in his attic room, he disturbed no one.

He had offers of several concert engagements which he had to refuse. He had a feeling of terror lest he should never be able to play in public again.

He had not seen George Fennel since the day of Eden's funeral, and one rainy Sunday morning he felt the sudden need of a talk with his friend. George would be at home, for he was unpresentable, Wragge had informed Finch, because of a face swollen from toothache.

He met Finch at the door of the Rectory looking even more cheerful than usual, his square face a little chubby on one side.

"Why," exclaimed Finch, "what's this I hear about toothache? Just bluff?"

"Had it out yesterday. A relief, I can tell you. My soul feels as peaceful as a pond."

Finch regarded him enviously. "I believe you," he said. "I'd have all my teeth out if it would make me feel like that."

George asked—"Where shall we go? We have the house to ourselves."

"Your room, if you don't mind. I believe I'm happier in that room than anywhere."

George led the way up the stairs to the shabby room where he and Finch had spent so many confidential hours. This room never changed. It seemed that its furniture, which had been almost worn out when placed there, would last for ever. Finch fitted himself into the accustomed hollow in the couch. He took out a cigarette-case, offered it to George, then took a cigarette himself and, breaking it in two, lighted a half with a shaking hand.

George stared at him. "Well—have you come to that?"

"Yes. I never smoke more than a half now. I think it's better for me."

"How are you? You look rather seedy."

"I am. It's the spring, I suppose."

George's hazel eyes beamed at him compassionately. "You've been through a good deal, Finch."

"Oh, well, no more than the others."

"But you're not quite as strong as the others. And you were with Eden through it all, weren't you?"

"Renny sat up with him at nights. But he seems as well as ever."

George said, in a tone that invited confidence:

"He's rather a queer chap, isn't he?"

Finch took the second half of his cigarette and lighted it from the stub of the first. He said:

"What do you mean, queer?"

"Well, there's a kind of fire in his eyes like there was in your grandmother's. I remember her so well. I thought she was magnificent. And he's magnificent, too, in his own way. But he strikes me as an uncomfortable chap to live with. I hope you don't mind my saying so."

"He is uncomfortable—in a way. But he's easy to get on with, too, if only——" He hesitated.

"If only you do just what he says, eh?"

"No, I wouldn't say that. I think he rather likes opposition, of a certain kind. But I think he feels himself spiritually alone at times—I don't know just why. Just now he's terribly cut up over Maurice's subdivision. Maurice has sold two more lots. Small ones, and at a much lower price than he asked at first. I can't blame Maurice, but it's going to make things very different at Jalna, there's no doubt about that. Yet Eden's death has left the rest of us rather numb—excepting Renny—and we can't work ourselves up over it as he does, and I think he feels alone—that we're not with him."

"What about Piers? He must feel it too."

"He does. But he's a fatalistic fellow. If things must be, they must be. He doesn't waste his energy fighting the inevitable. I think it's taking all his energy to keep his farm afloat. And he's got a family coming on, you know."

"How is the newcomer?"

A tender smile crossed Finch's face. "Oh, he's a splendid little fellow! He hardly ever cries. I think he's going to be the image of Piers. Same blue eyes. They're calling him Philip, after my father."

"The third Philip! I say, what's the good of limiting yourself to half cigarettes when you light them one off the other that way?"

Finch laid the one he had just broken on the table beside him. "No use, I know. I've no self-restraint." He looked despondently at the two halves.

"Well," said George consolingly, "you'll soon be quite fit again when you've had a little time. Are you playing much now?"

"That's the worst of all. I can't practise. I've had to refuse several offers of concert work." He wrung his fingers together and avoided George's eyes.

"What you need is a change," said George briskly, his affectionate eyes studying his friend's downcast face. "I wish we could get away together for a week at Easter."

"I wish we could," said Finch heavily. "But Aunt Augusta is sailing then, and I may have to go with her to Quebec."

"Your uncles will miss her."

"We'll all miss her. She's so wonderful for her age—a wonderful woman for any age. Weeks ago she wrote home to England to her housekeeper to send out some jig-saw puzzles she had. It seemed rather a silly thing to do—at such a time—but you wouldn't believe the interest the uncles are taking in them. The puzzles arrived last week—at least a dozen of them—and Uncle Nick and Uncle Ernie and Wakefield and Pheasant, and even Piers, were working with them all yesterday afternoon. It was pouring rain, so it was something to do. For my part I think they're getting a little too intense about it. I can't stand the concentration. It unnerves me."

"What about Renny? Is he interested in puzzles?" There was amusement in George's tone.

Finch was not conscious of the amusement. "No. I think his life is puzzle enough for him." He reached out, took one of the half cigarettes and lighted it.

"I must tell you," said George, "that he was in a terrible temper the day of the funeral. When he came here, I mean, to look for Dad."

"You could scarcely call it temper, George. He was upset. And no wonder."

"Well, it may not seem like temper to you, but I was afraid of him. He'd fallen down and cut his head, and he was in such a rage he didn't know he was hurt. The blood was running down his face and his eyes were blazing. Do you know what he said? He said he'd a mind to read the burial service himself and lay Eden in his grave with no help from anyone."

"Did he say that to the rector?"

"No. He just glared at him. Dad remarked afterward that Renny looks more like his grandmother every day."

"He does. And young Adeline is the image of him. The temper too. She's a thoroughly bad youngster."

The church bell began to ring. Finch rose and went to the window. From there he could just see the door of the church. It was the last bell, and it clanged its summons militantly against the heavy spring air.

"Who is the bell-ringer now?" asked Finch.

"The same. Noah Binns."

"If he put half the fury into his hoeing that he puts into his bell-ringing we should have no weeds."

Wakefield, Piers, Mooey, Augusta, Nicholas, and Ernest were presented for an instant to Finch's gaze before they disappeared into the church.

"They're almost late," he said. "I scarcely think that Renny will come. Cora dropped a foal this morning and he was up all night with her." He watched the procession of his family with an almost morbid interest.

The bell continued to clang, and, while Finch still stood at the window, the master of Jalna appeared for an instant on the steps as a significant figure and then disappeared into the church.

Noah Binns, through a crack, was able to observe those who entered. Now he had got his man, he muttered to himself: "I'll deafen 'm. Dang 'm!" And, with a last violent pull of the rope, he flung it writhing from him, and, composing his features, took his place among the worshippers.

Finch turned back into the room.

"I don't know what to do with my life," he said. "Something

went out of it with Eden. I'm left floundering about. I've no grip on anything. I want to compose. That's one thing I feel I could do. But my nerves won't stand it."

"I wish," returned George, "that you'd fall in love."

Finch gave an embarrassed laugh. "I don't believe that would help me."

"Well, of course it would depend on the girl. If it were the right sort of girl, it would have a most revivifying effect. Look at young Wakefield. He's become a man since he's in love with Pauline Lebraux."

"He's become more selfish than ever—if you call that being a man."

"I don't agree. I think he's improved in every way. Sometimes I can hardly believe it is little Wake talking. He's got such—well, such mature ideas."

"He always was precocious. He loves an audience."

"You're not fair to him, Finch. You don't see him as an outsider does. I remember when he used to come to Dad for his lessons. A sickly little chap, and precocious, as you say. Since then he's improved, of course, but he's always seemed self-centred till lately. Now it's all Pauline and his plans for her. He often drops in to talk about her."

"Does he!" said Finch jealously. "He's never mentioned it to me."

"He is probably shy of you. One often is shy of one's own family. You know how that feels. . . . But I think he and Pauline are perfectly matched and I do hope it comes off."

Finch regarded his friend's honest face with dislike.

George went on—"And he's so tremendously grateful to Eden. He's told me over and over again of Eden's generosity. He says he'll never forget it as long as he lives."

Finch interrupted fiercely:

"Well, I want to forget it. I tell you, it cuts me to the heart to remember it. I wish to God I could forget it—and Eden too!"

Now George brought out his mandolin and sat solidly playing, while Finch fretted up and down the room striving to gain composure. He did regain it but he did not forgive George. George had failed him, he thought, as he went homeward through the flat, damp, lifeless April day. He had gone to George for comfort and had got only irritation. Wakefield. . . . To have Wakefield's praises sung to him!

He tramped through the mud, turning his steps away from Jalna and toward the fox-farm. The leaf-buds, after swelling to make a mist across the trees, now seemed to shrink. The coarse grass in the ditch lay sodden and tangled in every futile shade of drab and brown. Oh, for hills and valleys, moor and sea! He pictured the lake lying beyond the stifling woods, flat as wax. Oh, for love! he thought—a wild and passionate love, to lift me out of this mental and physical slough. Revivifying, George had said. Sickening word! But to lift out of the slough—to give spiritual hills and valleys, moor and sea. . . . A passion to kindle in one a divine insanity. He was capable of such a passion, he knew, and he desired it.

He stood in the field facing the fox-farm, his arms folded on a gate. The dingy house needed painting. It looked flat and drab as the landscape. He thought: Why do I wait here? For I shall see nothing to lighten my heart. Even if I should see Pauline—what is the use of that? She can be nothing to me. Still, I long for a glimpse of her. Perhaps because there is something in her that is like the wind and the moors, the sun on the high hills. . . . Oh, if only Eden were back, I should not ask for anything! But he has taken my youth with him and I can find nothing to replace it. He shivered in the damp, still air.

He was about to turn away when he saw her coming down the road. She was returning from Mass, carrying a little book in her hand. He thought: "I wish she weren't religious. I can see the devout look overcasting her face and I should like to take it away. It is like this cold, still air that so badly suits the spring."

He drew back among the bushes by the gate and watched her approach. He tried to define what there was in her he found so beautiful. It was something that survived the wrong clothes, for she wore a blue mackintosh and a brown hat that hid her hair. It was not her walk, for she was moving slowly, with bent head. It was not her eyes alone, for they were covered by her downcast lids. . . . But what lovely, full, and classically cut eyelids! He could almost love her for the lines of those white lids. . . . But the mouth—the mouth was music, though it drooped silent. He compared its pouting curves to the small, delicate, in-drawn line of Sarah's mouth. . . . Yes, it was her mouth that made her so movingly beautiful to him. Her mouth and her eyelids. . . . If Sarah had eyelids he scarcely remembered them. They were no better than a lizard's. They were like a lizard's. He hated the thought of her.

Was it possible that Pauline loved Wakefield? But how could she love him—that boy—that child? What had he to offer her but a game of pretence—a playing at being in love? One had only to look in his face to see the child—laughing in his eyes, throned on his mouth. Why, Pauline was the sort of girl who might love a man years older than herself—a man like Renny, for instance.

He stood gazing at the house after she had disappeared into it. He put his hand on the gate to open it and cross the road to follow her, but his impulse died and he retraced his steps in the direction of Jalna.

XXII

JIG-SAW

IT was true that the jig-saw puzzles, for which Augusta had sent to England, had done good service in whiling away the hours of that late spring. Augusta kept the boxes containing them in her own room and she would not bring out a fresh one until the last was complete to the most minute, captiously shaped portion. Some of them were fairly simple and were achieved with just a pleasant surmounting of difficulty. These she handed out first, when the power of concentration of her brothers was wayward and feeble. But, as their skill increased, and as they took more interest in the life around them, she produced the more intricate puzzles and, knowing herself just how the pieces fitted in, she would stand behind the table over which they bent with the enigmatic smile of a Fate.

Others beside the two elderly men were interested. As soon as Pheasant was about again she would leave her newborn infant to hang over the puzzle, sometimes pouncing with exclamations of delight on the elusive piece. To Alayne the absorption of Nicholas and Ernest in such a trivial pastime was pathetic, but she would occasionally draw up a chair beside them and evince a pretended interest. Her real interest was in watching their faces. They were both aged by what they had passed through, Nicholas the more so because of the pouches under his eyes and the thinning of the cheeks behind the drooping ends of his grey moustache. He was not so good at the puzzles as Ernest. But he was more aggressive in his desire to be the one to place the wanting piece. He would try one after another, disarranging the entire picture as he fumbled with his large nervous hands to thrust the new bit into place. Usually it was the wrong bit, but, when he did succeed, he would give a triumphant laugh and exclaim— "There, now, Ernie! I told you I would get it. You're too slow for anything, you know!"

But though on the surface Nicholas seemed the most absorbed it was really Ernest who took the working of the puzzles to heart. He would sit drooping over them so long that, when he got up, he could scarcely straighten himself, and when he lay down for his rest the irregular pieces would dance before his eyes, here a bit of sky, there the hoof of an animal or a tangled patch that might be beard or grass.

Wakefield's help was invaluable, for he came to the work clear-eyed from out-of-doors. The spring labour of the farm was beginning and he was happy in it. He asked nothing better than the life he was living, and the study he had promised Renny he would undertake was more and more pushed aside for active things. When Renny thought he was at his books he would be in the library bent over the puzzles with his uncles.

Mooey, too, was fascinated by them, but his presence was not welcomed because his small quick hands were only too likely to displace the pieces. Ernest was irritated by him, but Nicholas would hold him on his good knee and, while he did not encourage him to finger the pieces, he would sometimes allow him to put one into place.

Augusta announced one day that there were only two puzzles left. They had worked their way through all the rest. Ernest looked almost relieved, for, in truth, they had been a strain on him. But he would fling himself with all his might into the solving of these.

Nicholas exclaimed—"Well, well, that's a great pity! They've been entertaining—very entertaining. It was a good thought of yours, Augusta, to send for them. I don't know when I've enjoyed anything so much." He looked at her out of his tired old eyes, and tried to smile.

Augusta emptied the second-last puzzle on to the table—a provocative and jumbled heap.

"This will keep you busy for some time," she said. "Mrs. Thomas Court worked at it for three solid days, playing a tattoo on the floor with her heels all the while, she was so wrought up."

Ernest selected a corner piece and placed it. "You'll find," he observed, "that I shall do it in a day, as I did the last one."

"Well—I like that!" exclaimed Nicholas. "Who was it that fitted the piece of torn trouser into the dog's mouth?"

"Of course, you helped," returned Ernest, "but you must admit that I did the bulk of the job." Already he had several bits fitted together.

Nicholas snatched up a handful, put on his glasses, and peered into them.

Augusta gave his heavy shoulders and Ernest's slender ones an encouraging pat and left them. They settled down to their task.

At first they got on fairly well, but there was a great deal of land-scape in the picture, mostly formed by bending reeds, and several female forms with Eastern draperies intricate and confusing. Ernest had indigestion and it made him nervous. Nicholas made a sucking noise on the mouthpiece of his pipe that was irritating. Pheasant spent an hour with them and was a great help. But it was Rags, lingering near the table, duster in hand, who discovered that the picture represented Moses in the bulrushes.

By evening it was three-parts done, but there were pieces that could not be fitted in, though Alayne, Piers and Wakefield all took a hand in it. At eleven o'clock weariness forced them to desist.

"It was far better," said Alayne to Renny, "when they played bridge. Now they care for nothing but these dreadful puzzles. I'd be demented if I went on as they do. Yet all you others encourage them."

"Of course we do. It keeps their minds off other things."

Ernest was up early the next morning. Betimes he entered the library and advanced with a determined tread to the table where the jig-saw puzzle lay. But he drew back, scarcely believing his eyes, when he saw that it was thrown together in a confused heap. His expression of dismay was so ludicrous that Nicholas, following close after, burst into laughter.

"Whoever did this," cried Ernest fiercely, "will regret it!"

But they could not discover who had done it. There was universal astonishment and innocence. Nicholas suspected Wakefield, and Ernest Mooey, though the little boy denied that he had been near the room. It was the subject of discussion all through dinner and tea. By supper-time the puzzle had reached the stage of the night before but Ernest was too tired to go on with it. His face was flushed and he could scarcely sit still. He refused to lock the door of the library and he slept with his bedroom door ajar.

Before he had breakfast he thought he would look in at the puzzle to assure himself that it had not been tampered with. But he was too late to prevent the disaster and Mooey not quick enough to evade him. Moses and his bulrushes were scattered over the table and even on to the floor. Mooey was trying to again put them in order.

Ernest was upon him in two strides. He had not for a long time felt such a desire for violence in himself. He gripped the small boy by the arm and cuffed him, first on one side of the head and then on the other.

"You young devil!" he stormed. "Take that—and that—and that!"

Mooey's howls brought the rest of the family from the breakfast-table. Ernest stuttered out his explanations. Nicholas said brusquely —"Well, you needn't make such a pother about it. Children will do these things!"

"I have seen," said Augusta, "for some time, that he has been getting out of hand."

"He's a young ruffian," fumed Ernest. "To think of his daring to repeat the offence!" He turned to Piers. "What he deserves is a good thrashing."

"He'll get it," agreed Piers grimly.

Mooey opened his eyes and looked at the faces about him, but, seeing that his mother's was not among them, he again shut his eyes and broke afresh into weeping.

Renny threw Alayne a mirthful glance.

"I think you're very cruel," she said, in a tense voice.

"I like to see the old boys up in the air," he returned.

Wakefield put in—"It's not any time since young Mooey put my kodak out of order."

"Yes," seconded Finch, "and he put a sponge down the lavatory yesterday."

"I didn't!" cried Mooey, in a strangling voice. "It was Adeline!"

"Well, she said it was you."

Nicholas looked down on his small favourite with severity mingled with compassion.

"What made you upset the puzzle?" he demanded.

"I didn't upset it! I didn't! I didn't! I want to go to my mummy!"

Ernest said to Piers—"If you don't take this sort of thing out of him now he'll be a heartbreak to you later on."

"I'll take it out of him."

He gripped his son by the arm and they were heard descending the basement stairs to the wash-room where many a chastisement had taken place.

Ernest and Nicholas were established over the puzzle and had already got young Moses in his basket when Pheasant appeared, leading Mooey.

"He wants to tell you," she said, "how sorry he is and that he's always going to be good in future."

Mooey held up a tear-stained face to Ernest and said:

"I'm sorry, Uncle Ernest. I won't never do it again."

Ernest bent and kissed him but his expression was still severe.

"If you had done it only once, my boy, it wouldn't have been so bad. But to do it twice—that was indeed terrible."

Nicholas took Mooey on his knee. "Was it pretty bad?" he whispered. "Poor old boy!"

So far but no farther could they complete the puzzle. Yet they were indomitable. By night all the family were engaged in the problem and the room was filled with smoke and loud voices. Even though the child had been punished Ernest did not quite trust him, and that night he locked the door of the library and took the key upstairs.

But he slept badly. His dreams were tortured by Moses in his uncompleted bulrushes and the sandalled foot that would not fit any of the female figures. He grew more and more excited and at last opened his eyes in the grey morning light, to find himself seated in front of the puzzle with all its pieces in disarray before him. Some were even on the floor.

He crept back to bed humiliated. Now he understood why he had had a cold in the head on the last two mornings. He remembered that as a boy he had been a sleep-walker. He was too just to keep the truth a secret and at breakfast he stammered out his story.

"What I most regret," he said, "is that poor little Mooey was punished unjustly."

"I told you you were making too much bother about it," said his brother.

"Still," amended Augusta, "the child was getting out of hand, in any case."

Piers said—"Down in the basement he told me that he had thrown it about because he was sick of seeing it."

"And I don't blame him!" cried Ernest. "I never want to see another jig-saw puzzle as long as I live!"

"Aren't you going to do the last one?" asked Augusta.

"No, no," said Nicholas. "We've had enough. We'll stick to bridge."

Augusta carried the discarded puzzle up to her room. There she took out the pieces which had been the stumbling-block to its completion and replaced them in the box with the last puzzle, which was a picture of Rebecca at the well, and from it extracted the pieces pertaining to Moses. She had thought, in this way, to make the puzzles last a little longer. She gave a sly smile as she sorted them.

She sighed then. What should she do with them? She would need them no more. They had served their purpose well. She went to the door and called Mooey.

He came running, for he distinguished kindness in her tone. He was bewildered by all that had passed but exhilarated by the laughing attention of his father and uncles.

"Mooey," one of them would say, "go and ask Uncle Ernest where Moses was when the light went out."

Mooey would shout the question.

"Come, come," Ernest would answer, reddening a little, "you need not rub it in. But I dare say I deserve it. Where was he?"

"Doing jig-saw puzzles!" Mooey would shout.

He came running now, to Augusta. She filled his arms with the puzzle-boxes.

"Here," she said. "You may have them all, and, if you work at them diligently, you will learn a great deal."

He flew to where his mother and Alayne were talking at the foot of the attic stairs. Pheasant held the infant Philip in her arms, and Alayne smiled down at him, his tiny hand clasping her finger.

"Look! Look!" cried Mooey. "See what I have!"

Nooky appeared and screamed at once:

"Me too! Me too!"

"No!" shouted Mooey. "You can't have one! Aunt Augusta gave them to me! Look, Mummy!"

Alayne said—"You might give Nooky just one." She loved Nooky.

Mooey flung one of the boxes to his little brother, then, seeing Adeline emerge from Alayne's room, a predatory light in her eyes, he fled with his booty up the stairs to the nursery, pursued by the other children, Adeline on hands and feet screaming as she went.

Alayne watched them, standing rigid. She said to herself—"Let them go! I don't care what they do to each other." Aloud she asked:

"Is Alma up there?"

"Yes," answered Pheasant. "Oh, that girl! She's impossible! If only we could afford a proper nurse!"

"The children are like gipsies," said Alayne. "I can do nothing with Adeline."

"Did she sleep last night?"

"Sleep! There was no sleep in her till I was worn out. I have never known her worse. She not only laughed and shouted but struck herself on the eyes to keep awake."

"Tck! How awful! Piers says he would spank her till she would ask for nothing better than sleep."

"Piers is cruel. When I think of poor little Mooey! The injustice!"

But Pheasant was loyal to her mate. "All the evidence was against Mooey. Piers only did what any good father would. He doesn't want his child to grow up into a menace to society, does he?"

She looked so pale, so ingenuous, as she said this, with her dark hair soft on her forehead and the child with Piers' eyes in her arms, that Alayne suddenly kissed her.

"You're a sweet thing, Pheasant," she said.

There came a concerted howl from above and Pheasant hastened up the stairs.

Alayne returned to her room. "Let them do what they like," she repeated to herself. "I don't care."

She was glad that Adeline had left the room. What peace without that fiery energy! The spring rain streamed down the pane and bounced on the sill. Under the eaves nesting birds talked together in the budding Virginia creeper. She stood looking out. Her thoughts were on Renny.

"Oh, my darling," she thought. "Oh, my darling. I wish you were here at this moment. If you were here now, I could show you all my love. I would kiss that abstracted, dark look out of your eyes. I know I could. Oh, Renny, Renny, I wish you were here!" Yet he was only in the stable. There was only that space of spring rain between them.

Augusta appeared in the open doorway. She said:

"I think, my dear, that we must speak seriously to Renny about the dilapidations of the house. The wallpaper in my room is disgraceful and I did not sleep half the night because of the clanging of a loose shutter."

"I did not sleep either," returned Alayne moodily.

"But why?" Augusta gave her a searching look.

"Oh, it was Adeline. She would not sleep—nor let me."

"I have heard Renny's mother complain of the very same thing. You must be patient. But I am going away now and I should like to think that the dilapidations would be repaired this spring. My father and my brother kept the house in perfect order."

"Times are different," said Alayne sullenly. At the moment she felt antagonistic toward the older people who were always talking about the perfect conditions of the past.

Wragge came down the passage bearing a scuttle of coals. He set it down with an air at once deprecatory and impudent.

"I 'ope you'll excuse me, madam; I 'ope you won't tike it amiss me drawing your attention to this 'ere coal-scuttle. But w'at you see in there are the very last coals we've got. I'm on my w'y with them to Mr. Ernest's fire. But the furnace fire's out and there's no more ordered that I knows of."

Alayne fixed her eyes on the opposite wall. "I shall order coal this morning," she said coldly.

Wragge gave a wry smile. "Excuse me, 'm, but the dealer said as 'ow 'e wouldn't deliver any more until the last was paid for."

Alayne was angry, humiliated. She said:

"I shall attend to that. Please take the scuttle away."

Augusta said—"I hope Mr. Ernest's room is comfortable, Wragge."

Wragge answered oilily, for he had in mind a farewell tip from Augusta:

"Oh, your Lidyship, I'd never let Mr. Ernest be uncomfortable! Not w'ile I'd a lump of coal in me cellar."

"Well, I'm very glad of that," said Augusta gravely.

Alayne thought—"One moment more and I shall scream. Renny told me that the last coal was paid for. Oh, what a liar he is! Oh, how can I endure this life!"

Pheasant came running down the attic stairs.

"Whatever do you suppose has happened? The roof of the nursery has been leaking and just now a quantity of plaster fell from the ceiling on to poor little Nooky's cot! If he had been in it he would certainly have been killed! Oh, dear, it seems sometimes as though the whole family was bent on killing my poor little children— between neglect and cruelty!" She sat down midway on the stairs and buried her face in her hands.

"It's not my fault!" said Alayne. "It's not my fault if the roof falls in and the shutters clang and the wallpaper sags and there's no coal in the cellar! If you must complain—complain to Renny! I've really as much as I can cope with." She hurriedly descended the stairs to the hall below. Augusta and Pheasant were left staring at each other.

Alayne had scarcely reached the bottom of the stairs before she was ashamed of herself. She had never so lost her temper before in front of the others. She regretted that Aunt Augusta should carry away such an impression of her, and she half-turned back to apologise but could not quite make up her mind to do it. She stood looking doubtfully at the door of the drawing-room deeply scored by the scratching of dogs seeking admittance there. Jock was sleeping now by the stove, his muddy feet turned toward the warmth. Piers' wire-haired terrier, who had had her leg injured and wore a bandage smelling of carbolic, sat shivering on a chair by the hat-stand.

Alayne drew a deep breath and went into the library to the telephone. She arranged for coal to be sent collect.

From there she went to the drawing-room, where she found Finch doubled over a book. His presence was comforting to her. She sat down near him and asked:

"What are you reading?"

He looked up, a strange smile flitting across his face.

"Eden's poems," he answered.

She drew back rebuffed. It was morbid of Finch, she thought, to sit crouched there reading those poems of his dead brother, to smile in that hallucinated way, as though he would draw the image of Eden between them, but she said gently:

"I think they are good but they have not the freshness and rapture of his earlier ones."

"You could scarcely expect that. He was changing. The poems are full of inequalities. But there's no indifference in them. His mind was on fire. . . . Look here—I wonder if you'd care to see what the critics are saying about him. I've subscribed to a press-cutting agency." He laid down the book and took an envelope filled with cuttings from his pocket.

He began reading them to her in a loud, rather tremulous voice, stressing, even re-reading, the passages of warmest praise, one long hand holding open the book against his side, as though from its pages he drew some sustaining virtue. His presence overshadowed for her the words he read. What was to become of this lonely boy whose face showed the suffering and the strain he had been through!

She heard the side door open and close with a bang. She heard quick sharp steps, and the thought flew into her mind, scattering all else before it—"Here is my darling—the one I am longing for—the one who means more to me than all else in the world! . . ."

He came, dripping with rain, into the hall, followed by a bull terrier he had just acquired. Jock sat up and saw the newcomer. He could bear much. He was no fighter, but he could not bear the sight of a bull terrier. With a low growl he advanced toward him. In a moment the two were rolling over together, and young Biddy, unmindful of her injury, leaped in to aid Jock. Nip, hearing the hubbub from where he slept on Nicholas's bed, came bounding down the stairs and stood on the last step uttering ear-splitting yelps. Mrs. Wragge, just coming up from the basement, screamed.

The bull terrier had Jock's foreleg gripped in his teeth. Renny was astride of them but he could not loose the bulldog's hold. "Water," he said to Finch, who, with the abandon of a hobbledehoy,

198

flung down the basement stairs and reappeared with a bucket, slopping the water at every step. Mrs. Wragge had run to the dining-room for a pepper-castor. "No, no," Renny warned her away.

At last the dogs were separated; the bulldog led to the basement by Rags, Jock's paw bandaged in Renny's handkerchief, Biddy's bandage replaced, and Renny, Alayne, and Mrs. Wragge looked at each other across a pool of water on the rug. Nip still barked from the stairway.

"My word," said Mrs. Wragge, "them dog-fights do give me a turn! As many as I've seen I can't seem to get used to 'em." She pressed a fat hand to her bosom.

Renny glanced at Alayne's face and away again.

"You'd better," he said to the cook, "have Bessie come and mop this up at once."

"Yes, sir, though where to find her I don't know, for she's always hiding in corners. What I was going to say is that the kitchen range is smoking like all possessed an' will do until the chimbley's cleaned. Me eyes is smoked almost out of me 'ead along of it an' the blood's still running out of the joint an' it a quarter to one by the kitchen clock though goodness knows it may be wrong for it's been gaining on me this twelvemonth an' I've asked times an' times to 'ave it seen to. I 'ope you don't mind my speakin' so, out of my own basement, sir."

He grinned at her genially. "I'll have the chimney cleaned tomorrow. Did the fishmonger bring the salmon? And did the cases of stout come?"

When Mrs. Wragge had gone, Alayne said, in a tone too low for Finch, who had re-entered the drawing-room, to hear:

"Do you know that there is always twice as much fish ordered as is needed? And must you have a case of stout? The bills for provisions in this house are appalling."

He gave her an admiring look, as though he thought—"You are a shrewd little thing!"

He said—"I am used to seeing plenty of food on the table. I dislike cheese-paring. As for the stout—that is for Uncle Ernest. He needs it—poor old chap!"

"I've ordered coal," she said, in a self-conscious voice. "It is to come collect. I'll pay for it."

He arched his brows. "My rich little wife!" he exclaimed. He put his arms about her and laid his head on her shoulder.

She clasped his hard body and thought—"He has no conscience. He is without conscience and he is as aloof as a tree, though he lays his head on my shoulder." Now that she held him in her arms she was not thinking—"My darling—my own darling!"

He was aware that she was not approving of him. He straightened himself and, to change the subject, asked, with a jerk of his head toward the drawing-room:

"How is that boy getting on? His nerves, I mean."

She drew a loosened strand of her hair into place and answered, half-petulantly:

"Oh—Finch! I don't know. He never plays the piano. He is in there now . . . reading Eden's poems."

"Is he really! He was very fond of Eden. We all were, weren't we? We, all of us, miss him. . . ." He looked at her challengingly.

She thought—"He is angry with me because I am not mourning for Eden. Was there ever such a position!"

He went to the door of the drawing-room and looked in. Finch was sunk in a deep chair, his hands clasped on his chest, his legs stretched at full length.

"Hullo, Finch," said Renny, "is your cold better?"

"Yes, thanks," he answered, without looking up.

Renny frowned at him speculatively, then said:

"There's just time before dinner for you to play a piece. Play me something nice, will you? I'm a bit tired and I'd like some good music."

"I can't play," growled Finch.

"Come now—just a short piece—a fugue or a gavotte—or something of the sort."

Finch looked at him, suddenly suspicious. Was he being baited? "You know I'm off colour," he growled. "Why, I—I'm hardly able to play a scale. I daren't try."

Renny came into the room and turned over some music on the piano. "This looks easy," he said. "Try this."

Finch began to laugh. He laughed suddenly, naturally.

Renny grinned. "Come now. Try this over. To please me."

Alayne, in the doorway, was making signs to him to desist.

Rags intervened by a prolonged sounding of the gong. The noise swelled to a deafening clamour, diminished, swelled again and, at last, as the family were collected, died away, and Rags, with a grand air, appeared at Renny's elbow. Renny looked up at him and asked an inaudible question to which Rags replied by a humorous pantomime affirmative.

Ernest had seated himself with a sigh. Nicholas had not appeared.

"Where is Uncle Nick?" asked Renny

"He can't get out of his bed," answered Ernest. "His gout is very bad. He's having a tray. No wonder he feels the weather. It is terrible. Terrible." The rain drove against the pane. "I'm afraid I shouldn't take roast pork, Renny," he said, "but it looks very nice. And apple sauce, too. I'm very fond of that."

"It will do you good," encouraged Renny, and cut him a juicy slice.

But when it was set in front of him, Ernest did not begin to eat. He stared, seeing nothing, and then he yawned without restraint. "Oh, ho, ho, ho," he yawned.

Mooey, with poised fork, was entertained.

"Oh, ho, ho, ho," he imitated, in his pretty treble.

"Don't imitate me, boy," said Ernest sternly.

Pheasant commanded her son to attend to his dinner.

"But," she observed, "there's an old saying that yawning is contagious and I really believe it is, for I feel like yawning myself this very minute."

Piers pinched her thigh and she laughed instead.

Laughter was pleasant in Renny's ears these days. He gave a bark of laughter himself, though he did not know what the joke was about.

Pheasant, seeing his good-humour, said:

"Have you heard about the plaster? A huge piece of it has fallen off the nursery ceiling right into poor little Nooky's cot."

The master of Jalna was noisily crunching a bit of crisp rind.

"Was Nooky in the cot?" he asked.

"Good heavens, no!"

"Why worry then?"

"But he *might* have been killed!"

Piers asked sharply of Renny—"Aren't you going to send for the plasterer? The entire ceiling should be done."

Renny dropped a piece of meat to one of his spaniels and watched the dog devour it without replying.

"Very well," said Piers, "I'll telephone for the mason this afternoon."

"If you do you'll pay him for the job yourself."

Piers' eyes grew prominent. The air became electric.

Boney, on his perch in the library, seemed aware of this. He flapped his wings and uttered incoherent screams that resolved themselves into "*Shaitan-ka-batka!*"

"The ceiling in my room," said Finch, "has been leaking as long as I can remember, and it has not fallen yet."

Augusta said—"I entirely approve of your decision, Piers. It cuts me to the heart to see my father's house going to wrack and ruin. The shutters in my room are ready to fall from their hinges."

"I'll have them mended too," said Piers.

"You'll pay for them too, then," said Renny. He continued to eat his dinner imperturbably.

Alayne felt a queer rocking motion inside her that was half sympathy for him and half anger against him.

The parrot, once roused, continued to scream.

Rags appeared with a glass of stout on a small tray and set it before Ernest.

"Well, well, that looks nice! Just what I needed, for I have no appetite at all!" He drank a little of it, beamed at Renny, and began to take an interest in his dinner.

Renny threw Alayne an intimate, laughing look that was almost a wink. It said—"I know how to cheer up the old boy."

Pheasant said, wistfully—"I don't see where in the world Piers is going to get the money to pay for all those repairs."

Renny returned—"He should have married a rich wife, like I did!"

There was appreciative laughter, shot through by Finch's hysterical giggle. Alayne turned scarlet.

Ernest, seeing this, observed—"Dear Alayne, she has been a blessing to us all."

"Please spare me, Uncle Ernest," she said sedately. How could Renny, in front of the family, refer to her pitiful possessions! Especially after the affair of the coal, that very morning. She remembered his proud refusal to benefit by Finch's legacy. What had come over him since then?

Throughout the meal Wakefield had paid little heed to what was being said. There was a secret, smiling look in his eyes. When they were leaving the dining-room, side by side, Finch said to him:

"Well, and what are you looking so smug about?"

"I suppose I feel smug."

"You may—but it looks damned silly, I can tell you!"

"No sillier than your sulks."

Alayne overheard them. Was there ever such a disagreeable family, she thought. She spent a part of the afternoon reading aloud to Nicholas.

Renny was out that evening, ostensibly to see a prospective buyer in town, but she suspected that he was playing poker with his horsy friends, Crowdy and Chase. She had discovered that they sometimes went to his office in the stables to play where they felt themselves more welcome than in the house, and she had, with a sense of shame, heard Augusta censure him for having Wragge join in the game.

She was asleep when he returned but the sound of his light step woke her. She called softly:

"Renny, can you tell who it is that is coughing? It's keeping me awake."

He came to her door and stood listening. The loud insistent cough came from Piers' and Pheasant's room.

"It's Pheasant," he said. "I suppose she's getting this beastly cold, now. God, how I hate the sound of a cough!"

"She takes no care of herself," said Alayne. "She kept me awake for quite an hour and when I did fall asleep from sheer exhaustion you have waked me again!"

"Too bad! I wonder if she has taken anything for it."

"No. She thinks it isn't safe when she is nursing the baby."

"Was Adeline good tonight?"

"Angelic. . . . What about your business? Was it good?" She succeeded in purifying her tone from suspicion.

"Very. The man—he's from Buffalo—is coming out tomorrow. I think Boniface is as good as sold."

Adeline stirred and snuffled.

"Sh," warned Alayne and he bent over her and kissed her.

Adeline laughed.

Renny went round to her cot and put his hand on her soothingly. She caught it in her strong little fingers.

"If she misbehaves tonight, I can't bear it," whined Alayne. She heard the whine in her own voice and was ashamed.

He whispered into the child's ear—"Be quiet and Daddy will give you a ride on his big gee-gee tomorrow."

"Now!" she exclaimed.

"No. Tomorrow. If you go to sleep."

She was quiet. He tiptoed to his own room. "My two darling girls," he thought, and he felt pensive, almost weak, in his tenderness for them.

Wakefield flung his arm across his eyes against the light. His lips pouted in a smile, as though he had been in a happy dream.

A violent spell of coughing came from Pheasant's room. After that it was repeated every little while. As Renny lay uneasily listening, he thought at first only of Alayne's distress. She would have another bad night, poor old girl. But, when a sustained cough came from Finch's room above, a sudden feeling of panic gripped his heart. What if the girl and the youth were both affected as Eden had been?

Finch had helped to nurse Eden. The doctor had warned them to be careful of infection. But—had they been careful? He knew that he himself had not. Finch was delicate—born of a consumptive mother —probably—good God, inevitably susceptible! He should never have been allowed to go near Eden. And there was Pheasant, just at the time of child-bearing—well, if she had it, she would last three months! What had he been thinking of? He was a fool—a brute! And there was Eden—poor boy—he'd told Eden to help Maurice with the work—the worst thing he could have done—he'd helped to kill Eden. . . . He clenched his hands, set his teeth to hold back a groan.

The coughing from the two rooms continued as a terrible duet in the blackness. Renny saw himself burying first Pheasant, then Finch. Gran would have three young people about her. Wakefield murmured in his sleep. . . . Little Wake—perhaps he'd be the next!

Renny found himself in the middle of the room quivering like a terrified horse. He stood so a moment, then felt his way to the door and groped along the passage, a pale pencil of light under the door at the end guiding him.

He tapped, but Pheasant was coughing and did not hear him. He pushed open the door and went in.

Pheasant was sitting up in bed and a night-light threw her enlarged shadow grotesquely on the opposite wall. She looked up at him with the wistfulness of a child.

"I can't stop it," she said. "I'm sorry."

He came close and looked down at her. He saw that Piers was fast asleep.

He said—"You don't think there is anything wrong with you, do you, Pheasant?"

She repeated, startled—"Wrong with me? What do you mean?"

"Like Eden had. . . . Your lungs."

"My goodness, no! It's just a common cold. I've had dozens like it."

"And what about Finch? Do you think he——" He looked at her tragically—"I'm afraid he's going the way Eden went."

"Finch smokes too many cigarettes. It irritates his throat. But he's perfectly all right. He was worried about himself—a little, and he went to a doctor in town. He's perfectly sound. So now you know." She began to cough. "Oh, if only I had a hot drink!"

Relief surged through Renny, followed by anger at Piers.

He went round to his side of the bed and, pulling down the bed-clothes just far enough, gave him a rousing slap.

"There," he said, "take that! You good-for-nothing lout—sleeping here like a swine while your wife coughs her head off!"

Piers sat up, furious. "Why doesn't she take her rum and honey?" he demanded.

"I have taken it!" declared Pheasant. "And it's making me ill!"

"You ought to be ashamed of yourself," continued Renny, "to show no more feeling than you do for Pheasant—or anyone else in the house! Do you know that Alayne hasn't slept tonight because of her coughing? I haven't slept. Nobody has slept—but you!" His fright, his relief, combined to make him thoroughly lose his temper. "You've never shown any consideration for other people! If Pheasant died at your side—you'd go right on snoring! You had no pity for Eden—no, by God—you'd no pity for Eden! You're colossally selfish. You act as though you owned the earth. You act as though you owned Jalna—sending for masons and carpenters without my permission! Now you'll go down to the basement and get this poor girl a drink of something hot."

During this tirade Piers' face had gone from flushed and sulky sleepiness to white anger. In one movement he was out of bed and on his feet facing Renny. He said:

"If you think I'll stand this sort of abuse, you're mistaken! I won't stay in the house. I'll get a place for myself!"

"Yes—I can see you!"

"Well—you shall see me—and before the month's out, too!"

"Come, come, don't get in a rage!"

"You like to do all the raging yourself, don't you?"

"I'm annoyed—and no wonder!"

Pheasant broke in—"Oh, please don't quarrel." Then, to drown out their voices, she threw herself into a fit of coughing. She kept it up until she saw Piers put on his dressing-gown and Renny leave the room. Then she took a spoonful of rum and honey and lay down.

Renny stopped at the door to say to Piers:

"You'd better bring a hot drink for Finch, too. I'll take it up to him."

Piers kept a stony silence.

Renny saw a light under Alayne's door and went into her room, closing the door behind him. Adeline was asleep, but Alayne was pacing the room with a blanket about her shoulders.

He looked at her mischievously.

"They're going," he said, with a nod toward the other room.

"Who?" she asked blankly.

"Of course, I don't really believe he'll do it, but he says he will.

205

He was lying there, beside that poor girl, fast asleep, simply paying no attention to her—well, I couldn't stand it and I gave him a wallop that made him sit up, I can tell you." He gave the arch grin of old Adeline.

<h1 style="text-align:center">XXIII</h1>

<h2 style="text-align:center">AUGUSTA'S FLITTING</h2>

PIERS stood by his word, and chance had it that the opportunity of renting a furnished house was offered him inside the week. The Miss Laceys wanted very much to spend a year with a cousin in California, and were eager to have friends as tenants for a low rental. Theirs was not a house that could be let easily, and they had a dread of strangers.

At first Piers' pleasure was damped by the fact that he had, in his hastiness, ordered mason and carpenter to repair ceiling, roof, and shutters of Jalna. Now that he was leaving, surely he could not be held responsible for the cost of these. Yet he dreaded to suggest this, for fear of exciting the anger of his inflammable brother. He did indeed approach the subject once or twice, but Renny shied from the mention of bills as a horse from fluttering paper.

Then Piers told his trouble to Augusta, and she, with a grand gesture of generosity, expressed herself willing to pay all from her own purse. Piers kissed her, gave her a hug, almost painful in its vigour, and went off to find Pheasant. In her relief and delight Pheasant rushed off to tell Alayne. Alayne, whose feeling at the moment was one of pessimistic tolerance toward them all, passed the news on to Renny.

He was honestly delighted.

"What a good thing!" he exclaimed. "It would have been a pull for the boy. And it's quite time the old lady toed the scratch. She hasn't laid an offering on the altar of Jalna for a dog's age."

He forgot that he had been angry at Piers, and that day called on the Miss Laceys and tried to beat them down a little more in the rent. He did not succeed in this, but they had a jolly afternoon together, and he returned home feeling happier than he had in many months. Perhaps, after all, it was a good thing that Piers and his family were going. The house was overcrowded. The noise of the children was trying to the uncles, and Pheasant seemed to be heading toward a large family. Piers would still spend his days at Jalna and would be living so near that there would be constant coming and going.

Alayne, he felt sure, would be more contented for the change. It was hard on her not seeing more of him—having more of a private life of their own—and she would see more of him with Piers and Pheasant and their kids out of the house.

Alayne, he thought rather ruefully, would have been a happier woman if she had lived quite by herself all the day, with a tired husband coming home at night to a perfectly ordered house, to a tidy and well-behaved child who would sit on Daddy's knee and stroke his tired head before she went to her cot. And, after a perfect little dinner, there would be a concert or intellectual conversation. Intellectual conversation—that was what hit him in the weak spot. He had it not nor ever would have. Still, they had their happiness. There was that other side of Alayne's nature, the passionate self-forgetting side which, it seemed to him, she was learning to keep under control.

But he felt cheerful. For one thing Maurice had not sold any more of his lots, and the two families who were already building bungalows there seemed to be quite decent folk. Perhaps they could be endured. Then the spring was forward. There was a quick rush of budding and unfolding, and the sun, in the height of the day, gave a generous heat.

Renny became jovial on the subject of the removal of the young family. He would say at table—"Well, I wonder where you'll be this time next year! Sneaking back to Jalna, I'm willing to bet!"

"I don't see why!" Pheasant would retort, hotly.

"What about the rent? What if you can't pay your rent? I suppose you think Auntie will pay it for you, but you won't, will you, Auntie?"

Augusta would look down her nose.

Or perhaps he would urge Mooey to a third helping of pudding. "Eat all you can, old man, while you have the chance! God knows how you'll fare when your dad has the providing to do." And Mooey, forcing down his third helping, would look downright alarmed.

But no matter what Renny said, Pheasant could not feel angry with him. She remembered the night when he had come in to her when she was coughing and been so tender with her and so rough with Piers, who, she could not help thinking, had deserved all he had got. In conversation with Piers she was always referring to that night "when Renny was so perfectly sweet to me."

Piers' eyes would grow prominent and he would perhaps repeat: "Sweet to you! What the hell do you mean, sweet to you?"

"Well," she would return, "you mightn't have had me with you today if Renny hadn't got thoroughly alarmed by my condition and sent you down for a hot drink for me. Whatever he has done or may do, I shall never forget that night, and there is no use in your trying to make me forget it."

"I only wish I could get a reputation for benevolence as easily."

Nicholas and Ernest had never been so unobservant of what took place about them. Even the budding spring did not arouse them from their dejection. They felt old, they felt ill, and the departure of their sister hung over them like a cloud. The day approached only too quickly.

Renny was to accompany her to Quebec from where she sailed. She would have preferred the company of either Piers or Finch, for she was feeling annoyed at her eldest nephew. But Finch's nerves were so unstrung that she hesitated to ask him to undertake a tiring journey, and Piers, with so much on hand, could not get away. The master of Janla could always get away.

On the last morning Augusta went from room to room through the house, from attic to wine cellar that had been so well stored in her father's time. With a feeling of melancholy reverence she said good-bye to each room with the conviction in her heart that never again would she see it. She gave a good-bye present to each of the children and carried a lump of sugar to Boney on his perch in her mother's room. He clutched it in his scaly grey claw but did not attempt to eat it until she had gone. He looked at her out of his shrewd grey eyes and made chuckling noises that ruffled the feathers on his throat.

The car, laden with her luggage, was at the door. All the family, including Maurice, Meg, and little Patience, had gathered to see her go. The sunlight intensified the lines in the faces of the three old people. They stood close together as they had stood on the same spot when they were tiny children.

"Well, well, Gussie," said Nicholas thickly, "so you've got to go! We must say good-bye, eh?" He took her in his big arms and held her tightly to him for a moment. The familiar strong smell of tobacco came to her nostrils.

"Good-bye, my dear, dear sister," said Ernest, in a trembling voice. "I am sure that next year you will come back to us for a visit. Say you will, Augusta, for just one more visit!"

"I will try, dear Ernest," she answered, and kissed him tenderly. She looked back just once at the group left behind, then pressed her handkerchief to her eyes and sat so for quite a long while. After that she was her composed self again and looked at the hurly-burly of the station platform with her accustomed air of dignified offence.

It was indeed a long journey to Quebec. The great powerful train raged and swung its way from province to province, from budding spring to lingering winter. "Never again, never again," thought Augusta, "can I undertake this!"

At Quebec the Citadel towered above them purple against an azure sky. The dark ramparts told their story of another day. She said to Renny, as they stood together on the pier:

"How strange to think that I was carried ashore here from a sailing vessel an infant, in my father's arms! My ayah, you will remember, died on the voyage and was buried at sea."

"Yes," he agreed, "things have improved greatly since then."

"I do not think they have improved," she said.

He was silent for a moment and then said:

"Speaking of burial at sea, Auntie, makes me think what a pity it is that you won't be buried with the rest of the family at Jalna."

She looked at him out of her opaque dark eyes where, on the iris of one, there was a whitish spot. She said:

"Well, my dear, my place is beside my husband and he is buried at Nymet Crews."

"I know. But—in spite of that—it's a pity. And I see no reason why—if you'd prefer to be buried in the family plot—you shouldn't have your wish."

They were jostled by the crowd as everyone moved toward the gang-plank.

She answered—"I do not see how it could be managed."

There was such a noise that he had almost to shout his answer.

"I'd gladly go for you myself and fetch you back."

She had no opportunity of answering him, such was the confusion, until they were on deck. Then she said:

"It is very kind of you, Renny, very kind indeed, to offer to take so much trouble for me. But I think, when my time comes, I shall prefer to lie beside my Edwin. . . ."

He stood on the pier watching the liner move slowly down the St. Lawrence. The river gave back the sublime reflection of the morning clouds. It ran swiftly toward icebergs, whales, and open sea, dandling the river craft on its way. Renny pictured his grandfather, fresh from military life in India, standing where he now stood, with his belongings about him, his handsome, hawk-nosed, brown-eyed wife whose bonnet concealed her luxuriant dark-red hair, whose strong arm negligently held the infant he had just surrendered to her. The delicate dark infant was now Aunt Augusta, steaming away on the wide water, probably never to return.

Renny pictured himself and Alayne and little Adeline in a like position and he thought it would have suited him very well. He would have liked the country as it was then, noble, wild, with forests full of game. He stood, tall and lean, a noticeable figure, with his air of impetuous pride and the disciplined strength of his body. The War had left its mark on him. His association with horses, his familiarity with the saddle, his long years of responsibility, had marked him. And on his features was the stamp of old Adeline, tempered with his manhood.

His reverie was broken by the passing of a long tail of black-coated schoolboys in charge of two priests. They were pale-faced boys who chattered in French as they passed him. He gave a last look at the liner, now growing small, as though drawing into herself, and turned back along the steep street.

XXIV

PIERS' FLITTING

Piers had chosen the days of Renny's absence as an agreeable time for his own removal from Jalna to the Miss Laceys' house. Pugnacious though he was, he rather dreaded the jocularities of his elder and he was afraid that he might be driven by them into a serious quarrel. He felt himself in the mood for a serious quarrel. For one thing Renny, after much pressing, had paid him his entire bill for the winter's fodder, and inside of a fortnight had, apparently being driven to desperation, borrowed it back. Since then it had not been possible to extract a penny from him.

The morning was the gayest possible, for the cherry-trees were in full blow, the apple-trees in pink bud, and the blue of the sky was an arch of forget-me-not. The breeze stayed in no direction for long but darted out like a playful child from first one hiding-place and then another. Sometimes it scattered a handful of petals, sometimes flung a feather from a bird, but always it lingered a moment to whisper through the shutters or ruffle the Virginia creeper on the old house.

Pheasant was in a state of bliss, but to Piers the day was unreal. He was exhilarated but, at the same time, unbelieving that he, Piers Whiteoak, was going to sleep from henceforth under a different roof. It would have been less impressive to him if he had been going far away. To go to a house of which every corner was familiar to him was a mental upheaval.

The young pair owned nothing save their personal belongings, the silver cups which Piers had won in school athletics and horse and cattle shows, and an armchair which he had once bought at an auction sale. The children's cots they took as a matter of course, and the children themselves came out to the waiting car clutching armfuls of toys.

Baby Adeline strode up to Nooky and snatched a stuffed blue rabbit.

"Mine," she said.

Mooey tore it from her grasp and returned it to his brother. "It's Nooky's!"

"Mine," she reiterated and charged again.

Mooey pushed her to the ground.

Wakefield lifted all three children into the car beside Pheasant, who was holding her youngest. She cried:

"But you shouldn't have put Adeline in! Heaven knows I have enough without her!"

There was a scene as Adeline was lifted out and carried into the house by Finch.

"All ready?" asked Piers, one hand on the wheel, the other steadying the toppling tower of bandboxes beside him.

Wakefield stood on the running-board. He was going to help them settle in.

"All ready!" cried Pheasant joyously.

"Good-bye, Uncle Ernest! Good-bye, Uncle Nick!"

"Good-bye, children! Come often to see us."

"Bye-bye! Bye-bye!" shouted the children.

Alayne came running down the steps to kiss them.

Finch appeared carrying Adeline.

"Wait a moment," he said. "She wants to kiss and be friends." He projected her, in a horizontal position, into the car and she pressed her rosebud mouth on each face in turn.

As Finch was withdrawing her she snatched the blue rabbit from Nooky and the car sped away, wails issuing from its interior.

Adeline smiled divinely and embraced the rabbit.

"Deah Bunny," she cooed. . . .

The Miss Laceys' house had been built just ten years later than Jalna, but their father (a retired naval officer who had named it The Moorings) had been a poor man and it was small and unpretentious. Now its grey plaster walls were weather-stained and it seemed to have sunk lower against the little hill-side from which it had sprung. It had an old-fashioned garden, a wicket gate, and a veranda across its front. The charming interior came as a surprise and there was an air of delicate femininity, for only women of a retiring type had lived there for many years.

They had left everything spic and span, even to freshly washed dusters in the duster bags of each room, and lavender was scattered in the dresser drawers.

"We must try to keep it this way," said Piers, looking about with great gravity after Wakefield had gone.

"Yes, indeed," agreed Pheasant. "Oh, darling, isn't it wonderful living in a place of our own after eight years of married life in the house of a domineering man like Renny Whiteoak, to say nothing of Gran and the uncles and all the rest? Even Alayne sometimes got on my nerves with her highbrow ways and her fussing over her child."

They had brought Bessie with them as a general, and Alayne had gladly surrendered Alma Patch as nurse. The little boys were in the garden feeding Mooey's pigeons. The infant was upstairs asleep. When they returned to the dining-room they found that Bessie had already laid an inviting tea on the small oval table. They looked across it into each other's eyes. Their toes touched beneath the table.

"*Isn't* it cosy?" she cried.

He nodded and grinned, showing the white bread behind his white teeth.

"And *me* pouring tea! Do you know, I've never poured tea since I was in my father's house, and there was no great prestige in that."

He nodded sympathetically and then asked:

"What about grub? Have you ordered things?"

"Not yet. Mrs. Wragge gave me a good supply to start with. She's really a generous old soul. She said she'd more on hand than she knew what to do with. She says she'll never forget us when she's baking."

"Good for her! I sent vegetables and eggs along with the load. Then naturally we shall get our fruit and milk from the farm. We killed a nice young pig yesterday and I sent a leg and some chops over here. We can manage pretty well for food. The rent will be the only difficulty."

"Never fear, darling! You will feel so much more self-reliant in this house that making money will come easily. Won't it be great fun having the family over to a party and showing off our house?"

"Yes, and having Renny jeer at everything!"

"Let him jeer! I'll not mind. And—after all—he's rather a darling. I'll never, so long as I live, forget how sweet he was to me that night when I lay awake coughing and you——"

Piers interrupted—"We shan't have any time in the garden, if you don't hurry with your tea. I must get the pigeons and try to find Biddy. I suppose she's digging up the flowers."

At this same moment Finch and Wakefield were standing in the middle of the room just vacated and looking about it with very different feelings. Finch was regretful of the break in the family. His mind went back to the time of Piers' marriage and his own delight in at last having a room of his own. . . . That attic room which he and Piers had shared together and where Piers had so often ragged him and made him unhappy. Now Piers and Pheasant had left their mark on this room. Would not the room hold for ever some essence of their joys and sufferings there? In here Piers had once locked her for three weeks after the affair with Eden. In here she had borne three children. His mind went back further and he remembered being led into this room to see his mother when she lay with the infant Wakefield at her side. She had been white as marble. In this room she had died.

Wakefield considered the furniture and the wallpaper. The carpet was quite good, if a small rug were laid on the worn spot in front of the dressing-table. He liked the walnut furniture, but the wallpaper was an abomination. He examined a small medicine cabinet. It was worth examining, for it had been fixed into the Sheraton frame of a mirror, the arched top of which served as a decoration for the cabinet. The mirror having been broken, someone had thus made ornament of the frame.

"Who did that, I wonder?" said Wakefield.

"God knows! But it's a monstrosity."

"I rather like it. I think it's neat."

"The room should be changed in some way."

"I agree! It's the wallpaper that's wrong. And, as I want the room for myself, I shall tear off the old paper and buy fresh and put it on. I'm sure I could. Perhaps you would give me a little help."

"*You* want the room! What for?"

"To sleep in, of course. Don't you think it's time I had a room of my own?"

Finch said roughly—"Oh, I know what you have in your mind! You make me sick—a kid of your age!"

"The trouble with you is that you're envious."

"Not a bit! Marriage is the furthest thing from my thoughts. But you're so damned ignorant, so unsophisticated——"

"I'll be all the better husband for that," interrupted Wake proudly. "And you needn't help me if you don't want to."

"Oh, I'll help you paper the room—if Renny says you may have it."

Renny, returning the next day, agreed. He was willing, as always, to give the boy what he wanted, but he felt that he would miss him from his side. But Wakefield was growing up and changes were in the air.

He was anxious to see Piers and Pheasant in their new surroundings, and just before one o'clock he appeared at their door, with Biddy at his heels.

"Here's your dog," he said. "She doesn't seem to approve of the move."

"Little fool," said Piers, patting her. "Won't you come in?"

Renny entered the house and, it seemed purposely to Piers, knocked his head on the door of the parlour. He pressed his hand to the spot and said:

"I'd forgotten how ridiculously small this place is. It's a good thing you're not so tall as I am."

"We like it very much," said Piers rather stiffly.

They were about to sit down to dinner. The roast of pork was on the table. Pheasant nervously asked him to share the meal with them.

"I'd like that," he said, and his eagle eye at once noticed the joint. "Some of our own pig, eh? And it looks good, too. And well cooked. I hope Bessie is doing all right."

"It's rather soon to judge," said Piers, beginning to carve.

He felt nervous with Renny's eye on him, for he had never carved before.

"Put up the guard, you idiot," exclaimed his elder, "or you'll cut your knuckle off!" He stretched his long legs under the table and looked disparagingly at its appointments.

"Poor old Miss Laceys," he said. "They haven't too much luxury about them, have they?"

"We think the house is perfectly adorable," said Pheasant quickly. "Oh, Piers, how could you?" For Piers, in his nervousness, had cut off the first slice of pork so energetically that it landed on the snowy tablecloth.

"What a duffer you are!" said Renny, rising. "Change places with me and I'll show you how it should be done."

Piers meekly took his accustomed place at the side of the table and Renny, after a short dissertation on the intricacies of carving, served all with dispatch. Mooey and Nooky stared at him wonderingly.

He in his turn stared at Bessie as she removed the plates and brought in the sweet.

"It's a pity," he said, "that you hadn't had Rags give that girl a few lessons before you set up housekeeping with her. She'll break all these pretty dishes and then the fat will be in the fire."

"I'll train her," said Pheasant, "when I have more time."

"Well, remember that it takes time to get things into the order they are in at Jalna. I wish I could tell you that your room is waiting for you if you can't stick this out, but, as a matter of fact, Wake has already taken possession and I left him tearing the paper off the walls."

Piers and Pheasant looked at each other. What cheek! they thought.

After dinner he went over the place with them, romped a while with the boys and kissed the infant Philip again and again. Piers had to restrain Biddy from following him. She writhed in her master's arms, licked his chin affectionately, but was all for Renny and the road.

He went toward the fox-farm. For a reason he could not, and did not try to, define, he felt exhilarated, pleased with himself. He cracked his leg with a stick he had picked up, and when, after a few hundred yards, Biddy overtook him he threw it far down the road for her. So they progressed, throwing and retrieving, to the ugly house with the white stones on either side of the walk that led to the door.

It was the first summer-like day and Pauline had put on a thin white dress. She was sitting in an old swing that hung from the branch of an elm. He came up behind her and, taking the rope in his hand, turned the swing so that she faced him. She knew who it was before she looked up. He was startled when he saw that she had been crying, and wished he had not come. But she said at once:

"I'm so glad you've come! Mother and I are terribly worried. Our landlord has closed down the mortgage." She spoke with the French accent of her father as she did when moved.

Renny was aghast. "Foreclosed, you mean?"

"But yes—foreclosed! We shall lose everything."

"Why are you only telling me this now?"

"We have just heard it ourselves. He was here this morning. Mummy was so rude to him. She told him she didn't care. But we are ruined. Where shall we go?" She raised her beautiful eyes to his with gathering confidence in his invincibility.

"I'll see him. Something must be done. Where is your mummy?"

For answer Clara Lebraux herself appeared. She came toward them with a queer fixed smile on her face and a cigarette between her fingers.

"It's all up!" she exclaimed. "I suppose Pauline has told you."

"I haven't had a hand in this yet."

"No use. The old man wants the place for himself. He is going to pull this house down and build himself a new one. Oh, my dear fellow, I've seen this coming for a year! It's not a great surprise to me."

"Why haven't you told me?"

"What could you do? You've worried over us enough as it is. Oh, we shall find something to do!" She stuck the cigarette between her lips with a jaunty air.

Pauline said—"One thing I will not do. I will not go to live with Uncle Bob."

Renny said bitterly—"If only things were as they used to be with me! But they're worse, Clara, than ever I've let you know."

She gave a sympathetic grunt. Then she said:

"Things are looking up with the Vaughans. I hear that they sold three new lots of their subdivision yesterday."

His face darkened. "I knew that people were looking at them, but I'd no idea that they'd come to the point."

"I am glad for their sakes," she returned.

"Well, nothing troubles me so much as this affair of yours. Would you mind letting me have a look at the papers? Have you them here?"

She assented and they went into the house.

Pauline sat in the swing looking after them for a moment's immobility. Then she let her hands drop from the ropes of the swing and laid them in her lap. They were golden against the white of her dress, so was her neck, dappled by the sunlight falling between the leaves of the elm. She felt profoundly her impotence against the forces of life. She felt a child's bewilderment on finding those on whom she depended unable to turn the tide that threatened. All about her the summer day glowed in honeyed brightness but she felt only fear. Her spirit reached out toward Wakefield but it could not find him. He was elusive as a summer cloud. She loved him but she could not bring his face before her eyes save as a laughing glance, an aloof profile. She saw his ring on her hand and closed her eyes. She laid her cheek against the rough hemp which Renny's hand had grasped.

XXV

STEMMING THE TIDE

Renny spent a sleepless night. He had never before faced such a situation as now confronted him. He had always been able, in whatever financial circumstances he found himself, to make some move toward release. But he was now baffled, faced by a blank wall. Clara and Pauline Lebraux were to be turned out of their house. They would be literally penniless and he could find no way of helping them. He could face his own troubles, but the predicament of these two who leaned on him, who had in a manner been left under his protection by his dead friend, discovered him helpless.

He had interviewed the landlord, an old enemy of his, found him obdurate, even taking a sly pleasure in his power. He had insinuated by look, as he dared not by word, that Renny's interest in the affairs of Mrs. Lebraux was the subject of lively speculation.

There was young Finch and what he had left of Gran's fortune. But no, it would not do to borrow that, for the boy must be assured of his future, and it was a matter of pride to refuse contact with that money. Still, it was not for himself. Finch could lend it direct to Clara. Surely he would be moved by her desperate situation, and Pauline's. They were going to be turned out—actually turned out. Clara had said that they would have to get positions. But what sort of indoor work were they fitted for? She had confided to him, with a wry smile, that the landlord, a widower, had proposed marriage to her.

There was Alayne. There was the legacy from her aunt. But there was no use in letting the mind dwell on that. She was close as bark to a tree. "I must provide for my child's future," she would say. It was an insult to him. He was quite able to provide for Adeline himself. Adeline was a chip of the old block. Nothing of her mother or her mother's people in her.

With these thoughts still in his mind he went down to breakfast. Wakefield had already gone to his work. Nicholas, Ernest, and Finch had not yet appeared. Adeline had had her breakfast and was playing out of doors, so Alayne and he were alone together. There were fresh roses on the table.

"Why do you so often wear blue?" he asked irritably. "It's such a cold colour."

She looked at him out of eyes the very shade of her dress.

"Cold? Why, I thought you liked it on me."

"Oh, it's becoming enough, but it's cold. Look at those roses. They're not in blue."

She laughed. She liked having him to herself.

"You don't expect me to look like a rose, do you?"

He did not answer but grimly tapped the top of an egg.

"What is the matter?" she asked teasingly, for she did not take his mood with seriousness.

He tried to smile. "Nothing. I didn't sleep."

217

"Poor darling! Was anything—anything special—worrying you? Oh, I know what it was! Those lots of Maurice's!"

He nodded and, at the same time, gave her a searching look. Perhaps, if she knew he lay awake at night . . .

But she only said—"I'd give up worrying over them, if I were you. It can do no good."

He said, in retaliation—"God knows where we shall all end."

"Are things any worse with us?"

"No. I suppose not."

"I think they are much better with Piers and his family gone. And Bessie and Alma, too."

He sighed. Then he asked—"What are your letters?"

"One is from my aunt, who is very well. The other is from Sarah. She asks me to spend a few days with her. She has no friends in town. She gets very lonely."

"Hm. . . . She should make friends."

"She can't. It isn't in her. But, for some reason, she likes me. And I am attracted by her."

"Hm." He leant his head on his hand, while the thought of Sarah filtered like a moonbeam into his mind. Like a golden moonbeam she came into its darkness. Her entry there was followed by other thoughts in brilliant confusion.

He was thus motionless so long that Alayne had a sudden feeling of apprehension. This particular moodiness was unlike him. She got up and went to him and laid her arm around his shoulder.

"Renny, what is the matter?"

He raised his eyes and she saw that there were tears in them. She had never seen him cry. She was frightened. She caught his face between her hands.

"Tell me what is wrong!"

He looked at her through his tears. "Nothing."

"Then why are there tears in your eyes?" Her own eyes were filling in response. Surely she loved him so that, if his heart ceased to beat, hers too would stop.

He pushed back the fresh blueness of her sleeve and began to kiss her white arm, mumbling his lips against it, making as though to bite. She gave a sigh of relief. There could not be anything terribly wrong. She drew her finger along the outline of his hair where it made a widow's peak on his forehead. She persisted:

"Why are those tears in your eyes?"

"I'm crying——" He cast about in his mind for something to say. Well—why not the truth?—"I'm crying because I'm so happy."

"Renny, you are ridiculous! One cannot believe a word you say." But she hugged his head to her.

"Don't you believe I'm happy?"

"I'd be glad to, heaven knows! But why so suddenly, so strangely?" He raised his eyes and she looked into their brown depths, trying to fathom them.

Adeline pranced into the room waving the fine, dark-petalled tulip whose bud Alayne had been watching for days. "Look! Look!" she cried.

Renny went into town that morning. It had been arranged that he should see Sarah and tell her that Alayne would go to her for a short visit.

He found her in the garden behind her house, a stretch of green turf enclosed by shrubs in bloom and a border of white and mauve flowers. She was throwing a ball for her pug, which trotted after it with a perfunctory air of amusing her. Her skirt touched the closely mown grass.

He stood watching her a moment before he spoke, admiring the picture she made, amused by, and very tolerant of, her ineffectual handling of the ball. Soon she saw him and came toward him without haste and took his hand in her strong velvety grasp. The pug dropped the ball and sniffed his legs, appearing to sniff out rather than in.

"Alayne will be glad to come," he told her. "She sticks at home too much. The change will do her good."

"I get so lonely," she murmured, "and the few I care for never come to see me unless I beg them to."

"You should come to us. You're always very welcome." He smiled as he added—"Finch especially would welcome you."

"There you are wrong! No one cares so little for me as Finch. And we used to be friends." She led the way to garden chairs on a brick terrace. The pug picked up the ball and followed her with an air of disdain.

Renny took the cigarette she offered. "We all love you," he said. "But you mustn't mind Finch's way of showing his love. He's depressed, poor devil. We all are, in fact, since Eden's death. And now Auntie's gone and the poor old uncles are more down in the mouth than I've ever known them."

"It's all very sad," she answered. "I don't think that, as a family, we're made for happiness. We don't conform to the pattern, and people hate us for that."

He looked at her a little doubtfully, for he did not, in his mind, include her in the family. She was a connection but not one of the family. Still she had Gran's hot blood in her veins. She was no mere outsider. And if she married Finch, she would be one of them. He felt sure that she wanted to marry Finch. He said:

"Well, I think most of us are fairly conventional—all perhaps but you and Finch—and poor Eden, of course. You and Finch are artists and you should be together more."

"He hates me, I tell you!"

"And you love him?" He spoke in a matter-of-fact tone.

She bowed her head and the pug in her lap peered inquisitively into her face.

"Finch doesn't hate you but he's very nervy just now. He's avoiding everyone. Sometimes when I come into a room I catch a glimpse of him gliding out. He has always been a queer fellow. The right sort of woman could do what she liked with him. Make a man of him. He's a genius, but he's not a man."

"What can I do?"

"Have him here."

"When he comes, he draws into himself. We are farther apart than ever."

"He is afraid of being alone with you. You should ask someone else as well. Why not have him here with Alayne? She'd like to see you two marry. She told me so. She thinks it would be the happiest thing for you both."

A pale light, as though from within, lighted Sarah's face. "Oh, if Alayne would help me, I'd do anything on earth for her. I've never had initiative. I wait in corners, reaching toward what I want, but I won't venture out. I'm helpless. My aunt broke my will, as she put it, when I was a child."

"No, no, my girl!" thought Renny, "you've a will like iron." He said:

"Alayne and I will do all we can to help. It is more perhaps than you think."

"I wish there were something I could do for you. I know it's a difficult time."

He looked at her a little distantly. "There is nothing."

They fell silent, lost in their own thoughts. The pug smacked his lips repeatedly, tasting something imaginary, and, at last, swallowed it.

Renny asked then—"How are your investments? Everything all right?"

It was a moment before she could recall her mind from her thoughts. Then she answered:

"No. Some stocks have gone down terribly. The real estate is all right."

His eyes glowed. "It's the only thing.... I've just been wondering how you would like to take a mortgage on Jalna. It's a beautiful place, isn't it? We've never borrowed a penny on it but I'm driven now. And I'd rather it was you—in fact, you are the only person on earth I can bear the thought of holding a mortgage on it. You're one of us—or will be soon. It would be a family affair."

His weather-beaten face looked eagerly into hers. He was so afraid she would refuse that he talked excitedly, giving her no opening to reply. He poured out his love for Jalna, extolled its unique beauties, urged its soundness as an investment. She sat listening, looking at him out of her narrow eyes, breathing quickly through her narrow nostrils, her small, secretive mouth compressed. The sunlight played on the intricate black braids of her hair, it discovered no flaw on her white skin.

When, at last, he was silent, waiting almost miserably for her reply, she answered:

"I shall be glad to do as you say." She was willing as a child to be guided by him. He could have embraced her.

But he insisted that he should pay a high interest on the mortgage. It was agreed that nothing should be said to the family of the transaction until it was necessary to tell them.

They lunched in the exhilarating intimacy of conspirators. She confessed to him that she had never loved Arthur Leigh, and he confided to her that Alayne often misunderstood him and that occasionally they quarrelled.

XXVI

LOVE'S AWAKENING

When it was suggested to Finch that he should go with Alayne to visit Sarah, his impulse was to refuse. But Alayne urged him and he gave way, partly to please her, partly because Jalna was becoming unbearable to him. He missed Augusta, in whom he woke the only motherliness she ever felt, and the burden of his uncles' depression pressed down on him. He despised himself for being irritated by the sight of Wakefield's happy sunburnt face, his ready laughter when there was so little to laugh at. He felt ashamed of the brutal way in which he sometimes spoke to the boy, but the words would blaze forth before he could help himself, and he was the more ashamed because of the magnanimous spirit in which Wakefield accepted his roughness.

The other members of the family were relieved by his absence. They were tired of seeing him always going out of a room as they entered it.

Renny drove Alayne and Finch to Sarah's house, wearing the mysterious smile that was puzzling them in these days. When he met Sarah the smile was replaced by a look of concentrated innocence that sat strangely on his hard, highly coloured features.

Sarah's attitude toward Finch was aloof. Her hands, when they touched his, cool and renunciatory. Still, his spirit responded to the quickening influence of her nearness. He could not be in the house with her and not feel the old enchantment circling them about. Even though Sarah spoke little to him he knew that she was always watching him.

She and Alayne sat together on the terrace and left the hammock-couch under its striped white-and-green awning to him. There was a garden pool circled by irises and a magnolia-tree. Most of the flowers in the garden were white and heavy-scented.

Alayne thought that a marriage with Sarah was the perfect thing for Finch. She was not too sensitive but she was strangely and subtly alive.

The weather continued in settled loveliness. Each day imitated the one preceding, adding to it the brightness of advancing summer. Only occasionally a small cloud stole shyly across the steady blue of the sky. It was hot by day but at night a coolness came. The gardener soaked the lawn from the hose and the flowers went to sleep with wet petals.

Finch improved in looks and spirits more quickly than Alayne had dared hope. He sought out Sarah and her instead of shunning them.

At the end of the week Alayne left. Meg had been keeping her child for her and she dreaded to hear what mischief or tempers might have upset Meg's house.

When she was gone and Sarah and Finch were alone together, they were startled by the change her going made in their relations. They did not know what to say to each other. This new intimacy frightened them. Alayne's presence had held them together and kept them apart. They wandered about house and garden, avoiding each other. When they were together every word they spoke seemed profoundly significant. Sarah would think—"Oh, why did I say that? I shall drive him away!" Or—"That hardness in his voice is a sign of his hate."

Finch would think—"Why did she say that? I believe that she is trying to tell me that I mean nothing to her." Or—"I must not give myself away—must not let her know how being alone with her affects me."

Hour by hour his strength and vitality increased. He was getting well and strong. He felt life and the desire for life abounding within him. A reaction against the melancholy of winter and spring had begun. The hot summer sun, the warm moonlit nights, filled him with a sense of power to enjoy. A sensual magnetism drew him toward Sarah. He began to realise that he drew a strange nourishment from her. He was stronger for her nearness. Yet, if she had her way, she would hold him a prisoner. The thought of bonds was horrible to him.

When they went out together he was restive to return to their isolation.

She said, at the end of the second week:

"I am going to sell this place."

He hid his surprise.

"I thought you were quite settled here."

"Me settled here? Oh no. I'm too much an outsider. I shall sell it and go back to Ireland."

He said politely—"We'd miss you, Sarah."

"The others may—a very little. Not you. You're too much absorbed by yourself—your music—and that is right."

"You are unjust. I should miss you terribly." He added quickly —"You are a link with so much that has been beautiful in my life."

"Well, perhaps—a link. But a link is not in itself important. . . . It will soon be as though you had never seen me."

"And what about you? Will you forget me so easily?"

She was desperate. She threw off the veil of her concealment. "You will be always with me."

"Sarah, I can't let you go! I—I need you. I'll lose something, if you go, that no one else can give me. Why should you want to leave me?"

A quiver trespassed the immobility of her lips. She said:

"I must leave you. It is because of you that I must go. Don't let us talk about it. . . . But I had to tell you."

He rose quickly and left the room which opened on to the garden. He went to the far end and stood among the flowering shrubs, listening to the hurried beat of his own heart. "I'll go home," he muttered aloud. "I'll go home. I won't stay here. She's cruel. She wants to torment me."

He could not see her side of any question. It was always that she was cruel—that she wanted to torment him.

The tea was set on the brick terrace and he saw her waiting for him. He crossed the warm sun-splashed grass and approached her with a dark brow. She saw his strong lithe movements, how his face had filled out in the past fortnight. But, when he drew close, she looked down at the tea-cups.

He said, after a silence:

"I must go home. I really should not have stayed so long. It's been frightfully good of you to have me."

Her fingers were pressed to her cheek and he saw the pressure increase against its white firmness. But she said, almost coldly:

"I think the change has done you good. I'm glad of that."

She did not oppose him when he suggested going that evening. They spoke little to the time of his leaving, when he held her hand for a moment and thanked her stiffly for her hospitality. He left her standing by the magnolia-tree, the pug sitting at her feet.

As the train moved past the summer fields and the lake he began to feel that he had torn himself from all that was most desirable in life. Torn himself from one who desired him, to return to the intricate relations of his family, to not one of whom he was necessary, a house heavy with memories of Eden. He shrank from the house and the people in it. He sank lower in his seat, staring gloomily out of the window.

He was roused by the name of the station preceding his own. The woman in the seat opposite was alighting there. She was old and laden with packages. He found himself helping her with them, then following her to the platform. He found himself watching the train steam out of the station, with no thought of the suitcase he had left in the rack.

It was growing dark as he stood waiting for a bus. It came and he climbed into it, found it almost empty and, pulling his hat over his eyes, settled himself in a corner. He did not ask himself why he was returning to Sarah moved by an impulse stronger than that which had driven him from her. Without question he accepted the fact that he could not, at this moment, do without her. He did not even ask himself what he would say to her in explanation of a so abrupt change of mind. He slumped in his corner, clasping his knee in his hands, his bony wrists projecting from his sleeves, thought almost suspended. Only instinct was alive, turning toward Sarah.

The light had faded from the sky and the street lamps passed in blurred procession outside the pane. In the town the streets were beginning to fill with the evening crowd, working men, clerks and their girls, walking arm in arm, and sometimes groups of laughing girls together. Finch gave them a sidelong glance from under the brim of his hat but there was an unseeing look in his eyes.

After the bus it was necessary to take a taxi. As he got into it he remembered the suitcase he had left in the train and he gave a growl of derision. What a fool he was! Rushing away like that. . . . Losing his suitcase. . . . Rushing back. . . . But he must return to Sarah—come what may.

What if she had gone out? He pressed his face to the window and peered out to see if the house were in darkness. The street was dark and quiet. Yes, there were softly shaded lights in the house. . . .

He paid the driver and went slowly toward the door. Sarah had given him a latch-key which he had forgotten to return. He went into the house and stood motionless in the empty drawing-room.

The pug had heard him come in and it now entered and came to him with an amused, cynical expression. There was a cool, detached, humorous expression in its wrinkled face. It seemed to be saying—"You are a fool, but it is not yet too late. Escape while there is time."

What irrevocable thing was he contemplating? Offering himself. Binding himself, for ever and for ever. That pale china clock was ticking away the hours, ticking away the life which he was passionately eager to make the most of. And he was going to offer his young, free life to another . . . to be bound . . . to be enslaved . . . not to art . . . but to Sarah's white flesh, to Sarah's black hair, to her desire. . . .

No, no, he could not do it! Now he was awake. He could see clearly the danger of it. Why had he ever thought of coming back! But yet. . . . Indecision moved him this way and that as a reed in conflicting currents. He stood pulling at his lip, staring, with an expression of fear, at his reflection in a mirror.

When Sarah opened the door he backed away from her as though she were a ghost. And like a ghost, she was so pale, she moved glidingly toward him.

"I—I've come back," he stammered.

"Yes?" She looked at him expectantly.

"Sarah!" He ceased to move backward and she to move forward. They stood rigid. The pug stood between them with an air of resentful solemnity.

Then the enchantment of her presence overcame his fears. Fate could not touch him with her always beside him. She would always be there to pour out his love upon. Aphrodite to whom he might offer his body. . . . From retreating he advanced, and she stood waiting.

XXVII

THE FAMILY AGAINST HIM

MAURICE and Meg were overheated when they reached the shady corner of the lawn where Nicholas and Ernest were sitting, each with a glass of barley water in front of him and a slowly swaying fan in his hand. Alayne had been reading aloud to them and had left the book upside-down on her chair while she went into the house in answer to the telephone. It was ninety degrees in the shade.

The two uncles smiled their welcome at the advancing pair, for a call from them was an unexpected pleasure on such an afternoon.

"Meggie does look hot, poor creature," observed Ernest, "but then she's getting so stout."

"Maurice is heavy, too. He looks older." Nicholas then called out:

"You are courageous! Come and have some barley water. There's nothing better for cooling one."

"Oh dear, oh dear!" cried Meg. "This is the hottest day yet! But how comfortable you are here! There's always a breeze stirring Jalna. It's so different from the hollow where we are stuck." She sank into a chair.

Maurice, dropping to the grass, uttered a deprecating grunt. "I can't feel much difference," he said. "It's hellish everywhere."

Nicholas quickly drained his glass and refilled it for Maurice, his handsome old hand with the heavy seal ring shaking a good deal, so that some of the liquid was spilt on the rustic table.

Meg took up Alayne's glass. "Whose is this?" she asked. "Alayne's? Well, she won't mind if I finish it. . . . Oh, how delicious! . . . And how cool!"

"It must have been very hot coming through the ravine," said Ernest, fanning her. "You should have waited till later in the day."

Maurice replied—"As a matter of fact, we wanted to get here before Renny returned. We've something we want to talk over with you."

Meg refilled her glass to the brim. "Yes, Maurice, tell them about it quickly, while we are alone. For I suppose Alayne will soon be out. I've never known anyone who seemed to be always on deck as she is."

226

"She's a good girl, a good girl," said Nicholas.

Ernest leaned forward with intense interest but still fanning Meg. "Do tell us what you have in mind. As you say, we shan't be alone for long."

Maurice gave a grim laugh. "She'll soon have to know all about it. Perhaps she will be able to solve the mystery."

Ernest drew a deep breath. "The mystery! What mystery? I do hope there is nothing wrong."

"As far as I am concerned," answered Maurice, "there is nothing wrong. As for Renny—he's got his own way—as he usually does. He's bought the land I was subdividing—lock, stock, and barrel. Paid me cash for it!"

"Good God!" ejaculated Nicholas. "But how could he? Where did he get the money?"

Ernest exclaimed—"But what about the lots you had sold? There were two bungalows going up! What about them?"

"Oh, they were barely begun. But he bought them and the lots too. He bought everything. The first time any land has been added to Jalna for a good many years, eh?"

"Well, well, well," said Nicholas, grinning with satisfaction, "this beats all! I must say I admire him for that. A slice of Vaughanlands for Jalna, eh?"

"Mamma would have been pleased to have seen a stop put to those bungalows," said Ernest. "I've known for several days that Renny had something up his sleeve. Some scheme or other. And I worried a little, for I don't always see eye to eye with him in his schemes. When did the transaction take place?"

"This morning. He came over in a most hilarious mood. He laughed and ragged me about the bungalows for quite a while before he came to the point. Then suddenly he got rather disagreeable. Demanded what was my lowest price for the damned land. I told him and he wrote me a cheque on the spot. Then he told me that he had bought the four lots and the buildings. Of course, I'm awfully glad for your sakes and ours too, but I'm wondering how it all came about. Meg thought perhaps you'd know."

"There is only one way," said Ernest, "and that is Alayne's private means. She must have handed that over to him."

"Well, and I think she should," said Meg. "If I had money I should consider it my duty to give it to Maurice at such a time as this. A wife must sacrifice herself."

They saw Alayne coming toward them across the lawn. Temperate greetings were exchanged.

"Shall I tell her?" Ernest had whispered, and Meg had nodded an affirmative. He therefore said, with a playful air:

"Alayne, dear, we've heard the news! And we're delighted, every one of us. It's such a relief to think that the subdivision is no longer necessary."

"All we wonder," said Meg, "is that you didn't do it before."

"Do what before?"

"Why, buy the land and the lots before!"

"I'm quite in the dark," Alayne returned, sitting down on the seat beside Nicholas. There was both coldness and apprehension in her voice.

"Oh, well," said Maurice, "if you don't want us to talk about it, we won't."

"I have not the faintest idea what you refer to. Perhaps if you explained I should understand."

The other four looked at each other blankly. Then Nicholas said:

"Maurice has just been telling us that Renny has bought the land he was subdividing as well as the lots already sold. We thought you would probably have talked it over with him."

"It is news to me," said Alayne, and a flush came into her cheeks.

"But where else could he have got the money?" asked Meg.

"I don't know, I'm sure." She spoke with intense irritation.

Nicholas demanded of Maurice—"Why didn't you ask him plump and plain? I think you'd have been quite justified."

Ernest asked gently—"Have you cashed the cheque?"

Maurice grinned. "Yes, I went into the bank at once. Not that I had any doubts of him!"

"Well, I should hope not!" exclaimed Meg hotly.

"Of course not, of course not," Ernest hastened to say, "but it's all so extraordinary! I thought perhaps the heat—it's very intense—might have gone to his head. He's really been rather odd lately."

"The money was there in hard cash," said Maurice. "In the mood he was, I didn't like to ask him where he got it. . . ."

"I know!" cried Meg. "Finch!"

The certainty of this conclusion pricked the bubble of their conjecture. They only wondered it had not been thought of before. Alayne was aghast.

"But," she said, "Finch has so little left of his grandmother's money! Not more than fifteen thousand dollars, I think. It would take all of it, wouldn't it?"

"Renny gave me a cheque for twelve thousand dollars," said Maurice tersely.

"What a pity he is not here!" cried Ernest.

"We could call him on the telephone," suggested Meg.

Nicholas said—"I cannot quite believe that Renny would borrow from Finch. He's always been against touching that money. I know he wanted Finch to buy the land himself and that Finch refused. No— I think we're off the scent! I think he's got it in some other way."

"May he not have sold some stocks of his own?" suggested Ernest.

"Any stocks he has are of little account now," said Maurice. "But he holds a mortgage or two, doesn't he?"

Nicholas rumbled—"Can't get anything out of those. He told me so. And he'd never foreclose—unless Jalna itself was at stake." He turned his eyes toward the house steeped in sunshine. He asked of Alayne then:

"Who was it on the telephone?"

"Sarah. Finch is staying a little longer with her."

Ernest frowned. "I don't think it is quite proper. People will be talking."

Meg exclaimed—"I wonder if it might possibly be Sarah! She is such a dear girl! I'm sure it would make her very happy to help Renny."

The eyes of the sisters-in-law met with only half-concealed dislike. Alayne said:

"I hope and pray that she has done nothing of the sort."

"She never would," said Nicholas, "without good security. That girl is as shrewd as the devil."

"But however Renny got the money," cried Ernest, "what a relief to think we shall not have those terrible neighbours!"

"And a new piece of land is added to the estate," said his brother. "That's very nice. Augusta will be pleased."

The sound of horse's hooves moving in a walk came to them from the drive. The group on the lawn turned their heads as one. Between the branches of the evergreens they saw the gleam of a bright chestnut flank and in a moment horse and rider appeared and hesitated before turning in the direction of the stable.

Nicholas called out impatiently:

"Come here! We want you. We're on tenterhooks of excitement."

Renny turned the mare's head in their direction, crossed the intervening stretch of lawn, and slid from the saddle. A glance at the faces about him discovered on what their minds were bent. . . . An aeroplane was flying overhead and he raised his eyes to its swift glitter and stood thus, reins on arm, as though enthralled.

"One would think," observed Meg, "that you'd never seen an aeroplane before!"

"I've never seen a prettier bit of gliding."

Ernest peered skyward. "It hurts my eyes," he said.

"Come, come, come," urged Nicholas. "Enlighten us about this amazing deal. You can't get out of that, you know. Maurice and Meg have been telling how you've saved the situation—and acquired new acres for Jalna into the bargain."

The aeroplane had disappeared. Renny turned his gaze inquiringly to Maurice. "What have you told them?" he asked.

Maurice's tone was impatient. "All I know. That you bought the land and paid cash for it, and are going to tear down what has been built on it."

Renny grinned genially at his uncles but avoided the eyes of his sister and his wife. He said:

"Well, then, there's nothing more to tell. It'll be good fun pulling those shacks down, won't it?"

Ernest stretched out his hand and clasped Renny's.

"My dear boy, this is a happy moment for me!"

The slender white hand and the muscular brown one gripped.

"I'm glad of that, Uncle Ernie."

Alayne, unable to contain herself any longer, exclaimed:

"It strikes me that you are all very optimistic. I am wondering what is to be made out of that land in return for the investment."

"It's good land," said Maurice, "but I don't think Renny bought it for crops."

"He bought it," said Meg, "for an ideal."

"Then how," asked Alayne, her voice trembling with anger, "is he to repay his debt?"

"He has probably arranged that," returned Meg stiffly. "I suppose it depends on whom he borrowed from."

Nicholas sent a sudden penetrating glance at Renny.

"Meg was wondering," he said, "if it might be Sarah."

Renny sprang up and caught the mare, which was now cropping the grass near them, by the bridle. She had one of her feet planted on the flower border. He spoke roughly to her and cuffed her head. She bit at him and reared. They showed their teeth at each other, but there was a subtle understanding between them. She reared, danced, dipped, like a plunging ship while he held her bridle, cuffed her, encouraged her. It was upsetting for those about the table, but it made them certain that it was Sarah who had given him the loan. He had not been able to face them.

But his expression, when he rejoined the circle, was brazen. "Yes, it was Sarah," he admitted.

"I'd never have believed it of her," cried Nicholas. "She's a trump!"

"To think of Sarah coming to the rescue!" said Ernest.

Meg looked complacent. "I was the one who guessed."

Alayne stared at Renny, dismayed.

Before there was further comment Piers appeared suddenly from the direction of the stables. His face was crimson and his thin shirt clung in damp patches to his body. He cast a quick look about and said:

"So you've heard the news!"

"Yes," answered Ernest; "and it has made us very happy."

"A great day for us," added Nicholas.

Piers was bewildered. "Happy! A great day! You must be talking about something else. I was speaking of Mrs. Lebraux losing her place." He turned to Renny. "I suppose you know all about it?"

Renny nodded.

Meg exclaimed—"Oh, the poor thing! Whatever will she do? Who told you, Piers?"

"Stone, who holds the mortgage. He's foreclosed. He came to see me just now about buying some corn. He mentioned it quite casually, as though he expected I'd know all about it, and then told me that Renny had bought the house from him. He'd been going to tear it down. What are you going to do with it, Renny?"

There was too much mystery in all this. There was something sinister in it. They looked at each other, they looked at Renny, and waited with misgiving in their hearts.

"Well——" He tried to speak confidently, as though he expected their approval, but how could he tell them what he had in mind to do?

"Do sit down," said Meg, "and tell us all about it!"

He dropped to the grass beside her chair. Piers remained standing.

"Well " he repeated, and began to laugh to drown out his own voice. He looked toward his mare as though hopeful that she might again offer distraction, but she stood immobile, her eyes fixed on him, inquiring like the others.

Meg said—"I've always hated this way of laughing when there's nothing to laugh at."

Nicholas, chin in hand, stared compellingly at him.

He ceased laughing. His face hardened and he said abruptly:

"I'm going to move the house from the fox-farm and put it on the land I've just bought from Maurice."

For a moment they could scarcely take in his meaning.

Ernest stammered—"But—I don't see—but why in the world should you do that? Why, it would look appalling there! It's a particularly ugly house."

Nicholas said—"It would look as bad as—even worse than—the bungalows. You can't do it! It's impossible!"

"What is the idea?" asked Piers. "Are Mrs. Lebraux and Pauline to live there?"

Renny looked up at his brother challengingly.

"Have you anything to say against them as neighbours?"

"But the foxes!" interrupted Meg. "They wouldn't bring their foxes, would they?"

"Of course they'll bring their foxes."

"But it would be horrible! A pack of yapping, evil-smelling wild animals. And the hideous house! And the more hideous wire enclosures——" She turned to Maurice. "We're against that, aren't we?"

Maurice replied—"I'd never have sold him the land if I'd known of it. It will depreciate both our properties."

Nicholas heaved himself forward on the garden seat and leaned toward Renny.

"It's doubtless very compassionate of you," he said sonorously, "to have thought of helping Mrs. Lebraux and her daughter in this way, but—I forbid it—yes, I must forbid it in the name of my mother, who would turn over in her grave if she knew of it."

"But she can't know of it," returned Renny; "so why harrow ourselves over what she would think? As for the fox-farm—you will scarcely know that it is there."

"It will be there for every passer-by to see," put in Ernest, striking his hand on the table. "As Maurice says, it will depreciate the property on both sides. We shall hear it, smell it, be disgusted by it, with every breath we draw!"

Meg interjected—"It's the menagerie effect that's so appalling to me. Wild animals raging about. Peering through the netting. And Mrs. Lebraux, in a man's overall, working among them like a man!"

"I shouldn't worry, Meggie, if I were you," said Piers. "The house will fall to pieces when they move it."

"No, it won't!" said Renny. "It's a well-built house. I have engaged a good man for the job."

"I have never known you, Renny," said Nicholas, "to do anything so callous as this!"

Ernest said—"To think that we were feeling so happy over the acquiring of this new land and the abolishing of the bungalows—and then to have to face—but we won't face it!" He rose and began to walk about excitedly. "It must not be. Alayne, surely you have some influence with him! Surely you can use it to make Renny see how wrong this is!"

Alayne said icily—"I'd rather not interfere. If you wish to influence Renny—it would be better for you to go to Mrs. Lebraux."

"I shall! I shall!" cried Ernest. "Surely she can't be so brazen as to come where she's not wanted!"

"It will be a joke for the country-side," said Maurice, "if the scheme is carried through."

Renny turned on him savagely. "What the hell do you mean? There is no joke about it. I have bought the land and I will put on it what I damned well choose."

"You bought it under false pretences! You said that you couldn't stand the thought of a dozen small houses there, and now you're planting a fox-farm."

"I am allowing two women—friends of ours—to keep foxes there. Very different from the thirty or forty people who would have swarmed over your lots." He turned appealingly to his uncles. "Surely you can see the difference. And what was I to do? That child and her mother are losing everything!"

Piers broke in. "I'm all at sea. When did you buy the land? And how?"

Meg answered for Renny. "He has just bought it. Sarah lent him the money."

Nicholas said—"Very well. If you must help those women, do! Let them have land, but, for God's sake, let it be at the back of the estate, not the front!"

"Yes, yes," cried Ernest, "there are fields back there—bits of wood behind which they would scarcely be noticed. Let us, by all means, give them a few acres there. I'll be the first to agree to that."

"There are two things against that," replied Renny. "One is that it would be almost impossible to move the house so far, and too expensive. The other that they would be much too isolated. They must be on a main road. For their business and for their own sakes. They have no car. They're obliged to walk to village and bus. Things are hard enough for them as it is. What surprises me is that you should all take the high and mighty stand you do." He turned

233

his eyes accusingly on Alayne. "I should have expected you to be more broad-minded."

"I have said nothing to oppose you."

"You have said nothing to help me. Disapproval has stuck out all over you."

Piers said—"I guess that Alayne is like I am—speechless at Sarah's generosity. We're both wondering what security you've given Sarah. Have you given her Finch? Or a mortgage on Jalna?"

At the first question a quiver, as of sardonic mirth, passed through the circle. At the second an electric tremor shook them into horrid confusion. The air was stifling. It was full of thunder. Every eye turned, startled and menacing, on Renny.

They needed no answer from him. The muscular contracting of his face, the quick intake of his breath, was enough. The question shot by Piers had caught him unprepared. He made a grimace, expressing both chagrin and defiance. He said:

"I was driven to it."

If only he had denied it! If he had made them believe, against the evidence of his guilty grimace, that he had committed no such outrage against them and against Jalna! Then perhaps Nicholas would not have turned so ghastly grey in the face; Ernest would not have clutched his throat and tried in vain to utter a sound; Meg not have burst into tears; Maurice not have looked at him with such horror; Alayne with something like hate; and Piers might have restrained the blasphemous oath.

Wakefield, still harbouring his childish fear of thunder, had left his work at the signs of approaching storm and now came running toward them, half laughing, wet with sweat. At sight of them the laughter died on his lips. He cried:

"What's the matter? Has the house been struck?"

Nicholas answered in a terrible voice—"Yes, the house has been struck! Look at it, all of you. It's been blasted!"

Meg threw herself into Piers' arms and clung to him. They all turned their eyes to the house which faced them, clothed in its creepers, their greenness and the dark red of its bricks intensified by the sulphurous light from the low, threatening sky. The house looked at them unblinkingly from its windows, not in reproach, it seemed, but in threatening aloofness. It appeared to recede from them, to draw away. "I am no longer yours," it seemed to say; "you are no longer mine. A barrier is between us."

Wakefield cried—"But I don't see it! I don't see the fire! Where is it? Oh, Meggie, don't cry! Renny, what's the matter?"

Nicholas caught him by the arm.

"The house has not been struck by lightning—but in another way," he said. He pointed to Renny, who had sprung to his feet. "He'll tell you. You've admired him. Let him tell you what he's done to Jalna."

Renny exclaimed—"By God, I won't have you turn the boy against me!"

"But what is it? What is it? I don't understand!" Wakefield drew away from Nicholas and faced Renny.

Renny said—"They're all after me because I've borrowed money on Jalna. I had to stop that building on Maurice's place and I had to help Pauline."

"That's shrewd of you," said Piers. "Why didn't you say Clara?"

"Oh, the deceit of him!" wept Meg. "If Gran knew of this!"

"It will be the end of me," Ernest got out in a strangled voice and supported himself against the table.

Renny said harshly—"You talk like an old fool! I have not lost the place."

"I'll thank you," said Nicholas, "not to insult my brother."

"Oh, he doesn't care what he does," said Meg, wiping her eyes. "None of us means anything to him."

A few heavy drops of rain fell. A roll of thunder came jarring from the black west as though it overthrew obstacles to approach them.

"I'll stick by you, Renny," said Wake. "I'm on your side, always."

Piers sneered—"You'd stick to the devil if you could get anything out of him."

"You'll see!" cried Ernest. "Sarah will be the mistress of Jalna! It will kill me."

"And Finch will be the master," said Piers. "Mark my words, he'll marry her. He'll line his nest if he plucks the down from our breasts to do it."

Alayne looked wildly about her. "I'm going in," she said, and turned toward the house.

Meg had never felt in such accord with her. She went and put her arm about her. "Poor dear," she said, "you look as white as a sheet. You're breaking your wife's heart, Renny. Anyone can see that. I've watched her failing for months."

The words, Meg's tender touch, were too much for Alayne. She too burst into tears.

A tawny radiance illumined their figures. The mare's side shone like metal. She lifted her lip in a wry distortion.

Piers fixed his prominent eyes on Alayne.

"No wonder she cries," he said. "This news is enough to make a man cry."

"It's killing me," reiterated Ernest, pressing his hand to his side.

Nicholas swept out his arm. "All this is on your head, Renny!" His gesture included the house, with its air of receding from them, his distraught brother, the weeping women, and the mouthing mare.

As Nicholas spoke the thunder pealed like a bell in simultaneous consent with a dazzling flash that struck the oak-tree near them, ripping off a strip of its bark from top to root. The sun disappeared and the rain began to fall in torrents.

Ernest cried—"There's a sign! There's a sign! The oak-tree blasted. I see the end of this!"

"Take him in the house," Renny said to Piers. "Give him a spot of brandy." He spoke coolly, but his lips were pale. He cast a bitter look after his wife and his sister, who had now reached the shelter of the porch.

Nicholas was trying to heave himself out of the garden seat. The rain beat on his grey head. Renny took him by the arm, but he planted his spread hand on his chest and thrust him away, growling:

"Don't touch me! I don't want your help."

Wakefield went to him and helped him up.

Renny caught the reins of the mare and sprang into the saddle. She stood a moment rigid, fierce, beautiful in her naked symmetry, divided between love and hate of him, then, tossing her head as the hailstones struck her, fumed galloping toward the stables.

Nicholas hobbled houseward, weighing heavily on Wakefield. He muttered to himself—"It's come to this, eh? Well, well, well. A pretty pass. I wish I'd never lived to see this day. . . ."

XXVIII

SULTRY WEATHER

THE storm did not cool the air or disperse the thunder-clouds. They lingered, shouldering each other on the horizon, their edges burnished by the blazing sun, now and then a troubled mutter echoing through their sultry depths. Every grass-blade held its jewel, and the timid movement of the birds among the leaves scattered bright drops. The scene was highly coloured and still, but without tranquillity.

Was it cooler indoors or out? Alayne wondered. Should she go up to her room where she would be undisturbed, or seek peace out of doors where these walls would not press in on her? If only some other people had once lived in the house it would not be so permeated by the essence of the Whiteoaks. They had built it, lived in it, quarrelled and loved in it, died in it. Even Eden, who had not died in it, had left his restless spirit there. Strangely the thought of him gave her pain at this moment. She had never sorrowed for him. In her secret heart she had resented Renny's grief for him as a shadow on their love. But now she found her heart yearning over Eden. As though to protect herself against today's unhappiness, she reached back toward something in her past that might justly claim her tears. She saw herself and Eden, a happy girl and boy, new-married, just come to Jalna.

How gay he had been! How full of hope! She could see him springing up the stairs, light and strong, or sitting at his desk, his face upraised to hers, while she scarcely heard what he said for watching the play of his lips, the light in his eyes. She was glad she could remember him like that, glad that she had never seen him after he was ill.

She stood in the doorway and started as Piers came up behind her. She moved aside to let him pass, avoiding his eyes, but he stopped. He gave her a curious look.

"Well, I'm off," he said.

"I hope the hail has not injured your grain," she remarked, for the sake of saying something.

"I don't think so. It didn't last long. But the storm is not over yet."

"You think those clouds will come back? Which way is the wind?'

He stepped on to the drive. He wet his forefinger in his mouth and held it up. "South-east," he said. "They'll come back."

His usually fresh-coloured face looked pale and heavy. She was sorry for him.

"I regret this for your sake," she said, "more than for the others."

His mouth went down at the corners.

"It's rough on us all. For my part, I feel as though the earth weren't solid under me any more. It's given me a nasty jolt. I didn't believe it was in Renny to mortgage"—his tongue stumbled on the word—"to do such a thing."

"I know how you must feel," she said quickly. "But Renny—he is not always easy to understand, is he?"

"Do you seriously try?"

The question surprised her. She stammered.

"Yes—I think I try very hard." And she added bitterly—"I know that you think I have no influence over him."

"Well, I cannot help thinking that you might have more. He strikes me as a man who would naturally be greatly influenced by a woman he loved—and who understood him. Pheasant influences me a lot, though you wouldn't suspect it. I should think that Renny would have been afraid to—do what he's done without giving you a hint of it. It's your show, and your kid's show, as well as his. He should have been made to feel that."

"I know," she answered miserably.

He continued—"I don't know Mrs. Lebraux very well, but I do know that she understands him. If I were in your place——"

Alayne, looking at him, tried to picture him in her place.

"If I were in your place I'd tell him that if he brings her on to our land, I'd leave him and take my child too. He'll think all the more of you if you're firm. I've heard Meg say how much good a sound hiding did him when he was a boy. He loved the one who walloped him. If he thinks you'll stand *anything*—well, there's no knowing what he'll do."

Advice on her marriage relations from Piers! She was both embarrassed and touched. Yet his advice was not ingenuous.

Wakefield came out of the house. He cast a look of apprehension at the sky. Piers said sternly:

"You've been wasting a lot of time. Get a move on now. You must drive the milk-truck to the station tonight."

Wake puckered his forehead but moved resignedly toward the stables.

Alayne called after him—"Is Uncle Ernest feeling better?"

He answered over his shoulder—"Yes, thank you, Alayne. He is lying down. Uncle Nick and Meggie are with him."

Piers followed his brother without another glance at Alayne. She slowly descended the shallow steps to the gravel drive and, crossing the wet lawn, passed through a wicket-gate and went into the ravine. She stopped on the little rustic bridge that spanned the stream, reduced now to a trickle. She was startled to find Renny leaning against the railing, his unlighted pipe in his hand and a look of complete self-absorption shadowing his face. She turned away, thinking he might not see her, but he had heard her step and threw her a negative glance as though her coming had scarcely roused him.

If each had come here for privacy or coolness they were disappointed in both. The luxuriant growth of honeysuckle, rushes, and

238

long moist grass, the branches meeting overhead, kept out any breeze, and he and she stood face to face.

In emotional coherence pictures of the events of the last months rose before her, culminating in the picture of him standing on the bridge, as it were at bay. She saw the defensive light gathering in his eyes. He waited for her to speak.

She said—"It is very close here." She put her hands on the railing of the bridge and looked down into the stream.

"We have chosen a bad spot," he said. "There is no coolness here."

"Except between us."

"There is no coolness," he exclaimed, "in my feeling toward you! I'm hurt—yes, I'm terribly hurt that you'd say what you did!"

"About Mrs. Lebraux, you mean."

"Yes. I've given you no reason for that."

She flashed at him—"No reason! Think before you say that, Renny! Think of the hours you have spent in that house—when I was lonely!"

"You might have heard every word that was spoken! You might have been there with us—if you had not been so high and mighty. But no—you look down on her. She is not your intellectual equal, you think."

"Have I ever shown that attitude toward Pheasant or Meg?"

"They are in a different relationship. Clara Lebraux is my friend. Consequently you dislike her."

"I dislike her for herself. The thought of her as a near neighbour —brought here in such a theatrical way by you—is distasteful to me."

He said, broodingly—"You were never even kind to Pauline. You would not read French with her when she was getting no proper education. You've been hard."

"You accuse me of hardness—when it is you who are hard! Do you realise what a blow you have given your family today? Did you see Piers' face? I have been talking with him and——"

He interrupted—"Talking me over!"

"And why not? There's only one thing in Piers' mind—your borrowing money on Jalna."

"You didn't speak of Clara Lebraux?"

Denial was impossible to her. She did not reply.

"Everyone is against me!" he exclaimed. "And what is it all about? I have raised money on my property. Borrowed it from a friend—a cousin who is in love with my brother. I had to have it. I could not let things go on as they were. I've only done the decent thing."

239

Alayne's mind hovered about the thought of Clara. She said, in a cold voice:

"Mrs. Lebraux has a brother, hasn't she?"

"If once you met him, you'd expect nothing of him."

"And she and her daughter are as capable of looking after themselves as other women. Why should they lean on you?"

"They have no training of any kind. They couldn't find anything suitable for them to do."

"So we must be saddled with them!"

"You need never speak to them."

"As though I could ignore them, when they'll be at our very door!"

"You ignored Eden when he was dying at Vaughanlands!"

Good God, what was this he was throwing up at her? She steadied herself by the railing.

"Eden!" she said harshly. "What did you expect me to do about Eden?"

He answered with obvious effort—"I thought you might have gone to see him. You scarcely asked after him."

"But what would it have looked like—for me to go to him—he my divorced husband—and your brother?"

"Eden never hurt us. He made the way clear for us."

"He was unfaithful to me."

Renny made an impatient movement.

"He knew that you didn't love him any more."

"But I could not go to see him! I could not!" Desperately she turned and looked into his eyes. "Less than an hour ago I was thinking of Eden—feeling so terribly sorry about him."

"That was because you were angry at me."

"Be careful what you say to me, Renny! You have the power to cut me to the heart!"

"But not to make you happy!"

"You know very well how to make me happy! But you don't try. . . . You know better still how to make me unhappy. And—and——" Her voice broke.

"Go on! Go on!"

"You seldom miss an opportunity."

"Alayne!"

"It's true."

"You make me out a brute!"

"I say that you don't care how you hurt me. You even blame me for Eden's——"

He broke in—"Good God! I only meant that Eden had not hurt you by it. He must have seen that you didn't love him any more."

"He didn't see. I kept it hidden. He could not have known."

"You're very clever but you couldn't deceive Eden."

She cried furiously—"*Will* you leave him out of this? You are like all your family. You never let the dead rest. You think yourselves so strong. But you are neurotic, I tell you. You see everything distorted." She pointed to the pool beneath the bridge. "Like our faces down there. . . . You never see things clearly."

He looked down into the water.

"Do you?"

"I see that you're infatuated with that woman."

"I repeat that you might have heard every word we have exchanged and not been made jealous."

"Words are not all. Even Piers has remarked how well she understands you."

"I should think you would have too much pride to discuss our affairs with Piers."

"How can I have pride and live here?"

He had been nervously twitching at a bit of broken bark on the rustic railing. Now in his anger and hurt he tore it off in a long strip, leaving the smooth wood exposed. It dropped from his hand and fell into the stream. He turned and walked quickly away, leaving her alone on the bridge.

XXIX

BROKEN CHORDS

Renny found Clara Lebraux standing on a chair while she took down the curtains from the window of the dining-room. Standing so, with arms upraised and head thrown back, she gave the impression of a free and careless energy, but when she looked down at him over her shoulder, her face showed tired lines and it was troubled.

"I knocked," he said, "but no one came. I'd seen you at the window so I knew what you were doing. But—what a job in a heat like this!"

"I must get things ready," she answered. "Here, take this from me." She slanted the curtain-rod toward him.

He took it, and the brass rings slithered against his hand. He asked:

"Couldn't the curtains be moved as they are?"

"They must be washed." She proceeded to take down the other pair and, in stepping backward, would have fallen from the chair had he not caught her.

He set her on the floor. She was a solid weight.

"Well," he exclaimed, "it's a good thing you weren't alone! You might have hurt yourself."

"Oh, I don't think so," she answered. "I did that very thing when I was taking down the curtains in the parlour and I only rasped my ankle." She tilted her foot, which was covered only by a canvas sandal, and showed a raw spot on the ankle-bone, from which a trickle of blood stained the brown skin.

"I am getting a very stupid person," she said. "I turn dizzy for no reason at all."

"It's the weather." And he added compassionately—"And the worry."

"Oh, I'm as strong as a horse!"

"You have good blood apparently. But that spot should be touched with iodine."

She shrugged, and began to gather up the curtains. She said, in a casual tone:

"Wake has been here. He says your family is upset by the news of our moving to Jalna."

"Did he come here to tell you that?"

"No, no, I got it out of him. I knew you were telling them today. I really think we ought not to go. I shouldn't feel comfortable."

He expelled his breath sharply and sat down on the edge of the table and faced her.

"For heaven's sake!" he exclaimed, "don't ask me to talk any more of this affair. I thought it was all settled. My uncles and Piers are angry because I have raised money on the place. They were hilarious when they heard that I had bought the subdivision. It was the mortgage that upset them. But Sarah would never do anything against me. Finch would never let her. You'll see that they will marry. And, as soon as the times improve, I shall pay off my debt. In the meantime you might as well be living on that bit of land as not. I've bought your house and I must have somewhere to put it. Sometime I'll renovate it and perhaps Wake and Pauline will live there."

His look was both sanguine and masterful.

She asked—"How does your wife feel about it?"

"She is like the rest of us—rather unnerved by the heat."

"Well, she need scarcely know that we are there. With the

ravine between—we shall not see much of each other." But she frowned doubtfully as she folded the curtains.

As he watched her he recalled scenes in which they had taken part together. Times when he and she had held Lebraux in his bed by main force during his last delirious illness. Times when he had helped her with the farm-work or done things about the house for her. He had told Alayne the truth. Not a word had been exchanged between them which she might not have heard without cause for jealousy. Unless she might have been jealous of their tranquil understanding. . . . And Piers had tried to make trouble between him and Alayne—as though there were not trouble enough without his putting a finger in the pie!

Pauline came in, followed by Wakefield. She looked pale from the heat and she carried some drooping flowers in her hand. She said:

"I went to the station with Wakefield—on the truck. There was quite a breeze. He brought me back in it. It's at the gate."

"You seem to have got over your fear of storms," returned Clara. "Do you remember the day I came home and found you here with Renny—quite upset by the thunder?"

Pauline flushed. "I was very silly," she said in a low voice.

"Tell me about it!" cried Wakefield. "As my grandmother used to say—'I like to know what is going on about me.'"

Renny interrupted—"Did you leave the engine running?"

"Lord, yes!" He dashed out of the house.

Renny touched Pauline on the shoulder. "You must not let your mother back out of this move," he said. "We must get you away from here."

She drew back a little and Clara said:

"No need to worry over that! I shall be glad to part company from my old landlord."

Wakefield returned. He said—"When I was a lad I used to amuse myself by wondering whether I should be a bishop or a judge or a Prime Minister. But I turned out to be a truck driver and I'm absolutely happy! Tomorrow we begin to raze the foundations of Maurice's bungalows. I've always loved the word *raze*. It is so smooth and yet so deadly. Don't you love it, my mother-in-law?"

"I have no imagination," returned Clara stolidly.

"I'm afraid Pauline hasn't much, either. But I have enough for the three of us."

"Will you stay and have some supper?" asked Clara.

A roll of thunder answered her. The storm was coming back.

243

Renny and Wakefield got into the truck, the elder watching, with some trepidation, the erratic sidlings of the machine along the rough road. He had scarcely ever been in it before, and the sight of Wakefield driving such a vehicle was grotesque to him. Before they reached the sheds the storm was on them. By the time they reached the house they were wet through.

The work of obliterating all signs of building from the newly acquired land was soon under way. Renny himself took part in it, evincing a ruthless pleasure in tearing down the flimsy erections that had caused him so much chagrin. Maurice showed the same good-humoured interest in watching them pulled down as he had in their putting up. He had made up his mind that there should be no hard feeling between himself and Renny over the affair, but Meg, meeting Renny on the road, had refused to speak to him, had turned her face away. The house was shadowed by a feeling of bitter reproach. Ernest was resuming, one by one, his invalidish ways. He and Nicholas both avoided Renny, and at table they either addressed themselves to Alayne or talked in melancholy undertones of days gone by. Alayne would rather not have been so singled out by them, so definitely drawn to their side against Renny, for she felt something irrevocable in the tide thus moving them along, but she could not help herself. Something in her made it impossible for her to reach out to him, and he on his part felt himself in the position of one definitely in the wrong in the sight of his family. Wakefield alone was on his side, but he was still too much the child to oppose himself openly to his uncles. He sat silent at meals, wrapped in his own thoughts or perhaps teasing small Adeline, urging her to forwardness. She needed little urging and, young as she was, she was quite aware of the conflicting emotions about her. She would look long and speculatively upon the faces of Nicholas and Ernest or cast a defiant prideful look at her mother. She watched Renny's every movement, tried to handle her spoon and fork as he did his, and refused to touch any food he did not like. If he said his bacon was under-cooked she would not eat hers, and her infant opposition caused Alayne an irritation quite beyond its significance, for she saw in it a forecast of the future. At every opportunity her child would run from the house and follow Renny to the stables. He encouraged her in this, and Alayne, in proud resentment, let them have their way, so Adeline was nearly always dirty and smelling of the horses and with horsy words on her lips.

When Finch returned from his visit to Sarah the state of affairs was concisely put before him by Piers. Shut in the piggery together, Piers poured out the sorry tale of the spiritual disruption of Jalna and prophesied to Finch that he would one day be its master.

All Finch could do was to pull at his sensitive underlip and reiterate—"Well, well, well."

He slunk to the dinner-table not knowing, but feeling sure that he must soon declare, which side he was on. The haggard looks of the elderly men distressed him. The rings under Alayne's eyes, her compressed lips, moved him to compassion. The look, reserved, suspicious, and hang-dog, on Renny's face, his sudden staccato outbursts of mirth at Adeline's capers, repelled him. But it was Wakefield who hastened his decision. Wakefield's attitude of intimate understanding toward Renny, and his encouragement of Adeline's naughtiness, roused Finch's resentment. The boy was modelling himself on Renny.

When Renny dropped a bit of meat to his spaniel and Adeline threw half hers on the floor, Wakefield said, apparently addressing the portrait of his grandmother:

"She is a perfect Court."

Renny grinned at Wakefield. Alayne kept her eyes resolutely on her plate. Nicholas and Ernest, cloaked in gloom, seemed scarcely conscious of what went on about them.

What a home-coming! Finch thought. Why had he been kept in darkness as to the state of affairs at Jalna? Probably the family had decided that his mind must not be distracted from his love-making. And Sarah had kept her share in the business a secret from him. Was that a sign that she would always tell him just what she chose? Or had Renny perhaps exacted a promise of secrecy from her? The food stuck in his throat.

After the meal he lighted a cigarette and went out into the porch. It was a warm, sunless, sultry day in August. The chorus of locusts was subdued. The heavy air was scented with new-mown grass. All this was of the essence of home.

Renny followed and stood beside him. He said:

"I can't tell you how pleased I am about your engagement to Sarah. I don't know when I've been so pleased with one of you boys. Sarah and you are just suited to each other." He gave Finch's shoulder a squeeze. "And she has means, too. That's not to be sneezed at."

By God, thought Finch, he should not have mentioned her means! He mumbled:

"I'm glad you're pleased. I don't know if we are suited. . . . I—we—we're awfully in love. . . ."

"Of course you are! There's nothing like it. You two will be perfectly happy. Now, when are you going to get married?"

"In the spring. Then we're going to Paris. I want to study there. And Sarah likes it. She'll sell her house here."

"Good! But don't be away too long. You will stay with us when you come back. Alayne likes Sarah. It makes things so much more comfortable when the women like each other. You'll find that out."

"Yes," returned Finch heavily. He hoped Renny would not speak of the mortgage, but he did.

"It took a load off my mind, I can tell you," he said, "to get that loan from Sarah. It eased things up all round. I had a number of small anxieties—as well as the big ones. But everything is all right now." His tone was determinedly happy. His brown eyes looked challengingly into Finch's.

"The uncles aren't very brisk," answered Finch. "Uncle Ernest seems rather weak on his pins."

Renny's face fell. "I know, I know. They took it very hard. In fact"—he lowered his voice—"they and Piers and Meg have been pretty disagreeable to me ever since. But I pay no attention. Simply let them stew in their own juice."

They could hear Ernest draggingly ascend the stairs for his afternoon rest. Nicholas rumble a complaint to Wragge. Adeline scream as Alayne prevented her following her father to the porch. Wakefield whistle "Live, Laugh, and Love" as he strolled toward the barn.

"I must be off too," said Renny, and went down the steps to the drive.

Finch looked at his tall, sinewy figure. What a source of strength he had been to the family. For twelve years Gran had lived on his bounty while she hoarded her own fortune. Now, for nearly twenty years, his uncles had lived on it. Meg had been provided for till she was forty. Eden had never been off his mind. He had always backed Piers. No one but him had had a kind word to offer young Pheasant when Piers had brought her to Jalna. He had been a father to Wakefield and himself. Yet—there was something in him that roused antagonism. He was too taciturn or too expansive, too arrogant or too demonstratively affectionate. When he was in the room others were overshadowed.

Adeline came running on her sturdy legs to follow him, but Finch caught her.

"No, you don't," he said, while she, half laughing, beat him with her fists.

Alayne appeared and Renny asked of her:

"Can't she come? I'll see that she does not get dirty."

Alayne answered sharply—"She is washed and dressed for the afternoon Can't you see that?"

The child was indeed dainty and in white.

Renny gave her a wry smile.

"Bye-bye," he said, and waved his hand.

"Bye-bye," she gasped, through her tears. She watched him disappear without further ado.

Alayne said—"I do so hope, Finch, that you and Sarah will be very happy."

"So do I. But—sometimes I wonder if any one of us is cut out for marriage. Excepting Piers, of course."

"If you two are not happy it will be Sarah's fault. The love you both have for music will be a great joy in your life together. Having the same tastes means so much."

"I don't believe it means anything to me. I love Sarah most for what is so different in her to myself."

"Yes. Now. But wait. Later on you'll rejoice in your companionship."

He was aware of the longing in her tone and it embarrassed him. To change the subject he said, rather irritably:

"I think this engagement of Wake's to Pauline is idiotic. He is just a kid. She is making a great mistake."

"He is terribly in love, poor child."

"But he's so smug about it! Of course, he always has been a self-satisfied little beggar."

"Well, I think that is a good thing. All this unhappiness around him does not touch him. He is secure in his own fortress."

"Hmph. . . . As for the fox-farm, I think it's a ghastly business transplanting it to Jalna."

She made a gesture of resignation. "I suppose it must be endured "

And he observed that attitude of almost tense endurance in the days that followed. Nicholas and Ernest poured out their feelings to Finch in the privacy of their own rooms, for Rags was always about downstairs, and he —although he was supposed to know nothing of the situation—showed himself definitely on Renny's side by hovering about him at table as though he were an invalid, speaking to him in a peculiarly hushed and sympathetic tone that set the nerves of the others on edge. On a particularly hot day he set before him an appetising omelette at dinner.

Renny's eyebrows shot up.

"What's this?"

"A homelette, sir, as Mrs. Wragge thought might tempt you. We noticed that you 'aven't been eating well, along of the 'eat and the worry, if you'll excuse me, sir."

"Damned impudence," growled Nicholas to his cutlet.

Ernest's fork trembled. He eyed the omelette resentfully. His own appetite, he thought, needed tempting.

Wakefield said heartily—"It will do you good, Renny. I have heard my grandmother say that nothing else gave her appetite the fillip that a well-made omelette did."

Renny slid the fluffy mixture to his plate with a glance of gratitude at Rags.

The day of the removal of the fox-farm followed a night of wind and rain. The sun came up red and stormy but the clouds passed, his colour paled to gold, and a jocund breeze swept gaily across the harvest fields. The air was of that sparkling coolness which gives a man strength.

The great lumbering lorry crawled slowly down the road cumbered by the bulk of the Lebraux's house. The house had a startled but submissive look, like a poor beast going to market. The face of the driver of the lorry was puckered with anxiety, but the master of Jalna, at his side, wore a grin that was almost hilarious.

He had put an end to Maurice's obnoxious subdividing of his property. He had added the subdivision to his own land. Now he was about to place on it the house of two friends whose welfare was irrevocably bound up in his heart. The land was his own. The house was his own. He was going to improve it. No one would be able to say justly that it was an eyesore. Clara and Pauline would live there happily as long as they wanted. When times were better, as they soon must be, he would pay off the mortgage.

His bull terrier sat at his feet. His spaniels ran joyously barking on either side of the lorry, while inside the house, Piers' fox terrier, Biddy, raged from room to room infuriated by so unnatural a spectacle.

XXX

SEPTEMBER DUSK

IT was surprising how the transplanted house was improved in its new position. For one thing, it stood farther back from the road, and the clipped cedar hedge enriched its bareness. Then, in place of dingy white, Renny had had it painted a pleasant buff and its roof green. Wakefield had planted a young juniper tree on either side of the green front door. He and Clara had distempered the walls and ceilings of the rooms in varying shades of tan and green. Pauline had made curtains of pale yellow net and filled the window-boxes with nasturtiums in flower which she had brought from her garden. Even the enclosures for the foxes were half concealed behind a little grove. Ernest and Nicholas, spying on it from the shelter of their oaks, had to acknowledge that it looked quite respectable, and returned through the ravine with a slight lightening of their melancholy.

But they said no word in praise of it to Renny. Indeed his position at Jalna during these weeks was far from enviable. Silent reproach and disapproval sprang up in his shadow like gloomy weeds and, when he came into a room, what conversation survived was constrained. He and Alayne exchanged no more than was necessary for the sake of appearance. So he spent as much time away from the house as was possible. It was little better at Meg's or Piers'; therefore he made companions more and more of his horses and his stablemen.

One evening in late September when the breeze had begun to lisp through the leaves with the foreknowledge of their falling, he crossed the rustic bridge, hesitating for a moment to see his own reflection darkling in the pool, and climbed the steep path to the other side and so approached the fox-farm. He had an almost childlike wonder in the thought that he now came to it in a quite different direction from the one to which he was accustomed, and that the house, although the same, had an appearance so different. . . . Pauline had changed, too. She could not, it seemed, be his friend and love Wakefield. The Pauline he saw now was no more than the mirrored image of the girl he had loved with such protective affection. . . . But Clara was unchanged. There was comfort in that thought. She would greet him with her look of sturdy eagerness, distinct from facile feminine animation. Her silence would harbour no suspicion.

She was alone in the little grove that hid the fox-runs. She was in white, more nicely dressed than was usual with her. In that light her tanned face and throat were coffee-coloured and her hair sleek and shining like a boy's. The foxes were padding warily about their new quarters, of which they were still delicately suspicious, and a whippoorwill in the ravine threw his mournful exclamation on the air. A narrow rim of the red harvest moon burnt on the horizon.

She stood watching his approach till his face became clear to her, then she came toward him and held out her hand. When he had taken it and she had murmured a word or two of the beauty of the evening, they still stood linked, for from each hand a sudden and inexplicable happiness had been transmuted to the other.

It was as though a shadowy something between them had in that moment become tangible, manifesting itself in a tremulous wonder at the nearness of each to each, and a fear that the moment would pass, leaving them to loneliness of spirit.

The scent of the earth they both loved rose to them, filling their nostrils with the breath of its secret life. A night bird, like a blown leaf, fluttered past them, the beat of its pale wings troubling the quiet air.

"Are you alone tonight?" he asked, and she answered, almost in a whisper, that she was. Wakefield had taken Pauline out in a canoe on the lake.

Soon this moment will be gone, she thought, and will never come again, and she held it to her like a jewel she had found in the darkness.

She had loved for all these years and had cloaked her love beneath a man's work, a man's language, and a matter-of-fact companionship. It was beyond her hopes, nay—against her will, that he should recognise it. And now . . . here were his fingers clinging to hers, his hand trembling in startled happiness. . . .

"A good moon," he said, with an odd tremor in his voice; "it promises well for tomorrow."

"Yes. A good moon," she agreed. "The farmers are having fine weather for the harvest."

"It's a nice time of year." He sniffed the scented air.

"Yes. It's rather a nice time of year."

"Are you warm enough in that thin dress?"

"Oh yes, I'm plenty warm enough." She gave a little shiver.

"It looks thin."

"It is thinner than I usually wear."

She tried to withdraw her hand but he held it tightly. She acquiesced then, and her fingers closed on his.

"Clara——" He hesitated.

"Yes?"

"Oh, nothing. . . . I'm not quite myself tonight. . . . Well. . . . Perhaps that's wrong. . . . I'm too much myself."

"Not for me!"

"Do you feel"—he gave a short laugh—"anything new in yourself tonight?"

"No."

"Does that mean that I am to keep my distance?"

"No."

"It means then . . . that you want me to be near you?"

"Yes."

He tried to see her face but the gently moving shadow of a tree lay across it.

"How long," he asked, "have you felt like this?"

"Don't ask me."

"But I do ask you."

"No, no, I won't tell you!"

"A long while?"

"Yes."

"And I never guessed it!"

He stopped beneath the pine-tree where the whippoorwill had been singing. They heard its frightened flight and then, far off, its faint repeated cry. The pine-needles lay thick and sweet beneath them.

Although he had touched her hand so often he had never before noticed how hardened it was through work. He raised it to his lips.

"My brave girl," he said.

He withdrew from her then and stood leaning against the rough trunk of the pine. His face was in shadow but she could see the brilliance of his eyes. She stood motionless, her heart beating strongly, waiting to see what he would do. She stood acquiescent, like a wounded animal.

He watched the steady rise of the hunter's moon as it climbed from branch to branch above the ravine. He felt happiness and strength welling up in him. "When the moon swings clear into the sky," he told himself. . . .

It swung clear and hung above them. The breeze lisped through the trees, not moving their branches but causing their leaves to vibrate. He came toward her, frowning. She felt only desire to surrender herself to him. She put a hand on each side of his head and drew his face down to hers. Their lips met.

"This will be our bed," he said, indicating the pine-needles.

He drew her dress from her white shoulders and kissed them.

XXXI

EBB AND FLOW OF THE TIDE

IF love was making a man of Wakefield, it was making a child of Finch. To Wakefield it was the opening of a window, letting in light and the stir of life. To Finch it was the closing of a door, shutting out the tumult and pain of living, making him an ecstatic prisoner. He could not bear to be away from Sarah, for then his happiness became shadowed by doubt. There came a fire in his head and an ache in his breast—and he longed wildly for the time when he would be able to work again. But when he was with her his spirit pressed, as it were, into her breast and abode there.

Sarah was as ununderstandable to the family at Jalna as ever, but they could not see her without being aware of an incandescence from within that lighted her every gesture. On the days when Finch did not go to her house she came to Jalna, her car gliding along the drive between the evergreens, while her pug gazed with tip-tilted nose through the window.

She brought little presents to Ernest and Nicholas, who roused themselves from their brooding to receive her. But, even while they were playfully gracious over their gifts, they looked on her with distrust, remembering bitterly her claim on Jalna. They were more than ever anxious that her marriage to Finch should take place as quickly as possible.

Between her and Alayne there existed an intimacy that could not be called friendship, yet was a source of acute interest to both. Alayne had known Finch since he was a schoolboy, and Sarah listened with avid interest to every incident of his boyhood which Alayne could recall. Any of these that related to suffering, she drank in with a strange triumphant smile. "We both had an unhappy adolescence!" she would exclaim.

Alayne, in her turn, sought in Sarah's mind some understanding of Renny which, she felt, Sarah possessed. It was as though Renny and Sarah had some quality in common which they wilfully concealed, and Alayne, if she could not discover it in him, might find it lurking in Sarah. No such definite thought was in Alayne's mind, but she faintly discovered in both the adumbrations of a calculated passion so alien to herself as to repel her. Around this passion Sarah's outer being irradiated palely like the faint nimbus of a star. Sometimes Alayne almost feared her and she wondered if perhaps she had not done wrong in throwing her and Finch together.

To Wakefield and Pauline, Sarah was a bright and lovely being. Her Paris gowns, her white, exquisite skin, the glossy convolutions of her black braids, filled them with wonder and admiration. Her voice, her smile, fascinated them. Pauline would say of her—"If I were a man, there is the sort of woman I should love!" And Wakefield would return—"And if I didn't adore you, I should fall for Sarah!"

Renny watched his young brothers in love with tolerant amusement. He was leading his own mature, secret life, and their loves were no more to him than the leapings and gambollings of young hares.

His attitude toward Alayne was at once taciturn and apologetic. He was taciturn because he wished to keep himself withdrawn from her, and apologetic because of the heaped-up faults which he was conscious she had accumulated against him.

One night, when it was close to twelve o'clock, he returned across the ravine and took, not the steep path that led to the lawn, but one scarcely perceptible which wavered alongside the stream and was lost at last in a pasture behind the stables. At the end of the path he came suddenly on a figure lurking darkly behind low-growing shrubs. He stopped, struck by suspicion. Was he being watched?

The figure came forward and in the pale light of the moon rising in her last quarter, he made out the face of Rags.

"I've been waiting for you, sir."

"Well, and what do you want?" His tone was surly.

Rags held out a yellowish envelope.

"It's a cablegram, sir. I thought I ought to deliver it myself as it might be important."

How had the fellow known that he would come this way? He hesitated, with the envelope in his hand.

Rags went on—"Perhaps it's about that 'orse you was talking of himporting from 'ome, sir."

Renny grunted. "That was just talk. I'm not importing horses. Wish to God I were! But I don't like this. I'm afraid Lady Buckley may be ill."

"That was my first thought, sir. And to tell the truth, that's w'y I thought I should bring it to you 'ere, because of the old gentlemen and the dynger of a shock to them in their present styte of 'ealth."

"How did you know I'd be coming this way?"

Rags bowed his head. "I'm one with you, sir, in all your doings."

"Hm. Have you a match?"

Rags ostentatiously produced a box and struck one. Renny tore open the envelope and bent his head over the writing. He read—

"Regret to tell you Lady Buckley suffered stroke last night proved fatal.   HOLLINGS vicar."

In the flare of the match Rags saw Renny's face turn not pale but, it seemed, almost green. The match burned Wragge's fingers and he dropped it with an exclamation of pain. He asked, in a trembling voice:

"Is she very ill, sir?"

"She's dead. Light me another match. I want to read this again."

Rags struck another two more after that, while Renny stared with horrified eyes at the cablegram.

"It'll be the end of the old gentlemen, sir."

"I'm afraid so. Thank God you didn't let them see it! Of course, I'll not tell them tonight. I'll go—I'll see—why, I don't know what I should do first...." He looked at Rags in bewilderment. Rags said:

"This is terrible news, sir. I had a great respect for her Ladyship and so had my missus. Her visits will be a great loss to Jalna."

Renny began to walk quickly, half dazed, across the pasture. At first he turned his steps in the direction of the house, then wheeled and went toward the road.

"I must tell my brother," he said.

At Piers' they found the lights out. During the walk Renny had talked incoherently, more to himself than to Rags, of the shock this would be to his uncles and of what must be done to ease the blow for them. A keen pain was in his heart at the same time for the loss of Augusta.

He rang the door-bell but there was no answer. Then he knocked loudly with his knuckles. There was a movement at a window above and Piers' voice demanded:

"Who's there? What's the matter?"

"It's me—Renny. I've just had a cable from England."

"Oh!" There was a moment's silence, then—"Anything wrong?"

"Aunt Augusta has had a stroke. She's dead."

"My God! I'll come right down. Are you alone?"

"No. Rags is here."

Piers appeared at the door in his pyjamas. He had switched on the light and Renny stepped into the hall.

"Have you told Uncle Nick and Uncle Ernie?"

"No. Not till morning." He looked almost pathetically at Piers. "I'm afraid this will kill Uncle Ernest, Piers!"

Piers' face was troubled but he said:

"Perhaps he will bear it better than you expect."

Pheasant appeared on the landing wrapped in a kimono. She was sobbing.

"Oh, how terrible it is! Tell me all about it, Renny. I did love Aunt Augusta and she was always so sweet to Mooey!"

Renny handed her the cablegram. He said to Piers:

"First thing in the morning you must get the doctor. Fetch him over to Jalna. I'll not break the news to them till you arrive."

Piers nodded. He looked shrewdly into Renny's face.

"I wonder," he said, "what brought this on?"

Renny scowled and bit his lip. "I can't imagine. She seemed perfectly well when she left."

"I expected her to live to be a hundred—like Gran."

"She had not Gran's constitution or her love of life. My God, Piers, this is a blow to me! I can't help wondering . . ." He could not continue.

"Wondering what?"

He turned his head away.

"Well," Piers said, "I'll be around with the doctor directly after breakfast. Let me give you a spot. You look all in."

"No, thanks." He hesitated, then asked—"Perhaps you had better break it to them, Piers. Perhaps you could do it better than I."

"No, no, I think it's your place to do it. Just tell them quietly that you've had word that she's very ill and they'll understand. But I'll tell Meggie before I go to the doctor's."

"All right. I'll be off, then. Good night. Good night, Pheasant! Get to bed, child!"

Pheasant ran down the stairway and clasped his arm in her hands. She looked up into his face out of wet brown eyes. "Poor Renny," she faltered.

He bent and kissed her, making an effort to control his lips that trembled. "Good night," he repeated, and returned to Rags.

After he was gone Piers asked her—"Why did you say 'poor Renny'? I feel just as badly as he does."

"I know," she returned gently, "but there was something in his face that made me say it. And then, I never can forget that time when he was so sympathetic and sweet to me when I had that frightful cough and you lay . . ."

Piers grunted and put out the light.

When Renny and Rags parted in the hall, Rags asked:

"Is there anything I can do, sir?"

"No, no. Don't speak of this to anyone."

"Not a word, sir. . . . It's a very sad ending, if you'll excuse my saying so, sir, to a pleasant evening."

Renny looked at him sharply. "Good night," he said and went up the stairs.

A deep rumbling snore came from Nicholas's room. Renny

paused outside Ernest's door and heard him moving restlessly in his bed, sighing, muttering to himself. Poor old boy! What might his condition be tomorrow! This blow might well finish him.

He moved on to Alayne's door and softly turned the handle. Her voice asked:

"Is that you?"

It was the first time he had come to her room since their quarrel. She sat up in bed. In the feeble light of the waning moon his face looked strange. There was a hungry light in his eyes, as for love. He came and sat on the edge of the bed beside her. She noticed for the hundredth time how beautifully his head was set on his shoulders. It was set there elegantly, warily, like the head of a thoroughbred. A rage of love for him mounted to her brain and, when he said, in a husky voice—"I must tell you something," she thought—"It does not matter. It does not matter what he confesses. I can forgive him anything!"

"Yes, yes," she whispered eagerly. "What are you going to tell me?"

He took her hand and held it tightly, as though to steady himself. "You must be brave," he said.

She drew his hand between her breasts. Her heart asked for his love. She thought—"Never again will I let anything come between us!"

She whispered—"I'll be brave."

"I have just had a cablegram. From the vicar at Nymet Crews. It is about Auntie. She's had a stroke. . . . I'm afraid we shall not see her again."

A shudder of revulsion ran through her. For a moment his words were nothing to her but a dreadful disappointment. She bowed her head over his hand and could not speak. . . . Then the significance of what he said pierced her consciousness and she gasped:

"How terrible! Oh, poor Aunt Augusta! When did you get the cable?"

"Rags was waiting up for me with it. I've been over to tell Piers." He went on to repeat the arrangements for the breaking of the news to his uncles.

"I think," he said, "that I had better wake Finch and tell him."

"Oh no! That would be cruel!"

"I think he ought to know. She was very good to him."

"But wait till morning! Surely you can see that he should have his night s rest!" Already irritation toward him chilled her voice.

256

"Very well." He rose and moved restlessly about the room. He asked:

"Shouldn't you like to dress and come downstairs? We might as well be up since we can't sleep."

"It is so cold," she answered, and somewhat petulantly pulled the blanket over her shoulders. "And it is so foolish and unnecessary to stay up. If you go to bed, I'm sure you will sleep."

He left her and went to his room but he could not stay there. He went downstairs to his grandmother's room.

He groped his way into it and lighted the night-light which stood by the bed. The air was heavy and the smell of old stuffs lingered on it. A film of dust dimmed the bright colours she had loved, and the maroon bedspread was rumpled by the sheep-dog who, when opportunity offered, snatched a nap there. Boney slept on his accustomed perch on the headboard. He was sufficiently disturbed to uncover one eye from the shelter of his wing and with its cold brightness scanned the unwelcome visitor.

Renny gazed at the bed, seeing with startling clearness the form of old Adeline resting there, her deep-lined, predatory profile, her handsome hands spotted with liver-marks and bright with jewels clasped on her stomach, her long limbs outlined beneath the bedclothes. Might not her eyes open at his coming and in their burning brown depths might he not see a mother's grief over her firstborn? But—mingled with the grief there would be a faint contempt, for she had always been contemptuous of Augusta. How often he had seen his aunt issue from that room with chin drawn back in deep affront! How that wicked tongue had scored her! "Lady Bilgely! Lady Bunkum!"—she never could remember the title she so resented! What a terrifying mother-in-law she must have been to little Sir Edwin!

Well—out of that staunch womb had issued Aunt Augusta and three sons, all big, well-shaped, fine-looking people. . . . He picked up a photograph framed in faded plush, the corners bound in silver, of a young family group. Adeline, in billowing skirts, holding a large-eyed infant Ernest on her knee, while at her side lounged Nicholas wearing a braided velvet jacket and a Thames tunnel on his forehead, represented today by his crest of grey hair. Philip, in cravat and tight trousers, held his daughter, her abundant dark curls confined by a circular comb, her white-stockinged legs dangling. The third son was not yet born.

Renny gazed at the small Augusta, trying to associate her in his mind with the elderly woman who had, a few months ago, waved her last good-bye to him from the deck of the steamer at Quebec. He looked long and sadly, for, in losing his grandmother and his aunt, he lost the two women who represented to him all he had known of love approaching the maternal. He could not remember his own mother and, between him and his stepmother, no love had existed.

He sat long at the bedside-table, the photograph in his hand, and, at last, as the slow greyness of dawn came through the curtains and settled on the objects in the room, he stretched out his arm and laid his head on it and slept.

There Rags discovered him and brought him a cup of tea, and, when he had drunk it, he took up his grandmother's yellow ivory-backed brush with the worn bristles and flattened his hair as well as he could. He gave a deep sigh and mounted the stairs to Wakefield's room.

With Wake following him, half-dressed, frightened, he led the way to the attic and roused Finch.

When the breakfast-gong had sounded he found Alayne in the dining-room ahead of him. He looked apprehensively at the chairs of Nicholas and Ernest.

"Have you seen them this morning?" he asked.

She shook her head. "No. But I heard Uncle Ernest sighing as usual."

Renny groaned. "Poor old boy! This will kill him."

"When are you going to tell them?"

"Directly they have something on their stomachs. Piers will be here by that time with Meggie and the doctor."

"Have you told the boys?"

"Yes. Wake was very brave but Finch lost control of himself of course. I told him not to come down to breakfast.... Good Lord, here they come!"

Heavy shuffling feet were indeed descending the stairs. Wakefield's voice could be heard, on a deep sympathetic note. He was giving Nicholas the support of his shoulder when they came into the room. Ernest followed after, tooting his nose into a large silk handkerchief. He had taken cold and went straight to the window and shut it. His eyes looked watery and the end of his long delicate nose was pink.

Renny sprang forward and drew out their chairs for them. He exclaimed:

"What a fine morning! There's a wind like the wind from the moors. Like Devon, eh?"

Alayne looked at him blankly. What was in his mind? Was he trying to prepare them by drawing their minds toward Augusta?

She sat down behind the large silver teapot and her own small green earthenware pot of coffee.

"I wish to heaven I were there," growled Nicholas, sinking into his chair and, as he did so, dragging the tablecloth askew.

Ernest also seated himself. "It blows like rain," he said. "There's a chill autumnal feeling in the air. Summer is over." He poured milk over his porridge. The milk dribbled from the lip of the jug and made a wet spot on the cloth.

"I hope you slept well?" asked Renny, addressing them both. "It was a good night for sleeping."

"Slept badly," returned Nicholas promptly.

"Well, you were executing a fine solo on the trombone when I passed your door."

Nicholas made no answer save to sup his porridge noisily.

"I," said Ernest, "lay awake most of the night. I heard every sound. I had to breathe through my mouth because of the cold in my head. My ears were making a buzzing noise and my left leg was numb. I could not help wondering if they were not forewarnings of a stroke."

Renny looked at him horrified.

"Oh, no, no, no," he stammered. "You must not think of such things!"

"Well, one is forced to think," answered Ernest.

"If you had my gout," said Nicholas, "you might lie awake. Every time I turned over it gave me a terrible twinge. You might have heard me groan."

Alayne tried to turn the conversation to impersonal things without success. She could not eat. Neither could Wakefield. Renny forced down his food with false gusto. With funereal solemnity Wragge set a platter of fish before him.

"What is that?" asked Ernest distrustfully.

"Salmon trout. It looks very nice, too."

Ernest shook his head.

"I couldn't think of it," he said. "Not after the night I had. I'm sorry there wasn't a bit of bacon for me this morning. I could have relished that."

"We'll have some cooked. Rags, get some bacon. . . . Uncle Nick, you'll have salmon, won't you?"

Nicholas had hidden himself behind the London *Times*, just arrived and twelve days old. From this shelter he growled:

"Bad for my gout. I'll take bacon too."

Renny was chagrined, for he had ordered the fish specially to tempt them on this morning. Silence fell while they waited for the bacon. Ernest looked disapprovingly at his nephew's unshaven chin. He observed:

"You'd have a really ugly red beard if you were to let it grow."

Renny passed a lean hand over his face. "Yes. I know. I'd look like the devil."

"How often do you shave?"

"Every day."

"Hmph."

"It's a fact. I didn't this morning. I——" He gave a mirthless laugh. "I'm off colour myself this morning."

Nicholas looked at him round the edge of his paper, then returned to it with relief.

An advancing tide of gloom crept into the room. Speech was impossible. Renny gave a noticeable start as the front door opened and closed. Low voices were heard in the hall. "Oh," said Alayne to herself, "why cannot they do things simply, like other modern people? Why must they create this overpowering atmosphere?"

She heard Renny say—"I must telephone Piers. I've a message from Crowdy for him." She saw him go into the library and close the door behind him. She knew he could endure the strain no longer. Her eyes met Wakefield's, and a tense look passed between them, intercepted by a sympathetic gleam from Rags' eager eye.

Renny sat down beside the telephone and buried his face in his hands. How was he going to break the news? Lead up to it carefully or simply blurt it out? His uncles seemed even more depressed than usual this morning.

Without taking down the receiver he loudly gave the telephone number and then said—"Is that you, Pheasant? I have a message for Piers from Crowdy. . . ." Then, in a mumbling tone he continued an imaginary conversation. The door leading into the hall opened and Piers came into the library. He said:

"We're here. Meg and the doctor have gone into the drawing-room. Is breakfast over?"

"Almost. I'm pretending to talk to Pheasant. I had to get away. Said I had a message for you from Crowdy. I'll tell them you've just happened in. God, I hear them getting up from the table now! They're coming in here! Don't go, Piers! I wonder if perhaps you had better tell them. Or Meggie! It might come easier from a woman. Has the doctor brought a restorative, do you think?"

Nicholas and Ernest, followed by Wakefield and Alayne, now

entered from the dining-room. Nicholas was already filling his after-breakfast pipe. Renny said excitedly:

"Piers has just come in. I was telephoning him when he walked in at the door. Sit down here, Uncle Ernie. I've something to tell you. I think perhaps Piers had better tell it."

"No," muttered Piers.

"What's the matter?" asked Ernest, looking from one face to another. Meg, drawn by curiosity, appeared in the doorway.

Nicholas went on stolidly cramming his pipe.

Renny turned to Meg. "Wh—what was it you were going to say, Meggie?"

She stared back at him, speechless.

"What is all this mystery?" demanded Ernest with dignity.

"Do you feel a draught?" asked Renny. "Shall I close the windows?"

"Thank you. . . . But why are you all here? Do I see Dr. Fairchild's car?"

"Yes, yes He came in to see Adeline's rash. It's nothing to worry about, he says. Isn't that what he says, Alayne?"

Alayne returned his look of appeal, stiff-lipped, frozen. Save in his passion she could not respond to him.

From upstairs, from the very attic, came the sound of loud crying.

"What's that?" cried Ernest, shocked.

"It's Finch," answered Renny.

"What have you been doing to him?"

"He's crying about Auntie."

Nicholas hit the table beside him with the flat of his hand.

"Explain!"

Ernest cried—"About whom? Auntie! Augusta! Has anything happened to my sister?"

"Oh, Uncle Ernie!" wailed Meg, and ran in and threw herself on his breast.

Nicholas heaved himself out of his chair and stood tall and commanding.

"Tell me," he said, in a hollow voice, "is Augusta dead?"

"A stroke," answered Piers.

"And did not survive it?"

"I'd a cable," said Renny, "last night. From the vicar. She's gone."

Ernest began to weep, clinging to Meg, who patted his back as though he were a child.

Nicholas ejaculated incoherently—"My sister dead! Gussie

261

dead! Poor—poor Gussie! Why—I can't believe it!" He looked about him bewildered. "Why, she was here such a little time ago! A cablegram, you say, Renny? May I see it, please?"

Renny took it from his pocket and handed it to him. Nicholas, with a shaking hand, adjusted his glasses on his nose and read.

"Let me see it too!" quavered Ernest.

Nicholas handed it to him. Ernest peered at it through his fast-flowing tears. He could not make out the words and handed it back to his brother, mournfully shaking his head. He said:

"To think of it! And I was going to write to her today! Poor, dear Augusta! Thank God, she did not suffer long!"

"I suppose," said Nicholas, "that you have all known of this since last night."

"All but Finch and Wakefield," answered Renny. "I told them before breakfast."

"And Finch broke down! Poor lad. Go upstairs, Wake, and bring him down! He must not be left up there alone."

"Yes, yes," echoed Ernest, "bring Finch down! He was very fond of his aunt and he will miss her sorely. Poor dear Augusta! I should not feel so badly if I had got my letter off to her."

"She'd not have been there to read it," objected his brother.

"I know, I know, but I'd have felt happier in my mind, just the same." He wiped his eyes on his large silk handkerchief.

"That's very foolish of you, Ernest. You were a very good brother to Augusta, and this is no time for futile regrets." Nicholas took out his own handkerchief and blew his nose.

Wakefield had gone upstairs to Finch. The doctor advanced cautiously across the hall to the door of the library. Renny met him with mingled relief and bewilderment.

"Do you need my help?" asked the doctor.

"Not yet! And I don't believe we shall! They're splendid. They're wonderful. They're thinking of others more than themselves. They're wanting Finch brought down. He has rotten nerves, that boy!"

Ernest and Nicholas came forward to greet the old doctor. He shook hands with them and murmured his sympathy.

"I had a great admiration for Lady Buckley," and he recalled an incident of her kindness to him.

Her brothers were pleased and joined in extolling her virtues.

Piers said to Alayne—"This is just what I expected. But Renny is always looking for scenes."

"Well, I suppose he has good reason to."

262

"I knew they would feel it terribly. But they've lots of character. They're not weaklings—like Finch."

"You're not fair to Finch! You never have been!"

"Perhaps. I don't understand him. But I think I do understand my uncles, and I expected them to show a certain amount of self-control. Thank God, they're showing it!"

Nicholas and Ernest were indeed controlled though their faces were white and drawn. They escorted the doctor to the door and, when they returned to the library, Piers had brought a small glass of brandy for each of them. They took it gratefully. After a few sips, Ernest remarked:

"She seemed so bright before she left Jalna! I can't think what can have brought this on. In her last letter she spoke of walking to the village and back."

Renny asked hesitatingly—"Was her last letter—written after—she had heard about the mortgage?"

"No—she had not heard about it then. But she must have had Nick's letter telling of it in a day or two."

"And you haven't heard from her since?"

"No, not since. It would be a blow to her." He exchanged a look with Nicholas.

"I wonder——" Renny began but could not go on.

Nicholas said—"If you're worrying, Renny, because you think that news brought a stroke on Augusta, you're quite wrong. No—she was too well-balanced for that. As a matter of fact, she complained to me, in an earlier letter, of sensations. I was more than a little anxious about her."

"Yes," agreed Ernest, "it would be wrong to blame yourself for that. Augusta's time had come and it is not for us to harrow ourselves with speculations." He laid a kind hand on Renny's shoulder.

Alayne looked at them wonderingly. One never knew what storm would sweep them apart or drive them together!

Wakefield returned to the room.

"Finch would not come down," he said. "He's quiet now. He's sitting by his window."

Nicholas refilled his glass. Colour returned to his lips. He said:

"There will be a lot of things to attend to. Someone will have to go to England at once."

"Oh, I wish I could go," cried Wakefield eagerly. "I've never been anywhere in all my life, and this would be a wonderful opportunity for me."

"Your turn will come later," said Nicholas.

"I could go," offered Piers.

"I don't think," said Ernest, "that you would know enough of my sister's affairs to be of any use whatever."

"The idea!" chimed in Meg. "As though you knew the very first thing about closing an estate! I am the only niece. Maurice and I will go."

"I like that," said Piers. "What the devil do you or Maurice know of such a thing?"

"Come, children," interrupted Ernest reprovingly, "this is no time for quarrelling. As for your Uncle Nicholas and myself, we should not consider shirking our responsibility for a moment."

"Do you mean to say," cried Meg, "that you will go?"

"Certainly we shall," said Nicholas.

"But who will go to look after you? You are ill and Uncle Nick's leg is so bad."

"We shall manage. I'll look after Ernie and he'll look after me."

"What about the expense?" Piers asked, but no one heard him. They were all talking at once.

It was a strange day. Mourning had returned to Jalna, not in pomp and mournful pride as in the passing of a century-old life, not in anguish as in cutting off a young life, but in ghostly bewilderment, in uncertain certainty. For while they knew Augusta to be dead, they knew nothing of her suffering, or whether or not she had experienced a moment of conscious pain. Her figure rose before them, as they had last seen her, upright, firm in her complicated clothing, her expression composed, no shrinking from death distorting her dignity. But she was gone, her spirit lost in the mist, while they (her brothers) were safe in the dear light of common life. The shock of her sudden departure had shaken them to their depths, but it had freed them from the creeping depression of the last months. It had turned their thoughts outward instead of inward. Through their tears they saw things the clearer. They had lost Augusta. They pressed closer to the breathing kin about them. Maurice and Meg remained for the day. All day, Alayne thought, they seemed to be eating, and drinking tea, and recalling the past and discussing the impending journey to England. Renny and Nicholas sat close beside each other. Ernest climbed the two flights of stairs to the attic and brought down Finch and made him eat. Piers and Wakefield did not work. Adeline and Patience, hilarious, ran up and down the house, calling to each other.

Boney, troubled by a growth of new feathers, scratched himself constantly.

XXXII

PRELUDE TO FLITTINGS

Two days after the news of Augusta's death the post was handed to Renny and he discovered among the letters one addressed to Nicholas in Augusta's handwriting. He was alone in his office and he laid it on the desk in front of him with a feeling of dismay. This was the first letter she had written to Jalna since hearing of the mortgage. What might there not be in its pages to distress his uncles, to harden their hearts against him? The writing was so natural, in its long spidery slant, that he had a moment's disbelief in her death. Surely she must be there, at Nymet Crews, thinking perhaps—"Today my letter arrives at Jalna. Today Renny will hear what I think of his actions."

He took the letter in his hand and turned it over, examining the sealing-wax with which it was stuck. He could not give it to Nicholas, and yet—how cruel to deny him the last words of his sister! He hesitated, then making his decision, took up a paper-knife and slit the envelope. Inside there were twelve closely written pages. He looked at them but would not allow himself to read them. He turned to the last page and read at the bottom—"Love and kisses to all from your—Ever affectionate sister—AUGUSTA," and beneath the signature, in clinging, childish habit, she had made a row of crosses to represent the kisses. Doubtless her lips had pressed those wavering marks. Renny raised the paper to his lips and so alone garnered them.

He went then to the small stove where the fire had not yet been lighted, and, removing the lid, thrust in the letter, and touched a match to it. It flared brightly, made the sound of a hurrying wind and its char flew up the chimney.

He sat down again and lighted a cigarette. His mind went back over the preceding day when their lawyer had brought Augusta's will to Jalna and read it in the presence of the family. It had been a just will, he thought. Augusta had left her income, amounting to twelve hundred pounds a year, equally between her brothers. Lyming Hall was also to be theirs. At their death the house was to be sold and the estate divided in equal portions among her nephews and her niece. Her personal belongings had been bequeathed, in a manner showing real understanding of the tastes of each, to Meg, Alayne, and Pheasant. Yes, it had been a just will, and no one could complain of it.

If Nicholas and Ernest had harboured any fear that the income might not be wholly theirs, they had been relieved of that, and if they had had hopes that the principal might be left to them direct, their disappointment was quickly lost in the thought that they were now independent men, free to do as they liked for the rest of their days without thanks to anyone. The effect on them of this knowledge was remarkable. No grief could quite beat down the wings of their exhilaration. They could not rest. They could not stop talking. They roamed from room to room examining things they had not looked at for years. They turned out unused drawers and from the contents made presents of no value to their nephews. Today Wakefield was in town procuring tickets from the steamship office for them. They were to sail within the week.

Sarah Leigh had arrived at Jalna. It was arranged that she and Finch, Wakefield and Pauline, should take a motor trip to Quebec. Pauline would visit her grandparents there and Wakefield experience, for the first time, the adventure of travel. They were to set out the day after the departure of Ernest and Nicholas. All was confusion and excitement at Jalna.

Finch put his head in at the door of the office. He said:

"They're having lemonade and cake on the lawn. They sent me over to find you and Piers. It's awfully hot, isn't it?" He held Sarah's pug, which had followed him, under his arm. Renny gave an amused grin at the contrast in the two visages facing him.

"You needn't grin at him," said Finch, rather huffily. "He is one of the most intelligent dogs I have ever known."

"Lap dog," sneered Renny.

"Not a bit of it. I'm carrying him because I'm afraid one of the horses might kick him."

When they were outside he set down the pug, which at once importantly led the way. Piers had preceded them.

It was Indian summer and thick yellow sunshine lay sultry on trees and grass. The grass was brown and the trees blazed, bronze and scarlet. The Virginia creeper was in a crimson cloak about the house. Zinnias and nasturtiums and fiery salvia challenged each other in the borders. Chairs and tables had been carried on to the lawn and there the family was established for the afternoon. The Vaughans were there and Pheasant had brought her three children. Mooey sat on the knee of Nicholas, drinking lemonade from a green glass in which bobbed a bright-red cherry. He was growing into a charming boy, thoughtful and sweet-tempered. His younger brother lay on his back staring up at the sky, his fair hair spread in a halo against the grass, while the six-months-old Philip snuggled on Ernest's arm, their eyes vying with each other in forget-me-not blue. Patience had ridden over on the pony which had once been Wake's. There was a tear in the seat of her riding-breeches and her hair was tumbled. As she ate her cake she rhythmically struck her leg with her riding-crop, the picture of care-free childhood.

Against this highly coloured background the black suits of Nicholas and Ernest, Meg's black dress, struck a sombre tone, but the faces of the wearers, though pensive, were not unhappy. A mellow undercurrent of affection buoyed up all the clan.

When Renny and Finch appeared, Wakefield advanced to meet them, one arm embracing Sarah, the other Pauline. The two girls were now definitely a part of the family circle.

Finch left Renny and joined the trio, drawn by Sarah's smile. Pauline, too, was smiling at him, avoiding Renny's eyes.

Renny sat down beside Nicholas and began to talk, but his bright glance moved from one to another of the engaged couples. Wakefield—his boy, growing into a splendid fellow, tall, free-moving, brown as a hazel-nut. . . . Finch—returned to health, his cheeks filled out, his future assured. . . . Sarah—well, she was a strange girl but he thought he understood her. . . . Pauline—his eyes clouded as they rested on her, for he was not sure of her happiness, and between him and her rose the firm figure of Clara and the thought of her compassion and her surrender.

Nicholas was saying—"Ernest and I went to say good-bye to Mrs. Lebraux this morning. It was the first time we had called there. But we thought we really should go, so that she would be assured that we harbour no ill-feeling."

Renny was immensely pleased. "Did you really? Well—I'm glad of that. . . . The place doesn't look too bad, does it?"

"It looks very nice indeed. We were agreeably surprised. And she has made the house so very nice inside. As for the fox-runs—they are quite inconspicuous."

"She has worked very hard there."

"She has indeed! She's not an attractive woman. She's not particularly well-bred. Neither she nor Lebraux were what I should call out of the top drawer, but—there's something very pleasant about her—something quite apart from feminine charm that makes her very companionable. We enjoyed our call and stayed longer than we had intended to."

Renny leaned forward and dropped his cherry into Mooey's glass. "Another cherry for you, old fellow."

Nicholas beamed. He turned to Maurice. "Mooey is developing wonderfully," he said.

Maurice regarded his namesake without enthusiasm. He paid little attention to his own child, toward whom Meg had an aggressively possessive air, and to Pheasant's children still less. In the midst of the family he addressed almost all his remarks to Meg—as though he did not see enough of her at home! Now he inquired of her:

"Would it be best to have the things your aunt left you sent on to you at once or brought back when your uncles return?"

Meg asked Nicholas—"How long shall you stay in England?"

"Till next spring. We could not exist long away from Jalna."

"All those we love are here," added Ernest, casting his eyes about the circle, and then kissing the baby.

Nicholas said—"We must find a good tenant for Lyming, if possible. I wonder if you'd like to spend your honeymoon there, Finch?"

Finch had come to the table for a piece of cake. He shook his head. "No, thanks. I should not like a honeymoon there."

Piers, from where he lay on the grass, looked up at him curiously. He asked:

"When is it to come off?"

"In the spring. I'm doing concerts all winter."

"I must be back to give Sarah away!" cried Nicholas.

"I think," said Meg, "that I shall have my things brought then. I'm so glad that Aunt Augusta left me her pearls. They go well with my skin."

"And don't forget the cameos for Pheasant," put in Piers.

Meg was content that Pheasant should have the cameos. "They will look very nice on her," she said graciously, "and they're coming in again."

Maurice asked his wife—"What about the sealskin coat?"

"Oh yes!" cried Meg, "don't forget the coat. It is real seal—even if it is old-fashioned—and certainly more valuable than the watch and the Indian shawl that Gran left me!"

"By the way," asked Maurice, "where are those things? I never see them?"

"Yes," said Piers, looking full at her, "where are they?"

Meg coloured. "Put away. I cannot use them."

"But where?" insisted Piers.

"Is that your affair?" she cried hotly.

"I don't believe they're in your house."

"They are!"

"Be careful, Meggie! You're an awful liar!"

"How dare you?"

Finch growled—"Let her alone!"

"*You* tell us, then," said Piers.

"What is this all about?" demanded Nicholas.

"Have you dared to part with my mother's bequest to you?" exclaimed Ernest, peering at her accusingly.

"Don't drop my little baby!" cried Pheasant.

"Here, take it then." Ernest spoke testily. "Let me get to the bottom of this matter."

Pheasant took little Philip and cuddled him.

Ernest turned to Piers. "What do you suspect?"

Piers smiled pleasantly. "Well, I went up to Finch's room one day when I was out of cigarettes and tried to find some. And there, in his cupboard, were the shawl and watch, done up together in paper."

"They looked like a package of cigarettes, didn't they?" sneered Finch.

"Not a bit. But some of the fringe was sticking out and I recognised it. And, as you have such a gathering eye, I said to myself—'Here's Gran's shawl, and probably her watch wrapped up inside it!' And so it was!"

"Meggie, Meggie," said Ernest reproachfully. "How could you give away the things my mother left you?"

Meg bowed her head. "I—I saw that Finch admired them. He had been kind to me and so—I let him have them," she faltered.

"Let him have them, says she!" jeered Piers.

"Foolish, generous girl!" exclaimed Ernest.

"Ask Finch what he paid for them," suggested Piers.

His sister turned on him angrily. "Will you stop your interfering? Really, you are abominable! As though Finch and I would do such a thing!"

"No, no," rumbled Nicholas, "Meggie would never do such a thing. Now my mother's watch and shawl will fall to Sarah and she will appreciate them and perhaps wear them. They will become her very well indeed."

Maurice's face was dark with suspicion. Piers' was bright with mischief. Meg's hot with anger. The squabble might have been prolonged but that the group was broken in upon by Pauline and Sarah pursued by Wakefield, pelting them with freshly cut grass from a barrow. Pauline subsided laughing beside Pheasant. Sarah glided swiftly to Alayne's side. On her other side was Renny and she took a hand of each. Wakefield emptied the last of the lemonade into a glass and drank it. Finch began to eat his cake.

Into this precarious peace the figure of small Adeline was then intruded. She was now three years old, tall and strong. She came running bare-legged, with flying red hair, across the lawn with something brilliant in her arms.

"Look what I've got!" she shouted.

They looked and, according to their ages, were delighted or aghast. For it was Boney she carried, flattened against her chest, his bright wings outspread, his beak gaping.

"Good God!" cried Ernest. "She has killed Boney!"

"If the bird is dead," sputtered Nicholas—"if the bird is dead—if the bird is——"

Alayne screamed.

Renny leaped up and ran toward his child. When she saw him coming she flung the parrot from her with all her strength and he fluttered into the midst of the circle with screams of fury and amaze. His Hindoo curses came from his throat disjointed and broken. None of them had ever heard him curse like this. It was chaotic but it was terrible. Beating his wings on the ground, it seemed that he would swear himself to death. Then, as by an inspiration, Finch threw him his cake. The parrot heard its soft thud on the grass and lowered his grey lids, exposing his furious pupils, and spied the cake. With marvellous dexterity he calmed himself and began to peck at it, ripples of pleasure soothing his throat.

"Well, I declare!" exclaimed Ernest, beaming.

"I have warned her time and again," said Alayne. "He might have pecked out her eyes. I do wish you would keep him in a cage!"

"No, no, no," said Nicholas. "It would break his spirit."

Sarah's pug drew cautiously nearer to the cake, but a scream from Boney and a warning arching of his beak drove him back. When the cake was finished he flew heavily to Nicholas' shoulder and, with sinuous movements, wiped his beak on Nicholas' moustache.

"Darling old bird," rumbled Nicholas.

Boney settled himself peacefully and, in a cooing tone, said into Nicholas' ear:

"Gussie—Gussie—Gussie Whiteoak—dear, dear Gussie White-oak——"

Nicholas looked about him bewildered. Boney had not uttered her name in years.

XXXIII

ALONE TOGETHER AT LAST

CAN it be possible that summer is over? The air is so tenderly warm. It smells of wood-smoke and ripe apples, and, when the breeze stirs, it touches the cheek as lightly as the breath of a child. A gentle vibration passes through the strong limbs of the evergreens; their long, sticky cones ooze sweet-smelling resin. The grass is warm and dry to rest on, and across it pass the shadows of migrating birds. Sometimes a feather is dropped by one of them, and it falls in an exquisite, slow decline to earth. Never has the old house been so quiet.

It is in good order too, for the repairs, paid for by Augusta, have been well carried out. The roof has been mended, the ceilings repaired, and the shutters painted a vivid green. Since the departure of Nicholas and Ernest and the young people, it has been cleaned, the windows made to shine, the carpets taken up and beaten, the curtains washed. To Alayne, coming out of the door and looking back at it from the lawn, it has an air of almost intolerable smugness. It seems to say—"My birds have flown but—they will come back. A price is on my roof but—my memories are without price." She stands looking back at it, a smile half tender, half deprecatory, on her lips.

She has been through all the rooms, giving the last touch, putting the last thing in place, preparing, not for coming guests, but for this space alone with the one she loves. She has looked with pleasure at the beds that will not be slept in.

Renny has told her that he will be back at this hour and she has dressed herself charmingly to please him. . . . A new flowered dress with little ruches and elbow-sleeves. For some reason she feels herself nearer to him spiritually than for a long time. She feels a warm, tender tolerance of his faults welling up in her like a happy darkling spring. She has perhaps, she thinks, judged him too harshly in the past. He is not sensitive or subtle, but he is full of fire and life, and, though he may not show it, craving for kindness. He is hers and she will accept him as he is. She feels a new pride at having borne his child. . . .

He comes toward her, up out of the ravine, a look of contentment in his eyes. He too is glad, she thinks, that we are alone together. Nothing must interfere, she thinks, with our time alone together.

Now we shall get to understand each other as never before. Now our misunderstandings shall migrate, like those birds overhead.

In his hand he carries a short green stalk crowned with red berries.

"What is that?" she asks, going toward him.

But he throws it away and will not let her touch it.

"It would stain your frock," he says.

She smiles up into his face.

"We are alone!" she says. "Can you believe it? Do you like it?"

He touches her cheek half timidly with his fingers. "How nice you look! What's that business about your waist?"

"A peplum. They're in again. All old fashioned things are coming in again. . . . Conjugal bliss will be coming in next."

Adeline darts out of the bushes, running between them, grasping a hand of each. They look down at her proudly and then smile into each other's eyes.